The Rainwater Secret

Shaw Publications, Dallas, Texas © 2016
Copyright © 2017 Monica Shaw
All rights reserved
ISBN: 9780998599601
ISBN: 9780998599618
ISBN: 0998599603

In memory of Eileen Paterson

Dedicated to the Medical Missionaries of Mary
"Rooted and founded in Love"

1

May 26, 1946
Maghull, England

Anna walked briskly down the deserted sidewalk, enjoying the spring breeze playing gently with her dress and delivering a pleasing embrace of warmth. School was out and summer was hitched to a lorry soon to be deposited upon her doorstep. Her hope was that the lorry carried produce from Clarence G. Pyle and Son Grocers. After all, she was dating the *son* of Clarence G. Pyle and Son, so this summer looked full of promise and brighter than any summer in her previous twenty-nine years of life.

Anna walked up two small steps to a street-level flat and knocked. As she waited for an answer, she looked up and down the streets. They were mostly deserted. It was Sunday. The streets were not likely to be crowded until noon or later. That's when the churches let out and the crowds made their way home to prepare a special dinner.

She knocked again. Still, there was no answer. This bothered her because usually Molly opened the door right away. And if she couldn't get to it, she would at least yell, "Enter!" Anna decided to try the door and found it open. Stepping in, she blinked in the dim entranceway and yelled, "Molly, I'm here!"

Seconds later, she received a response. "Come to my room please!"

Anna made her way down the hall to Molly's bedroom where she saw Molly sitting in front of the small vanity table, dabbing powder on her cheeks. She gave an exasperated sigh and said, "Will this be as long a process as always or can I expect you to be ready in time for Mass?"

"Oh hush up," Molly replied. "Just because you have personal objections to makeup doesn't mean you have to be miffed when others don't."

Anna stood behind Molly staring at her in the mirror. "I don't have any issues with makeup. It's just that I never got in the habit of buying it, much less applying it. So feel free to cake it on, especially if you think it will do any good."

"For the second time, hush up! I need all the help I can get since I'm not the one marrying the most eligible bachelor in this out-of-the-way bog."

Anna had already spied wedding dress flyers strewn about Molly's desk. She picked one up and studied the advertisement. "Well you must think you're marrying someone or you wouldn't be looking at wedding dresses, would you now?"

Molly replaced the pad back into the powder case and snapped it shut. Then she gathered her two crutches and put them into position. Slowly and patiently, she got her legs set and rose to a standing posture. When she had maneuvered herself to face Anna, she said, "That's not for me. It's for someone I know; someone who's dating the most eligible bachelor in the village."

Anna hadn't caught it the first time but now she did. "Are you talking about me?" She knew Molly and every other single girl in Maghull considered Clarence G. Pyle, Jr. to be something better than a good catch; he was *the* most eligible bachelor in town.

Molly shifted to her closet to pick out a purse. "Of course, who else?"

Anna's heart began to thump harder; so hard she wondered if her friend could hear it. Molly Tomlinson's reputation as the village busybody was well known and well earned. Anna knew if there was but the tiniest morsel of information hidden in the corner of a dark, locked closet, Molly would somehow know and pounce on it. Not wishing to appear too anxious, she calmed herself and said, "So what makes you think I'm getting married?"

Molly placed the purse strap over her shoulder, put her left crutch back under her arm and slowly turned to the door. "Oh, just something I heard somewhere, something about a certain someone. That's all."

Anna frowned for she knew well Molly's penchant for dragging out disclosure—the moment when she revealed her insider information or *gossip* as others called it. She actually enjoyed it. Yet Anna was practically dying to know what she had heard. "Are you going to tell me before Mass or after?"

"Well, I guess I can tell you now if you really want to know. And I mean *reeeee*ally!"

"Molly, stop it! Tell me what you've heard at once! I'm not kidding. Right now!" Anna could no longer contain her excitement. This was exactly what Molly was waiting for; a hungry, desperate customer, one whose interest had piqued to the point that their lack of knowledge was unbearable. "Alright dear, and it's real juicy." Molly stroked her lower lip, taking in her friend's anxious face and drawing the moment out a tiny bit longer. "I heard this morning that Clarence was supposed to take Susan Daughtry out to dinner last night, but he called her to say that he couldn't take her out because he would be getting engaged soon. Under the circumstances, he did not think it appropriate, nor would it be proper or respectful to Susan. He hoped she understood." Molly's voice trailed off as Anna's head was left spinning. She had to carefully consider the implications of what she'd just heard.

Clarence had been seeing both her and Susan ever since he had broken up with Florence Stilbury. The town of Maghull was sure Florence and Clarence was a match made in heaven because his father's desire to expand the grocer's locations fit nicely with her father's desire to lend him the money. After all, her father was president of the Maghull branch of the Hatterton Bank of Liverpool. Most of the main businesses of Maghull placed their money with Mr. Stilbury, and borrowed from him when they required operating funds. Florence, an attractive natural blonde, with an hourglass figure no man could fail to notice, was his only daughter. She had dated Clarence for just under a year before the two had parted ways. The village gossipers had put forth a number of reasons for the breakup but neither party was talking. Still, the event held enough intrigue and wonder that tongues were kept wagging about town for months.

Once Clarence started dating again, odds were immediately placed on who would win his heart. Whoever it was would most likely live in luxury, though a somewhat diminished luxury considering the relatively small size of the Pyle estate, its location in the small town of Maghull, and the devastating destruction experienced by all the British citizens from the recent war. The top two contenders were Anna and Susan Daughtry. Anna strongly suspected she would play a distant second fiddle to Susan, who most men also found quite attractive. She knew she had never been referred to in that manner, unless it was because of her hair, a lustrous, thick affair that grew past the small of her back. Other than her hair, she was an ordinary, natural-looking girl. And given her advanced education, the deliverymen, loaders and carpenters of Maghull would not likely be interested. At least they hadn't been, so far.

The two walked carefully through the hallway to the front of the flat where Anna opened the door.

"When he told Susan, did he mention my name?" Anna asked.

Molly negotiated the threshold and the two steps before answering. "He didn't but she did. She was extremely distressed; said she couldn't believe someone of your—and these are her words dear—'plain appearance' could win against her. And with her family status and experience from finishing school, she had already seen that ring on her finger. She was very upset and it appears, mostly at you."

Anna was stunned. She tried to process all of this as they continued in the direction of the church three blocks away, but her mind was reeling. When they were far enough past an open window, she lowered her voice and moved closer to Molly. "Did you talk directly to Susan?"

"No, I didn't but I heard it from a very reliable source."

Anna whispered, "Who?"

"Susan told her friend Helen who told her brother Bert who's dating Rose. And you know Rose is best friends with Beatrice, who couldn't wait to call me up this morning and fill me in."

Anna shoulders sagged. "Oh for heaven's sake, there are five people between you and Susan. And you insist to call this fifth-hand information *reliable*?!"

"Yes dear, but every one of these five hands is an excellent source. All of them have impeccable records for providing high quality gossip." Anna shook her head as Molly added, "Do you believe Clarence didn't actually break up with Susan? Because that's what's important, dear. Oh, and the about-to-be-engaged part? If that wasn't true, why would Susan allow such a rumor to spread?"

Anna hesitated. "You do have a point. Okay, we have just a few more moments until we're at Mass. I want you to tell me everything you left out and then repeat it all again."

Molly smiled. "I will if you tell me I'll be your bridesmaid?"

"Who else would it be?"

"I know I'm your best friend but I just wanted to make sure."

"Will you stop it? You're stalling. Tell me now!"

The two girls talked quietly as they made their way into the church. When they entered, they dipped a finger in the holy water, made the sign of the cross on their forehead and chest, and genuflected before finding their way to the front row.

"Molly I'm going to sit at the back with my mother, but I want to talk to you after church because I'm going to the concert tonight and *he* might be there. I believe his father will be too, especially since he's the sponsor."

Molly leaned her crutches on the short wall of the wooden pew and nodded. "Yes dear."

With assurances in hand, Anna left Molly and went several rows back to where her mother was already seated, waiting for her only child. Then the traditional Roman Catholic Mass began.

Anna had the entire event memorized for it never changed. First came the Entrance Procession with the priest, altar boys, servers and a new fellow she had never seen before. This group walked reverently and ever so slowly from the church entrance behind the parishioners, inching forward towards the altar. Side to side and back and forth, the priest swung a burning censer full of frankincense. This cast through the crowd a sweet, piercing and woody scent reminiscent of purification and sanctification. While all of this occurred, Anna rewound the information Molly had divulged and replayed it in her mind.

I'll soon be Anna Pyle or better yet—Mrs. Clarence Pyle Jr.!

There! She dared to think the words.

When the procession arrived at the front of the church, the priest at last gained the altar and the Mass proceeded in its regular fashion. Next came the Greetings followed by Gloria in Excelsis. Anna fidgeted, unable to still her hands through the Opening Prayer, the Liturgy of the Word and the Lectionary. It was hard paying attention when her mind was filled with thoughts of the field now being clear of rivals and Clarence gallantly taking a knee to ask her to honor him with her maidenhood. Yet, they had just gone out on Friday, not two days ago. She was puzzled as to why he had not proposed then. Perhaps he had just made up his mind.

Anna had told Clarence she was tied up Sunday evening. A concert being performed by a female opera singer from London was taking place in the school auditorium. School staff had been asked to help. The Superintendent had volunteered his services; however, a family illness had taken him away. He asked Anna to take his place and since she had no plans, she agreed. Besides, she knew Clarence G. Pyle and Son Grocers were the sponsors and even though she disliked operatic singing, it might be a chance to bump into Clarence Jr. Hopefully, she would learn more tonight.

The Mass continued with the singing of hymns and repetition of prayers. It was hard to concentrate even though the Homily, her favorite time of Mass, was starting. This was when the priest delivered God's message to His people. Usually, it was short and sweet. Today though, Father Thomas rose and said no more than a few words before introducing the stranger she had seen during the Procession. The man got to his feet, cleared his throat, and began speaking in a thick Irish brogue.

"Thank you, Father Thomas, for allowing me this time to talk to your parishioners today. My name again is Neel MacKenna. You may have already guessed I'm not from around here."

The English crowd laughed.

"I'm from Dublin and as part of our Catholic Missionary program, I have been assigned to a country in Africa called Nigeria. It is located on the west coast of Africa. Nigeria is a large country and its citizens are quite poor indeed."

Anna was desperate to stop thinking about what she had heard earlier regarding Clarence. It was causing her anxiety. Yet, when she heard the word Africa, she knew this was just what she needed to take her mind off her love life. She had recently read a book about Africa and was left wanting more. She took in a deep breath and tried to concentrate on the man at the front.

"During my time there as a priest, I traveled extensively spreading the Gospel to the people and in turn, learned much about their ways. On my many trips through their shockingly primitive villages, I found a startling and disturbing practice. At times, the village chieftain or elders will take a poor soul—one of their own—from the village and cast them out. This villager is sent into the bush to fend for himself or herself. Neither food nor water is provided. No farming tools or survival equipment. Nothing. They are told never to come back."

He leaned towards the crowd, gesturing with one hand, his eyes alight with a sort of excitement. "If these sad creatures are spotted in the village, they are chased out by whips or worse. After one or two attempts, it begins to sink in that they can never return to their birth home where their families reside."

The audience—along with Anna—leaned forward in their pews, fully engaged. Still reeling from the recent Holocaust, they wanted to hear more about this unbelievable travesty.

"At times, these outcasts come to our mission pleading for food. They are emaciated and often near death. It is quite disturbing to see, to say the least. As I made my way around Nigeria, I discovered that the numbers are not in tens or hundreds. From what I can tell, the number is in the thousands; it may be greater than 100,000!"

The audience gasped.

"But I must tell you that the most distressing part of this tale is not the numbers. No, unbelievable as it may seem, it is something much worse. These outcasts may be elderly grandparents who can barely walk. They may be teenagers who have no idea about managing their affairs. They may be children who don't know how to do anything for themselves. And they may be babies still nursing at their mother's breast."

Now the audience only sat in frozen, stunned silence. Several women dabbed at their eyes while more than a few men looked angry and agitated.

"All of these people—who are God's creatures—are left to themselves only to rot in the bush. Rarely do their families come to look in on them. The stronger ones construct very basic, crude shelters to live in. They live primarily by stealing, until they are caught. Some turn to begging. If they are very young and not taken in by an older outcast, they wander about as if lost, with no idea as to what to do. Eventually, they find a place in the bush to lie down and wait for death to arrive. It's a terrible practice indeed!"

By now, everyone was deeply affected by this disturbing story. After all, here was a tale about placing babies in the bush to die. It sounded purely evil.

Father MacKenna could see that he had everyone engaged. It was time to provide the rest of the story. "You may ask how the people of Nigeria can even consider, much less *do* such a thing. Why would they even contemplate abandoning their own flesh and blood? The answer is twofold: fear and survival."

"Each one of these creatures I refer to is afflicted with a disease called leprosy. These outcasts are referred to as lepers." One or two of the more well-informed parishioners nodded their heads. Apparently, they had heard of this disease.

"Leprosy is a disease initially of the skin, although it affects all of the body's systems. When a person comes down with leprosy, they can be contagious. The villagers fear they will catch it. Not knowing what else to do, they quickly banish these lepers to the bush to fend for themselves. Also, because they do not know our Holy Father, there is the pagan belief that some god is punishing the recipient and thus this person has brought shame to the family and on the village itself. Even babies are subjected to this treatment. The worst part is that the people of Nigeria have no medicine or ability to treat these lepers. There is a particular plant oil that may be injected into the dead skin of the leper, but it's more of a stabilizing solution than a permanent cure. Still, it's better than nothing."

Anna swallowed hard as she listened to these details. She couldn't imagine something like that ever happening in Maghull, people being rejected, being outcast from society.

Father MacKenna paused to review his notes, and then cleared his throat. "The progression of the disease to death can be rapid or very long, even up to twenty years or more. At this time, there exists no known cure, but the Church of Scotland has established a leper colony in central Nigeria. At this colony, they administer injections of the plant oil I mentioned, which provides some relief. There is also work for the patients who are physically able. Milk is imported for the abandoned babies.

"After seeing their good work, I wrote to the Medical Missionaries of Mary in Drogheda, Ireland which was formed by Marie Martin in Nigeria in 1937, just before the war. My letter submitted the question as to their willingness to provide several sisters who could act as nurses and help administer a leper colony in Eastern Nigeria where my prefecture exists. They have agreed to provide four wonderful sisters who are willing to take the trip to Nigeria and engage in this mission—a Roman Catholic Church mission, no, God's mission—to help these lepers. It will be an exciting adventure!

"So now you all must be wondering how you can help me—us, your church, your God, in sustaining this mission. Well, maybe I won't tell you."

Much needed laughter rippled through the church; Father MacKenna had timed it perfectly. After setting their emotions on edge, he knew it was time for some levity. He wanted them relaxed when he presented his case.

"Okay, I'll tell you. After all, I have come all the way from Dublin to tell this story." Again, there was a round of laughter. "You precious followers of our Holy Father here in Maghull can help in three ways. First, we need volunteers. We desperately need a doctor. If you know a doctor who would consider such a mission, I should be pleased for you to have him contact me. We also need nurses. We could use a secretary or two, someone skilled in organization. We could use a teacher. There are others with trades and skills that can help. I am leaving several brochures in the back. Please take one if you or some- one you know may be interested. My postal address is on each bro- chure. Also, this church will have my postal address should you need it. Please write to me, although my reply might be slow to arrive if I am in Nigeria. I ask for your patience."

"The second way you may assist us is through your donations. I know the war has at last come to an end and you are all recovering, but I remind you these lepers are in a war every day; a war that involves lack of food, water, and shelter. They also lack human contact and compas- sion. Please consider them when you think about your finances."

"Finally, we could use your prayers. As I said, it will certainly be an adventure and while we believe our personal safety is not an is- sue, it is a strange and faraway place. The customs are vastly differ- ent. The food too, is unlike ours. The only aspect close to life here is the language. They speak English, although it's hardly the King's English. Still, we are able to communicate well enough even though I am from Dublin."

Several people laughed out loud as they imagined an Irishman with a thick accent speaking to Nigerians who spoke a crude form of English. It had to be a hilarious scene.

"That's why we need your prayers, for our safety and for our success." He glanced at his watch. "I see my time is up, and I hope you will remember this important mission to save all of God's creations including these poor souls, and lead them to a life of salvation, one that you already have. Thank you."

The parishioners clapped politely, some already reaching into their purses or wallets to make a donation. Anna looked at the back and saw the brochures. She wanted to remember to take one when she left. It might be something she could organize for her students; a relief effort so to speak. That is, if she was still teaching in the fall. Since she was about to be married to Clarence Pyle, Jr., it was unlikely she would be working as a teacher any longer. Instead, she would be starting a family—a family of future grocery magnates.

Oh children! she thought. *My own wonderful children!*

The Mass ended, bringing Anna back to reality. She rose with her mother, slid from the pew and together they walked towards the main entrance. There on the small table were the brochures. As her mother was talking to another woman, Anna took one. Molly caught up to the pair moments later.

"Hello Mrs. Goodwill, how are you doing?"

Anna's mother looked in the direction of the voice. "I'm fine, Molly. And how are you doing?"

"Smashing! That was some shocking news today, don't you agree?"

"It was," Anna said, cutting her off. "I have a brochure for my students. I may organize a relief campaign and raise support funds somehow. I feel so sorry for those poor lepers."

Mrs. Goodwill agreed. "Yes, even with all the bombing and killing we've been through, we have it quite nice here, I would say."

Molly hobbled behind them. "Yes, though I do long to have my left leg back. That wasn't nice of the Germans. Dropping bombs on Maghull as if we were the very center of England's armament industry. Really!"

Neither Anna nor her mother said a word. It was a difficult subject, the fact that one of the last bombing runs the Germans had made over England just happened to land in such a way as to send hot shrapnel into Molly's leg. At first, the doctors thought they could save it, but then changed their minds. There was no sense in risking her life. A devastated and pained Molly finally consented to an above-the-knee amputation.

"I thought you were going to look into a prosthetic?" Mrs. Goodwill asked.

"Yes ma'am I was, but the doctors want it to heal for another year. Then they can fit it properly. Of course, by then I'll be thirty years old, just another hopeless old maid, well beyond the possibility of being married."

"Oh hush Molly," Anna said. "Your self-pity is more than I can take. Being thirty years old has nothing to do with it. After all, I'll remind you I'm going to turn thirty this fall. The lack of eligible men is the biggest impediment to your marriage, and that's the case for almost every girl in our town."

All three women knew full well how many men their small town had lost, as had nearby cities like Liverpool. Every family had sacrificed someone, including Anna's.

"You girls will find a man in good time, and Molly, if a man truly loves you, he won't be bothered by your 'situation' or your age. He will love you, your heart and mind and soul. You are far too lovely to have that stand in your way. And my dear Anna will produce dozens of grandchildren for me. I just know it. Perhaps that fellow Clarence will be the one."

Molly grinned mischievously. "Yes, he may just be the one, Mrs. Goodwill. He may just be the one."

Anna cast a stern look in Molly's direction. The last thing she needed was her mother pondering the latest unconfirmed gossip.

When they reached Molly's flat, Anna told her mother she wanted to talk to Molly about something and Mrs. Goodwill proceeded home alone, two blocks away.

Once they were inside, Molly spoke up. "Could I perhaps tag along to the concert with you tonight? I would so love to hear this singer."

Anna smiled. "Of course you would. I know how much you love a good opera." They both laughed. "I know you all too well. The truth is you want some fresh produce for your gossip stand. Don't you?"

Molly touched her chin with her forefinger. "Well, Miss Goodwill, I believe you've bitten into an apple or two from that very gossip stand, and I don't recall you asking for a refund."

Anna chuckled. "Yes, I can't deny it. All right, I can slip you in through the rear entrance. You probably won't be able to sit in the auditorium seats because they are sold out. Just act as though you have something to do backstage and stay near me. I'll come by at six. I need to be there before it begins so be ready or I'll be leaving you and your business behind."

"Certainly, Mrs. Pyle."

"Would you stop that!"

An hour later, Mrs. Goodwill was resting comfortably on the couch, well into her traditional Sunday nap. This was the time Anna cherished, for each Sunday afternoon, when her mother fell asleep, Anna went to the rear of their flat and walked outside to a large oaken barrel. There, she lifted off the wooden lid and studied the contents. It was rainwater—glorious rainwater—that was continually replenished by the passing clouds over Maghull.

Anna looked both ways to see if anyone was watching her. Hardly a soul ever bothered to come behind these flats unless they were taking out the trash. Since the barrel was tight against the rear wall, she had all the privacy she needed.

Ever since she was a child, she had learned the value of rainwater on her hair. At seven, she started with a simple bucket, and then moved up to a new procedure as she aged and her hair lengthened. Now, it was a fairly simple process.

Anna loosened several clips which let her dark caramel-brown hair fall to her waistline. Then she backed up to the barrel and carefully lifted her long tresses into the barrel to let them soak for ten minutes. Next to the barrel, she sat on a small wooden bench she had placed there, leaning her head back into the opening to get as much hair underwater as possible. It was at this point that she would look up at the sky and let her mind wander.

Today she thought about where she and Clarence would live; when she would get pregnant; what her in-laws would be like; what she would name her children; where the nuptials would be held. There was no detail so small as to escape her pondering. Before she knew, the ten minutes were up and it was time to move to the next step.

Taking the heavy wet hair out of the barrel, she brought it around to her chest where she liberally applied a simple shampoo from the general store. Patiently, she worked it in to every spot on her hair, combing over and over until she could hardly see any evidence of the liquid, except a few bubbles. Then she took a small bucket and filled it with rainwater. Standing away from the flat and leaning forward, she doused her hair with several buckets of rainwater, watching the suds form puddles around her bare feet and gradually drain away. After she was done squeezing the water out, she picked up the comb and spent the next hour combing and brushing it until that gorgeous dark caramel color reappeared and her hair was mostly dry. At no time did she ever use a towel. Except for the shampoo, everything was completely natural.

As far as she knew, no one had ever learned her secret. They simply thought she was born with incredible, luxurious hair. But Anna knew different because this was one secret she kept from even her mother and friends. It was all hers.

At a little past six, the sky was overcast. Molly, a half a block behind, struggled to keep pace with Anna's brisk stride. Yet, Anna didn't wait. She was too anxious. She arrived at the door and opened the latch of the rear entrance to the auditorium.

Anna looked around and saw very little activity, so she decided to wait for Molly and help her up the steep stairs that led to the rear of the stage. Once that was accomplished, Anna found a place for her friend to sit near an electrical panel, and out of the way.

With Molly's crutches stored, Anna found the stage manager and introduced herself. The stage manager explained this wasn't like a play where scenes changed. There was only a single piano on stage with a microphone in front. All Anna had to do was turn the lighting down and make sure it didn't change until the performance was over. After that, she could enjoy the show from the rear of the stage.

The manager took her to the lighting panel and showed her how it worked. It was fairly simple. Then the manager disappeared once the indoctrination was over.

With nothing to do but wait, Anna took the opportunity to push through the center of the curtains and stand on the stage. She looked out over the auditorium. There were only a handful of patrons in their seats, although that would soon change. There would be no empty seats tonight as performances like this were rare in Maghull. This was the event of the season for what scant society existed in this small, working class town.

Anna closed the curtain and took her place near a lighting panel at the very corner of the stage. This was about ten feet from where Molly sat. Since the curtain would be kept closed and the dressing area was on the opposite side, they would only be able to hear the singer. This would mean she wouldn't be able to see her soon-to-be fiancé, if indeed he showed up, though both Anna and Molly knew the chances were good.

Molly gave the thumbs up just as the stage manager signaled to Anna to lower the lights. She turned a knob and the crowd noise quickly diminished. Within a minute, Anna heard clapping. She assumed the master of ceremonies was approaching the microphone.

"Welcome ladies and gentlemen. Thank you for coming tonight to this prestigious event. We hope you enjoy Dame Angelina Fleming. She has a special performance planned for you tonight. But before we begin, we must recognize the underwriter to this fine event. Please show your appreciation for Clarence G. Pyle and Son Grocers."

The audience clapped appropriately. "Now, please welcome Mr. Clarence Pyle himself."

Both Anna and Molly craned their necks to get a glimpse of the man but it was futile since he entered from the opposite side of the stage.

"Thank you very much ladies and gentlemen of Maghull. And thank you for your patronage of our family business. Tonight, I was going to take a moment and talk about our fresh produce and new location, but something has come up that I wanted to share with you, something that is very important to our family."

The audience was silent.

"Let me bring out my wonderful son—my *only* son—Clarence G. Pyle, Jr."

More clapping followed. Anna left her station to gain a better angle but it was all in vain.

Mr. Pyle continued. "I have some important news involving my son."

Anna was absolutely positive that she had ceased to breathe. Molly glanced at her but she didn't notice.

"Tonight, I'm proud to announce that my son is engaged to be married. The Pyle family is blessed to soon have a new and wonderful daughter-in-law. "

Anna's heart missed a beat.

"Florence, please join us."

There was a brief pause followed by some light clapping.

"Citizens of Maghull, please welcome Florence Stilbury and soon-to-be Mrs. Clarence G. Pyle Jr."

This time the applause from the crowd was deafening. Anna failed to notice her friend, who was frantically reaching for her crutches. She was oblivious to anyone else, her face rigid and emotionless with cords standing out in her neck, and jaw muscles bunched and tense. She was still not breathing and her heart was beginning to hammer in protest. In fact, she was frozen.

Molly had her crutches and was almost upright when suddenly, Anna snapped out of her trance, spun towards the rear steps and disappeared.

2

At the second tap, Mrs. Goodwill pushed herself out of the easy chair and made her way slowly to the front door. Before she arrived, she could plainly see who the visitor was. There was no mistaking the shadow cast by her wooden crutches on the sheers of the sidelight windows. Mrs. Goodwill released the latch and opened the door.

"Hello Molly, won't you come in?"

"Yes, ma'am. Thank you." She worked her crutches through the opening.

Mrs. Goodwill closed the door behind her and pointed down the hall. "Anna's in her room, dear."

Molly lowered her voice to a whisper. "How's she acting?"

Mrs. Goodwill nervously rubbed her hands and whispered back. "When she came home unexpectedly, I-I saw her face. It was very dark. Then I heard the crying from her bedroom. She won't talk to me or come out. I can't find out what's wrong. It's distressing. You know I don't like to be upset. The doctor has told me often enough to avoid overexertion." She hesitated. "I want to go in and ask her if I can help but she's an adult. If she wants me to know something, she'll tell me."

Molly lowered her head but didn't move. Mrs. Goodwill noticed this.

"Do you know what's happened with her?"

Molly nodded. "Yes ma'am, I'm afraid I do. We were at the performance seated behind the stage when Mr. Pyle came out and announced that his son was now engaged to Florence Stilbury. Anna's face turned white as a sheet and she left right away."

Now it was Mrs. Goodwill's face that turned dark. "Oh dear, this is terrible! That young Clarence seemed quite attached to Anna. I saw him each time he came to call on her. They appeared to be a very smart couple." Mrs. Goodwill rubbed her cheeks and shook her head. "Oh dear! This *is* bad news. What a shame for my Anna. She must be crushed."

It was Molly who felt bad then; she barely lifted her head. "I'm afraid I may have hurt her worst of all. You see, I discovered that Clarence had called another girl he was seeing and told her he was about to be engaged. Since the only other girl he was dating was Anna, I assumed it was a foregone conclusion. There was no one else. I never dreamed he would get back with Florence Stilbury. It's all rather shocking."

Mrs. Goodwill's mouth worked but no sound came forth. She was at a loss for words. Now she understood her only child's distress. She patted Molly on the shoulder. "I need to rest dear. You go in and see if she wants to talk to you." She left Molly alone in the foyer and returned to her chair, the stress of the situation unnecessarily raising her blood pressure.

Molly looked down the hall then back to the front door. She didn't want to do this tonight but it wouldn't get any easier tomorrow or the next day. Besides, Anna probably needed her.

After much thought, she moved slowly down to Anna's room and lightly tapped on the door. "Anna, it's me, may I come in?"

She could hear a slight movement but no response came.

"Anna, please!"

Footsteps approached the door and the latch turned. "Oh, it's you... and your fresh produce. Have you any information for me tonight?" Anna's tone was mean, her eyes red and shining.

Molly put her right crutch in first followed by her left crutch. "I am so sorry Anna. I had no idea this was afoot. You must believe me. I'm as devastated as you. Please accept my sincerest apology. *Please?*"

Anna only looked at her for a brief moment, her chin trembling as she tried to hold back more tears. Without a word, she turned and went back to her bed as she began to cry uncontrollably, her face buried in the pillow. After several minutes of sobbing, she trailed off.

At last she lifted her head and in a choked, little girl's voice said, "I'm not mad at you Molly. I'm mad at myself for being so stupid, for allowing myself to even dream of being married to Clarence. The life, the children. Everything. I was taken in and now I feel empty inside. It hurts terribly." She reached for a tissue. "I do think most of all I will miss the children. The ones we would've had. The ones I would've loved."

Molly worked her way to the bed and slowly lowered herself down to her best friend. "I'm so sorry for you. I'm also sorry for my big mouth. I guess I'm just very sorry." She patted Anna's back much as a mother would do to a child. Then she prepared herself for what lie ahead: to remain by her friend's side for however long it took to comfort her.

❦

Two days later, Anna had somewhat recovered and was moving slowly about the kitchen making afternoon tea to share with her mother. When the hot water was ready, she took three measures of the black Darjeeling tea and dropped it into the porcelain teapot to steep. Then she placed some sugar biscuits on a tray, arranging them in a nice pattern, one she knew her mother would appreciate. Five minutes later, she was seated at the dining table where her mother was already waiting.

"Here we are Mother. Would you like a cuppa?"

She poured each of them a cup of tea. Then she tipped in a dash of milk for her mother and watched the thin, golden liquid turn a muddy brown.

"How are you feeling?"

Mrs. Goodwill bit into a biscuit and chewed slowly. "Better since I had a nap. I still feel the fever though."

Anna sipped on her tea while she studied her mother. Her coloring was better though she appeared to have aged tremendously in one day. "Would you like me to fetch that powder, the one the doctor wrote out for you? It might do you some good."

Her mother said nothing but instead quietly sipped tea. Anna watched her even more carefully. She decided that if by the end of the day her mother's constitution didn't improve, she would take her back down to the doctor and have her looked at.

Anna poured herself another cup of Darjeeling. The golden Indian tea was one of her favorites. She enjoyed the smooth, rich taste as it swirled around her mouth. It was one of the few pleasures she allowed herself.

She thought about how much her mother had aged since her father's passing, though she was only sixty-three years old. Her mother suffered from a heart ailment, one the doctors weren't quite able to heal. It appeared five years ago, right after the air sirens sounded as everyone was running for the shelters. A horse pulling a wagon had panicked and despite the driver using all his strength at pulling on the reins, he was unable to control the terrified beast. When the horse made an abrupt turn, the wagon raised up on two wheels before catching her father and crushing him under the weight of the wagon.

Anna had been at school with her children when it happened. Her father's death was a shattering tragedy, one of thousands to come out of the devastating war. Anna's mother had never fully recovered from this tragedy.

She finished her tea and set the cup down on the saucer. As she stood up she said, "Mother, I'm going to purchase that powder for you. Where is the slip of paper with the name written on it?"

Her mother raised a trembling hand and pointed to the desk. Anna walked over and pulled open a drawer. The brochure Father Neel MacKenna had left at the church the previous Sunday was lying on top of the heap. Anna picked it up and stared at the photo of the sick children in Nigeria. She read through the brief paragraph before setting it down and moving some scraps of paper around.

"Here it is Mother. I'll be right back."

When her mother didn't answer, Anna turned around. Mrs. Goodwill was sitting in the chair staring straight ahead. Anna approached from behind and placed her hands on her mother's shoulders. She leaned over and left a gentle kiss on the top of her head.

"Mother, we will get you feeling good again. I promise." She patted her mother's shoulders, and turned back toward the front door, leaving the flat.

The brilliant sun overhead lit up her face as she stepped onto the sidewalk. It felt good.

I need to take Mother outside to soak up some of this beautiful sun while we still have it. I'll do that when I get home.

Anna walked along taking in the sights of Maghull. People were bustling in one direction or another, all of them in a great hurry to get somewhere. With the war ended, the citizens of Maghull, and indeed all Great Britain, were catching up on lost time.

Ahead was Phil's Apothecary. She crossed the street and made her way to the main entrance. As she turned to enter, a man burst from the store directly into Anna. Feeling as though she'd run into a brick wall, his body weight caused her to lose her balance and fall backwards. A split second before the back of her head struck the sidewalk, strong hands clamped onto her arms and steadied her. The momentum of all this caused Anna's body to pivot upwards, falling directly into the man's chest. As he raised her to stand once more, she instinctively wrapped her arms around him to prevent herself from falling backwards again. She also felt his powerful arms encase her body, protecting her. She inhaled his scent; he smelled clean and good, and… familiar.

As they separated, the man blurted out, "Oh my goodness, I am so sorry ma'am…" He studied her face, a hint of recognition forming in his eyes.

"Anna?"

At the same time, Anna studied the man's face. She recognized him as well.

"Clarence?"

The couple disengaged while several patrons passed by to enter the store.

"Are you okay?" he said, dusting her off as if she needed it.

"Yes, I-I believe so. That took my breath away. You caught me just in time." Anna's mind flooded with strong, conflicting emotions.

"I apologize. Really, I'm truly sorry."

"No, no, I wasn't looking where I was going. It was an accident," she said trying to sound polite although her own ears didn't believe what she was saying.

"No Anna, not about this, although I am sorry for dashing into you. No, I'm talking about the engagement announcement. I meant to call you beforehand but events just spun out of control."

Anna straightened her blouse and skirt. This gave her time to compose herself. "Clarence, you're a single man and have the perfect right to do what you wish. I certainly have no claim on you. There's nothing to apologize for."

He frowned. "Oh yes there is. You see I was very fond of you... I mean, I'm still very fond of you. I truly enjoyed our time together. It's just that... well..."

A passerby on the sidewalk patted Clarence on the shoulder. "Good afternoon, Mr. Pyle."

Clarence responded. "Good afternoon, Mr. Helton. Look forward to seeing you in the store." He waited as a few more citizens passed by. "Anna, what I want to say is that everything happened so suddenly." He lowered his voice. "There are issues I can't discuss and I... I wanted to call you but then Dad orchestrated that announcement and..." His words trailed off.

Anna gazed into his eyes.

I thought we were perfect together. Don't you know the great life we could've had? The children we would've raised? I have so much I want to say to you. I can't believe you picked her over me. I'm sorry but I just can't.

Anna spoke up. "Clarence, I also enjoyed our time together. I know you'll make a wonderful husband and an even better father. I offer you only congratulations." She was stunned as the words left her lips.

Oh Clarence, are you sure you want to marry her? Tell me this isn't final. Please think about it. Please!

Clarence blinked several times before words formed at his lips. "Why, thank you Anna. I'm truly grateful you feel that way. I'm not sure I would feel the same if the positions were reversed. But I sincerely hope I see you in the store. Perhaps you will stop in occasionally and say hi?" He allowed the hint of a smile to play at his mouth. It was this cute look that Anna had fallen for.

"Of course I will Clarence. And maybe your store will begin stocking fresh boyfriends, as I see that I am clear out of them." She grinned back at him.

"Ha ha, you are something else. Truly something else. You will have men standing in line for your hand." His genuineness was apparent.

Anna blushed, glanced at her shoes, then back to Clarence. "Well, I must be getting what I need here and back to Mother. She hasn't been feeling well."

"Oh really? I'm sorry to hear that. Indeed, I'll let you go. But do say hello to her for me."

"I will Clarence. I will."

Of course there's no way I'm going say anything about her—your new fiancée!

"And please give my best to Florence." Again, Anna couldn't believe what she was saying.

"I will. She'll like that. I do hope I see you more often though. And I won't force you to fall for me next time just to say hi. "

Anna wanted to smile but didn't; his words striking a lonesome chord within her.

"Take care, Anna."

Anna nodded then stepped into the apothecary leaving Clarence behind. Her heart was beating fast as the urge to cry bubbled up to the surface.

I'm not going to cry. Stop thinking about him. I'm not going to cry. He's moved on with someone else. I'm not going to cry.

She wiped away a tiny tear, pulled the piece of paper from her pocket, and began looking for the druggist.

Twenty minutes later, Anna held the small package in one hand and turned the latch with the other. She stood on the front step, looked up and saw clouds obscuring the sun.

I wanted to get Mother outside. Now the sun's gone. My encounter with Clarence delayed me long enough to miss it. Maybe it will come back out in a...

Anna saw her mother slumped at an awkward angle in her easy chair, the color completely drained from her face. In less than a second, she knew she was all alone—utterly and completely alone.

3

July 8, 1946
Dublin, Ireland

Anna stood in the street, her small suitcase in hand, and checked the address against the slip of paper. It appeared to match. She was in Harold's Cross, a suburb on the south side of Dublin. Father MacKenna had given her this address as the place he was staying while he was back in Ireland. According to his letter, it was his brother's residence and from the looks of it, she guessed he was fairly successful at whatever he did.

Father MacKenna had explained he wanted to meet Anna first to see if she would be a good candidate for the brutal work in Nigeria. His would be the final word on the matter.

To improve her chances, she had studied up on Nigeria and the work the Scottish church was already doing there. Anna read about Britain's colonization of the country, and how they had put together all the competing factions. Standing there, she felt as prepared, knowledgeable and ready for the interview as possible.

The hackney taxi she had shared with another man pulled away, leaving her all alone. Anna looked both ways down the street and saw very little activity. With the suitcase handle in her left hand, she took a deep breath and strolled up the long sidewalk to the front door.

A small brass knocker rested against a large oak slab. Through the sidelights, she could tell the inside of the house matched the outside.

She took in another deep breath before lifting the knocker and banging it on the brass plate several times. It wasn't long before a figure appeared and opened the door.

"Miss Goodwill, I presume?"

Anna nodded. "Yes Father, that's me." She stuck out a hand which he shook in a gentle manner.

"Please come in. Here, let me take that for you." He took her bag and set it on the floor next to a closet, leading Anna to a well-furnished living room. "Please have a seat and let's get to know each other."

Anna sat down on a nice, overstuffed davenport upholstered in a floral pattern.

"It looks like it was a nice day for you to travel," Father MacKenna said, as he sat opposite of her. "I trust the passage was calm."

"Yes, it was," Anna replied. "And it was on time, which was a nice treat. One never knows with the Liverpool ferries."

"Fortunately, I've had little experience with them, other than the one time I crossed in May. That was when I visited your church, I believe."

"Yes Father, you are correct." Anna forced a smile, enduring the small talk although she was anxious to get to the heart of the matter.

"Well I'm glad you made it here safely." Sensing her anxiety, Father MacKenna changed the subject. "Now I suppose we should get down to business."

He lifted a small bell and rang it. An older woman dressed in an apron appeared. "Muriel, we would like some tea please."

"Yes sir," the woman replied before disappearing.

"My brother is a barrister in town and quite in demand. From what I understand, one side usually seeks to retain his services before the other can. As such, he is able to afford my presence whenever I'm in town, which is a nice savings for the church and my own purse. And I do fancy these lodgings." He held his arms open wide as a broad smile spread across his face. "I hear the other barristers call him the very devil himself, so I told my mother between he and I, one of us will be with you in the afterlife."

They chuckled at the comment as he kept talking.

"I understand from your letters that you are a head mistress in Maghull. Why do you want to go to Nigeria?"

This was the big question she had been anticipating. She sent up a silent prayer before speaking. "Well Father, I feel called to help these poor children in Nigeria. I have no children of my own, as I'm not married and my mother just passed a little over a month ago. There is no longer anything for me in Maghull."

"What happened to your father?"

"He was killed during an air raid." She left out the part about the wagon overturning and crushing him. People generally understood that air raids killed in many different ways.

"I am so sorry for the loss of both your parents. You are the only child I presume?"

"Yes."

Muriel appeared with a tray loaded with saucers, cups, biscuits and a steaming pot of tea. She set the tray between them on a table and turned to Father MacKenna. "Will there be anything more sir?"

"No Muriel. Thank you."

He served tea to Anna, asking if she took it with milk. Anna picked up the saucer with both hands, holding it close to her chest. Father MacKenna poured himself a cup and held it in his left hand as he continued gesturing with his right.

"I understand you are most anxious to be a part of this mission and teach in the leper schools, but I'm not sure you fully understand the conditions, food, climate and the work itself. I'm concerned you will be shocked when you see your living conditions."

Anna decided to take the initiative. "Father, I've studied up and know about the heat, the moisture, the huts we will be living in, everything. I assure you I know as much as possible about what I'm asking to do."

"Do you now?" he said with a questioning eye. "You have never seen a patient with leprosy. You have never seen the cruelty of this disease and its effect on people, especially the children, have you?"

"No Father, but that can be said of anyone you take there. If that was the criterion you wouldn't be taking anyone." For a brief second she thought she might have gone too far, too fast, perhaps even insulting him. But when she saw a smile, she relaxed.

"That is so true. However, for the sisters who are going, it's their assigned duty. They are conscripts so to speak. Certainly they could say no but they never do. You however are different."

"Father, I will not let you down. If I do, I will pay my own passage back and do my best to locate a suitable replacement."

Father MacKenna sipped his tea while he studied his potential recruit. He currently had no other prospects and this might be the only one. "Well you certainly are eager. You will need a visa. Do you have a passport?"

Anna smiled. It sounded like she just might make it. "Yes, I have a passport. I've also checked with the Foreign Service Office. They told me that travel to Nigeria from England does not require a visa."

"I didn't know that. I'm required to have a one since I'm from Ireland. You are very thorough." Father MacKenna paused as he sipped his tea once again. "Very well, the position is yours... on one condition."

"Wonderful!" Anna exclaimed. "What condition do you propose?"

"I want you to spend two weeks with the sisters in their convent at Drogheda. The Medical Missionaries of Mary are furnishing four nuns to help with the nursing and spiritual duties. After all, you will be living with them in the bush. I want to ensure you are compatible with these women individually as well as their living habits."

"Of course. When will all this take place?"

Father MacKenna had to think for a moment. He set his cup down and withdrew a piece of paper from his pocket. "Passage has been booked on Elders & Fyffes Ltd. for the fifth of October from Dublin. I suggest early to mid-September. Let's see, this is July so that would give you two months to get your affairs in order. Will that be enough time?"

Anna turned it over in her head. "I'll have to give notice to the administration. They may require me to teach the first several weeks until a new head mistress can be secured. I would suggest the last two weeks in September and then leave in October with your group. I'm confident I will be compatible with everyone. With the extra time, I should have no problem selling my flat, disposing of my personal belongings and arranging my finances."

"Well then it is settled. I will have the sisters provide you with a list of items you should take in your personal kit. Many items you now take for granted are not obtainable where we are going, which is Ogoja by the way. That is where my mission is established. Ogoja is very small and primitive, but the natives consider it a good-sized city. You will see for yourself whether or not it's a bustling metropolis. From there we will assess the situation and decide where to set up the first leper treatment center. I hope within six months of our arrival to begin providing treatment to the unfortunate lepers.

"Of course you will be educating the children in a school we will set up near the treatment center. You will be provided compensation for your work from the government, which will be deposited in your bank here. In Nigeria, we bank in Calabar—a city on the coast. You won't be able to make drafts in Ogoja as hard currency is all they take, although you will likely find nothing there to purchase any-way. If you do find something, it will be extremely inexpensive. Your money should go a long way; however, this is not a place to go if one wishes to gain wealth."

Anna chuckled. "No, I wouldn't think so. And thank you for this opportunity Father. I won't let you down."

Father MacKenna smiled. "I'm sure you won't. You seem very fit and eager. Are you traveling back tonight or staying in town?"

"I'm staying with a friend and taking the ferry back tomorrow morning. I wasn't sure how long this interview would take."

"I see. Then as you have just arrived, let me provide more details of the culture, the climate and the journey itself. I wish to prepare you as best I can."

"I'd love that Father."

Anna poured herself another cup of tea and settled in for a long conversation, while her mind was busy creating a long list of things to do.

September 17, 1946
Maghull, England

The bank clerk reviewed everything one more time and pushed the documents to Anna. "Please sign these, and we will post a letter to our agent in Port Harcourt to allow you to make drafts on your account. I understand they have an agent in Calabar—which is closer to where you are going—however, I can't vouch for the expediency of the Nigerians. You are our first customer to test the system. May I suggest you travel with a sufficient amount in your purse just in case the procedures we're setting up are delayed for some reason?"

"Yes, that would be a good idea. Thanks for suggesting that."

Anna signed the documents and pushed them back to the clerk.

"I was thinking of fifty pounds but perhaps one hundred pounds would be more appropriate. If you could provide me lower denominations such as crowns, shillings and pence, I should be most grateful."

"Certainly ma'am. Just give me five minutes to prepare the withdrawal and arrange the money for you. If you would care to take a seat, I will come and get you when it's ready."

"Yes, thank you." Anna backed away from the counter and walked to the seating area. Suddenly, a voice shouted out across the lobby.

"Anna! It's good to see you."

She turned to her left and saw Florence Stilbury coming towards her, striding purposefully across the white marble floor. Anna's pulse quickened. She was absolutely the last person Anna wanted to see today.

"Hello Florence," she said with a forced smile.

Florence came close and grabbed Anna's hands. "I understand you are leaving Maghull for Nigeria, of all places."

Anna thought she detected a smirk. "Yes, that's right. I'm going with the Medical Missionaries of Mary to teach the leper children."

Florence grinned. "I just think that's wonderful! I'm so sorry you will be missing our wedding. I know Clarence would have loved to have you there."

Anna couldn't believe what she was hearing. Of course she wouldn't have attended. Most women didn't attend the wedding of their former boyfriends. It wasn't proper and Florence surely knew it. Anna desperately tried to think of an appropriate response when she heard a familiar voice from behind.

"Anna, what a pleasant surprise."

"Clarence, it's good to see you too." Anna's heart dropped every time she saw him. The last time had been at her mother's funeral.

"I know you are leaving soon for the bush. I hope you write and let us know how you are getting on. And I pray you are safe out there."

The three stood in an awkward semicircle. "Yes, of course I will write. And I do believe I'll be safe, although Father MacKenna has repeatedly told me there are no guarantees."

Oh how I wish you were my protector. My knight in shining armor.

"I do hope you are very safe indeed." He stared at her a little too long. Or was it her imagination?

Florence pouted as she tugged on her fiancé's arm. "Dear, I'm hungry and you promised me lunch." It was clear she was ready for Anna to be gone.

"Yes, I did promise. I suppose we should go." Again, he gazed intently and this time it wasn't Anna's imagination. It seemed like he wanted to say something but with Florence glued to him, he couldn't.

The clerk approached and tapped Anna on the shoulder. "Ma'am I have your items for you."

Anna nodded and turned her head back to the couple. "It was good to see you both. I wish you the best. I truly do." It was a lie. Anna felt dizzy wondering what this scene would've been like if she was the one he had proposed to.

Clarence smiled warmly. "Take care, Anna." Before he could say more Florence pulled him away.

"Good to see you Anna," Florence said as they walked toward the exit.

"Wonderful to see both of you. Goodbye!" It sounded so final. Anna watched the couple exit the bank holding hands. A melancholy mood fell over her entire spirit making her both sad and depressed. Her eyes moistened as she made her way to the counter to complete the transaction. The consequences of her decisions were just now becoming apparent. She hoped her thoughts would improve as the day progressed.

Molly hobbled around on her crutches in her spare bedroom, watching her best friend lying on the bed, poring over photographs. Anna's head was down, studying each photo before moving on to the next one. A single overhead light illuminated the room save for the shadows created by Anna's hunched over form.

"Are you going to look at those all night?" Molly asked.

Anna lifted her head and looked into her friend's eyes. "There are just so many memories. It's sad leaving this town and especially you. I guess I underestimated my feelings. I just feel sad now."

Molly rested her crutches on the bed and sat down next to her best friend putting an affectionate arm around Anna. "You don't have to leave you know. It's not too late to say no. You could live with me for a while until you reestablish yourself. I would be grateful for the company."

Anna held up a photo of the two girls. They were standing in the still-smoking, scorched rubble of a nearby building, another victim of a German bombing raid. Molly still had both her legs and was standing at attention, her hand saluting Anna as if her friend were a superior officer. Anna was caught laughing the moment the camera snapped, which produced a photo capturing the essence of their relationship: joy in the face of tragedy. Molly was like that. Always making people laugh and cheering everyone up.

"Can I take this photo with me?" Anna said.

"I suppose, if you are bound and determined to go forward with this unnecessary adventure. You know you could find a man around here somewhere. You don't have to go to some far-off land to find love and adventure."

Anna set the photo on the nightstand and gazed into Molly's eyes. "I know that. I'm not going there to find love. I think I'm going to find myself, my purpose in life. I don't know if it's in Nigeria, but I have to go. There's something in my spirit that's pushing me out of Maghull. Something I can't explain."

"Gosh, with you gone, I guess there's one less female to compete with me for all the men here. At least I have that for comfort." Molly patted Anna on the leg. "Of course I'll be able to keep you informed of all the gossip floating around this backwater town. That should ease your loneliness in the bush."

Anna clasped Molly's hand. "Oh I know you're good at that. I'm counting on your letters to keep me informed. I wouldn't be going there without them."

Molly reached over and hugged her friend who winced. "Is something wrong?"

"No, it's just that when you hugged me it hurt my arm. That's where I received the yellow fever and anti-typhoid injection this afternoon. It's still tender."

Molly picked up her crutches and pushed herself up. "I'm sorry but I'm going to have to hug you at least one more time before you leave, so I want you to get a lot of sleep tonight and heal that arm. I'll leave you to it."

"Thank you, Molly," Anna said, her eyes glistening. "You've been a wonderful friend to me. I'm sure going to miss you."

Molly stopped at the door, pivoted on one heel and gave a slapstick salute mimicking the photo. "Private Tomlinson at your service, sir."

Anna waved at her saying nothing. Her throat had tightened up and she didn't want her best friend to see her cry. Molly turned and left just in time for Anna to bury her head in the pillow and give in to the tears.

When the door was closed, Molly hobbled to her room leaving her own trail on the wooden floor. Wiping away tears is impossible when one's hands are occupied with crutches.

4

September 21, 1946
Drogheda, Ireland
Medical Missionaries of Mary Convent

The bell rang a second time as Anna stirred in her cot. It was 5 a.m., much too early for her to rise even though she meant to. The Mother Superior had told her that even though she was going to be living with the sisters, she didn't have to follow the same routine as they did. They had committed to this way of life; she hadn't. Still, Anna was determined to follow their routine while she stayed in the convent for two reasons: first, she wanted to completely experience their lives for herself. It would be something she could write about in the future; stories to tell. The second, and perhaps most important reason, was that she didn't want to give the sisters any cause to reject her or have the opportunity to go to Nigeria pulled from her. She had already said her goodbyes and going back now would be humiliating. She was determined to see it through.

Anna sat up on the cot and saw that the other nuns had already moved towards the dressing area. She winced as her feet absorbed the frosty chill seeping up from the stone floor. It was an eye-opener.

She shuffled over to the dressing area. The one aspect of being a nun that she liked was the simple dress. A long black tunic slipped easily over her spare frame, with a cloth belt cinching it around her waist. They had not provided her with a white coif or headpiece, and she had not asked for one. Anna rightly assumed she wasn't allowed to have one since she wasn't a nun. She did put on her own pair of black shoes. That appeared to be the only piece of wardrobe a nun had any say over.

Anna moved swiftly to the chapel where she found the nuns already kneeling in prayer, waiting for the service to begin. Prayer would continue until 6 a.m., when a priest would appear and conduct mass. At 7 a.m., when mass was over, they were all allowed to have a small breakfast in the dining area before beginning various chores.

Anna was assigned to iron clothes because the nun that usually did the ironing had to take leave due to a death in the family. When she was told of her duties, Anna thought it would be fairly straightforward. She had ironed her own things all her life. How hard could it be?

Then she discovered it was not the same simple ironing she was used to. Each garment carried religious significance and had to be strictly ironed just so, with the creases in the exact same spot. It had been a challenge at first, requiring at least thirty minutes per garment. It took about six days but Anna finally mastered the various garments. Now, she was able to allow her mind to wander.

Clarence Pyle comprised a large amount of her daydreaming, as did Molly. Her mother and father too. Then she dreamed about the life in Nigeria she was going to have. Where would she be living? To what conditions would she be exposed? Would it be painfully cruel, or would she love the work and make it her life? Would she meet some new friends? Would she find a man there? She dared to dream about that.

At noon, as she was finishing her ironing, another bell rang for yet another mass. After that, a small meal would be served. Even though Anna wasn't a big eater, these meals were not what she was used to eating. Being a nun was a life stripped entirely of worldly noise and excess. If it wasn't absolutely necessary, it wasn't present in the convent.

By this time, Anna had learned the names of the four nuns who were going with her. Two were trained nurses and the other two would handle the secretarial duties, which apparently were significant. All four sisters would handle the spiritual duties of explaining the Gospel to the Nigerians, or at least those who showed any interest.

The two nurses were Sister Browne and Sister Flores. Sister Flores was from Bilbao, which was located in northern Spain. From the moment they met, Anna sensed this woman despised her. It didn't help that she had already run afoul of the nun several times. The problem was with their cots; they were right next to each other.

Her first night in the pitch-black sleeping room, Anna was rudely awakened by an angry nun demanding answers. Apparently, she had mistaken Sister Flores' cot for her own. Sister Flores worked late, put on her nightgown, and made her way along a well-practiced path only to find her cot already occupied. The commotion awakened a few nuns nearby. When she had understood her mistake, Anna immediately moved to the correct cot. Sister Flores insisted on changing her sheets and pillowcase which caused more noise and irritated muttering, and awakened even more nuns. Anna wasn't sure which side they were on, but she knew she was starting off on the wrong foot.

The next night, exhausted from a long day's work, Anna again mistook Sister Flores' cot for her own by laying some things on it. This time, the nun appeared, stopping her before she could crawl underneath the covers. It was now clear to Anna that Sister Flores was firmly against her and for whatever reason, there was no turning back.

Fortunately, Anna made friends with Sister Browne. Sister Browne was from Canterbury, England, on the east side of the island directly opposite of Anna's hometown of Maghull. She had pulled Anna aside and told her not to worry about Sister Flores.

"She doesn't care for anyone. Just steer clear of her and you'll be fine, dear."

The other two nuns were Sister Brigid Whelan and Sister Darcy O'Keefe, both from Ireland. Anna had yet to find out exactly where in Ireland they were from because with their thick Irish brogues, she had not spent a lot of time talking to them. However, both were very pleasant and welcoming.

The Mother Superior, Mother Walmsley, appeared quite capable of making any decision that was needed to ensure the convent continued running smoothly. She was supported by Mother Marie Martin, who had founded this convent and the resulting organization Medical Missionaries of Mary or MMM—as it was known. Its motto was: *"Rooted and founded in love."*

MMM sent trained nurses and staff to all parts of the world to treat and care for the sick, while at the same time exposing as many as possible to Christianity. They worked closely with the Foreign Service branch of the Roman Catholic Church, which used the designations Prefect Apostolic for priests who headed up a particular territory in a foreign country. The MMM would usually send nurses to currently established missions when requested *if* they had the money and people to do so.

Father MacKenna had been recently appointed Prefect Apostolic over some territory in Nigeria and had convinced Mother Marie Martin to send him nurses and staff to deal with the leprosy issue. Sending Anna—a qualified and competent teacher—was an added bonus. Of course, finding a doctor willing to go to Nigeria would be likened to finding the pot of gold at the end of a rainbow. At last check, they hadn't found anyone.

After the nuns finished their noon meal, the normal routine was to head to various locations for quiet solitude, reflection and prayer. This was followed by more work. By Saturday, Anna knew the routine and where the sisters would usually be, which helped her avoid Sister Flores. The big problem she had now was her hair. She had kept it bound up since her arrival and it was crying out to be washed. That morning, she had discovered a large oak barrel outside recently filled with fresh rainwater. It was in a relatively secluded area and was calling out to her, creating the strong desire to give it a try. But she was hesitant. She didn't know what was proper, especially with her elaborate ritual and extravagant tools. She thought about asking for permission but was afraid of receiving a no, and she didn't know how much longer she could go before her hair would have to be scrubbed by shower water inside the convent. The last time pipe water had touched her hair was longer than she could possibly remember. She decided the time was now.

Making her way to the kitchen, she found it empty. A small pot with a handle resting on a shelf was quickly removed and concealed in her bag, joining a glass bottle full of premium shampoo (a recent indulgence) and a towel. Anna moved towards a rear door near the rain barrel so she could accomplish her mission. Just as she pushed opened the door, she remembered she had left behind one very important item: her comb. It wasn't just *any* comb. It was an extravagant eight-inch whalebone comb, set inside an ornately embossed and engraved silver handle. The size of the handle made it easier to grip and also protected the delicate whalebone. This special comb was made in Portugal. Her father had given it to her as a present when he traveled back and forth from Portugal on business before World War II. He had explained to her that it was a birthday present and Christmas gift all rolled into one. That's how she knew it must have been very expensive. It was precious to her; Anna had loved it from the moment she saw it. She considered it a miracle that all these years later, the comb's teeth remained intact. After making the trip back to retrieve it, she was ready for her clandestine mission.

Once again Anna pushed open the door and closed it as quietly as possible, ignoring the complaints from the squeaky hinges. Walking softly, she stayed on the pavement that surrounded the convent and drained away the water from the exterior walls. It didn't take long for her to find her rain barrel.

Anna quickly and quietly untied her hair, letting it fall down her back. Wasting no time, she bent backwards into the barrel and dropped her long tresses in to let them soak for the required ten minutes. When time was up she pulled the dripping mass out and liberally applied the shampoo. Anna worked it in with her hands, making sure each strand received a royal treatment. Once she was satisfied with the shampooing process, she dipped the pot into the barrel and poured water over her hands to clean them. Then she picked up her unique comb and began running the teeth through her sudsy hair. She hadn't even gotten halfway through when a side door squeaked open, shielding her from the person on the other side.

Holding her breath, Anna froze. She knew it was time for prayer and since she was supposed to be following the rituals of the nuns, that's where she should've been. But she wasn't in prayer; she was washing her hair.

Anna hoped and prayed the person would simply go back inside and close the door leaving her undiscovered. From her vantage point she saw thick shoes exposed under the bottom of the door. Anna wasn't able to tell if it was a man or women, but she knew she probably shouldn't be out here doing this. Now she stood frozen, waiting to see if she would be caught.

As Anna focused on the thick black shoes, the door started closing. They moved away and Anna exhaled in relief. She thought the owner of the shoes had gone back inside but when the door closed they had only stepped away from it, allowing the door to shut and see what was behind it. Now they stood facing her.

Anna's eyes slowly worked upwards. She saw a tunic, just like the one she wore. She saw a cloth belt. It was definitely a nun. Anna saw a rosary hanging down over the tunic. A thick mound of foam fell from Anna's long hair and landed with a wet *plop!* on the pavement. When she saw two angry, fisted hands pressing hard on two mean-looking hips, she knew exactly who her captor was: Sister Flores!

November 30, 1946
Maghull, England

Molly heard the familiar clang of her mailbox just outside her door. Even though the mail was theoretically delivered each day Monday through Friday, post came so rarely for her that it was a nice treat when it did.

Fumbling a bit with her crutches, she carefully navigated the furniture, reached the front door and was promptly greeted by a blast of cold air. Fortunately, she could reach her mailbox simply by leaning out a bit and keeping her body half-screened by the front door. Glancing up at the sky, she could tell it was going to be another dreary English day, one that would likely bring rain, fog, and more cold wind.

As she reached inside the mailbox, she felt several items—one particularly large. This intrigued her. Not able to manage the crutches and open the mail at the same time, she gathered the envelopes to her chest, worked her way back inside her warm flat, and hobbled over to the kitchen table, spilling all three pieces onto it. Standing over the table, her heart raced when she saw Anna's handwriting on the large, thick envelope. Knowing that this would be something to savor slowly, she decided to make a pot of tea before tearing into it.

As the water boiled, she removed the lid from a small wooden box labeled Thomas Twining Fine Teas, and took out several bags of one of her favorites: Darjeeling Orange Pekoe. Lifting it up to her nose, she breathed in the heady aroma, already imagining the strong, but golden-light taste, one that was perfect for such a dreary afternoon and a long letter from a dear friend.

When the tea was steaming from her cup and properly adjusted with fresh cream, Molly looked at the two other letters and put them aside. One was from a prosthetic manufacturer, likely telling her it would be six more months before they had the material to make her new leg. The other was from a friend in Liverpool that surely contained gossip from the local scene. Both could wait.

She picked up the long thin metal opener and carefully slid it under the sealed flap, cutting the seam. Pulling out the letter, it was eleven pages front and back—a record for both Anna and Molly. She looked through the pages, making sure they were in proper order and then took a long sip of her Darjeeling. Another pause and one deep breath later, she began.

October 30, 1946

Dearest Molly,

I hope this letter finds you in excellent health and well-being. I have so much to tell you! I expect to be sending you many letters (and of course receiving many back), so I would be obliged if you would save each one in the order I send them. That way I shall have a complete record of my time in the bush when I return—however long that is. Perhaps I can draft stories for my future students or even compose an entire book. Who knows? But either way, please be a dear and save them for me. Thank you, in advance.

First, I have to say I almost didn't make it to the ship on the day of departure. I had several run-ins with one of the nuns—Sister Flores. She is a stout, rigid woman from Bilbao, Spain. If you knew her, "inflexible" and "unyielding" would be the first two words that come to mind. She does not suffer fools gladly, and sadly, on many occasions I was one of those fools.

As you know, Father MacKenna instructed me to spend two weeks living with the nuns in their convent, since I would be living with them in the bush. And even though he did not require I follow the nuns' routine, I thought it only proper to try to fit in and not hamper any chance I might have of being allowed to come to Nigeria and teach. I think now that might have been a mistake.

The very first day I made a number of errors, each involving Sister Flores. For some reason, she seemed to not want me to go with them. I sensed this and did everything I could to please her. I then changed strategies and tried to avoid her. By the third day, she was ready for me to leave. I had slipped away from my assigned chores and prayer to take care of some personal items such as washing my hair. As the nun's hair is continually tied up and covered, they seem to never worry much about it. Well, as you know I worry about mine.

And it was there that she found me and made a report to Mother Walmsley, the Mother Superior of the convent. I felt like a little schoolgirl trudging off to the headmaster's office to await my punishment. I couldn't help but assume the worst.

Mother Walmsley closed the door and turned back at me with the look she usually wore: serious and no-nonsense. I had heard that Sister Flores was voicing her strong opinions for me not to go to Nigeria by listing them out: I wouldn't be up to the work; I'm a city girl used to fine things, therefore the bush would eat me alive; I wouldn't relate well with the natives. There are several others I can't recall. While Mother Walmsley didn't explicitly say so, I gathered Sister Flores was making an "it's-her-or-me" proposition.

Sister Flores is scheduled to be the head nurse at the mission. She has been trained to deal with leprosy patients, and will be supervising the other three nuns and training the locals to provide medical care as well. This means she is vital to the mission, certainly more vital than I. But Mother Walmsley explained they really want a teacher with my credentials to go, because an educated native can teach others. Furthermore, to have locals become nurses would mean they must first be able to read. Their duties will include creating and maintaining charts, reviewing medicine records, keeping an inventory of supplies and understanding many other subjects. So my teaching work will be important too.

As we talked (although she mostly talked while I listened), Mother Walmsley gave me the real scenario that was at play here. Sister Flores is very close with another nun, Sister Fent. During the war, the two of them worked closely together with the field doctors tending to men on the front lines. They were known as, 'the Two Generals' for their rigid determination in getting things done. Most nuns disliked working under them but they all had to admit what-ever the Two Generals did, it was successful and economical. She told me the Pope recognized both women for their work.

After the war, they managed to use their clout to obtain the same assign-ment: this Nigeria leprosy mission. However, someone high above Mother Walmsley wanted Sister Fent to run a large mission in India, so they had her reassigned. When that happened, both sisters raised quite a row. There were several high-level meetings and it was agreed Sister Fent could go to Nigeria to teach if there was no certified teacher who applied. When I volunteered, Sister Fent was rescheduled for India, upsetting them both. As such, Sister Flores is doing her best to be rid of me so her friend can jump on the ship to Nigeria. Mother Walmsley wanted me to be aware of the headwinds I was facing.

We continued talking and I got the distinct impression that Mother Walmsley was looking forward to saying farewell to Sister Flores and restoring peace and harmony to her convent. I must confide, dear friend, she appeared as eager to see her go as Sister Flores is for me to stay behind. After much thought and prayer (about two minutes), Mother Walmsley came up with an ingenious plan: she would personally supervise me and make the decision at the end of the period as to whether or not I could go. Then she moved me to a small room that was a supply closet with my first duty being to clean it out and move the supplies elsewhere. We arranged my schedule so as to interact as little as possible with Sister Flores, though that unfortunately also included avoiding/not interacting/not getting to know the three other sisters going on this great adventure.

Well, it worked! I managed to stay out of sight and mind my own business, so when the day before our departure arrived, no one could prevent me from going. When Father MacKenna later joined us, he knew nothing of the entire affair and remained in quite a jovial mood, having recently secured two additional financial benefactors for our trip.

The next day was October 5th, and a local bishop arrived to perform a departure ceremony and farewell address. He performed the blessing with such a thick Irish accent, I wasn't sure whether he was sending us all up to the North Pole or Nigeria. I'm sure thankful he's not going. One thing I am thankful for, however, is my tea shipment sent directly from the Ceylon plantation! It arrived with no time to spare. This is the one comfort from home I'm sure to be able to manage, for all I need is a proper tea cup and saucer (I'm taking one from Mother's excellent collection) and hot water (which I pray they have there). Surely they are at least that civilized. If I'm lucky, I may even find a tea pot there, perhaps one rugged enough to withstand open flame.

I must confess I was a bit melancholy right before departing. Leaving England… you and Maghull—it all seems so permanent, like I may never return. It's just a feeling and I'm probably being silly. I'm sure everything will be fine.

(I composed this letter up to this point and meant to send it to you before we departed Ireland, but events conspired against me, and I regret I was not able to post it in time. So, during the time at sea I added to it and that starts here.)

The journey began on the steamer *Medina*, which I later learned to be a cargo ship that only incidentally carries passengers. The *Medina* routinely carries manufactured goods to Nigeria (bales of fine cloth, rubber tires, cars, and roofing zinc), and after unloading those, picks up bananas, cocoa, timbers, and palm oil which she then brings back to England. The crew makes this journey every month.

Because of this arrangement, the ship has very few amenities as Father Neel (that's what he likes to be called in the bush) explained. Father Neel is well traveled and informed me that most proper seagoing vessels transporting people have a First Class and Third Class designation. For First Class passengers, they have the use of a Lounge, Dining Saloon, Library, Cardroom and Smokeroom/Bar. He showed me a postcard from one ship that had a shopping arcade with glass display windows from floor to ceiling, as well as small palm plants in the lobbies. They even had a children's playroom complete with a small slide, playpen, and toys cars. I am sad to report that the *Medina* is not burdened with such fine amenities. According to Father Neel, we will have no trouble finding our way around this ship (a prospect one cannot be sure of on the large passenger ships where the choices are apparently endless).

I was immediately shown to a two-berth cabin which I shared with Beverly Stanton, an older woman traveling to Nigeria to deal with her father's passing. He was with the War Department and, despite having a wife in a London institution, took up residence there to handle postwar activities. He died leaving a large house, numerous belongings and, from what I can tell, a native woman who claims to be his wife, or at least his mistress. Beverly has been trying to have his property and money (which I gather is extensive) transferred back to England, but has been unsuccessful due to this woman's legal claim. Since Beverly's mother cannot travel or handle her own affairs, Beverly now has to go on her own adventure to resolve the mess. She is not looking forward to it!

My sullen traveling companion, Sister Flores, berths with Sister Browne who is from Canterbury and seems to be entirely of the opposite temperament. Sister Browne is jovial and never lets conflict affect her. I like her, although I have had very little time with her. The other two sisters—Sister Whelan and Sister O'Keefe—are Irish girls and berth together. They mostly keep to themselves, and seem pleasant enough.

When we finally pulled out of port and made it to open sea, the ship began rolling. Walking was far more difficult than I ever could have imagined! At least I wasn't the only one having problems; the four sisters were having troubles, too. (Father Neel, however, seemed unaffected.) It took a whole four days before I became accustomed to the roll of the ship and could confidently make my way around. Occasionally, the direction of the waves or wind would change, forcing us to adjust for that day and making the trip that much longer. Honestly, I can't imagine how someone could make their living at sea!

Because there are only six cabins, the ship can only hold twelve passengers. Two of the cabins are comprised of four Nigerians traveling back to their homeland. Two of them are men who were in England on business. The other two are husband and wife who were trapped in Poland during the war (of all grim places!) and worked hard after the war to save up enough money to go home. They are very excited to say the least.

Father Neel is berthed with a man who is thirty-nine years old, and I must say, quite dashing. During the first several days I avoided talking to him for fear of it looking unseemly, but then I found out from Father Neel that his name is Grant Eaton and he is a widower—his wife and son were killed in a German air raid. He is travelling to Nigeria to perform a wide-ranging assessment of the land and update maps in case there is another war—God forbid! I guess he's something like a scout.

When I began talking to him in the dining room, he explained that when war breaks out, there's no time to update maps and fix locations of buildings and roads. It's only when things are peaceful that this work can be done. As such, he will be travelling all over Nigeria for quite some time, perhaps even years. He seems swashbuckling and I have to admit, we get along famously, always chaperoned of course.

Grant has coal black hair (which he wears slicked back) and round wire frame glasses that add a sense of intelligence to his finely chiseled face. He is quite a bit taller than I and appears very fit. I see him each day on the deck doing calisthenics, something I should probably be doing. To my delight, Father Neel arranged a card game with Grant, Sister Browne and me.

The two men took us on and we demolished them, after which a rematch was demanded the next night and the men won, but barely. We were planning on having a rubber (playing a round of bridge) when the ship touched at Funchal, Madeira to offload two vehicles and some supplies. That's when my adventure truly began!

Authorities boarded the ship and demanded to see all our paperwork, including the crew's. They were angry as they searched the entire ship. At first, they appeared interested only in the cargo, so we were forced to sit in the dining room while the search was transpiring. Of course, I happened to sit next to Grant. He was unconcerned and told me this was fairly common. When he saw my concern he laughed, and said a bribe proposal would be forthcoming and the ship's captain would be forced to pay something or remain in port. He said sometimes they even grab a passenger and throw them in the local jail until they are ransomed out. It all sounded so evil to me. While we were talking, Father Neel quietly slipped unnoticed back to his cabin and donned his formal attire, giving him a glittering if not royal appearance.

While Grant and I were talking about things and laughing, a rough looking Portuguese officer came in and pointed to the two of us. My heart stopped. Grant clutched my arm, as Father Neel jumped up to protest. He can put on a mighty good show when it comes to it and it nearly stopped the officer. But then his boss came into the dining room and away they took us, literally grabbing our arms as they led us down the gangplank. At the bottom, the officer talked to some port officials and Grant used this distraction to reach over and whisper in my ear, "Let me do all the talking. Say nothing. Simply agree with me." I nodded, fearfully imagining what my last days withering away in a Madeiran jail would be like.

When they had cleared up the problem with the port officials, the officers took us to a dark, dingy room just off the dock. Here, I must admit my heart was about to explode with fear. They began treating Grant roughly, pushing him around and even slapped his face one time. When Grant started speaking in Portuguese, it caught them by surprise. During the English words, I could hear him explaining how he was affiliated with the government and they had booked him passage at the last minute. That's why the paperwork wasn't exactly in order. One of the officers asked me if I was with him and I saw Grant's head nodding in the background. I nodded and they went back to speaking in Portuguese. After an hour of this, Grant grew very angry and they got nervous. I have no idea what he said, but all of a sudden they became very polite, even bringing us Madeira wine, water, juice and fresh seafood to eat. Grant told me to enjoy it as a sign of their apology, which I did, still praying a jail cell wasn't in my immediate future. No sooner had we finished, then were we carefully escorted back on board and the captain called us immediately to the bridge. Grant told them to cut the stay short and disembark as soon as possible. The captain revoked all shore leave, quickly offloaded the cargo destined for this port, and soon we were headed back out to sea. Honestly, he couldn't sail away fast enough—I was so glad to see Madeira disappearing over the horizon!

The next night things had settled down and we got to our rubber match. Of course the men won. Oh well! Grant explained to everyone what happened, politely leaving out the part about me agreeing I was with him. I thought it was the gentlemanly thing to do, especially since I was traveling with a priest and four nuns, all who have made a vow of poverty, obedience and chastity.

On Sunday, we held mass in the dining room. It was just our missionary group and Grant. Father Neel had trouble administering the Eucharist when the ship began rolling, but with Sister Flores' help he managed.

On the sixth evening, a nasty thunderstorm overtook us. I must admit, the wind and waves tossed us about, so I was relatively certain of imminent death! My cabin mate, Beverly, was even more frightened. We confined ourselves to our bunks and prayed for the best, and an hour later the lightning disappeared as if it had never come. It was smooth sailing from then on out.

It didn't take long to learn the ship's layout, at least of the few places we were allowed to go. The dining room is the common place for every activity: we eat there, play cards, read, or just sit and have conversation. There are several exterior deck chairs on either side of the dining room, and we can sit in those at any time. However, when the seas are up, the mist can often sur-prise you and coats the entire body. And since the chairs are not well shaded, if the sun is fully out one can end up a lobster, even with a nice breeze. Beverly stayed out in the sun too long and has been suffering from burns the last two days.

There are two bathrooms at the end of hallway where our cabins are—one for women and one for men. There's room for two women at the same time, and I must tell you that taking care of one's personal business is a different experience when there is someone next to you. It tends to speed some bodies up and slow others down.

After seven days at sea we passed the Canary Islands. Grant had some binoculars and pointed out several landmarks, including a tall spire on one of the larger islands. It was like having my own personal tour guide. Once the Canary Islands disappeared behind us, the air turned decidedly hotter. The crew informed us this was normal, as the Canaries (that's what they call them) are the dividing line between the two climates. We were now officially in the tropics.

On October 14th, we eased into the port of Dakar, Senegal for refueling and fresh food. It was a dry and dusty, orange-colored world that looked like what Father Neel described as a version of hell. Grant warned us to possibly expect a repeat of the Madeira adventure, but Father Neel didn't think so. He had sailed many times and never had an issue like that in an African port. He said they rely on trade too much to hassle the cargo ships. Without ships from England and Europe, their bananas would simply rot on the dock.

Thankfully it was as Father Neel predicted and our ship left port without any problems. A relieved Grant lit up his pipe and puffed like a merry Lord. I was relieved as well.

After that, all was calm until we rounded Africa and were heading south-east along the coast. That's when a swarm of locusts and other insects invaded our ship. The crew said this happened sometimes when the wind was strong off the land. Be assured it was—strong and hot. We all began wearing the light-est clothing possible to avoid melting into a puddle. At one point, I touched a metal railing on the deck and thought I had burned my hand! I made sure not to do that again.

On October 23rd, we saw Lagos off the port bow and waited some distance until a pilot was brought onboard to navigate our ship into the dock. Once docked, we were free to spend some time on shore, which of course we all did.

Our four Nigerian passengers and my cabin mate Beverly permanently disembarked, leaving just our original six missionaries and Grant. With an extra cabin available, Grant moved into his own, leaving one cabin vacant. I thought one of the sisters might move over, but no one did.

When we exited the ship, it was hard to walk straight—it was like the earth wouldn't stop rolling—truly a strange feeling! Grant, Father Neel and I traveled away from port to a restaurant Grant knew of. He bought our meals—some exotic dish that was completely foreign to me. Except for the thin soup, it was quite delicious. During the meal, Grant took notes from Father Neel as to where we were setting up the ministry and where exactly in Nigeria we were going to be. He told us both that he had to travel all over and intended to stop in at some point, although it was clear he had very little inclination for missionary work or lepers. I couldn't help but wonder if I might be the reason.

On the way back to the ship, Father Neel showed us the Ekeyia Cemetery where all the missionaries who had died in Nigeria were buried. I found it somewhat depressing, particularly imagining what it was they could have died from. Father Neel explained that in the last part of the 1800s, the average lifespan of a missionary coming to Nigeria was five years! He said a prayer for their departed souls and we turned to leave, which relieved my soul! I'm certainly not intending to end up in a Nigerian cemetery.

We stayed at the port in Lagos two days, since this is where the ship was offloading most of its cargo. Day and night endless lines of shirtless black stevedores carried away the ship's cargo. At night, their path was lit by electric lights and lanterns, which must have been enough to help them find their way. But from where I was watching, the lights cast eerie shadows over everything.

Our second day in port Grant took the chief mate and me to dinner. The next thing I knew, the chief mate had departed our company, leaving me all alone with this exciting man! I was going to protest, but everywhere I looked I saw nothing but black faces. Besides, I had no idea where we would find a proper chaperone. I could only pray that no one from my party stumbled upon us.

After a fabulous dinner, he secretly asked the waiter to bring me a piece of cake with a candle in it. He had found out it was my thirtieth birthday and told me, "We can't have you entering a new decade without ringing it in properly." The entire scene was magical.

Afterwards, we strolled through the market simply enjoying each other's company. My heart nearly stopped when I saw my nemesis Sister Flores looking at some housewares. I grabbed Grant's arm and pushed him into a tobacco shop where he pretended to shop for cigars. I didn't need any more problems from her. When she disappeared, we snuck out like two spies and made our way back to the ship. At all times, I assure you Grant was entirely proper.

While I'm sure you will read a great deal into this letter, let me say I honestly didn't come to Nigeria for romance. I came to serve the missionary effort and to help teach the afflicted here. I can't deny, however, that I have grown quite fond of Grant. I would be very happy and, yes, even excited for a visit from him. He has spent a great deal of time learning what things I like and I believe he will appear one day in the bush bearing gifts for me. I'll be careful to catch myself if I become too romantic. So have no worries Mol, I'll soon be back to my normal unmarried, unprospected self.

On October 26th, we departed for Port Harcourt and were told we would arrive late on the 29th. The plan was to disembark on the morning of the 30th. Around noon on the 29th we reached Bonny Island, which sits at the head of Bonny River. From there we were required to slow down to a crawl as we navigated this narrow and crowded river up to Port Harcourt. When we pulled into the river, the sun was high and we stood in the shade near the bridge staring at the massive mangroves and palm trees. They seemed taller than any building I have ever seen. The vegetation everywhere consisted entirely of large leaves and the land was so prehistoric I half expected dinosaurs to emerge out of the bush at any moment.

As I'm writing this, I'm fairly used to the salt air, but the heat is still too much. We are only a hundred and fifty kilometers north of the equator and the sun shines relentlessly. Father Neel said my body needs two or three weeks to adjust, and that drinking plenty of water will help. I added that not overexerting myself might be wise—laughing of course—and he smiled then chuckled a bit, surely hoping I was kidding.

As the sun fell on our port bow, we moved to the starboard side and enjoyed a cool breeze in the shade. The African dusk cast large shadows over the land. It's truly hard to describe. I must admit it's all I imagined and more. I can only wonder where we are going and what it will be like. Such adventure awaits on the other side of the day!

On the last day, the ship's cook presented us with a farewell feast of a large grouper bought off the bow earlier in the day from the local boats that come alongside the ship. We also shared some port and Madeira wine, and relaxed, telling the crew goodbye. Grant made his way around saying his goodbyes, explaining he would be off the ship as soon as it docked. He told Father Neel that the Ogoja Province was very much like an untamed jungle—the last frontier. "Beware the Bight of Benin, for few come out though many go in!" He was joking, of course, but he made it sound ominous.

He caught me alone, near the door and said he would be seeing me again. I smiled and told him I would love that dearly. Out of sight from the others he held my hand briefly and then left to pack. The next morning at breakfast it was just us six as Grant was gone, perhaps forever.

I asked the captain if he would post this back in Liverpool and he agreed, so I gave him some money and he assured me it would arrive before December. Hopefully it has.

Molly, I will be writing you frequently and I hope you will be writing me as well. Please know, I so look forward to hearing from you and hope you will keep me informed of everything that's going on back home. Father Neel again confirmed the Calabar address I gave you previously, so please use that. I find it amazing that my writings will reach you so just think, each letter you receive will have traveled a great distance and have the dust of many different countries on it. Make sure you enjoy them properly, preferably with a nice cup of your favorite Darjeeling Orange (which I somehow can't imagine you without).

Know that I miss you dearly and already wish you were on the adventure with me. But you would probably be complaining by now. (Smile!) Take care and write often.

Your loving friend,
Anna Goodwill.

Molly put down the last page and wiped away a tear.

Yes Anna, I sometimes do wish I was there with you!

Then she helped herself up onto her crutches and prepared to go to work.

5

October 30, 1946
Port Harcourt, Nigeria

Anna stepped aside as two large Nigerians walked down the hallway and began collecting the baggage the six passengers had set out. Each Nigerian was dark and lean, with well-defined, rippling muscles exposed by their bare chests. Anna followed them out and stopped as they made their way down the gangway.

"Go ahead Anna, "Father Neel said, "We'll be right behind you."

Anna stared out over the large port, which was a furious bustle of activity. Several ships were either being loaded or unloaded with long, never-ending lines of black workers. It was early morning. The sun illuminated the top half of the gangway, the same gangway she was about to descend and leave the last vestiges of civilization behind. This was it for her—the moment of truth. She could stay onboard, unpack her bags and be back home in less than a month. Or she could push her foot out over the gangway and take the first step towards a new life, a life of uncertainty, a life where danger may await. It was time to decide.

As if possessing their own will, her feet began moving, slowly at first, then faster with purpose. No sooner had they touched the dock was she greeted by an official looking man. He emerged from a crowd of stevedores and presented himself.

Pointing to a small office he said, "Be it pleased to follow me."

Anna glanced back up to the ship—her metal cocoon for the last three weeks—and saw Father Neel nodding, waving his approval. Without hesitation, she turned back to the man and fell in behind him.

As she walked, she noticed he wore navy blue shorts that stopped just above the knee. His shirt was also navy blue, constructed of a strong, durable wool fabric not suited for hot climates like this. And he seemed to enjoy an air of importance. After her experience in Madeira, she was wary of any official no matter how odd he looked.

When they reached the small office—actually more like a shack—Anna went in and stood at a small counter no more than two feet long. The man lowered himself underneath the counter and popped up on the other side. It was a comical set up, again designed to make him appear important.

"Please to see me your papers," he said, hand out and palm open.

Anna had been advised to have them ready and handed him her papers for inspection. He unfolded the three small documents and looked through each one while Anna took in his office. There were neither personal items nor anything of value. Not even a spare pencil or eraser was anywhere in sight. It was at this moment that the pungent reek of body odor assaulted her nose. Apparently, the clothing this man was wearing hadn't been washed in some time, and perhaps neither had the inhabitant.

She blinked several times and turned to the door to get some fresh air. Not wanting to offend him for fear of any power he had to detain her or worse, send her home, she held her breath and prayed for the end.

As quickly as he started he was finished. "Thank you," he said with a broad smile that displayed his brilliant white teeth. "You may go."

Anna snatched her documents from the man's sweaty palm and left the tiny structure, gasping to fill her lungs with fresh air as she tried to orient herself as to where she was. Brushing by her was Sister Browne who had to make her perfunctory visit to the stinky shack. Anna decided to wait some distance off to see what happened next.

Quite recovered from the ordeal, she observed a dozen or so Nigerians standing on a distant curb with palms out, talking to each passerby. They were all dangerously thin. There were several missing limbs. Some had legs horribly mangled, having improperly healed from no medical care. One young boy had a massive growth protruding from his back and neck. It was a hideous sight. When Sister Browne joined Anna, she was dismayed as well. It made them want to open their purses and help these beggars. Yet they stood perfectly still, waiting for further instructions as they were in a strange land and fearful of making a mistake.

In ten minutes, all six missionaries had satisfied the local official that their paperwork was in order and stood on the long dock waiting for Father Neel to lead them. One of the stevedores who had offloaded the baggage approached and said some words to him, pointing as he spoke.

Father Neel glanced toward a dusty lane clogged with old broken down vehicles and said, "Ah, there he is. Patrick! Here we are!"

A young boy heard the voice and instantly recognized him for he was hard to miss in his flowing white robe.

"Come hea! Come hea!" he shouted back waving furiously.

Father Neel led the women to one of the battered cars. It looked like it used to be a small truck, but now there was another row of seats fastened to the floor behind the driver. The side panels had also been removed leaving a supported roof over the rear passengers to protect them from the sun yet still providing an open-air ride. All the luggage, though, had been piled on the seats leaving no room to sit except for the driver and one passenger.

The skinny black boy looked at all six missionaries. "Oh my! I know you sey dey come but I no know you sey plenty."

Father Neel pursed his lips. "I know Patrick. We need to hire another vehicle. Can you do that for me?"

"I sabi one man. No mess with area boys. Dem dey bad." He pointed to the ground and said, "Here," then walked off in a hurry.

Anna took this opportunity to speak to Father Neel. "What language is he speaking? Can you explain what he just said?"

Father Neel chuckled. "Patrick is speaking Pidgin English. Even though Nigeria has been an English colony for a long time, the population has not been quick to pick up the language, and there were no teachers to instruct them. So, like most everything in Nigeria, they worked around it using a few words here and there to reach an understanding. Patrick said he didn't know I was coming with five others so he thought the luggage was all mine and loaded it accordingly. When I asked him if he could hire another driver he replied that he knows a driver and won't waste time with the street boys who are troublesome. When he pointed to the ground and said 'here', he wants us to stand next to the kit car and make sure the luggage doesn't disappear. Most everything in Africa can sprout legs and walk away the moment you turn your back."

Anna nodded. "I see I have some learning to do myself. Those beggars over there, do they just stand in the lane begging and do people give them money?"

"Sometimes. They stand over there because they will be beaten if they set foot on the dock area. It's considered government property. That's why they're waiting until we get in the street. But by then we shall be in the kit car and it will be too dangerous for them to approach. Although from the looks of them, I'm sure some have tried. Sadly, they have no way to make a living and unless they have family taking care of them, they don't eat. But beware: once you start giving out money, the rest become a mob and surround you quickly. Some may even be pickpockets. It's always better when there are only one or two. Just wait until we reach our destination. You'll find plenty of charitable opportunities there—so much that you might drown in them!"

Anna got the message and decided to keep her money safe for now. She continued taking everything in, looking at the dirty streets and the sweaty people. Although she had seen ports in England and

Ireland, the heat, dust and poor conditions of this one were something completely new. It took time to adjust.

Their small group continued to cluster together, nothing but a few dots of white among an ocean of black. They stood out, drawing a few open-jawed stares from the men waiting in line to unload the ship. No doubt they were just as curious about the missionaries as the missionaries were about them.

Patrick soon reappeared as a passenger in a similarly looking car. He jumped out of the seat and said, "This one, dey honest."

The man began unloading pieces of luggage while Patrick watched, refusing to help. When the loads were finally balanced, he pointed to the cars. "We dey comot now o. (*We are leaving now.*)"

Father Neel turned to the women and said, "Let's have three in each car. I don't trust this new driver so I'll ride with him. Anna, you and Sisters O'Keefe and Whelan ride with Patrick. I'll take Sisters Flores and Browne with me. We may be separated on the road but don't worry, we'll catch up. If Patrick has to stop, he'll take care of you. He works with us in Ogoja."

Sister Flores spoke up. "How long is the trip?"

"It's almost two hundred kilometers and will take all of six hours. We will stop in three hours to use the facilities and eat. So sit back and enjoy the scenery, though it will be quite dusty and bumpy. And hold on tight!"

The women put on a brave face as they climbed into the death-traps. Nothing anywhere on the vehicles looked original or displayed the manufacturer's name or emblem. Instead, the cars seemed to be rigged together from scrap.

Anna sat up front next to Patrick who crossed himself, whispered a prayer, and engaged the engine. The car had just started moving when he began yelling. "Comot! Comot the road! (*Get out of the way!*)"

The beggars in the street barely acknowledged him but they did have enough sense to step aside and not get run over.

Dodging people and cars, it took them thirty minutes to navigate the few paved roads of Port Harcourt before they reached the countryside. These roads were mostly dirt and gravel, with the occasional large pothole to dodge. Patrick held the wheel with both hands while leaning forward, staring intently out the windshield at the rough road.

At first, Anna stared out the window too so as to possibly assist him. But she eventually relented when the sun, heat and lack of water took their effect. Besides, there was very little she could do. She wasn't willing to reach over and turn the wheel. She would have to trust that Patrick knew his job.

About ten minutes outside of the city, the road narrowed and became little more than a pair of bumpy dirt trails. When a car approached from the opposite direction the journey became frightening because the road wasn't wide enough for two cars. Anna's eyes widened as the two cars came closer and closer, each one firmly occupying the entire road. Just when it looked like they would crash into each other head-on, both vehicles swerved, barely missing the other, their left tires leaving the road to smash down weeds and other vegetation. Then they swerved back to the right, resuming their place in the middle of the road. This scene was repeated over and over again, and each time Anna was certain she was about to meet her maker. In fact, she was so sure there was no possible way they would make it to the midpoint without a violent crash, she began to mutter Hail Marys. Yet somehow, they made it to the first stop intact with Father Neel's kit car pulling in one minute behind them.

Up to this point they had traveled over three hours. Anna was tired and thirsty and glad for the stop. It was hot, dry work traveling in this land, much more than she had anticipated. She relished the chance to stretch her legs and dust herself off.

Patrick pulled next to a small house just off the road. He showed them inside, taking them past a few shelves that made the place look more like a store selling dry goods than anything else. It was only when he pointed to some small tables in the corner that she understood this place doubled as a restaurant.

"Come chop (*Come eat*)," he said.

Sister Whelan responded in an Irish brogue, much deeper than Father Neel's. "I should love to use the toilet. Could you please show me the place?"

Patrick couldn't understand her dialect so Anna tried squatting slightly. "Loo? Privy? Lavatory?"

After seeing Anna's posture, he understood. "Yeah, com wit me, make I show you." The three women followed him as he walked through the house, past black women seated in chairs preparing food. Patrick opened the back door and pointed to an odd structure in a field. A small area was enclosed by four rough wood panels, each beginning a foot off the ground and ending at about four feet high. It was exposed to the sky and offered little modesty; a primitive beginning to a necessary ending.

Seeing it, Anna said, "You go first and come get me when you're done. That way we can all have some privacy." She made her way back inside with Sister O'Keefe and went to the tables where the other three were seated. A pitcher of water along with a plate of dough balls welcomed their return. Anna saw a large basin of water on a side table and joined the others in washing her hands.

Father Neel stood, giving instructions. "Sit and eat. We have a long ways to go yet. These little balls are fou fou. It's made from the yam or cassava plant and it's very filling. You dip them in this sauce which may be quite spicy, so be careful."

Anna tried one and had trouble swallowing. The red sauce bit hard on her tongue and inner cheek, and her sinuses were flooded with fiery spice. She drank some water before trying a ball without the sauce. It tasted very bland.

"Careful sisters, this stuff expands in your stomach—filling you quickly. A little goes a long way. That's why they eat it."

Anna ate one more waiting to see what would happen. When she saw the other five women had used the outdoor toilet, she knew it was her turn. It was quite a thing to see. Upon closer inspection, she saw a hole perhaps eight feet deep, with a small wooden platform over it. The boards had been cut away to create a jagged, semi-round hole. There was a movable wooden chair she could slide over the hole.

As she sat down on the already-warm seat to relieve herself, a small dog approached and sniffed furiously at her shoes through the short opening. She wasn't sure if the dog was going to bite or just wanted to know where the shoes had come from. Either way, she twitched her feet and the dog scampered a short distance away.

From her seat, she peeked over the top of the wood panel and saw Patrick urinating against a tree. The other driver was standing nearby, ignoring his companion.

When she finished, she found the way back to the dining area and once again washed her hands in the now murky water, and dried them on a well-used towel. She shook her head and thought to herself, *You're definitely not in Maghull any longer.*

After the meal, they were back on the road with Anna thinking about what she had just eaten. A woman had served them what looked like chicken broth, but told them it was grasscutter soup. Father Neel explained that a grasscutter was a large, hairy rodent that lived all around and provided the population with a lot of protein. Between three small balls of fou fou and the grasscutter soup, Anna was surprisingly full. Now it was time to watch Patrick dodge potholes and cars again while hanging on for dear life.

During this first leg, she occasionally noticed deep tracks leave the road and end a short distance into a field. Back at the restaurant, she had asked Father Neel about them and discovered they were caused by drivers going off the road where they likely died.

"When a car breaks down in Nigeria," he explained, "it swerves wildly off the road, often plowing into a field. Sometimes the driver loses control due to mechanical failure, lack of maintenance or simply falling asleep. It's a dangerous business as there are no emergency vehicles to arrive on the scene and help."

This reality was frightening. Anna understood that here in Nigeria, she was truly at God's mercy.

This second leg seemed even longer. It took three more rugged hours yet felt like six before Patrick pulled into a small lot next to a large river. Her hindquarters were sore from bouncing up and down in the seat and her hands cramped from holding on so tightly. Patrick turned off the engine and motioned for them to get out.

"We don arrive. You go like here. (*We are here. You will like this place.*)"

Anna stepped from the kit car somewhat dizzy with fatigue and took in the vast area. She had no idea they would be setting up the mission next to a river this large. This was too good to be true. Sure, it was a brutal six-hour ride through dry, hot country but this could work nicely. There even appeared to be some commerce in the area, unlike what she had been told. A nearby market was selling fresh fish and other meats along with massive vegetables. They were so close to the coast she could still smell the salty air.

Six hours back to the port and three weeks to get home. It's fairly easy to leave this place—if I ever want to.

The more she thought about it, the happier she was.

A few minutes later, the second car arrived. Father Neel got out and pointed to a small barge.

"The boys are driving the cars onto the ferry and we will be off shortly. Just make your way over there."

Anna followed the nuns and boarded a flat vessel with thin wire rails around the edges. The railing would in no way stop a man like Father Neel from going over the side. As far as stopping a woman, it was a fifty-fifty proposition.

When Patrick parked the car and turned off the engine, she decided to stay far away from the railing and sit in her seat for the ferry ride. It seemed to be the safest approach.

Somehow, she thought the trip would take only a few minutes since she could almost throw a stone to the other side. But the ferry turned left and went between two small islands to a deeper and much wider waterway. She could hear Father Neel explaining they were in the main part of the Cross River heading upstream to the Calabar River. The ferry would dock in the city of Calabar.

The name rung familiar with Anna and confused her. Her postal address was in Calabar and she knew they weren't staying in Calabar. She slid out of her seat and found Father Neel to ask for clarification.

"Dear," he said, "we are staying in Calabar tonight at St. Luke's hospital. They have some extra rooms there. That is where your mail will arrive and Patrick will pick it up when he comes into town. Tomorrow we get up early and begin our journey north to Ogoja. It's over 300 kilometers and will take us close to ten hours. We must travel during daylight because it's too dangerous at night. Most vehicles have no lights."

Anna politely nodded then lowered her head in exhaustion and walked away. She had forgotten about the next leg of the journey. Lacking water in the heat of the tropics, her mind had tricked her into thinking she was at the end. Instead, they weren't even halfway. It was hard to swallow.

An hour later, they arrived safely at the hospital, with each passenger covered in sweat and light red dust. With no proper bath or shower available, they washed up as much as they could. The locals treated them to some fruit and plenty of water. Anna almost choked as she gulped down large mouthfuls of tepid water, realizing how dehydrated she had become. Father Neel purchased some bread and cheese and told them to eat their fill, then showed them to the sleeping area.

Anna unpacked a few items from her personal kit and immediately collapsed in her assigned bed. She was sharing a room with Sister Browne, yet it could've been the devil himself for all she knew. The only thing she recalled was the groggy, deep sleep she fell into and the black face jostling her shoulder saying, "Wake please. Wake please."

Anna opened her eyes and looked out the window at the sky, which was pitch black. The next thing she knew Sister Browne was jostling her.

"Wake up Anna! You fell back asleep." Sister Browne was bending over her, fully dressed, while Anna was still in her nightgown. This time though, Anna pulled up her arms, supported her tired body on her elbows and raised herself out of bed. The instant her feet hit the cool floor she wanted to go back to bed. Instead, she forced herself to dress and pack her baggage for Patrick who came around to collect it.

After she had used the restroom and washed up, she met the rest of her group outside the hospital where they all stood, apparently waiting for her.

Father Neel handed her a brown sack and a canteen. "This is for you," he said before turning to address the entire group. "We will be stopping briefly three times to use the restroom, take on fuel and stretch our legs. This is your food for today. There should be plenty and I have two extra bags in case we need more. At each stop you need to refill your canteen at the water pump. We must push hard to make it before sunset, otherwise we'll have to stay somewhere along the road and it's not always safe. So, I need each of you to be quick and efficient at each stop. Understood?"

The five women nodded.

"Good. Patrick says he can now see well enough so let's get in and go. But before we do, I will bless this trip." He said a brief prayer in both English and Latin, after which everyone—including the two drivers—crossed themselves and found their seats. Then the engines started up and the two kit cars pulled away from St. Luke's leaving Calabar for the deep bush.

It didn't take long to get clear of the city. When they did, the elevation began sloping upwards. A few miles later, and a massive, forbiddingly dark forest appeared on the right. Although the road was dry, run-off from previous rains had swept across the surface causing deeper holes and treacherous crevices for the cars to navigate. Patrick was even more challenged now. If the road on the first day was rough, this one was at least twice as bad.

After thirty minutes of bouncing around in their seats, the terrain smoothed out. The sun was now high enough to provide light to see a good distance in front of the vehicle. Anna looked ahead and saw this relatively flat portion continued for a long way so she immediately dove into the bag of food. She quickly learned that one bump at the wrong time could send anything in her hand onto the filthy floorboard or worse, flying out the window lost forever. That's why she took very good care to firmly hold one item at a time with both hands. Using this method, she was able to eat part of a banana and a piece of dried meat then wash it all down with several swigs from the canteen. She repeated this every thirty minutes or so until they made their first stop at a small town called Abini.

Anna stepped out of the car and stretched her legs watching Patrick and the other driver congratulate themselves for safely getting this far. They acted like they hadn't seen each other in years. At the station, several other drivers with various junk heaps came over to congratulated them. They all spoke in a tribal dialect, one she didn't comprehend. She later learned that they were talking about trading parts and what to be on the lookout for ahead. This vital information could help them successfully make it to the next town. It was quite different than Maghull where she couldn't ever imagine people congratulating themselves for simply driving to the grocer or picking someone up from school. Yet with the condition of both the road and the vehicles, she understood their excitement.

Anna fetched her canteen and headed to the water pump to refill it. The pump was located under a shade tree where two of the sisters were already working hard on the iron handle. Water shot from the nozzle, allowing Anna to top off her canteen without having to work the pump. She thanked them and no sooner had she put the cap back on did she see Father Neel heading to his car. This was the signal for everyone to get moving so she jogged over to her car and climbed in.

Up to this point in the journey conversation had been kept to a minimum for several reasons. First, everyone was so tired that they didn't want to expend the effort. Second, it was difficult to hear inside the car because the engine was so loud and without windows the wind raced through interior, making the comprehension of any words almost impossible. But probably the most important reason was the nature of driving in Nigeria. It was a serious and dangerous business. Each passenger wanted the driver's full concentration on the road and not listening to unnecessary chatter from the passengers. As such, everyone simply hung on to whatever they could and bounced around in their seats praying they'd make it to the next stop where the drivers would once again celebrate.

It took almost three hours to reach the next stop at Abba Omega. The two kit cars pulled off the road into a primitive service station to fill up. Here the terrain was quite steep and Patrick was forced to take out some wooden blocks and stuff them behind the rear wheels to keep the car from rolling away. He topped off the tank with petrol while Father Neel inspected the three passengers in Anna's vehicle.

"How are you ladies holding up? Do you need any food?"

All three shook their heads. Sister Whelan appeared slightly pale considering her normal skin tone, while her Irish companion Sister O'Keefe looked like she could keel over and fall asleep instantly. Anna knew how they both felt. This was now a deep journey into the bush. There were long stretches of nothingness. No humans, no vehicles, no structures. With every kilometer they logged, she felt farther and farther from home. She wondered how anything could make it here from England—even a simple letter. Before, it had all been talk and lines on a worn-out map. Now, this new life she was undertaking was real. Very real!

Father Neel spoke loudly. "Make sure you fill up your canteens. We stop in about three more hours so cheer up. That will be the last stop."

Anna smiled and forced herself out of the car over to the water pump. As she worked the lever and filled up her canteen, Sister

Flores came over, stout and energetic as ever. Without saying a word to Anna, she filled her canteen and walked away looking as if this journey was nothing but a trip to the bus stop or taxi stand down the street. Anna couldn't believe it. Maybe, she thought, Sister Flores was meant for this kind of work.

In no time, they were back on the road again, leaving the huge forest behind and crossing over mostly barren land. Occasionally a small patch of forest appeared but soon the landscape returned to the rolling fields of weeds and scrub. Anna began figuring out when a town was approaching as fields of crops would come into view, sometimes with people working in them. A few structures would then emerge from behind a hill followed by a few more fields before returning to barren land again. It was a monotonous pattern.

Patrick said almost no words to the passengers but had plenty to say to other drivers. During the rare time another vehicle approached, he waved his arm out the car and yelled something in another language as if the other driver could hear him. Of course, the approaching driver was doing the same thing. Once the two vehicles had passed each other, Patrick would shake his head and go back to driving as if nothing had happened.

Anna thought he was quite a character. She judged him to be in his mid-twenties or perhaps younger. He was wearing the same clothes as the day before and Anna had picked up a slight smell of body odor as the wind whipped around the car. She knew it was something she would have to get used to.

Anna fished out the last of her food and finished it off. Surprisingly she was not very hungry and assumed she would have no trouble making it to the end. She was, however, going through her water fast. She now understood the importance of Father Neel's instruction to top off the water at each stop since they were all losing fluids fast. Until her body acclimated, this would be the norm.

The final stop occurred in a town whose name escaped Anna. For the first time Father Neel looked haggard. So was everyone else— except Sister Flores. Even the drivers appeared to be ready for the end.

Father Neel trudged over to the pump and splashed water on his face. He did this several times, wiping himself off with some cloth he'd been carrying. When he was done, he offered the remaining bags of food to the women and only Sister Flores took some. Sister Whelan, whose pale face was getting worse, looked nauseous at the thought of more food. Anna hoped that if she had to get sick, she did it over the side especially since she was right behind Anna.

A few vendors approached the weary travelers and tried to peddle some fruit. Anna saw that most were missing at least a few teeth. With everyone shaking their heads, the vendors retreated into a mud hut and the missionary group assembled in their vehicles for the last time. Just before Anna climbed into her seat, she took in several deep breaths and readied herself for the final push.

Father Neel guessed it would be about two and half hours. He didn't, however, promise them a paradise when they arrived. He knew better than to get their hopes up.

They were soon lumbering along with the sun setting to the rear of the kit car mostly on Patrick's side. This put Anna in complete shade which was a tremendous relief since she had been in the sun all morning and several hours past noon. The cool shade was a simple joy.

Steadily the group seemed to be climbing. They would come to a small hill, make it over and head down yet never reach the same level they had been at before the hill. With each kilometer, she sensed they were getting higher and higher.

Somewhere near the end of the trip, the vehicles turned south and threw what was left of the sun back on Anna's face. But it wasn't so bad now. The sun wasn't strong and a rise here or dip there kept the car mostly in shade.

Anna drained the last of her canteen assuming rightly that they were almost there. Ten minutes after her last swig, the two-vehicle caravan picked their way through a small town making several turns before finally pulling up to a church. Goats and chickens scattered before the car. Little children played haphazardly, seemingly oblivious to the danger a moving car presented.

"Ogoja!" Patrick announced before shutting off the engine. "Here."

Anna sat for a moment looking around at the place that would be her new home. For a girl from Maghull, she had traveled an incredible distance. It was twenty-six days from the time she left Ireland. This was certainly farther than any of her friends had ever traveled. Now though, she was literally on the other side of the world.

No sooner had she set her feet down on Ogojan soil did two naked children approach—girls—perhaps three or four, muttering something she couldn't understand. When Anna bent over to touch each of their bellies, they giggled and ran off. Anna giggled too. This was truly the beginning of her incredible adventure. After all the planning, she was finally here. From now on, this would be her new life—whatever that entailed.

6

"The land you see before you is the Lord's gift to you, a divine gift; march in and take possession of it… let there be no cowardice, no shrinking here."

Deuteronomy 1:20-21

Father Neel pointed to a spot on the floor. "Patrick, place Anna's kit there and set up a bed for her. The other four kits belong to the sisters and they should go on the other side of this curtain."

"Ya fada. I go do shap shap." Patrick turned around, yelled at the other driver and soon a steady stream of luggage and travel bags flowed into the small concrete block building. Anna stood nearby occasionally pointing to a bag that belonged to her and dragging it to the spot Father Neel had designated, but mostly she just stood out of the way, watching the boys effortlessly hoist each piece of luggage onto their shoulders. She wanted to help, but was already learning that here in Nigeria, the boys see their work as a right—a status symbol—not some dreary obligation.

Feeling sort of useless, she decided to check out the mission grounds. They were staying in Ogoja, in a building attached to the rear of the church near the center of the mission. The building they were sleeping in—a storehouse—had various oddments and supplies piled high in anticipation of their arrival. Aside from the church and a few other buildings, there seemed to be little else in this small village.

Anna walked towards a large knee-high field of grass surrounding the mission. It was dotted by the occasional cluster of trees. Small children ran here and there without any apparent supervision. Most were completely naked, unaware of any immodesty.

The sun was dipping below the tree line to the west when, for a moment, Anna thought she saw a young boy standing behind a tree peering at her. Taking a few steps forward, she shielded her eyes and blinked, but whatever she had seen was gone; if it had been anything at all.

A voice inches away startled her. "Sista abeg. Make we go river side. Dem no wan go." A young girl stood there waiting for a response.

"I'm sorry, what are you asking? Something about a river?"

From the building's opening, Father Neel's voice boomed out. "Her name is Kim and she's asking if you want to go to the river and wash. They have a private place where only the women go. If you want, you should do it now before it gets too dark. It will likely make you feel better after that long journey."

Anna pulled at her dress sending up little puffs of a reddish dust. Dried sweat had caused her clothes to stick to her skin making her even more uncomfortable.

"Oh well, I suppose I'm here. I might as well dive in with both feet so to speak. Are any of the sisters coming?"

"No, I think not," Father Neel replied. "They're busy organizing their kit and setting up the beds. Unfortunately, it appears Sister Whelan is a bit sick. But don't let that trouble you in getting clean and comfortable. After all, we can't have our only instructor getting sick, too. That wouldn't do."

Anna nodded. "Do I follow her?"

"Yes, and you should take along fresh garments and a towel. Kim, get Miss Anna a towel to dry off please."

Without saying a word, Kim ran off to a small building nearby.

Father Neel continued. "I believe you packed some soap?"

"Yes, I'll need to dig it out, but I do have some soap and shampoo. I confess I'll be quite pleased to get clean."

"Excellent. When you return, we'll have your bed arranged and a meal ready. I'll leave you to it then."

Anna went back inside to rummage through her luggage. While she was setting aside her carefully packed clothes, she heard Father Neel talking to the sisters and giving more orders. It struck her how she was able to understand every word of his thick Irish accent now that she'd spent almost a month in his company. That gave her hope that she would soon understand the Pidgin language of these Nigerians. In a way, the language was like just about everything else she'd seen so far: strung together with sweat, scrap, and ingenuity. Even the words Kim spoke made some kind of sense, "Sista abeg. Make we go river side. Dem no wan go." She wondered if 'Sista' was what she was going to be called, and whether it was because the Nigerians considered her a nun or that's what all adult females were called when the proper name wasn't known. She'd heard the boys call each other 'brudder', even though she was quite sure they weren't all related. Then there was the part about "Make we go river side." Even though it wasn't proper English, it got the message across in far fewer words—very efficient. It was going to take some time to get used to, but at least it wasn't a completely foreign language.

By the time Kim returned, Anna had filled a small cloth bag with fresh clothes, shampoo, soap and her special comb. Rising to her feet, she could see activity on the other side of the thin sheet-for-a-curtain and thought about asking if someone wanted to join her, but eventually decided against it. Her modesty would be challenged enough with Kim, not to mention three other nuns splashing around next to her.

"Lead on Kim," she said, picking up her bag.

"Yes sista, we dey go now."

Holding a towel underneath the crook of her arm, Kim selected a path through the grassy field and started down it. The ground around the mission was relatively flat until they came to the tree line, where it gently fell off. Anna noticed that most of the area around Ogoja was quite hilly, something she wasn't used to in Maghull.

"Is it far?" she asked Kim.

"E no far, sista. How una dey do?"

Anna took a second to process this. "I'm fine Kim but you can call me Miss Anna.

"Okay, Miss Anna," she said, followed by several murmured "Miss Anna's."

Anna grinned at the girl's willingness to please, then stopped suddenly in her tracks. Staring at a distant figure in the woods, she said, "Kim, come here please."

Kim stopped, stared back at Anna, and walked towards her. "Wetin dey happen?"

Anna pointed to a distant tree. "There's a young boy. I just saw him again,"

Kim squinted her eyes but saw nothing. "No mind the boy. E be wahala."

"What's 'wahala'?"

"Dem be trouble. Dem get spots, white spots," she said pointing to her arms and legs. "Make you follow me."

They continued on as Anna thought about Kim's words. The white spots she referred to were probably leprosy, which was why this boy was forced to hide out in the woods. The thought of him excluded from society, sleeping on the ground like an animal, eating wild nuts and berries gave her a chill, even in this heat. For the rest of the walk, Anna couldn't help wondering about him.

What was his name? How did he live? Did his family reject him?

She was musing on all this when she noticed Kim had stopped. They'd come to a stream, dimly lit among the tall trees and the fading light. The edges were filled with still waters, but the middle was turbulent, something Anna eyed cautiously before deciding it didn't look too dangerous.

Small pebbles embedded in compact red clay created a sort of sidewalk in the stream leading to large rocks, worn smooth from both the river and other bathers. Without saying a word, Kim lifted her dirty cotton dress over her head, revealing nothing underneath. She folded it up, placed it on a dry, flat spot on the bank, and stepped into the stream, wading towards the turbulent section. Once there, she promptly dropped down to her neck and motioned to Anna. "Come, Miss Anna, come."

Anna looked around, paused for a moment, and feeling a little self-conscious under Kim's steady gaze, slowly began removing her clothes. Once she had finally extricated herself from the last undergarment, she gingerly let herself into the water, feeling the coolness cover more and more of her aching, tired body with each step. Surprisingly, the footing was sound and she was able to safely move to a deep spot next to Kim, where she lowered herself entirely under the rushing water. Instantly, a feeling of relief washed over her as the stream took away all her fatigue. It was both surprising and invigorating.

The first twenty minutes was consumed by relaxing and washing her body clean of all the sweat and grime she'd amassed from the trip. Once her skin was gleaming, she waded back to shore for her shampoo. It wasn't going to be her special rain barrel treatment, but when she got back to the deep spot, the clear stream water would be a good substitute.

Anna shampooed and scrubbed her hair thoroughly. Then she rinsed it by bending backwards into the stream so that the strands drifted away from her, floating in a current of churning bubbles. On the bank, Kim gaped at Anna in wonderment—this was obviously the first white woman, or at least first *nude* white woman she'd ever seen.

The light had almost faded entirely when Anna waded to the bank to a waiting towel from Kim. Anna dried herself off and said, "We finished just in time, didn't we?"

"Yeah Miss Anna. Una enjoi?"

"Very much so. Thank you for taking me here."

"We fit come tomorrow."

Anna chuckled. "Well, we'll see. It depends on what we…"

Suddenly, the young boy reappeared.

"Kim, there he is, right there!"

Kim was right next to Anna looking down her arm. "I no see him o. Bone him." Then she yelled into the forest. "Why you dey give me wahala? Dem send you follow me?! Come Miss Anna, we go now."

Anna looked once more at the spot where the boy had stood before refocusing and then focused on Kim's back, which was rapidly disappearing in the fading gloom.

℀

Dinner was spread out over a table designed for four yet seating six. It consisted of tomatoes, fou fou, rice, pan fried sweet plantain and dried pork. The six cramped missionaries tried not to elbow each other as they ate. Sister Flores was right next to Anna and had already elbowed Anna twice. She couldn't quite shake the feeling that it had been done on purpose. When Father Neel asked about Anna's bath, for some reason the tension increased.

"So Anna, did Kim treat you properly?"

"Oh, she took good care of me. And the bath was lovely, really you should all try it."

Anna glanced at the four nuns and noticed a sarcastic smirk on Sister Flores' face.

"She showed me good spot in the stream to stand. The water was cool and felt refreshing in this heat. There was something though, I want to ask about."

Father Neel pulled on a tough piece of pork with his teeth. "What is it?"

"Well, I kept seeing this young boy in the woods. It was almost like he didn't want to be seen by the others, but he didn't mind if I saw him. When I showed him to Kim, she couldn't see him and I thought I was imagining it, though maybe I misunderstood what she was saying. She did mention he had white spots. That's leprosy, right?"

Father Neel chewed slowly, before swallowing. "The boy you saw is real. There are many of them. They live in the bush, and yes, they have leprosy. They're the ones we have come to help. You have just seen your first one."

"But what do we do about them?" Anna asked.

"All in God's time, girl. We're meeting with the chiefs tomorrow, and I need all of you dressed in your best clothes. We'll have a feast and I'll attempt to talk them into donating some land for us to set up our compound. If I'm successful, we'll start building immediately. It all begins tomorrow."

"I see. So the boy stays in the woods?"

"Yes, I'm afraid he does. You see, if you start helping him right now, we'll soon be inundated with them. The locals here in Ogoja will break out the whips and beat them back. No, believe me when I say this, the best course is to keep them in the bush until we're ready. Then we can help as many as we can handle."

Anna shook her head and frowned. She wanted to do something for the boy right now. Sister Flores watched her carefully during all this, but said nothing.

When they had all finished eating, Father Neel gave some final instructions. "Ladies, you will find the Nigerians' lives revolve around the sun. They are up working when it's light and they go to bed when it's dark. We'll need to fall into the same routine. Because of the heat that builds up in these buildings during the day, it'll be best to leave the windows open in your building while you sleep. They have no screens so we've set up mosquito netting. Please keep it tucked into your mattress at all times. These bugs are ingenious at finding ways to join you in your heavenly slumber. And, please use your oil lamps only if it's absolutely necessary. The bugs love them. Understand?"

The women nodded, including Sister Whelan, who seemed to be doing better.

"Excellent. I shall be sleeping in the other building and will leave you to it. I bid you all a good night."

The group pushed back from the small table and made their way to the sleeping quarters. Once they were inside, Sister Flores pulled a surprised Anna aside.

"I understand that you're not one of *us*, but to expect us to assemble and make your bed while you're out splashing around is completely out of order. We all expect you to pull your own weight here or go home, where you can have the comfortable life you are obviously used to. Do you understand?"

Anna drew back. "I never intended for you to assemble my bed much less make it. Who told you to do that?"

"Father Neel. Evidently, he feels you deserve special attention. Yet we have other chores to do and don't have time to do yours. Do you understand?"

"Yes, I do," Anna said, turning her back on Sister Flores. She decided to add one last comment. "Oh, and thank you for making my bed. Thank you very much."

Sister Flores said nothing and left abruptly, disappearing behind the curtain. The whole situation was very upsetting, but there wasn't much she could do about it now. Stifling a yawn, she studied her bed. Her lamp was beginning to attract a nice collection of insects—some grotesquely large. She turned it down, figured out her mosquito netting, and within minutes was nearly asleep before remembering to turn it completely off. Once her head touched the pillow, she was out.

"Help me!"

A loud scream echoed through the small building. Anna jolted upright from a deep sleep, only to be engulfed by a wave of mosquito netting.

Where am I? she thought. *What on earth is going on?*

It took her mind a few seconds to clear. She was in Nigeria. There was a sound of a match scraping on the floor. A small flame flickered.

A cascade of shadows danced on the curtain. She heard a woman crying in pain. Another lamp appeared in the doorway illuminating Anna's tent.

"Aaaiiiii!" This time it was Anna screaming. "What is that?!"

A large insect six inches long clung to the netting, giving her a full view of its hideous appearance. It had a three-inch, horn-like projection from its head and a needle sticking out from its lower jaw. These protuberances took up half the beetle's length, making its yellowish body look like a small plum. Three-inch legs enabled it to climb her netting in search of food, whatever that might be.

"Help me," Anna begged. "It's huge!"

Father Neel was in a night robe, standing next to Kim at the building's entrance. Anna pointed to the monster and Kim reached over and plucked it off the netting. A squeaky hissing sound pierced the night air as Kim took it outside still pinched between her fingers.

"What was that?!" Anna cried.

"A Rhino beetle I'm afraid. Ugly creatures, aren't they?"

"Are they p-poisonous?"

"I don't think so, although I tend to give them a wide berth. The locals collect the larvae and pan-fry them in palm oil with coconut. Quite tasty, actually."

Anna inspected her netting for more rhino beetles but instead found hundreds of flies, gnats and other flying insects all buzzing around the lamp.

"Anna, was that you crying?"

"No, it was someone over there."

Father Neel approached the curtain and said, "Ladies, may I come in?"

From the other side, Sister Flores pulled back the curtain wearing a scowl on her face. "It's Sister Whelan. She must have gotten up in the night and failed to fully tuck in her netting. The black ants got in and bit her all over."

Father Neel examined the whimpering nun. "Oh my! We'll get you fixed up soon enough. Kim, get a basin of water and a cloth to wash off the bites. Then get some baking soda and make a paste. That will soothe the sting."

Kim took off.

"Sister Flores, come with me to the storage room where we keep some powder that's fairly effective against these rampaging insects. We'll also find some brooms there to sweep the ants out with."

The curtain pulled back again and they reappeared in Anna's room, only to brush past her.

Just as they were out the door, Anna spoke up. "What can I do, Father?"

He called back without stopping. "Just remain in bed and seal yourself in tight. We don't need another disaster tonight."

Anna, wishing she could be of use, remained sitting upright for the next ten minutes watching the others come and go. Once the lights were finally out, she lay back down and she fell asleep almost instantly.

The next morning, Anna awakened to see Kim approaching the building with a small pot of hot water. Hurriedly, she brushed the sleep from her eyes and rummaged through her things for her English Breakfast tea and her mother's fragile cup and saucer. With that in hand, she made her way to a small table just outside and spooned some of the loose-leaf tea directly into her cup—a method she abhorred—before pouring the hot water over it. She let it steep for the requisite three minutes before scooping it out onto the ground. It was less than perfect—there were a few pieces of tea leaves still floating around her cup—but she would have to make do. The fog she had just come out of required a boost only tea could provide.

Once she took a few bracing sips, she felt herself begin to awaken. Apparently, she was the last to wake up. Somehow, the nuns had slipped past without waking her. She must have been tired, indeed! And, she was still exhausted. Granted, the nuns were much more accustomed to hard work; she'd watched them move tirelessly at the convent, either worshipping or working at something strenuous, rarely taking any time for themselves. Now, they were working rings around her. It was embarrassing to watch.

From the brief words she exchanged with Kim, she understood the two drivers had taken Father Neel and the nuns to a local market to purchase food for the coming meeting with the chiefs. Outside, two boys were already setting up chairs under a cluster of trees nearby. She was hoping to finish her tea and the two bananas Kim brought her before the group returned. At least she could make herself useful in unloading the supplies.

Some flies buzzed around her teacup as she swallowed the last drop. She thought of making another cup, but dared not. It was highly unlikely she'd ever find a tea supplier in the bush and she needed it for moments like these. As she was eating one of the bananas, she saw the boy from yesterday, but this time he was standing clear of the trees no longer hiding. Anna looked around to see if anyone else was watching but they weren't. Holding a banana up she motioned to the boy to come and get it. He began to take a few steps towards her, then froze, cocking his head to the left. Anna looked in that direction and saw two cars rumbling towards the compound. When she turned back, the boy was gone. With little time left to think about it, she hurried to her room, deposited her cup and saucer, and prepared to meet the group.

One car pulled up near the chairs and trees while the other drove to the entrance of the church. Father Neel, Sister Browne and Patrick jumped out of that one. Anna hurried over to them and asked, "May I help?"

Father Neel surveyed the supplies and said, "Yes, you and Sister Browne may go inside and help organize the supplies. Patrick will bring them to you. I need to go over to the other car and give them their instructions."

Anna followed Sister Browne to the pantry and began working.

It took a quarter of an hour to stack all the tins of food, bags of spices and flour, and other cooking necessities on several shelves. Just as they finished, several local women barged into the small pantry, including one large woman who claimed to be the cook. Stepping out of their way, Anna and Sister Browne leaned against a wall and watched them set to work.

Sister Browne said, "It sure will take a bit of getting used to."

"Yes it will," Anna responded. "No matter what they tell you beforehand, it's certainly a shock to the system. That nasty bug on my netting looked like something straight out of a comic book or movie picture."

"I'm glad I didn't see it. I hate things like that. Besides, I had to look at the terrible welts on Sister Whelan's legs and arms. That made it hard to get back to sleep. I couldn't help but imagine they were crawling all over me."

"Yes, it's something we need to watch out for." Anna patted down her dress. "Do you think we should find Father Neel and see if he has more work for us?"

Sister Browne agreed and the pair soon found the sweaty priest beneath a cluster of trees, arranging tables and chairs in a rough semicircle. Sisters Flores, Whelan and O'Keefe were there with him.

"Father Neel," Anna said, "Is there anything else we can do?"

"Yes and no," he said, wiping his forehead with an oversized handkerchief. "The chiefs will be here in a few hours. The males run their society and make all the important decisions, so you will need to sit apart from the negotiations, but still in plain view. Perhaps over there, in the shade near the mission where we can see you but you can't hear us. Please be aware, you're not to serve anything to the chiefs, or for that matter, let them see you doing any manual labor whatsoever. We need to distinguish you from the local women. I'll have Kim and the others serve the wine and hors d'oeuvres. Please dress your best, as I will be pointing at you and explaining how you will benefit their tribes. If everything goes as planned, we'll have a feast where I will formally introduce you. Any questions?"

Sister O'Keefe spoke up. "Do we have time to bathe? Sister Whelan could use a chance to get that baking soda off."

Father Neel nodded. "I suppose so. They won't be here for another two hours and you'll soon learn that out here, appointments are more advisory than mandatory. It's extremely rare for anyone to be on time. So by all means, clean yourselves. Any other questions?"

Since there were none, the group disbanded with Kim gathering up the four nuns and their fresh clothing and leading them to the stream. Anna stayed behind and found another girl to help iron Anna's formal outfit. A crude flat iron was placed on a warm stove and served nicely to push out most of the wrinkles. It was a luxury to have some time to herself, and Anna made full use of it.

Once her outfit was ironed, she organized her things along two shelves near her bed and hung what items she could from nails projecting out of the concrete blocks. She also brushed out her hair, braiding it and tying it up properly. She was just finished with all this when the nuns returned from the stream, all sporting smiles and generally in a far better mood than she had seen them in since their arrival. Even Sister Flores seemed content.

At the appointed time, all five of them were assembled in the chairs, sitting in the shade of the mission wall watching Father Neel standing before a small band of tribal chiefs, gesturing emphatically. Each chief was draped in vibrant colored clothes and elaborate headpieces. They contrasted strikingly with Father Neel's attire, as he was clothed in a somber, all-black soutane with a black zucchetto covering his head. From his neck hung a large, silver cross, its recent polish glinting as he moved around in the sunlight.

Father Neel knew enough of their language for them to follow what he was saying. As he spoke, the chiefs occasionally nodded, once in a while taking a bite of some of the snacks laid out before them or sipping out of small wooden cups that were frequently refilled from a large calabash (gourd) containing palm wine. After thirty minutes or so, Father Neel bowed to the tribesmen and walked over to the five women.

"Well ladies, that's it. The chiefs are now discussing my proposal. Let's hope I was persuasive enough."

Quietly, Anna said, "Can we ask what you told them?"

Father Neel took a seat, sighed deeply, and said, "I explained how the leprosy problem may decrease if we're allowed to care for them. I also explained educating the lepers would make expelling them from the village easier. With any luck, they will allow us to take full charge of the lepers, and the beatings and killings will stop. I also told them it would be a comfort for those parents who are heartbroken after casting out their child or loved one, to know they're going to a nice place where they'll be educated, fed and taken care of. That may ease their conscience."

He motioned to Kim. "Please bring out that bottle of whisky I set aside." Turning back to the nuns, he said, "It's time to up the ante, so to speak."

Kim returned with the bottle just as one of the chiefs rose, motioning the bishop over.

"Say a prayer, ladies. We will now receive their verdict."

As he walked over to the tribesmen, each chief fixated on this new bottle before beginning a heated discussion. To Anna, it looked ominous. She whispered to Sister Browne, "What do you think?"

Sister Browne whispered back, "I think we aren't going to get our land."

During a lull, Father Neel pointed in the direction of the land he desired, and then poured an ounce of whiskey in each of the chiefs' glasses. The chiefs downed the whiskey, clearly enjoying it. Once they'd drained their cups, Father Neel said something else and they all rose to walk in the direction he had pointed. One of the chiefs hung back and surreptitiously poured himself another shot, downing it without any of the other men seeing him. Of course, Anna and the four nuns—whom he completely ignored—had full view of this and smiled. Then he jogged to catch up with the others in the group, and quickly disappeared into the bush.

It was a full hour before they reappeared. The previous discord had transformed itself into smiles and laughter.

Anna whispered to Sister Browne, "It looks like you were wrong. We have our land."

The verdict was confirmed when the men resumed their seats and Father Neel poured out another shot of whiskey. After they raised their glasses and tipped them over, he signaled Kim and two other girls to bring over the pans of food waiting in the kitchen. All of a sudden, the feast was on.

Beautifully prepared dishes made their way to the banquet area, after which Father Neel motioned for the women to join in the festivities. When each one had been introduced, the women were poured a dainty portion of the palm wine while the men drank cup after cup of whiskey and gin, both of which were flowing freely. It didn't take long for the volume of voices to rise and more than a few glassy stares to appear on the chiefs' faces. Anna enjoyed the wine along with the sisters and talked more openly with them.

Sister Whelan was now fully recovered and in a very jovial mood. Sister Flores still kept her distance from Anna, but nonetheless appeared to be having fun. Sister Browne turned out to be the best conversationalist, enjoying both Anna's stories and the palm wine.

As the day dwindled into evening and the oil lamps were lit, a few of the tribesmen passed out from too much liquor. Patrick and the other driver pulled up and helped the chiefs stagger into the cars, driving away slowly so that none of them opened a door and fell out. It had happened before.

Father Neel finished his plate and stood up with a glass of gin. "Ladies, we have our land. Here's to God's blessing on our endeavor."

The nuns raised their glasses and drank down the last remnants of wine.

Anna, mystified, asked Father Neel, "How did you not pass out like the chiefs? Do you have some secret weapon?"

Laughing loudly, he said, "Why yes my dear, I do! I'm Irish and an Irishman can hold his liquor. Besides, the bottle of gin I've been drinking is mostly water. That helps, too!"

They all laughed merrily, before retiring to their beds and a well-deserved long night's sleep.

7

December 28, 1946

Dear Mol,

It's hard to believe I have been here for almost two months. It truly seems like a lifetime since I was back in Maghull. I haven't received a letter from you, but I'm hoping to receive one soon. We're sending our driver Patrick to Calabar to pick up the mail and supplies, and he should be back in a few days. I'm hoping there are letters from you waiting for me.

I have so much to tell you it's hard to know where to begin. In late November, we had a big meeting with the local chiefs and they gave us the land Father Neel wanted (only after drinking a large quantity of spirits). The next day two of them came back and set up the boundaries for the land. It seemed like they were just randomly setting down large stones, but I'm sure it had some meaning to them. The ground where the leprosy school is going to be constructed is fairly level and near a nice all-season stream called Monaiya or 'daughter of the main river'. It's barely a mile from the mission in Ogoja. I must tell you that after a month in the bush, the town of Ogoja feels like visiting Liverpool—it's a thriving city compared to our tiny outpost on the new land. I can only imagine how I'll feel when I go back to the real Liverpool one day.

Construction began on four huts the moment they dropped the last stone. It was fascinating to watch—the workers started by chopping down bamboo to make crosshatch for the walls. Once that was done, they smeared one side with mud, let it bake hard in the sun, and then flipped it over, doing the same thing to the other side. While the walls were baking, they lashed together a bamboo cone and left it on the ground before erecting and tying the walls together. The cone was, as you can guess, the top of the hut and somehow it fit perfectly. Three hours later they had already thatched the roof and made it as dry as a breadbox. Now I have my own little hut with one rickety door and two windows. I have to duck each time I come in because all the roofs in Africa hang low to keep the sun out. We haven't had much rain yet, so I'll be interested to see how waterproof they actually are, although Father Neel is trying to procure some zinc to replace the thatched roof. We will see how that goes.

Speaking of rain, we just started the dry season, the worst of which runs from December to February and sometimes lingers on until March or even April. It brings with it the Harmattan—a hot, dry wind blowing right off the ground, spreading dust and dirt over everyone and everything. Most of us (including me!) have come down with a hacking cough. It takes some getting used to.

The same men that built our huts are also building a concrete foundation upon which they intend to make buildings out of handmade concrete blocks. When we move into the concrete block buildings, Father Neel's plan is to convert the huts into homes for the lepers. Hopefully, the lepers will add to the hut village themselves. Unlike the huts, the concrete compound seems like it's taking forever to build, though Father Neel keeps telling us they'll have it completed before the end of the dry season.

Both Father Neel and I have our own hut. The two Irish Sisters Whelen and O'Keefe share a hut, as do Sisters Browne and Flores. Sister Browne and I are now very close, while Sister Flores continues to despise me. I'm still walking carefully around her. I don't think she can get me sacked, but I certainly don't want to find out.

In addition to the four huts for our living quarters, the workers also constructed three larger huts: one for my school, one for the infirmary and the other for general religious instruction and mass. In my tiny school, I have six leper children from five years old to fifteen. They call me Madame and they're all very sweet and obedient, feeling blessed to have some place to go, rather than just living in the bush all by themselves. They want very much to please me, which, I have to say, is quite a change from some of my students back in Maghull.

I have learned that the area we are in is called the 'Lost Province'. The reason appears to be when Nigeria was created. This area had difficult roads that washed out and rivers that couldn't easily be crossed. As such, the British and Nigerian governments did little to develop it. Many in the rest of Nigeria still refer to our area as the frontier—a place that's wild and untamed. Some days I tend to agree with them.

Even though we're in the Lost Province, nothing is lost on Father Neel. He is ahead of every problem and always worrying about what might pop up next. He is an excellent leader and a good motivator—a man born for this work! He is also quite funny. When we need a part for the kit car, I'll hear him tell our driver, "We are in the Lost Province! That means others have lost a great deal of items in our land. Now go and find the part somewhere!" Our driver will look at him funny before taking off to find it. God sure knows what He is doing because I can't imagine another man getting all this built. His dedication to the lepers and helping them survive their leprosy is unmatched!

Speaking of leprosy, it's such a malignant disease! It affects each one differently. For some of them it causes vision problems. With others, they may get organ difficulties or simply painful patches on their arms and legs. It took a week or so for me to get used to it, but I've finally managed to stop feeling sorry for them because I can't teach while I'm so emotional over their wellbeing. (Easier said than done!) There is one very familiar saying here in the bush that helps: "You get used to it."

One boy refuses to come into the school or be treated by the nuns. I'm not sure what he's about. He watched me from the forest for several days when I first arrived, before finally sneaking up to my hut for a banana. They warned me not to do this, but I could not simply shed my humanity and ignore him. My hut is the farthest from the group and closest to the tree line, so it's easier for him to go unseen. How small and skinny he is—he can't be more than twelve years old. I asked him his name and he said he didn't have one. I've been told that children are sometimes cast out into the bush so young (essentially to die) that they don't remember their given names. So he'll never have a name unless someone takes him in and gives him one. It's so sad! After a few visits *he actually asked me to name him! I thought for a while and came up with 'Clarence,' and told him it was the name of someone who was once very dear to me. Usually, in the evening when I'm reading in my hut by the lamp, Clarence sneaks in and eats whatever I have for him. He doesn't ask for much, other than to be near someone who cares. One evening I saw he had a scrape on his elbow and used some bandages to fix him up. He couldn't stop smiling. It was probably the first time he'd felt a loving hand on him. The locals believe leprosy is highly contagious yet from what we know, it may not be. Anyway, I had no hesitation, touching him carefully, and he loved it.*

Clarence is a very sweet boy and I'm afraid I've become quite attached to him. I've tried to get him to see the nuns, but he refuses and I'm worried because it appears he's in an advanced state. One night I went to bed and heard him come in to lie on the ground next to me. In the morning he was gone before I awoke. This has only happened twice and I don't know why he did it or if he'll be doing it again. I know with time I might be able to integrate Clarence into the settlement as more and more children come in from the bush and my class fills up. But for now, this little secretive relationship will have to do.

Speaking of guests in my hut, I was awoken ten nights ago by the local goat sniffing at my mosquito netting. (Mol, you wouldn't believe the variety of nasty flies, gnats, mosquitoes and other hideous flying insects who would consider it a feast to land on us!) Somehow, the goat nudged open my rickety door. In the moonlight, all I could make out were his eyes, so I leaned over and stared him down before I heard him scoot out the hut. I assume he smelled some food decorations we had put up for Christmas. The next morning I was getting ready for class when several workers began raising a fuss. They came walking around my hut pointing to the ground and talking excitedly in their tribal language. Before long, I drew a visit from Father Neel who had just completed the morning mass. He came, looked on the ground, and asked me if I knew I'd had a visitor in the night. I told him about the goat's visit but he just laughed and showed me the tracks. They were from a leopard! It was a very dangerous situation and he couldn't believe I'd stared it down—it could have killed me! After visiting the missionaries' cemetery in Lagos on the way over here, I can see how so many of them ended up there. He immediately ordered the men to stop working and fashion better doors over our entrances with good rope for hinges. They work quite well, and we've slept without incident from then on.

As for other wildlife, one day I was calling my school children back to class after taking a break. Uncharacteristically, they didn't come. Instead they continued banging sticks into the ground or at each other, I couldn't tell which. When I went to investigate, I saw a long brown snake—perhaps four yards long and very fat—heading away from camp. Its head looked like it could swallow an entire rabbit! I ordered the children away from it and allowed the large reptile to slink away unmolested, although later I wasn't sure why. Perhaps soon, it will be visiting my hut too! I hope not, though.

As for maintaining some modicum of civilization, I have to say bathing in the stream comes closest to keeping me sane. It is quite invigorating and I go perhaps three times a week. Usually Sister Browne and I go together, for as I said, we've become good friends. It's like we have known each other for years. This gives us a chance to talk, away from the other sisters. Father Neel has a bathing spot upstream from ours and bathes by himself as the stream has a hierarchy that gives men precedence. He, being white and the leader, gets the best spot. White women are second, with the locals downstream of us: men first and then the women farther down from them. The lepers are bathed from water out of our barrels as they're not allowed in the stream. If anyone is caught out of their designated spot they are verbally chastised and perhaps beaten, especially if they are lepers for no one wants to catch leprosy.

When evening comes, a cool breeze flows over the hot, dry fields and enters our huts. I say cool, but it is all relative especially since our huts lack ceiling boards to hold the heat above us. Ten nights ago, I was enjoying one of these cool breeze evenings when a bicycle appeared out of the darkness. I guess he stopped at my place first, being the first hut on his path. To my surprise, he was a Brit. His name is Dr. Thomas Chapley. He was working temporarily with the Nigerian government at Obubra and was not needed anymore since they now have a new doctor there. He heard of our need for a doctor and wanted to talk to Father Neel. When I pointed him in the right direction, I wondered if he would stay. In the morning, I discovered he was still here. That night he came to my hut and we played rummy with a deck of cards he had.

He is a pleasant looking fellow and very polite and, of course, very single. He's going to stay with us for a few months until it's clear whether we'll get our own doctor. (Father Neel's been corresponding with someone, but apparently they haven't made up their mind.) Thomas is very familiar with leprosy and experienced in its detection and treatment. When I told him about Clarence, he said that perhaps the boy would come to the hut while we were playing cards. Then he could have a look. So far, on the nights we've played, Clarence hasn't shown up.

Father Neel is about to send Thomas, as he likes me to call him, on a survey of the area to try to determine how many lepers there are. Thomas is from Bootle and has actually been in Maghull for a day or two, so we have a few things in common. Now before I go on, I want you to wipe that smile from your face. He is likely to be gone soon and that will be that, but at least for a brief time there's a man here who's not committed to a life of service in the clergy and all the restrictions that entails.

It's evening time right now and the flies are buzzing around my lamp, bothering me. Clarence has just appeared at my door with a forlorn look, perhaps because I've been spending so much time with Thomas. I've handed him some crackers and he is content for the moment but I'm going to seal this letter now and send it with Patrick in the morning. You should count the days until you receive it and write back as to how long it took to reach you. That way I'll know how long I'll be in the dark awaiting news from back home.

With great affection and surviving in the bush, your best friend,
Anna.

❧

December 31, 1946

Anna stood next to Father Neel, watching dozens of workers as they carried concrete blocks and containers of sand and cement on their heads to the building site. Several men were already at work, fashioning the walls by setting down concrete blocks into a layer of mortar and then wiping them off with a trowel before moving on to the next level of block. They were progressing so quickly that Anna was beginning to see the outlines of the building.

"Soon, they'll start erecting the columns with those steel rods over there," Father Neel said, pointing to the staging area full of construction materials. "Then the beams and wooden rafters go on top, followed by zinc for the roof."

"Do you think the zinc will come in soon?"

Father Neel nodded. "Yes, I do in fact. I've made inquiries and it looks like it'll be delivered by the end of the next month. The roofs on our huts will have to suffice for a good while. The rains aren't really so bad, it's the wind that matters. It blows the thatching out of place. Even though the leaks are fairly easy to fix, it's small consolation when you've got water dripping on your face all night."

A supervisor approached Father Neel and showed him a sample of the powdered cement. When he left, Anna asked another question. "How do we have the money to pay all these workers?"

"It's all up to the Lord. The money we receive from MMM is not enough, so I've received a little from the church and some other benevolent givers. Still, we're desperately short of funds. This Leprosy Settlement in Ogoja, as I've taken to calling it, will need to be self-sufficient. We'll have to grow all our own food, make all our own clothes, and improvise as best we can. I'm still planning on saying many more prayers that the Lord might grant us the funding we need. I hope He comes through."

"I hear the word 'hope' often. It appears to be a common theme in this part of the world."

"I'm afraid hope is all we can provide these poor lepers."

Anna pointed to part of the structure. "I believe you told me this will be the infirmary?"

"Yes, almost all of it is an infirmary with the rear of the building forming an open-air intake center. The plan is to have the unconfirmed lepers line up there," he said, pointing, "and one by one be inspected for leprosy. If they're confirmed, they'll begin treatment on the other end at the edge of the infirmary. The interior will be where we have beds for the terminal cases and storage for our medicines and records while the second floor will be our quarters. I think it's a good set-up."

The sun was just rising over the trees, and Anna shielded her eyes. "Is this the only building being constructed?"

"Oh heaven's no! God willing, we'll have the funds to construct a large open-air building for you to teach more children. Eventually, I'll build a real church here so we can hold a proper mass and give the Eucharist to those who believe. It's a grand plan but remember, God can do grand things."

"Yes," Anna replied. "He sure can. He's allowed me to survive a leopard in my hut and that nasty looking bug."

Father Neel laughed. "Yes, we're all still alive and well, too. We can be grateful for that."

Anna touched his arm. "I must begin my lessons, Father. I'll leave you to it. Happy New Year."

"Happy New Year to you, too. I'll see you at dinner tonight."

With a cordial wave, Anna walked over to her school, ducked under the low roof, and clapped her hands loudly. "Children, it's time to begin."

A cool breeze pushed and pulled the mosquito netting in Anna's windows. The sun was down and the night had taken over. Anna was sitting in a chair when a knock on the bamboo pole holding up her front door startled her.

"Are you ready for our nightly session?"

She recognized the voice. "You mean am I ready to administer your nightly thrashing?"

Dr. Chapley entered and took his seat at a small table. This gave her a chance to study his strong jaw and neatly combed black hair while she waited for his reaction.

"Sadly," he laughed, "that may be true. But tonight is New Year's Eve and perhaps my luck will change."

Grinning mischievously, Anna cleared the small table. "Of course, it's New Year's Eve for me as well. Perhaps the luck will be mine."

Thomas laughed. "Perhaps so. We shall see, but I'm afraid you must get in all your licks tonight. I'm leaving tomorrow morning to ride a circle around the entire Ogojan Parish. Father Neel wants me to assess all the lepers. It will only be a guess, but at least it's a start."

Anna shuffled the cards. "How many did you have in Obubra?"

"Let's see," said Thomas tilting his head back. "I think it was about four thousand or so."

"What?! Are you teasing me?"

"Absolutely not! The Nigerian government estimates there are over two hundred thousand lepers in all of Nigeria. I'm guessing there will be close to four thousand here in the Ogojan Parish, alone."

Anna contemplated all this as she dealt the cards, letting Thomas see her mood shift.

"What did you think?" he said. "That there were just a few hundred to treat and minister to?"

"It's hard to imagine so many," she said. "Right now, we have barely ten adults that come in for whatever treatment we can give them, and I have just six children in my class. I was thinking it might grow to a hundred or so, but thousands?!"

Thomas frowned as he picked up his cards. "Leprosy is widespread in these parts. The villagers try to stop it from spreading by casting out anyone they think might possibly have it—regardless of age, love or relationship. But it's not stopping the spread. And the condition of those cast out! At the Scotland Mission in Uburu, they'd approach the church resembling animals more than humans, with nodules all over their face. Some were missing toes and fingers. And all of them were starving. They'd touch their stomachs then their mouths, hoping for a dash of food or a few pence. Their misery would pierce your heart and make any miser open his purse."

Anna sorted her cards and laid down a deuce. "The ones I've seen pull hard at my heart. Father Neel tells me when the workers finish all the construction, more will come in from the bush. Right now, though, they're afraid of getting beaten or killed by the construction workers."

Thomas fanned out his cards, picked one from the deck and then discarded another. "In Obubra, they were tolerated up to a point until one of the elders had his temper piqued for the smallest of reason and flew into a rage. Then he'd randomly beat them, regardless of age. We were told not to intervene or they would swarm us, possibly destroying all that we hope to accomplish while putting ourselves in harm's way. It was terrible to watch. All I could do was treat their wounds when they next appeared at our clinic."

Anna shook her head. "I'm here to help these people, but it's hard for me to stomach some of the things I see."

Thomas paused and held her gaze. "I understand. In Efik they say, 'Nkpa Afia', which means 'White Death'. You must understand, these people believe leprosy is the curse of evil spirits and greatly fear it. Many despise what we're doing here. They believe that we're helping the evil spirits continue and prosper."

Anna looked away and they played the rest of the hand in silence. Suddenly, a noise at the entrance distracted them.

"Clarence!" Anna said laying down her cards. "Please come in and meet Thomas… uh, I mean Dr. Chapley."

Thomas stood up and moved aside hoping to draw Clarence farther in. It worked.

Anna reached out and touched his shoulder. "Clarence, I would like for Dr. Chapley to take a look at you. I promise he won't hurt you. Right Doctor?"

"Exactly," he replied. "I won't even apply any treatment unless you wish it."

"I no know," the boy said.

Anna kneeled in front of him. "Clarence, please do this for me. *Please?*"

When he nodded, Thomas pulled up a chair and gently lifted the boy's right hand. Working his way up the arm he switched to the left hand, and then down to the legs past the dirty cloth wrapped tightly around his waist. After looking intently at his eyes, the exam was complete.

"Clarence, you did fine. I'd be most pleased if you'd allow me to put some chaulmoogra oil under these white patches here. You won't feel anything at all, I promise. Will you agree?"

When he didn't respond, Anna, still kneeling, grabbed his shoulders and turned his body to face hers. "Clarence, will you allow him to help you?"

The boy looked around the small hut obviously thinking it over. Then he looked down at his feet. Finally, he silently nodded.

"Excellent," Thomas said, rising to his feet. "Let me grab my kit and I'll be right back."

When he was gone, Anna gave Clarence some food which he devoured as if he hadn't eaten for days.

"Dr. Chapley will make you feel much better. You know, soon we'll have huts for you to sleep in and you won't have to live in the bush anymore. We'll be able to see each other during the day too because you'll be in my class. We'll have a great time together. Won't you like that?"

Again, the boy nodded silently, still unsure of everything.

Once Thomas returned with his kit, Clarence looked wide-eyed at the doctor as he opened the worn leather casing and extracted a couple of needles. Even though the boy was fearful, he allowed the doctor to inject the oil into the white patches.

"See how I'm doing it, Anna? Depending on the size of the patch, I may have to make injections in two and three places. I'm injecting it until I see the orange color appear underneath the white."

Anna moved in closer. "That needle is broad and quite blunt."

"Yes, it has to be because the oil is so thick and heavy. The white patches are dead skin and they can't feel it, so long as I inject it at an angle and don't go too far down it won't hurt. Their nerves are all gone under these areas."

"How often do I treat him?"

"We like to treat them at least once a week, but it is better if you can do it twice a week. The oil appears to retard the spread of the disease and, in some cases, will even clear up the white patches. At the very least it usually makes the disease more bearable for the patient."

Thomas withdrew the needle for the last time and wiped it off with a rag. "There you go, Clarence. Your first treatment and you did wonderfully. Why, I've seen grown men who didn't do as well as you."

The boy looked at his orange patches and smiled. "I dey leave now."

"Wait," Anna said handing him a roll and two bananas. "Here, take these. And come back tomorrow evening. Dr. Chapley will be gone so we can talk more."

He nodded and disappeared through the opening in the darkness.

Twenty minutes later, Anna had to know. "How does he look?"

Shaking his head, Thomas frowned. "Not well. The disease is spreading rapidly in him, as it sometimes does. If you can begin applying the treatment regularly, you may save his limbs. But I'm afraid he'll lose some toes or fingers before it's all over. When you begin to smell a terrible odor from one of the patches, the rot has spread to the blood. Then he has two weeks left at most."

Anna stared down at the table. "I understand. Let's just play cards and talk of other things. It's your last night here for a while, so let's just enjoy ourselves, shall we?"

"Sure," Thomas said as he picked up his cards. "Sure."

The next morning, Anna dressed and went to breakfast but Thomas was already gone. He had taken his bicycle to conduct the survey. Somehow, the table seemed less lively. Even the fried eggs, sliced tomatoes and fresh goat's milk tasted less enjoyable. What talk there was seemed centered around their problems. Father Neel and Sister Browne, both of whom had hacking coughs, wore the most serious demeanors. Anna was suffering too, but not nearly as bad as they were.

Father Neel, sitting directly across from Anna, coughed several times into his handkerchief. "This Harmattan cold is rather tough to get rid of this year. I've had it before, but this year it seems particularly harsh. The locals tell me it portends a brutal rainy season. Let's hope not."

There was that word 'hope' again, Anna thought.

Sister Browne endured a coughing fit that lasted almost two minutes. Once she caught her breath she said, "With every swallow, I taste the dust and grit. All night I'm coughing and sneezing. In the morning, I feel exhausted before I even get out of bed. I'm simply not getting enough sleep."

"Perhaps you should stay in bed today," Father Neel said. "It won't do you any harm to get caught up on your sleep. That is, if you can sleep in this oppressive heat. Why, even the candles are bowing over during mass. We'll have to be careful or we'll burn the place down."

Sister Browne rubbed her eyes. "I believe I shall stay in today. Maybe it will set me up for the rest of the week. I can only hope." She let loose another hacking dry cough to punctuate her decision.

Anna had heard enough. She didn't feel great either but didn't want to sit around a table being reminded how harsh the conditions were. She pushed back her chair and said, "I pray you get feeling better, both of you. And I wish you all a Happy New Year."

They returned the same wishes and Anna walked to her school to begin class.

When she arrived, Esi—one of the young girls in her class— pointed to her dress and said, "Madame, somtin dey do una dress. (*There's something wrong with your dress.*)"

Anna looked down at the spot she was pointing to. "Oh my, it's a rust stain. My dress must have touched some metal."

The girl offered a solution. "Madame, I can do new."

Anna shook her head. "No thank you, Esi. We need to start our lessons. I can work on it later."

"No mind. I go do ham." With that the girl sprinted out of the hut before Anna could stop her. She ducked under the low roof and watched Esi pick up a long stick from the fields and run to a nearby lemon tree. In less than a minute she had knocked off a lemon and was running back to the school, dropping lemon peels along the way. When she was standing before Anna, she took the dress and squeezed lemon juice over the stain. Using the leftover peel as a scrub brush, she removed the stain completely. Anna inspected the fabric closely, amazed.

"Thank you, Esi! That was excellent. You'll make a great housewife for someone."

The young girl beamed with pride. "Shey I feel leave now?"

Anna chuckled. "No, you did a nice thing, but that doesn't allow you to miss class. Please take your seat. Now children, let's get started on our lessons."

The day dragged on with the wind getting hotter by the hour. When all the classes were over, an exhausted Anna retired to her hut to enjoy some afternoon tea. Seeing Kim carrying a pot of hot water towards her hut, she went to the shelves to get her mother's cup and saucer, but couldn't find them. Knowing exactly where she left it and finding the spot empty, she began to worry.

When Kim entered the hut, Anna told her to just leave the pot on the table. As the girl left, Anna frantically removed her belongings from several boxes, scattering everything haphazardly. When she opened the box that contained her silver-handled whale comb—the special gift from her father—it was gone too. Now she panicked.

After a few more minutes of searching yielded nothing, the realization that she had been tapped (*robbed*) set in. Stealing was so prevalent in Nigeria that it was a wonder she hadn't been victimized before.

Anna forced herself into a chair and slumped down. Hot tears dripped off her dusty cheeks. What precious few possessions she'd brought from home were now gone, vanished into the bush only to be sold for a few pence to some unappreciative buyer. Now she had nothing physical to remind her of her mother or father. It was a disheartening moment.

Suddenly, Patrick appeared at her hut. "Madame, I dey here. Na you get dis letter o." Ignoring the obvious mess in her room, he leaned over and set a letter on her desk. Seeing the tears in her eyes, he turned and left as quickly as he had arrived.

It was a letter from Molly. Turning it over and over in her hands, she finally broke the seal and scanned the seven pages. In the coming days, Anna knew she would read it in depth many times but she caught the most important news: Clarence's wedding had been a big affair and now, his new wife was pregnant and soon to continue the line of Pyles. Tossing the letter on the table, Anna sat in her chair struggling against despondency.

What was she doing out here? Was she actually making a difference? Did anyone care?

Before long, she found she had missed dinner and the pot of hot water had long gone cold. Darkness enveloped the hut. The incessant crickets kept up their choir of noise, sometimes distracting her from her dark thoughts and other times merely annoying her. Somewhere around eight o'clock, a hot breeze blasted dust through her hut which set her to hacking and wheezing. She lit a lamp, found her handkerchief, and began wiping away the tears and dust from her face while continuing to cough into the white cloth. Anna was wondering if she would ever "get used to it" when she picked up the photograph of Molly standing in the rubble of the burned-out building, saluting her. Even that failed to register a grin.

What am I doing out here? she thought, when someone knocked on her hut. Lifting the lamp towards the door, she said gruffly, "Yes, who is it?"

A man's head ducked under the low roof and straightened himself up. "A wise man bearing gifts."

Anna blinked twice then blurted out, "Grant!"

8

"Grant, you found me! What a surprise!" Anna threw her arms around him and held on tightly, allowing her anger and frustrations to completely dissolve.

His hands were full so he was unable to return the favor. "Whoa, take a look at what I've brought you."

Anna pulled back and adjusted the lamp so she could better see him as he reached into a bag that produced several bars of soap—the elegant kind that was sold back in England.

"This might feel refreshing," he said handing a bar to her.

Anna lifted it up to her nose. "Grant, it smells wonderful! Thank you."

"Wait, that's not all. I have some shampoo here—the good kind. And the pièce de résistance—ta dah!" He pulled out a bundle of small tins.

Anna's eyes widened followed by the appearance of a big smile. "Tea! You've brought me tea! I can't believe you're such a dear. It's like having my own butler right here in the bush."

She turned over the tins taking her time to inspect each one.

"Oh Grant, I can't thank you enough," she said, leaning over to kiss him on the cheek.

"Well it's the least I could do for the woman who's bringing knowledge to the lepers of Nigeria. Wouldn't you say?"

"I would say anything after receiving these gifts. Please, take a seat and join me, won't you?" She hurriedly pulled back her hair and patted the dust off her dress.

"Actually, I can't. I have a driver waiting for me in Ogoja. He refused to drive up here. I'll be back tomorrow though, and we can have dinner together if you're willing to walk into Ogoja. I'll meet you at the mission church, say six o'clock, and we can go from there. What do you say?"

Anna's glowing face gave away the answer. "It's a date!"

"Super! Oh, and before I leave, do you know if I received any correspondence? I gave this address out as one of the places I might be."

"No, not that I've heard."

"I see," he said his face growing serious. "By any chance has anyone come looking for me?"

"No, but Father Neel would know all that. You can talk to him tomorrow if you like."

He nodded. "I'll do that. Well, I'm off. I'll see you tomorrow, then."

"I look forward to it!"

Grant lowered his tall frame through the doorway and disappeared into the darkness, leaving Anna to smell her gifts and decide where to store them.

Ten minutes later, she was still in a euphoric state when Clarence appeared at her door. Anna motioned to him. "Please come in, won't you?"

The young boy looked around making sure nobody else was present. "Madame, how una dey do?"

"Both good and bad, I'm afraid." An idea popped into her head. "Say Clarence, I had some items stolen from me today. These items are very dear to me. Would you know who might have taken them?"

"No. I go find ham. No mind."

"Please try, Clarence. I'll pay you something if you can bring them back, especially the comb."

The boy shook his head. "No no. Tell me wetin dem steal."

Anna gave him food to eat while carefully detailing the comb and the china. He stood still, staring intently at her as she described the items a second time. Seeing he'd eaten everything, she reached back for some more food, but when she turned around he was gone. Now she was hungry. Anna picked up Molly's letter and began reading it, eating the food she'd saved for Clarence. It took her over thirty minutes to get through it, rereading certain portions several times but a few things stood out. First, the Pyle's wedding was a spectacular event for Maghull. It had taken place while Anna was still in Ireland living in the convent. Most of the town had turned out for it. Then surprisingly, two months later, Clarence's wife Florence had taken ill. Apparently the cause was pregnancy. The doctors recommended she stay in bed until the baby was born. Since Florence didn't have to work, this was no big imposition.

As far as Molly's life was concerned, she'd been on several dates with a delivery man from Clarence G. Pyle and Son Grocers, and he was able to give Molly the inside story on both Clarence and Florence. The man treated Molly very well, but she wasn't making any wedding plans soon.

Molly said she absentmindedly went to Anna's old flat thinking she'd be there and stopped herself just before she knocked. She missed Anna and it was clear she hadn't received Anna's first letter, the one sent from Calabar the day she arrived. The rest of the letter was filled with gossip about various friends and current events in Maghull.

Anna set the letter down and sighed. On one hand, she was grateful for news from home; it warmed her heart knowing she still had that connection even though all her family members were deceased. On the other hand, it was depressing and not just because she'd received confirmation Clarence was married and now expecting. The time difference between Maghull and her location was so great that by the time the letter arrived, it was almost like reading a history lesson. For all she knew, Molly could be married and pregnant at this very moment. Or one of her friends' dead. It was a hard concept to get used to. But then when she refocused on her life in Ogoja and the children who not only needed her but loved her, the physical distance from home no longer mattered. It was that thought that reminded her to write down on Molly's letter the exact date she'd received it: January 3, 1947.

Anna studied her new teas again and was about to locate some hot water when she decided she had a big day tomorrow. It would be best to go to bed, rather than stay up all night. Within the span of a few seconds, she locked the door, doused the light and climbed under the mosquito netting with thoughts of Molly's letter and Grant's visit all fighting for space. It didn't matter which side won—she was asleep before she knew it.

❧

The evening sun was still hovering above the trees as Anna left her hut to make the one-mile journey into Ogoja. She stayed on the thin dirt path, occasionally venturing onto the dirt road when the path crossed over it. The path led straight to town while the road zigzagged back and forth making a walking trip longer. Everyone stayed on the path to not only cut down time but avoid the dust that a vehicle kicked up when it passed by. This was something she had to avoid because she wanted to look her best. She'd taken great pains to wash her hair in the stream with the fancy shampoo Grant gave her. The stream wasn't as good as a barrel of rainwater, but it did add a nice luster to her hair.

When Anna arrived at the mission church, Grant was already there waiting in a chair. Seeing her, he sprung to his feet. "Don't you look lovely!"

Anna beamed. "Why you look nice, too. How did you manage to press your clothes?"

"That's the great advantage of Nigeria. A two-pence will buy just about anything." He thrust out his arm for Anna to take hold. "Shall we? I assume there's no need for a chaperone."

Grabbing it with her hand she said, "No, I think we've left most of civilization behind, especially the *civilized* part. By the way, where are we going?"

"My driver introduced me to a woman—her name escapes me—who operates a small establishment on her veranda. I'm told she makes delicious dishes and she just happens to have a table available for tonight."

Anna chuckled then stopped. "Wait, it might be Mama Mimi. She cooked the feast we held for the local chiefs. It was very delicious!"

"Mama Mimi! That's her! I guess we'll have a meal fit for a chief."

"Now I'm definitely looking forward to this, not that I wasn't already."

They made small talk while they found their way to the makeshift restaurant, arriving to find a beautiful table set with a vase of local flowers. Although the table sat directly on the dirt, it was adorned with real silverware and linen napkins—an oasis of civilization in a desert of unsophistication.

"Madame?" Grant said as he pulled out her chair.

"Thank you, sir," Anna replied, sliding into her seat.

Grant took his seat which brought out the famous Mama Mimi, who was carrying a small plate of appetizers. She set them on the table and turned to leave without saying a word.

A few minutes later she returned with two glasses of water and a bottle of wine Grant had obviously given her earlier. This time Mama Mimi smiled, poured the wine, and left just as quietly as she had come, taking the bottle with her.

Grant whispered, "I've learned the locals don't really know how to run a restaurant so they tend to say nothing until you do. We'll eat some of this, and then see what she has in mind for the next course."

Raising his wine glass, he made a toast. "Here's to a wonderful meal with a wonderful person."

Anna raised her glass to meet his. "Thank you, that's sweet. And thank you for this wonderful evening."

When Grant smiled at her, she could tell their friendship was rapidly progressing beyond mere shipmates.

For the next two hours, they sat talking, eating and drinking, occasionally swatting away a fly or mosquito that threatened to ruin the evening. During the meal, Anna learned he was staying one more night before moving farther north to Kano, and then on to Katsina.

"When will you be coming back this way?"

Grant rubbed his jaw and thought for a moment. "I could probably come back around Easter. I assume the mission will have a huge feast and celebration especially with Lent ending. Am I correct?"

"Gosh, I don't know. I assume so. Surely, they will have something. Of course, you don't need to wait until then to come back."

Grant nodded, smiling again. "I know, but the rainy season will be starting in March and that makes a lot of the roads impassable. Easter will likely be the first I can make it back, perhaps later."

"Well I hope you're not in any danger when you travel."

"Not likely, but it is the bush you know. Most locals assume a white person is carrying valuables and can waylay them at any moment. It's not like there's a policeman or constable standing around the corner to nab them. Right?"

"I see what you mean."

"I'm always extraordinarily careful in the bush, particularly in making sure no one is following me. I have to carry substantial funds with me, as there's no reputable bank to make a withdrawal from until you get near the coast."

Anna listened and sipped the last of her wine. Grant did likewise, creating a lull in the conversation. After a moment of silence, he set his glass down purposefully.

"Anna, I have something I want to ask you tomorrow evening and it's something important. I want you to think about it while I'm gone and give me your answer when I return around Easter. Is that alright?"

"My, you're sounding serious."

"Yes, perhaps I am. Will you be available tomorrow evening at your hut? I'd like to talk to you in private, without the good father or the sisters listening in. Is that acceptable? I won't be able to stay for long, though."

Anna breathed in deeply. "Yes, I'll simply be sitting in my hut like I do most nights. The others are usually in their huts too. I'll look forward to your visit… and whatever that entails."

"Wonderful. Oops, there's that word again." He laughed. "Perhaps I should get you back." Grant placed some bills on the table.

"I suppose you should, even though it's been a *wonderful* night."

At that, they both laughed heartily as they left Mama Mimi's one-table restaurant.

❧

The day seemed to fly by for Anna. At breakfast, no one mentioned the visit by Grant or the fact that the locals were all abuzz with the two white people who'd come into town to eat. It was a certainty that at least one of them had told Sister Flores and Father Neel. Still, some privacy boundaries had developed among the missionaries, if only in regards to the few yards separating each other's huts. When Anna noticed Sister Browne smiling at her, she knew she'd be telling her all about it when they had some time together at the river. But for now, whatever talk there was covered the weather, the hacking Harmattan coughs and the construction progress.

When breakfast was over, Anna went to her lessons in a cheerful mood and the children responded warmly. Teaching came naturally to her. It was something she was made for. Her abilities helped them progress faster than even she thought possible. They seemed to have hungry minds as well as hungry stomachs. Even though most of them were starting from zero, their happiness at being accepted by a non-leper person coupled with doing something meaningful, gave them incentive to learn as much as they could, as if the school might up and disappear at any moment.

When class was over for the day, Anna walked back to her hut to check on her teas and soap and ensure they were still there. Ever since the theft, she'd been watching her hut closely, hiding her valuables as best she could.

As she looked through her things, she found the box of medical supplies Thomas had given her to treat Clarence. A quick inventory told her she needed more gauze. Knowing she wasn't allowed to treat Clarence in her room, she would need to pilfer it from the infirmary. Its normal hours of operation were from 9 a.m. to 4 p.m., and as it was just a little after 3 p.m., she still had plenty of time left to get to the infirmary before it closed.

Pretending to be inspecting the construction, Anna stood at the site, biding her time. The men had been making real progress. Blocks had been laid around the entire perimeter reaching high enough to begin the second floor which was far sooner than she'd imagined. As she thought about it, she realized that unlike back home, there were no inspections, no work rules, and no electricity or plumbing pipes to worry about. Construction in Nigeria was much simpler and faster.

The men who worked on the project were ones who weren't afraid of leprosy. Or they needed the money so badly they overlooked the risk. Either way, they worked long, hard hours with no gloves and mostly barefoot.

Anna continued watching for a while longer until she saw Sister Flores leave on time. This was odd because she usually stayed longer, always finding something more that needed to be done. With her gone, the infirmary was now empty, with the only people nearby being the workers, who were occupied with making mud and laying block. She tried to act casually as she walked to the infirmary, carefully opening the bamboo door and going straight to the small cabinet where the gauze was kept. Next to it was a locker with needles and medicine, secured by a padlock. They too had suffered thefts. Grabbing a small quantity of gauze, she stuffed it into her pocket and exited the small structure, making sure to properly latch the door.

Just as she was finishing up, she turned around and a voice boomed out. "There you are. I was looking for you!"

Anna's heart stopped. Father Neel was coming along a path from the huts and had caught her coming out of the infirmary.

Or had he?

"Hello Father Neel, what can I do for you?"

"I'd like to talk to you in private about an important matter. Let's go into the infirmary and sit down, shall we?"

"Certainly," she said, hiding the bulge in her pocket and the nervousness in her hands.

Spinning back around, she undid the bamboo door and walked inside, selecting a chair as far away from the medical supplies as possible. Now she had to wait it out and see if she had been caught.

Father Neel took a seat across from her, slumped down in a chair and sighed. "Anna, I need you to review some letters for me. I'm drafting them to ask for more funds, as I'm afraid we'll be running short soon. I would be ever so grateful if you could check them for grammar and such, and see if you can make my words sound desperate enough without sounding *too* desperate, if you know what I mean?"

Anna felt relieved, although she still kept her hand over her stuffed pocket. "What happens if we don't receive the money? Do we leave and go home?"

Father Neel was disconsolate. "I suppose the best answer for you is that if it's God's will that we should be here, then we'll be here. If not, we'll go somewhere else."

"How long do we have?"

"We have enough money to get us to Easter. If we don't receive more funds by then, I'm afraid we'll have to halt construction, pack up our things and ship back to Ireland. The letters Patrick brought back didn't contain the funds I was hoping for. That's why it's urgent to get these letters out now, to hopefully bring in the funds before it's too late."

Anna bit her lip and nodded. "Sure, I'm happy to help in any way. Where are the letters?"

Father Neel fished inside his pocket and produced five sheets of paper. "Please feel free to make whatever changes necessary."

Anna took the papers from him and was about to place them in her pocket when she remembered the gauze was there. Instead, she held them to her chest, smiled, and hoped to end the interview. "I'll get to them right away. Is there anything more you need?"

"Yes, your confidence in this matter. No sense in anyone else knowing our predicament."

"Certainly. I won't say a word."

"Thank you," he said rising. "I would like Patrick to take it tomorrow and go into Calabar. I know he just came back, but if you have any letters to go out, by all means include them. I hate to rush you, but if you could return them before dinner, I'd be most grateful. That would give me time to make any rewrites and go to sleep with an easy mind, at least as easy as a poverty-stricken priest can sleep."

"In that case, let me get to it. I'll let you close up here." Without waiting for further conversation, she left the infirmary and breathed easier with every step away from Father Neel.

When she was safely inside her hut, she pulled out the box of medical supplies, removed the gauze from her pocket, and stored it away. Then she sat at her bench and began working on the letters.

By dinner, she had the project completed and discreetly handed the papers over to Father Neel. No one seemed to notice.

They dined on dishes of yam mash—a concoction of yam, salt, goat's milk, pepper spice and ground grasscutter—tomato slabs, leafy lettuce, and fresh bread. Anna ate her fill and made light conversation before excusing herself and hurrying back to her hut to await the dazzling Mr. Eaton.

It was very dark when Grant finally appeared. The moon was gone and the sky was inky black. Even the stars were hiding. Swinging an oil lamp at his side, Anna could follow his progress along the trail and thought he would never arrive.

When he finally did, he bent down at her open door and said quietly, "May I come in?"

"Of course you may, but please leave the bugs outside."

"If that were only possible, I surely would." He set his lamp on the bench next to Anna's and turned it down. "How are you? Did you have a nice day?"

"I did," she replied. "It was easy, because the children make it so. However, tomorrow is treatment day and that means the nurses look them over and make any necessary injections. It doesn't appear to hurt them although they don't like the process. But, like a passing shower, once they're finished they are extremely sunny and happy."

"I would be too. I don't like to see needles."

They smiled at each other allowing the moment to stretch out. After a long silence, Grant finally spoke.

"Anna, as you know I lost my family in the war. It was a devastating time for me—my family was everything to me. I couldn't imagine ever being without them. Now, I find myself a widower and childless. When I took this position, I thought it would be good for me to get away from England and all the pain I felt there; just leave everything behind. And truthfully it has been good. Not that I've forgotten them—that's not possible. But it feels like I've started a new life. Then, when we were put on the same ship and I got to know you, it seemed like we shared a common bond. Even the incident in Madeira, as terrifying as it was, brought us closer together."

Anna sat motionless, barely breathing. Grant paused to let it all soak in.

"Seeing you again and getting to know you even better, I've found hope in you. Hope that I may one day have a wife and child again, something the Germans ripped from me."

He leaned forward from his chair, closer, to see her expression.

"Anna, in a perfect world, we would spend weeks if not months getting to know each other better. But this is the bush. My work doesn't allow me to circle back here more than once, maybe twice a year at best, and even then it would only be for a few days. Certainly not enough time to have a proper courtship. With each year, I'm getting older and, of course, lonelier."

Reaching over, he took her hand. "So, my lovely Anna, I'm asking you to marry me. Although I can't marry you this very moment, I will be back around Easter for your answer. If it's yes, please tell me then and we'll make the proper arrangements. Once we're married, we can travel together through Nigeria as I continue my work. It's possible I may be sent to other countries, so you would get to see the rest of the world. Eventually, I'm sure my position will end and we'll go back to England. When that will be, though, I don't know."

Grant kissed her hand and let it go, leaning back in his chair as Anna let out a deep breath. Taking a moment to collect herself, she said, "I've never had a man propose to me and certainly never imagined it would be in the bush. But life is full of sweet surprises. I thank you for giving me some time to think about it. Getting married would mean leaving my work here, and I'm just getting started. I have to admit, I've come to love these children, these unloved and rejected little piccans (children). But I'd like children of my own too, and unless God intends to bestow a miraculous conception on me, I'll need a man for that."

Grant laughed. "That's what I love about you Anna, you're such a deep thinker, even when comparing me to a car battery, like I'm necessary to crank up the engine."

Anna laughed too. "Come now, you know I'd never compare you to a battery. Perhaps the tires and petrol all rolled into one."

They continued laughing until Grant said, "Being your auto part would be good enough for me, so long as I'm with you for the ride. Speaking of rides, I must get back to my driver and get going."

As he stood, so did Anna. Suddenly and without warning, he pulled her close, wrapping his arms around her before kissing her full on the lips.

With their lips still close to each other, he said, "This is something to remember me by."

He removed a tiny square box wrapped in paper and placed it in her hands.

"Hold this for me. When I come back, if you say yes, we will open it up together. If the answer's no, I'll retrieve it and be on my way."

Anna stared at the box, understanding clearly what it contained. "Grant…"

"Hold that thought, dear, for the next time I see you." He turned up his lamp, walked to the door and said, "I'm not saying goodbye Anna. Just *Easter*."

Before she could reply, he was gone.

Anna watched as his lantern faded down the dark path and disappeared. Her head spinning, she plunked down in a chair and turned the box over and over, shaking it several times. Nothing moved inside.

Looking around her small hut, she had no idea where she could put it to keep the thieves at bay. It would be something she'd have to really think about, not to mention Grant's proposal. The whole thing was difficult to believe. She'd been in Africa barely two months and already had a marriage proposal. What else could happen out here?

She was about to turn down her lamp and crawl underneath the netting when another person appeared at her entrance: Clarence.

Anna eyes flew open when she saw his hands. Each one held something precious to her: the comb, the saucer and the cup.

"You got them back! Why Clarence, that's wonderful."

She took the items and set them on her bench, grabbing the boy and hugging him hard. Having never been hugged before, he kept his arms by his side not sure how to respond. When she finally released him, she studied the items. "This makes me so happy. Here, I'm going to give you some money."

Seeing his troubled face, she wondered what she had said. "Clarence, what's wrong?"

Tears dripped down from his eyes as the words left his lips, "You dey get man now, you dey go and leave me here—*alone*."

9

Anna awoke the next morning with the memory of all that had happened the previous night still fresh in her mind. There was so much to comprehend it was almost overwhelming. Events like these, had they happened back in Maghull, would've been easily dealt with. Yet out here in the bush, the daily routine hardly varied. Rarely was there anything new happening so it was easy to get used to everything being the same all the time. Nevertheless, in just over the span of an hour, Grant had proposed, her precious items had been returned, and the mysterious Clarence was crying because he heard what Grant had said. She had gone to sleep and experienced deep dreams about all of this. Now, as Kim sat the pot of boiling water in front of her on the breakfast table, she hoped her special blend of tea leaves from Ceylon, Kenya and Assam would reorganize her mind.

Anna removed a spoonful of black tea from her square container and carefully dropped it into a metal tea infuser, the one she'd brought from home. She was very precise in making sure none of it spilled over the edge and was wasted. Six minutes later, the tea had steeped, been poured into her favorite cup, and was almost drained when she noticed another diner coming. Feeling extravagant, she went ahead and made herself another cup just as Sister Browne arrived.

"Where is everyone?" Anna asked.

Sister Browne took her seat and poured a glass of water. "Father Neel and Sister Flores are still suffering from the Harmattan cough. Sisters O'Keefe and Whelan are tending to them. I think Sister Flores will be up and about this afternoon, but who knows? Breathing in dust all day is enough to bring anyone down."

"Thank God it hasn't put me down yet."

Kim returned with their food. "I guess now is a good time to give the blessing. The honor is all yours."

Sister Browne said the prayer and the two started in on a large portion of sweetened mashed yams and fried bush-bird eggs. The ever-present large loaf of bread sat waiting to be sliced, a job Father Neel usually handled with enthusiasm. Today, though, Anna performed the task, handing the first piece to Sister Browne. They took turns slathering on a good dose of fresh butter and marmalade. Meals were one aspect of the bush Anna enjoyed.

Sister Flores had hired in a rotating group of cooks and serving girls who not only kept them well fed, but did an excellent job of changing up the fare. Though meat wasn't often on the menu, gorgeous fruits and vegetables from Nigeria's fertile land always were. Everything here grew well and fast. Anna was continually amazed at the incredible size of the vegetables. The yams were double the size of the ones back home. It was the same with tomatoes. And the large leafy lettuce was big enough to hide a rabbit in. She was sure Pyle and Son Grocers would be astounded.

Outside, a breeze sprang up, forcing Kim to adjust a covering over the window. They tried very hard to prevent the breeze from coming inside. This was yet another aspect of their meals: avoiding the dust. When they had first arrived, meals were eaten in the open air, usually under a tree near the mission. It was a nice, pleasant experience. After they received their land from the chiefs and moved, they had continued the practice while their personal huts were being built. But then the dry season arrived, and with it the dust. Usually, it wasn't too bad in the morning when the hot winds hadn't yet built up. But by dinner, it was terrible. The wind carried dust onto everything. No matter how well the food was covered, it had a thin layer before it entered one's mouth. Anna found it hard to chew, especially with grit grinding against her teeth. It turned even the best-cooked meal into trash. Father Neel joked that they would soon all have teeth as white as the Nigerians. The joke was funny for the first few days, but by now no one was laughing. Instead, they were coughing.

Fortunately, the workers had quickly built the large hut for the infirmary and made a good shelter. Since it was the only building beside the small church that someone was not living in, and it had a table in the back—one the staff used to go over patients' records—it made a nice place to have meals. With a little planning, they could cover the window with thatching and eliminate the breeze (and thus the dust). The only problem with that plan was the hot air. With no circulation it could be unbearable, especially at dinnertime. Mornings, though, were usually pleasant, as the cool air from the night had not yet fully departed.

When the two were finished, Kim took away their plates and left them alone. This was what Anna was waiting for. "Can you join me for a bath this evening?" she whispered.

"Yes, I need one," the nun replied.

"Good. I have much to discuss with you." Anna said, smiling playfully. She would've loved to tell her everything right then, but a combination of impending work schedules and the fact that the locals seemed to be everywhere, constantly listening in, made her put off any discussion. The river was one of the truly private spots they had.

"I can't wait," Sister Browne whispered back. "It'll give me something to look forward to. With everyone down and the doctor gone, I'm the only nurse left standing. I'll be running the clinic all by myself."

"Gosh, I wish you the best. I have testing this morning. This is where I find out if I've been doing any good with these children."

Sister Browne pushed her chair back to leave. "I guess we'll compare notes at the river then."

"Come by my hut when you're ready and we'll walk together."

"Will do. See you later."

Anna went to her small school and like always, found the kids under the large roof milling around, waiting for instructions.

Clapping her hands, she said, "Children, take your seats please."

As they scrambled for their places, she saw a lurking figure at the rear. Because his lower half was standing in the shade and the upper half was in the bright sunlight, she couldn't tell if it was a new student or someone else.

"Would you like to come in?" she shouted towards the figure.

The students turned around just as the boy ducked under the thatched roof.

"Clarence!" Anna said. "So wonderful to see you. Please take a seat."

A murmur went through the class as most of them knew who he was. Clarence took the first available seat at the rear of the classroom wearing a look of a kid ready to bolt.

"Children, today we are having a test. I will pass out your paper and I want you to keep it turned over until I say to start. You will have thirty minutes to complete it. Does everyone have a pencil?"

The students held it up for her to see.

"Excellent. Clarence, I need to take down some history on you for our records, so we will do that while the rest of the class takes their test."

Clarence said nothing, and instead busied himself with studying the exits. Once Anna had passed out all the tests, she glanced at her watch and said, "Begin." Then she walked to the rear and motioned for Clarence to follow her.

"Please sit at this table. We'll whisper so we don't disturb the other students."

Clarence took his seat, his eyes darting this way and that. Sensing his anxiety, Anna softened her voice. "Tell me where you are from?"

"I no know."

"That's okay. What are your parents' names?"

Shaking his head, he said, "No mudder. No fadda."

"I don't understand. You had to have a mother and father or you couldn't have been born. Do you not know them?"

Clarence shook his head. Anna asked a few more questions before finally, the boy opened up and explained in Pidgin all he knew about this past.

At a very early age he was cast out of his village and left with other lepers like him. He thought his village might be farther north, around Adikpo, but he wasn't sure. At times, he almost starved to death before a kindly woman named Kissa, who'd also been cast out of her village, took a liking to him. Kissa fed him when she had food and showed him how to take care of himself. She called him Okey. He was with her three dry seasons when one day, he awoke and waited for Kissa to get up. When she didn't, he pushed her several times and learned something new: death. Burials among lepers didn't take place, because no one had the tools or the strength. The group simply got up and moved away, leaving her for the animals.

Without Kissa's protection and nurturing, he was constantly harassed. If he found food, someone would beat him up and steal it. One day, he stole some food from a nearby village and to prevent it from being taken from him, he hid in the bush to eat it. He had to eat slowly, because his stomach was so shrunken he couldn't eat much and got full quickly. After a few days, a bigger boy found him and ripped the food from his grasp. While the boy turned away to eat some of it, Clarence picked up a rock and hit him in the head. The boy fell to the dirt causing blood to splatter everywhere. Clarence took the food back and stayed where he was, since he knew the other boys were out looking for him too. The next day the boy's breathing slowed before finally giving out. He was dead. With nowhere to go, Clarence stayed there and ate all the food, then scavenged anything of value off the boy and left him for the animals. It was truly survival of the fittest.

Over the next few years, he hid out and scavenged, stole, and begged. He got big enough to defend himself and was generally left alone by the other lepers. At times, he came into contact with non-lepers through begging or stealing and picked up more language. It was long slow process but he had lots of time to sort it all out.

Anna wrote all this down and wiped her brow several times. She had already heard horrendous stories of young kids sent away with not even a yam in their hands to die in the bush, but this story was one that pushed her understanding of the leprosy epidemic to new heights. Now she understood why he acted the way he did.

"Clarence, listen to me. Please come to school each day. We will feed you and help you with medicine. No one will beat you up or take anything away from you. Please believe me."

The boy said nothing.

Anna glanced at her watch. "You stay right here while I pick up the tests and grade them. Later, we will have some food for you. After school is over, I'd like to take you to the infirmary. Okay?"

The boy remained silent.

Anna went to the front and announced, "Children, time's up. Please pass your papers to me and remain silent while I grade them. I'll just be a minute."

Sitting at her desk she quickly graded the six papers, pleased with the results. Her students were learning almost everything she was teaching them. Even though she was a very experienced teacher back in England, this gave her a lot of confidence that she could teach in the bush. It was also encouraging to see that their enthusiastic attitude towards learning was not just a show, unlike so many other things here.

"Well children, I am very pleased with the grades. During our break, I will go over each one with you and explain what you missed. And then we will…" Anna stopped short. At the very back, the seat Clarence had been in was now empty. The boy was gone! She shook her head in frustration. He was going to be a tough catch.

Around two in the afternoon, a young Nigerian girl approached Anna and whispered in her ear. Anna nodded and sent the girl on her way.

"Students, we are short on staff at the infirmary and I'm needed to help out. We are going to end class early today, but you can stay here in the nice cool shade and work on your lessons. I hope you choose to do that. Class is dismissed."

Esi raised her hand. "Madame, may I come to help?"

"Why Esi, that's an excellent use of English. I'm very proud of you. However, you have not been trained in nursing, so I'm sorry, you should stay here and work on your lesson."

Esi was not deterred. "Remember you the dress?"

Anna laughed inside. This young girl was reminding her how she had removed the stain from Anna's dress using a lemon and thus, was somehow qualified to help in the infirmary.

"Yes, I do remember. But my answer is still the same. I have to leave now so end of discussion."

Esi shook her head in disagreement but stayed at her desk to work on her lessons like the rest of the students did.

Anna exited the school and found Sister Browne in the infirmary treating a patient. "Are you all by yourself?"

Sister Browne looked up. "Yes. Both Father Neel and Sister Flores are feeling worse. Sister O'Keefe is helping them get to Ogoja so they can stay in the church tonight. It has less dust than anywhere else around, though inside, it's as hot as an oven. Sister Whelan is packing up some clothes for both of them and I have these three people to treat. Can you help?"

"Sure, tell me what you need."

"Can you fill some of those syringes with oil?" she said, pointing to a rectangular metal container.

"How many do you need?

"Just three."

"Certainly." Anna took three large syringes and filled them with the yellow-orange chaulmoogra oil.

When she was done, Sister Browne asked her for another favor. "Can you inject it into the white patches on the woman? Do you even know how?"

"Yes I do. I'll take care of her." Anna took a seat in front of a woman who appeared to be close to her age. Two fingers and a thumb on her left hand were nothing but stubs, while the remaining two fingers were beginning to rot. One finger on her right hand was also disappearing. The staff called these patients 'burnouts', for the way leprosy reduced fingers and toes to nubs. After this stage, the disease would work its way into the upper limbs, and death soon followed.

Anna smiled at the woman and quietly began injecting the oil the way Dr. Chapley had shown her. It was a slow, tedious process, but she had discovered with Clarence that this process did more than provide some medical relief. The mere touching of the woman triggered an emotional reaction bringing an immediate smile to her face.

Lepers were destined to a life of seclusion from the rest of the world, yet they longed for human companionship. They rarely touched one another, since they had their own hierarchy. It was like, "I have it bad, but not as bad as you do." That attitude kept them from touching each other for fear of making it worse. As Anna touched this lady, she appeared overjoyed.

Another result of the injections was giving the patient the feeling that someone cared about them. Someone was trying to make them feel better. They might be drowning, but help was rowing out to them with a life vest. And maybe, just maybe, they could be cured and return to their families. After all, they could dream.

The patient and Anna were the same age. Anna wondered how she would feel if the roles were reversed. What would her life be like? Would she even be able to survive in the bush? It was too scary to think about.

Because of the woman's advanced stage of leprosy, it took Anna an hour to complete the injections. She also applied salve and wrapped a cotton strip around the oozing wounds. When she was done, Anna smiled, patted the woman on the shoulder and sent her on her way, leaving behind a gigantic smile as payment for services rendered.

"Sister Browne, is there anything else can I do?"

"Help me finish up with this gentleman. If you can bandage these two wounds, I'll finish injecting the oil."

Anna made short work of her task and began cleaning up while Sister Browne completed the injections.

"I can't wait until we have the building constructed," Sister Browne said. "Then we'll have a better organization of medical services and patients. Right now, they just come in here and find a place to stand."

"I'm also looking forward to having a room to live in, one a leopard can't come into."

Sister Browne chuckled. "I'm glad that didn't happen to me. I don't know what I would've done." She patted the man on the shoulder. "There you are, Buki. Please come back in three days. Perhaps the doctor will be back by then."

"Sista, I go come come chop tomorrow."

"Oh yes, of course they'll be serving food at noon, but please wait three days from today before seeing the doctor." She held up three fingers to make sure he got the message.

"I sabi. Bye bye sista."

When he was gone, Sister Browne put away her things. "I think I'm ready for that bath now."

"Grab your kit and come to my hut. I'll need to get my things together."

"Be right there."

The two were soon walking on the long path to the river, where their secluded section awaited them. The brown grass was dry and dusty, barely reaching their knees.

At the stream, it didn't take them long to remove their clothes, wade into the cool water, and find their spots. By now they knew every rock, especially the two hollowed out seats which allowed them to rest comfortably on the riverbed while the water swirled around their necks. The current was strong enough to easily remove the day's dust and grime. Because it was so hot, baths often took an hour or more with most of the time dedicated to relaxation rather than actual washing.

"So," said Sister Browne, "are you going to keep me in suspense?"

"No, I was waiting to get the first layer of grime off before I started in. But I think it's gone now. The first thing I have to tell you is that Clarence came by my hut last night and had all the stolen items with him—the cup, the saucer and the comb."

"That's wonderful! How did he get them?"

"He didn't say and I didn't ask. I was so happy, I could've hugged the life out of him. But before I could, I noticed he was crying."

"Crying? Why?"

Anna built up the suspense. "He's worried I'm going to leave him."

"Why would he think that?"

Lowering her voice, she said, "Because he overheard Grant asking me to marry him."

Sister Browne shifted in the sand so she could sit more upright. She wanted to make sure she heard every word. "Grant asked you to marry him?! How did this come about?"

"He said he was coming to see me the next evening after our date in town two nights ago. I didn't tell you because I didn't know what he was going to say. I didn't want to embarrass myself with assumptions; I've done it before."

"This is certainly big news. How did he put it? And what did you say?"

Anna detailed Grant's proposal, his projected return trip around Easter, and the small box he'd given her.

"Did you open it yet?"

"No, I wrapped it up in some cloth and buried it beneath the floor of my hut. That should keep the thieves at bay."

"Are you going to accept his proposal?"

Anna stared at swirling water. "I don't know yet. It's all so sudden. I've only known him since the journey on the ship. What do you think?"

"Well, I'm probably not the best one to ask. I've taken vows that you haven't. I will surely miss you if you leave. But on a purely objective level, he is rather handsome. I happened to glimpse him in town when you two were meeting for dinner. He looks even better than he did on the ship."

"What?!" Anna said laughing. "Why Victoria, you're a spy!"

"Perhaps, but we had to return some items to the mission and I was the one on task."

Anna splashed some water in her direction. "At the exact time I met Grant in town?!"

"No," she said grinning. "Thirty minutes earlier. I just stayed behind in case you needed help. Besides, I thought he might want to say hi to another former shipmate."

Anna giggled. "I should've known. Have you told anyone?"

Sister Browne held up her hand. "As God is my witness, no. But the sisters and Father Neel heard that you had a date at Mama Mimi's. I didn't hear anyone discussing it, though. At least, not around me. I don't think they even know it was Grant."

"Please don't say a word. Promise me that."

"I promise. Not a word."

"Good, now let me tell you more about what Clarence told me today when he appeared at school."

❧

A week later, Anna sat in her hut reviewing some papers from her students. The afternoon was crawling on towards evening. The winds outside were gusting, blowing dust through the cracks in her walls. She had the windows closed and a piece of cloth wrapped over the opening to keep it out, but it wasn't much use. The inside of her hut was so dim, she had to turn the lamp up as bright as it would go, even though it was still very bright outside; not the easiest conditions for a school teacher. A knock came to her door.

"Yes, what is it?"

Kim was standing there with a message. "Miss Anna, fada Neel wan make you tea with him."

"I thought he was staying in the church."

"Yeah-ya. Make we go see fada Neel."

"Walk to the mission in this wind?"

Kim shrugged her shoulders.

"Okay," Anna said turning off her lamp. "Let's go and have that tea. I sure hope it's good."

On the path, Anna wore a cloth tied around her nose and mouth to breathe through. She also kept her eyes mostly closed, hoping to keep the dust at bay, yet still see enough to follow Kim who was ahead of her. She wondered how in the world the locals survived this year in and year out.

It seemed like a long walk, certainly longer than normal. When they arrived, Kim showed her to Father Neel's makeshift bedroom in the sanctuary, separate from Sister Flores' room.

"Father, how are you feeling?" she asked.

He coughed several times. "Not good. Kim, bring the pot in, please."

"Yeah-ya," she said, before running off to the kitchen.

"Please take a seat Anna. Thank you for coming. I'm sure the walk was not pleasant."

"No it wasn't, but perhaps the wind will die down before I have to make the return journey."

"Perhaps. I'm very sorry to bring you here, but it's important I talk to you."

He gathered up some papers in front of him. This gave Anna the chance to look around the church and see dust everywhere. And it was hot! Hopefully, her visit would be short.

The pot arrived and Father Neel dropped in the tea to steep. "It's the construction. I'm worried about the roof. They should be getting close to putting the zinc on, so I need you to personally talk with the foreman and convey my thoughts to him. Can you do that?"

"Of course," Anna said growing concerned. "What thoughts would you like me to convey?"

"The roof supports. They must be placed on mud blocks first. Sometimes these people cut things short and don't do it correctly."

He coughed several times. "The mud blocks are very hard and the white ants can't chew through them to get to the wood supports. If the workers fail to do this, it may be just a few seasons before the ants chew through the wood. When that happens, the roof collapses. People can die, you know."

Anna nodded. "Don't worry. I'll talk to the foreman first thing in the morning and make sure he's doing that."

Father Neel poured her some tea. "But you must also watch the construction. Can you take some time to watch it? Perhaps after your classes?"

"Yes, of course," Anna said patting his sweaty hand. "Don't trouble yourself. You need to get well."

He poured himself some tea, slowly swallowing it. "This cough has really got me. Normally, I'm traveling and don't have to deal with it too much. I guess it caught up with me this time."

"Maybe when Dr. Chapley returns, he can give you a tonic or powder to relieve some of this." How he was able to drink hot tea in this furnace, she had no idea.

"Maybe so," he said, holding the cup close to his lips. "I'm wondering where he is. He should've been back several days ago. I'll have to send Patrick out looking for him if he doesn't return soon."

"I hope he comes back soon, too. I had to cut class short today to help Sister Browne with the patients. I don't mind doing that, but the children will have trouble learning if I have to do it too often."

Father Neel shook his head. "Oh no, that won't happen again. With the Irish sisters helping both Sister Flores and me all day today, we simply had a…"

The church door swung open letting in a strong gust of dirt. Anna and Father Neel turned their attention to the entrance and the first thing they saw was a bicycle wheel. This was followed by a set of handlebars, and finally, Dr. Chapley. He had a bandana wrapped around his mouth and nose and was completely covered with dust.

"Why, there you are Thomas," Father Neel said. "We were just talking about you!"

Dr. Chapley leaned the bicycle against a pew and removed the bandana, dusting himself off on the doorstep. His black hair was so dirty it was now a light brown. "I was hoping to be here days ago, but between the winds pushing me back and the winding trails, I lost my way. I was severely delayed. Seems I've made it just in time."

Father Neel coughed loudly. "In time for what?"

"The babies. The towns from Adinya to Katsina heard we had an infirmary for lepers so they took up a collection for us."

This got Father Neel's attention. "Collection? How much did they come up with?"

The doctor downed a glass of water. "Not money. Babies. They have two kit cars bringing them here. I asked them to give me three days before they came so we could be ready to receive them."

Father Neel nervously rubbed his hands together. "Oh my! Babies. How will we manage that? And three days is hardly any time to get everything ready, especially with everyone so low with the cough."

Dr. Chapley poured himself more water and took a long drink. "No, you don't understand. I asked them for three days because I thought I could get back here that same day. That was two days ago. They're coming with the babies and we need to be ready—tomorrow! *Morning!*"

10

Around ten a.m., the kit cars pulled up to the infirmary and were met by the entire medical staff. Two women eased out of each car, each holding a crying baby. The sisters gently removed the babies from their arms and carried them to makeshift cribs inside the infirmary. Dr. Chapley looked in the car and found a surprise—there were babies everywhere—neatly packed throughout the cars. Immediately he knew they weren't going to have enough cribs.

"Temidayo, come here please."

The tall muscular construction foreman dropped a saw and came over.

"Wetin Doctor?"

"You built six cribs. I need six more cribs, immediately! No, make that eight, just in case we receive more."

Temidayo nodded and left to find some lumber. Just hours earlier, he and his crew had finished the six cribs that were already set up in the infirmary. Now, he'd have to do it again, yet neither he nor his crew complained. They were paid by the day and felt lucky to have the work.

"Dr. Chapley, I'm deeply concerned about this arrangement." Sister Flores said, her hands on her hips. "We are overwhelmed here in the infirmary. We simply must have more space!"

She was right. The six cribs had taken up the entire staff area. Eight more would definitely not fit.

"I agree, but I hate to split up the babies. We should have everything in the same area. That way we won't have to go back and forth and one nurse can watch all of them. Where do you suggest?"

"The only place that's available right now: the school."

Dr. Chapley rubbed his lips. "Yes, but won't it interrupt the schooling? Father Neel has made education a priority."

"That may be, but it's either take over the school or risk some of the babies dying. After all, each crib needs proper netting over it along with additional protection from the insects. Which do you prefer?" she said sarcastically.

He frowned knowing the consequence. "Well, when you put it like that I suppose you're correct. I guess I should be the one to tell Anna." This was said more as a question than a strong declaration.

"No Dr. Chapley, you stay here and supervise the transfer of the babies. I'll tell her."

"Thanks," he said, relieved.

Anna was in the middle of lessons when Sister Flores entered through the rear. The look on Sister Flores' face made it clear that she needed to talk to Anna right away. Anna noticed this and made an announcement. "Class, give me a moment please."

She walked to the back and approached Sister Flores. Interaction between them was rare. "Do you need me for something?"

"Not exactly," she said grinning. "We need your facility."

"For what?"

"For a nursery. The kit cars arrived with twelve babies and we don't have room in the infirmary for all of them. The men are building more cribs as we speak and they will be in here soon to make additional modifications. I'm afraid you will have to find some other place to hold your school."

Anna stepped back and clasped her cheeks. "Twelve babies?! Oh my. That *is* a shock." She paused as the ramifications of the request became clear. After letting out a deep breath, she said, "Yes, of course.

The babies are more important. Let me dismiss my class and help get the school ready. Once the babies are situated, we'll worry about the school."

She went back to the front of the class. "Children, we've had some new developments. Twelve babies have arrived and we need to convert this school into a nursery. Please come back tomorrow morning and I'll know then if we have another place to go. Any questions?"

Esi raised her hand. "Madame, can we hold the babies?"

Anna let a tiny smile slip out. "No, not right now. The babies need to be fed and put into cribs. If there are no more questions, class dismissed."

She began picking up the chairs. "I'll move these over here and you can decide later if you need them."

"That would be fine," Sister Flores said. "Now, I must get back to the infirmary."

"Do you need my help?"

"No," she said curtly. "I'm sure we can manage. Thank you."

Anna took all the teaching materials to her hut and leaned back on her bed. Since the new building wouldn't be ready for a few more months, she needed to find a temporary place for the school. She also wondered how this sudden development would affect the arrangements in the building. The plan had been for the staff to live on the upper floors while the infirmary occupied the entire ground level. The current infirmary would be converted into living quarters for the lepers as would their living huts. The school would remain until they had funds to build a one-story building and training center. Anna looked out her window and noticed the dusty winds had died down. With plenty of time on her hands, she decided to walk around and look for a new location.

The land they had been given was extensive. They lived and worked on the high ground, which was a large open field with a cluster of trees here and there. Ringing the north end was a forest, behind which the land sloped down to the river. It was through this that they walked to their bathing spots, and it was in this forest and the surrounding bush that the lepers lived, mostly hidden from view in their primitive lean-tos. Anna walked on the bathing path, and turned right (east) when she reached the forest. She traveled several hundred feet before finding two like-sized trees. They were the same distance apart as the width of the school. She studied the ground for a few moments and got an idea.

Father Neel was dozing when she entered his room. He was still staying at the church so she had walked all the way into Ogoja to see him. He heard her as she came near and his eyes snapped open.

"Anna, how are you doing?"

"Fine," she said taking a seat next to him. "There were twelve babies that came in the two cars and we've had to move them into the school. Now, I need to find a new spot to teach."

"Oh dear. Twelve babies? It seems word spreads fast. I suppose the bush is ready to give up its babies to anyone they can find. And with our financial difficulties…" He lowered his voice. "Of course, you know I speak to you in confidence. I still haven't told anyone else."

"Yes, I know. The good news is the men are making more cribs. When they're done, they'll make some adjustments to the school. I did talk to the foreman this morning to relay your concerns about the mud blocks. He said they had already made the blocks, but needed them to dry a few more days before setting them in place. As soon as the zinc arrives, he'll set the roof for the building then replace the roofs on the hut with zinc. He fully understands the white ants."

"That's great! But I need you to keep an eye on him. I'm hoping to be better in a few days, but who knows? This wind comes and goes. How will you teach without a school?"

Anna straightened herself up. "That's what I came here about. I've scouted out the area and found two trees on the edge of the field, just east of the bathing path. I think we could have the men fashion a crude sloping roof tied to the trees and set two posts in the ground. This would give shade all through the day and keep us relatively cool, though we wouldn't have any walls to stop the winds. Perhaps I could get the children to gather up some materials and make our own temporary walls. They don't have to be anything fancy since we only need it to last a few weeks. It might be a good project for them to work together. What do you say?"

"I think that's an excellent idea. If we stop educating the lepers, they lose hope and will never have the opportunity to care for themselves. We must continue the schooling. I'm sorry though, but I'll have to leave the details to you until I'm over this cough. The rainy season is almost here and I'm ashamed to admit it but I keep praying for it night and day. Back home, if I prayed for rain they'd lock me up."

Anna laughed. "Yes, that's true. But out here it's a different world."

Those words echoed off the church walls causing her to reflect more deeply. It *was* a different world, one far away from the one she'd always known. Now that she was a part of it, she couldn't imagine never having known it.

With Father Neel's blessing, Anna made the long walk back to the leprosy settlement. The babies had already been moved out of the infirmary and the morning's patients stood in line waiting to be treated. Only Sister Whelan was there working with them.

"Do you need help?" Anna asked.

"No, but they may at the school—I mean the nursery. The quicker they finish up there the quicker they can come back and work on these patients."

Anna went to the nursery and found the workers adding interior walls to further shield the babies from the wind and dust. Sister Flores had everything under control with six cribs full and temporary beds holding the others. Sister O'Keefe held a shears fashioning small blankets from a large one.

"Can I assist?" Anna said again.

Before Sister Flores could say no, Dr. Chapley spoke up. "Yes, we need more imported milk. The kit cars came with a small supply and we have a few cans, but not enough to last us more than two days. Without the aid of a wet nurse, we may be quite desperate and I hate to see what goat's milk will do to their digestion. Could you walk into town and find Mama Mimi? See if she knows where any imported milk may be. Also, check with the mission. I think they have a few cans. Gather everything you can and bring it back here. I need to plan ahead and know what I'm dealing with before I send Patrick off. Take a girl with you to carry it all in case you find a nice supply."

He put his hand on her back and pushed her to a corner, away from the others. Whispering he said, "Mama Mimi is holding a bottle of wine for me. If you could pick that up, I'd be grateful. I was hoping I could bring it by and play some cards. Are you available tonight?"

Anna blinked. "Uh, yes. That would be fine."

"Great! I'll be by after dinner and tell you what I saw out there."

"And I'll tell you everything you missed." Of course, she didn't mean the part about Grant asking her to marry him.

❧

Their two lanterns burned low as Dr. Chapley removed the cork and poured two glasses of red wine. Holding one up, he said, "Here's to the cans of milk you found today. Cheers!"

Anna touched his glass. "And here's to you, Thomas. You managed to get the babies *and* the patients taken care of today."

"Thank you very much. I have my moments," he said as he winked at his hostess.

"Yes, I suppose you do." Anna said, her dimples making a rare appearance as she sipped her wine. It was warm, yet still tasted better than palm wine. "How much milk do you think we have now?"

"Enough for a week, maybe longer depending on their appetites. This gives me time to talk to the bishop about sending Patrick to Enugu for more, or maybe even Calabar if he wants to fetch the mail. I'm going to need a month's supply, plus paying back the cans we've already borrowed. And that assumes we don't receive more than the twelve apostles, which is what the sisters are calling them now."

"Twelve apostles? Are there any wise men in the picture?"

Thomas laughed. "I guess that would be me or perhaps Father Neel. You choose."

Swirling her wine, Anna pointed to Thomas. "I choose you. Now tell me about your survey. You were gone forever. What all did you see?"

"That's going to call for a bit more wine," he said, refilling his glass.

"Was it that bad?"

"Bad? I'd say 'overwhelming' is a better word. My estimate is that there are more than four thousand lepers in our administrative area."

"Four thousand?!" Anna said, putting her wine glass down. "That's a tremendous burden. How will we ever manage?"

"Good question. If they all showed up here at once it would overwhelm us. As it is, I'm afraid we may be receiving more surprise deliveries of babies. They're hard to care for. But thankfully…" He stopped and looked up to the heavens. "… they're not very common. That gives us a fighting chance."

"A fighting chance to do what?"

"Expansion! I scouted out additional locations for more outposts. If we could set them up with locals running them, I could make the circuit on my bicycle every month. That way, the lepers could head to the nearest infirmary and be treated properly. I'd see only the worst cases. Of course, the key to this entire plan rests with one particular person. Do you know who that is?"

Anna knew. It all came back to money. With more money, new infirmaries could be built and stocked with medical supplies. Yet she didn't dare breathe a word of the current financial crisis, because the one person who the entire mission depended on was the man who'd sworn her to secrecy.

"Father Neel."

Thomas slowly shook his head. "Not quite." He tipped his glass to Anna. "It's the person sitting three feet away from me."

"Me?! Father Neel is the one who collects the money. If it isn't him, it has to be you. You're the only doctor around. I can't heal anyone."

"Believe it or not, this entire mission will be completely wasted if we don't reproduce ourselves in dozens of other locations. To do that we need locals—both lepers and non-lepers—educated and trained. With you, we can attack this problem like no one before us. Without you, we're just a single location helping a few hundred lepers a year, nothing more."

Anna stared at him in disbelief. "I've never thought about it like that."

"Well, you can think about it now. Once we have this settlement up and running, I'd like you to accompany Father Neel and me on a journey. I want to show him the sites I have in mind and the type of people we will need to run them. That way, you can scout out some people from these outlying areas and bring them back to be educated here. Then we can set them loose in their own infirmary, healing and teaching others. Of course, this would have to be after the rainy season when the roads are better. By then we should have this place in tip top shape."

A grin crept across Anna's face. "I'd like to go on a journey with you some day. It would be nice to see the surrounding areas. But at the moment, I'd like to beat you at cards."

He picked up the deck and began shuffling. "Again?!"

The next day, Anna organized the workers to construct a temporary school while she spent her time in the nursery (her old school), holding the babies and gently rocking them to sleep. At Sister Browne's suggestion, they'd each been given a Christian name like Mary, David, Peter and Grace. Not surprisingly, each missionary had their favorite. Dr. Chapley loved feeding John, while Sister O'Keefe fussed over Elizabeth. Anna was attached to two: Jonah and Lily. She even arranged to have their cribs placed next to each other so she could hold one and touch the other at the same time. Every spare moment she had was spent checking in on her 'little ones'.

"You drink all your milk and become strong," she whispered to Jonah. "Then you can help us build more schools and infirmaries one day." She had just finished feeding Lily, who was already asleep, and was working on Jonah when Sister Browne came into the room with a fresh bottle.

"We can't get rid of you, can we?"

Anna looked up from her baby. "I'm afraid I'm hopelessly smitten. You may have to pry these two from my arms to get me back to teaching."

"Or we may not. You're a big help. We're all just trying to keep up with the feeding. With the adult patients increasing every day, we've been overwhelmed."

"I'll do my best. At least we don't have to inject them."

Dr. Chapley said there was little he could do for the babies at this stage of their life. Some of them didn't have any white patches, but instead had the telltale white spots of film on one of their eyes. Others had no signs, but were born to a mother with leprosy who wouldn't feed them because she didn't have enough food to generate breast milk. Being sick with leprosy made it impossible to care for a baby. The village she lived in wouldn't feel safe taking care of a baby from a known leper. As a result, many babies simply died. But not these twelve. They would be loved and cared for.

It took two more days for the workers to complete the temporary roof and get Anna's school back up and running. The class still had only six students, but she was hopeful for more once the huts were ready for the lepers to live in.

After the daily lessons were completed, she spent all her spare time in the nursery holding and caring for Jonah and Lily. One day after school Anna came by the nursery and found Sister Flores pointing her finger at Sister Browne and Sister Whelan, speaking to them in a harsh tone. When she saw Anna, she redirected her wrath.

"There you are! Neither Jonah nor Lily were fed this morning. If they hadn't cried and cried, we might not have discovered it."

"I don't understand," Anna said indigently. "What have I done?"

Sister Browne gave Anna an apologetic look.

"These two said they thought you fed them. As a result, they didn't. Did you feed them?"

"No but..."

"There are no buts. From now on you are not to feed any babies in here. I'm creating cards for each one and we will initial and mark off the time they are fed." Turning back to the Sisters Browne and Whelan. "Is that understood?"

Anna walked up to Sister Flores, her neck and face burning hot. "I'm not going to stand for that! I can feed them when I'm available. Besides, you need the help." She was going to add that Sister Browne had said so, but decided not to.

"You will stand for it because I run the nursery and you don't! Now leave."

Anna stood there in place—frozen—the rage inside her building. She was not going to tolerate this. No one would keep her from her babies. No one!

11

April 4, 1947

Dearest Molly,

I have so much to tell you, but I'm a bit rushed because Father Neel has told me he is sending Patrick, our driver, to Calabar in the morning to collect the mail, so I apologize if you can't read the script. I'll try and write neatly.

First, I'm still having tremendous problems with Sister Flores but those details will have to come in a separate letter. I'm so mad that I'm afraid if I start with her, I won't finish this letter and tell you everything I have on my mind, the most important of which is our financial problems. They have come to a head. Father Neel is praying that additional funds have already arrived in Calabar, and we can keep this mission going. That's why Patrick has to leave in the morning. It's very desperate! I feel the weight too, especially since he has confided only in me. (I know you won't tell anyone!) I can see the stress on his face as he walks around inspecting the nursery and all the lepers we are helping. If we leave, the imported milk goes too and I have no idea how the babies will survive. It sickens me to think about it.

Poor Patrick is upset too. He was looking forward to experiencing our Easter celebration on Sunday. Yet Father Neel can't explain to Patrick why it's so important for him to go the day before Easter. And with the rains, Patrick says the trip will take longer. In the dry season, he would leave early one morning and arrive in Calabar late in the evening. Then he would collect the mail the next morning and come back that evening. Assuming he had no mechanical problems, he'd be back that night and we'd all have mail to read. Now, it could take four days or longer—the rains tend to wash out everything. It wreaks havoc on the kit cars, too, causing them to break down. But enough of my complaining.

In mid-March, we had the first good soaking of the rainy season. Fortunately, our zinc arrived just in time. The men first installed the roof on the new building then replaced all the thatched roofs. It was fascinating to watch them remove an entire thatched roof (a cone) and set it on the ground so it could be used on another hut—one that would soon be built. When the raindrops hit my zinc roof I can't fully describe how loud it is. At first it was hard to get used to, but now I hardly notice it. Unfortunately, the zinc took the last of our funds, so Father Neel told me my salary would be delayed. I told him not to worry since I had everything I needed. I think this relieved him a little, though I don't know what he's going to do with the construction workers and local staff who prepare our food and do our laundry.

When the rains came, the ground turned to mud and funny enough, green grass sprung up out of nowhere. It was like the grass had been hiding and all of sudden it came to life. The only thing that's muddy now are the paths we've beaten down. And then there's another unexpected feature of the rain: it reveals all the visitors we have each day. Let me explain.

The first morning after it rained hard, I got up and stared at the mud outside my hut. There were animal tracks everywhere. The locals trained me to read them. The harmless ones are the shrew, aardvark, hyrax, and mongoose. Then there's the ones I have to keep an eye out for: the leopard (it will attack people although not often—the lepers in the bush are the main victims, though you will recall when I first arrived, one visited me in my hut), the hedgehog (it doesn't kill, but it's needle-like quills will stick in you if you get too close—at least once a month someone stumbles into our infirmary with quills in their leg), and the viper (it's bite is lethal and while I haven't seen anyone die, the locals tell me it's only a matter of time). The viper, like all snakes, makes an endless back and forth line in the mud. They're everywhere. The problem is that there are many good non-poisonous snakes that eat the rats and bugs, but it's very hard to tell the difference so all the snakes that are seen are killed. The lepers value their meat, considering it a delicacy. There are a lot more tracks I can't read so I'm still learning, but at least I haven't seen a hungry lion or an angry elephant. When I have to bathe, the tracks in the mud make my trips down to the river adventurous. Before, I didn't even blink an eye, or for that matter have a dark thought. Now, I'm stopping every thirty seconds and studying the tracks. It makes my journeys somewhat longer and certainly a bit more stimulating.

One good consequence of the rainy season is that Father and the sisters have completely returned to health. I had a few small bouts with illness myself, but now it's like we are all new people. There is no dust floating through the air and the rain smells wonderful. Sometimes it smells like mud and yet we still smile. The locals we've hired spent the first week wiping all the dust off everything—our huts, furniture, and personal belongings. It's like a fresh new house. I breathe in deeply and have nothing but clean air in my lungs. At one point, Father Neel was so happy I thought he was going to do a dance. We don't like tracking mud around, but it's a small trade-off for not having the hot dust everywhere.

Another good feature of the rain is the bugs. Many of the nastier bugs had their habitats washed away. Gone are the scorpions, flies and soldier ants. Instead, we have spiders weaving webs everywhere to catch the new mosquitoes and gnats which have flourished in the rain. And the lizards are snapping up all the bugs the webs don't catch. Since we don't have screens, they like to sit on my window ledge and catch the mosquitoes trying to fly in. I see them as bodyguards—they keep the mosquitoes out and yet are respectful enough never to come into my hut. Sometimes I leave a few crumbs for them on the sill which keeps them coming back.

As you can guess, we are still in our huts. Even though the building has a roof on it, the workers are whitewashing the inside and outside, putting screens on the windows, and other small tasks. Father Neel has told everyone we are moving in after Easter. Of course, he hasn't told them about the financial problems. With the war so recently ended, the extra money people have for charity is small. Everyone is still rebuilding their lives. Helping lepers in a faraway land is a hard idea to grasp. Again, we are hoping for a miracle.

I've become good friends with Sister Browne, whom I described in previous letters. She lets me know about the matters Sister Flores keeps from me. Several *months back I had a nasty confrontation with her (Sister Flores) about feeding the babies and needless to say, I've done nothing about it. I thought about going to Father Neel, but because of his health at the time and financial worries, I didn't. So I'll just have to think of some other way to deal with her. I know there is more trouble brewing with her.*

Dr. Chapley—or Thomas as I call him—has been spending a lot of time with me. We often play cards and now he's invited me to go to the outlying areas with him and Father Neel to see about locations for new infirmaries. He wants me to select some locals and have them come to Ogoja where I can train them. Once they're trained, they can go back and run their own schools. He's very kind and polite and attentive. He even let me borrow some money to buy this beautiful fabric a vendor came across in Ogoja. I had a dress made out of it. Now, it's my special dress and fits in here with the culture perfectly—very African, yet very modern. Lord only knows how the vendor came to have it, since theft around here is like going to the river to draw water: everyone does it. Regarding the trip with Thomas, if Father Neel says yes, and if we get more funds, I think I may go. That's a lot of 'ifs.'

This brings me to another man—Grant. As I told you before, he said he would be back around Easter and it feels like a lifetime since I've seen him. Actually, it's been over three months, yet out here so much happens in that span that he seems like a distant memory. There are days when I hold the babies and hug my students and I can't imagine leaving this place. When Thomas comes to my hut to play cards, I feel that this is now home. Then I have those moments when things aren't going my way or I'm in a foul mood, and I want to run away with Grant. He is my African fantasy and his proposition is all so mysterious and exciting. It's hard not to seriously consider it. I don't know which way I will go when he returns. Matters of the heart are so tricky. I feel it could be at any time, so you will have to keep an eye out for my next letter. (How's that for suspense?)

My teaching is going well. I still have only six students but as soon as we move into the new building, everyone expects the lepers to take over our current huts, build more huts, and begin tilling the fields and planting crops. This Leprosy Settlement in Ogoja (as everyone calls it) must become self-sufficient. If we can get the money and stay another few months, I believe the school can obtain Standard VI status and produce many well-educated students, as well as plenty of Leprosy Control Officers. Apparently, the entire mission here depends on our ability to reproduce more of us. Otherwise we are simply a drop in a very large bucket.

One interesting facet of us being here is the contact we have with the lepers. Leprosy is a most disfiguring disease, yet I have never met a patient with a rebellious spirit. There is an amazing cheerfulness about them and a genuine smile of welcome for any visitor to the village. Their happiness and courage is simply amazing. As for the Nigerians without leprosy, well, they look at us white people differently. They consider us to be more educated and more advanced in many areas (including medicine) and this is challenging their views of leprosy. They see me teach lepers and hug them. We all hold the leper babies. Yet the Nigerians cast out a leper in their midst the minute they believe the poor person has the disease. Seeing us in close proximity to the lepers is causing them to stop and rethink their position. They are still removing all lepers in their midst, but the locals who help us, and at first steered a wide berth of any leper, have become less concerned after seeing our actions. I'm sure the locals go back to their families and villages and tell them what they are seeing. While Dr. Chapley believes we are safe from catching leprosy, he's not completely sure. That's why we take precautions, especially when medically treating the lepers. We constantly sterilize everything. Sterilization begins in the kitchen. The stove and water filter are the instruments of life and death out here. Father Neel and the sisters continually pray that we are safe from the disease, so I know God is watching out for me and that's all that matters.

Last but not least, there has been tremendous planning for the Easter celebration. Mass is supposed to be spectacular and the locals have formed a choir to entertain us. They've been practicing for weeks. I heard them the other day and they were truly wonderful. I can't wait for the show. Father Neel will be conducting mass for the non-lepers at the mission church in Ogoja. He'll then conduct a second mass for the lepers in our settlement. After the second mass, our local chef, Mama Mimi, is working with the cooks to prepare a huge feast. If you hear a loud commotion, just look to the south and know it's us having a grand time.

You should see our leprosy settlement. It's a world of contrasts: the old meets the new; pagans worship next to Christians; the bugs eat us then we eat the bugs. Yet everyone gets along. And why not? We are providing education, medical care and food. Hopefully, we will be providing more shelter soon.

Now I have to carry this letter to Patrick so he can carry it to Calabar to begin its own journey to your kitchen table. I can't wait for more from you.

Still your best friend,
Anna.

The next morning storm clouds parted and the sun shone brightly on the leprosy settlement. It was Saturday. Anna awoke, and instead of going to breakfast, gathered her kit and headed to the river for a bath. She wanted to wash her hair and get clean for the big celebration on Sunday. She knew she'd have very little time later in the day and certainly no time on Sunday. It was now or never.

She had just reached the forest when a noise to her left startled her. After seeing leopard tracks the day before, her senses were on heightened alert. She frantically looked for stick to defend herself with. But found none.

"No wahala Madame, it's me," a low voice said.

Anna whipped around and there was Clarence, partially hidden behind a tree.

"Clarence, what are doing here? You scared me!"

"Come wit me," he said waving her to follow to him. Since he was on the same path she was taking to the river, she followed. When they reached the rushing water, he waded in up to his chest and made it to the other side.

"Come," he said waving her over.

Anna looked around and, seeing no one else at her bathing place, held her kit and towel above her head and waded through the river to the other side. Clarence walked downstream for a short way before turning into the forest on a barely visible path. After making her way through a forest of large trees, she entered a small clearing. Just on the edge of the clearing was an old oak barrel exactly like the one she had back in Maghull. Clarence walked up to it and pointed inside. Leaning in, she saw it was filled with rainwater. Anna was stunned.

"How did you know?"

He shrugged his shoulders.

"You must've seen me when I was using that barrel on the far side of the construction site that one time. I thought no one was watching. Yes, that's it! Or you read my mind. Either way, you're wonderful!" She hugged him and said, "I'm going to use it right now!"

"I go watch for you and make sure dem no bother you. He took up a position just inside the forest, apparently looking for lepers who might disturb her or animals that might eat her.

It didn't take long for Anna to undo the ties in her hair, lean backwards, and let it fall into the cool rainwater. Her thick, luxurious tresses had been seriously damaged from the sandblasting she'd endured. Now that the rainy season was here, she hoped to restore her hair back to its original luster.

As the dark caramel hair sank towards the bottom, the cool water touched her scalp like a long-lost friend. When time was up, she pulled it out and gathered it around her chest to apply some of the special shampoo Grant had given her. It smelled and felt even better than when she had last used it in the river.

After brushing and combing it out forever, she realized she lacked a bucket to rinse out the suds. Her only choice was to dip it back into the rain barrel. With her hands, she squeezed and massaged her hair until the soap was gone. Then she combed it all out. It was a simple yet joyous return to an important part of her past.

When she was done, she gathered up her kit and looked around to tell Clarence how thankful she was, but he had disappeared—again. By now Anna was used to it. Sometimes, he was like a ghost.

With nothing else to do, she made her way back to the bathing spot to complete her bath, a chore made all the more difficult with the swollen river. She made a mental note to return with a bucket next time.

By the time she completed her bath, two full hours were gone. Anna dressed, gathered up her things and began the walk back to the settlement. She had missed breakfast, a fact her rumbling stomach was reminding her of. Since it was closer to lunch, she decided to see if there was something in the kitchen to hold her over. Just as she emerged from the forest, she saw two military vehicles leaving the settlement. One was large, with a contingent of soldiers in the rear. The smaller vehicle had three or four men, obviously the commanders. She went to find Sister Browne.

"Victoria," Anna whispered. "What happened?"

Sister Browne pulled her around the corner of the infirmary. "They're looking for a gentleman from England—a Mr. Gene Eppers. He stole a great deal of money from a war contractor and fled to Nigeria to hide out. London sent two men over here to work with the Nigerian military to find him. They've been hot on his trail."

"Why would they think he's staying at a leper colony?"

"They didn't answer a lot of questions, but I gathered he was seen in Ogoja at some point. By whom, I have no idea."

"What does he look like?"

Sister Browne glanced around to make sure they were still alone. "I don't know, but they showed an old photo of a young bearded gentleman to Father Neel and the other sisters. I was working with the babies, and they left me alone so I didn't see the photo. Before they left they searched the entire grounds."

"Hmm. I guess we'll have to keep an eye out for him. For the life of me, though, I can't imagine someone hiding out here."

"I agree. Of course this *would* be the last place someone would look—among the lepers."

"Yes, that's true," Anna said, growing concerned. "Well, thanks for the news. I need to find Kim and see if I can fill my stomach since I missed breakfast to bathe."

"Oh, I'm going to try and squeeze in a bath later today, though I don't think any amount of bathing will make my hair as beautiful as yours. It looks magnificent!"

"Thank you. Now I must go before I drop from fatigue." She left Sister Browne without saying what was on her mind: could Grant Eaton be Gene Eppers?

The remainder of the day, Anna helped with the Easter preparations. There was always something to do and she did a lot of it. It was way past dark when she trudged her tired body to her hut to prepare for bed. As was usually the case, Kim had been there and lit a lamp, making it easy to find her way home. All she had to do was put away a few things, slip into a nightgown and pass out on the bed. She was so looking forward to that.

She had just put her nightgown on when she heard some rustling outside her hut. Thinking it was Clarence, she continued getting ready for bed knowing he'd come in only when he was ready.

After a muffled knock on her door, she said, "Come in."

The door creaked open revealing a man.

"Grant! You're back!" She went to hug him, but remembered she was in a nightgown, and grabbed a blouse, holding it in front of her.

"Can I speak to you for a moment?" he whispered.

Anna studied him closer and saw a haggard man hunched before her. He hadn't shaved in days, nor likely bathed in a week.

"Where have you been? You look exhausted."

He carried a dark brown satchel and set it on her table. "I need you to hold this for me. I have to visit a man north of here in Gboko and it's not safe for me to be carrying it around in the bush. Can I trust you to keep this safe?"

"Of course, but you don't look well. Should you be traveling like this? Where is your driver?"

The lamp's flame cast eerie shadows on his face. "I'm on a bicycle now. My driver had an accident in Abakaliki and died. The kit car was destroyed too. I was fortunate not to be in it. My luggage was burned and the locals scavenged what wasn't ruined. When I got there, it was all gone. Now I need to meet this man and complete an assignment, or I could get sacked from my job."

Anna stepped back, away from him. "Listen, there were some military men here today looking for a man named Gene Eppers. That's not you, is it?"

Grant shook his head vigorously. "Oh God no! I'm surprised you would even ask that. But I have to admit they would detain me if they spotted me." He nervously licked his dry lips. "Anna, here's the truth. I'm not just here assessing land and updating maps. I'm a British spy who is meeting with groups that oppose the current Nigerian government. They're considering a revolt and Great Britain is examining all the options. That's really all I can say. That's why I need to steer clear of any Nigerian officials. They'd put me in prison and it would be a while before our government could set me free. I certainly hope this Gene Eppers fellow doesn't look like me. They might shoot first and sort it out later. They're not well trained."

"Okay," Anna said, feeling somewhat relieved. "When are you coming back?"

Grant rubbed his grizzled jaw. "A few days. A week. Maybe a bit longer. I don't know for sure. Regardless," he said pushing the satchel towards her, "hold this for me and when I come back we'll have that talk I promise." Focusing his eyes on a small shelf near her bed, he added, "Is that a dinner roll?"

Anna turned around to see what he was referring to. "Yes, would you like it?

"Very much so," he said, his eyes wide open.

"Here are some crackers, too."

She handed him the food and was horrified when he shoved everything into his mouth at once. With a full mouth, he waved goodbye and rode away on his bicycle, the full moon guiding him into the dark forest.

Completely stunned at all this, Anna sat down on the bed staring at the satchel. She pulled it closer and saw the initials G.E.

Grant Eaton or Gene Eppers?

The satchel wasn't locked, only secured by three leather straps buckled tightly. That was the only thing that stood between her curiosity and its contents. She had two options: open it up and see what was inside or shove the entire thing under the bed and go to sleep. Fiddling with one of the straps while she considered everything, she decided to check inside.

One by one the buckles were loosened and the leather straps pulled free. When the large flap was hanging loose, she paused one more time wondering if this was the right thing to do.

Would Father Neel look inside? Would any of the sisters?

She concluded they wouldn't and began lacing it back up when impulsively, she pulled the flap back. Inside were stacks of British pounds. It took her breath away. Doing a quick count, she could see it was a small fortune, certainly enough to live like a king in Nigeria for the rest of one's life. Moving the stacks around, she found nothing else. No papers. No identifying information. Nothing. Grant had left his entire fortune with her. Nobody had ever trusted her like this. Feeling dizzy, she quickly laced it back up, shoved it under her bed and turned off the lamp.

As her head hit the pillow, she thought about the military trucks and their pursuit of a criminal wanted back home, someone who had stolen a lot of money. Were they looking for Grant? How could he have boarded their ship without the proper identification? Certainly the authorities in Madeira wouldn't have let him back onboard. Or would they? Did they suspect Grant Eaton was Gene Eppers, but he convinced them otherwise? Was he telling the truth?

Thoughts collided in her mind as she tried to sort out all of this. Her brain told her this was wrong—*he* was wrong—but then her heart reminded her he may be telling the truth. Eventually—mercifully—she drifted off to an uneasy sleep.

The next morning, Anna sat at the breakfast table sipping her tea and trying to wake up. Several dark dreams had visited her in the night and she was feeling decidedly unrested. Before she could finish her first cup, Sisters Whelan and Browne joined her.

"Are you awake yet?" Sister Browne asked.

"Barely. I didn't sleep well," Anna replied.

"I don't blame you. You worked hard yesterday. But there's still work left to do. Sister Flores is looking over the decorations and Sister O'Keefe is feeding the babies. She'll need our help after breakfast."

"I'll come with you," Anna said pouring more hot water. "Besides, I want to hold my little ones."

She and Sister Flores still had not resolved anything. Anna didn't feed the babies, but held them whenever she wanted. So far, no one had complained.

Breakfast was carried in and they made short work of it. Since Father Neel failed to make an appearance, they left the table soon afterwards and went directly to the nursery.

"There you are," Sister O'Keefe said, removing her apron. "I'm famished! It's your turn now."

"We'll take it from here," Sister Whelan said.

Anna went straight to a crying Lily and picked her up. "Now now. Your bottle is coming."

A few seconds later, Sister Browne came over with the bottle and took the baby, allowing Anna to pick up Jonah, who was sleeping. The moment she brought him to her breast, he woke up, smiled and giggled.

"Who could not love these children?" she remarked.

"They won't be loving us if Patrick doesn't bring back a load of milk with the mail. We're almost out."

Anna froze. "Really? I thought we had enough for several more weeks."

"That was two weeks ago. I'm surprised Father Neel waited so long to send Patrick."

Anna said nothing more. She knew the real situation. Instead, she turned her attention back to little Jonah.

At eleven a.m., it was time for Anna and the sisters to make their way to the church in Ogoja. Locals were streaming in, most of them topless and barefoot, with a few covered in elaborate cloth and wearing sandals.

Anna took her place in the first pew next to the sisters and waited for mass to begin (which was ten minutes late as Father Neel was accounting for Nigerian time). When it did start, the service was elaborate, with palm leaves everywhere. Jesus was prominently displayed on the cross for all to see.

Communion finally came, with Anna and the sisters going first. She could see some of the Nigerians had no idea what they were doing. According to doctrine, they shouldn't be receiving it. Yet it was hard to tell them no when no one knew for sure what they actually believed.

As soon as it was over, Father Neel went to the rear of the church, greeted everyone and then hustled north to the leper settlement with Anna and the sisters in tow.

Surprisingly, it was a nice turnout. Guided by Father Neel and Sister Flores, a beautiful altar had been erected outside of the small church. It was covered with a nice drape and set beneath palm branches. Portable awnings had been erected for the lepers, keeping everyone in the shade.

Anna knew that many of the lepers saw the ornately decorated priest as some sort of god. Their pagan beliefs were very deep and hard to dislodge. They might one day accept Christianity, but they weren't going to give up their other gods. For them, the idea of only one God wasn't easy to fathom.

With the second service over, the settlement quickly turned into a large festival. The lepers retreated to their usual place near the woods, while the locals flooded the fields with running children and loitering adults. There were unsaid rules in the mixing of lepers with non-lepers.

An hour into the festivities, native dancers appeared, dressed in ornate costumes and danced to the rhythmic beating of tom-toms. Their headgear was made of four small mirrors, each in the form of a cube with a small figure sitting on top. At each corner of the cube was a different figure. Anna assumed they were saints, but she was too far away to make sure. Whatever it was, the dance excited the Nigerians since the display was apparently rare.

At first, the dancers formed a large circle. Then, one of the dancers began running through it at random angles. The male was the focal point of the entire ceremony and everyone clapped urging him on. For Anna and the other white people, they had no idea what was happening. Clearly, though, it was important to the Nigerians.

An hour later, the dancers finally stopped, allowing a loud applause to go on. The sweat glistening from their bodies told the audience how much they had exerted themselves.

"It was a very good show!" Sister Browne remarked.

Afterwards, while everyone milled around waiting for the food to be served, the missionaries and a few select locals sat down first, as custom dictated.

The feast was a large, extravagant event, with each course carefully planned. Father Neel was served first. Once his table started eating, the locals were served under a tent, followed by the lepers under another. Soon, everyone was stuffing themselves with Mama Mimi's excellent cooking.

One custom that amazed Anna was watching a particular Nigerian wash his hands in preparation for the meal. He put some water in his mouth, swished it around, and spit it slowly onto his hands. Soon after, several men did this causing her to wonder if it was some sort of ritual or if it was just their way of washing hands—by warming up the water first. She never did find out.

Midway through the meal, to everyone's surprise, Patrick arrived in his kit car back from Calabar. He had made the journey in two days, just like during the dry season. Sister Browne nudged Anna.

"I'll bet if we had a feast every time he had to go to Calabar, we might find he could make the journey faster."

"That's what I was thinking," Anna said. "He just tossed the mail bag to Father Neel and ran for the leftovers like a man possessed. But I am glad that he got back in time to enjoy this."

Sister Browne lifted her glass. "It looks like his arrival has also coincided with the wine, porter and whiskey."

Anna pushed hers away. "I noticed. I'm going to have to go slowly on all this. I don't want to begin acting silly."

The alcohol was indeed flowing. The wine being served was a cheap red from Spain, although most of its drinkers wouldn't have known otherwise. The beer, unfortunately, was not a stout Irish porter, but a weak local brew that passed as beer. And there was no Jameson Irish whiskey. Instead, a variety of both Nigerian and cheap imported spirits with a high alcohol content quickly made the rounds to most everyone's delight.

It was after seven when the coffee was served, black and steaming. By now the celebrants were somewhat giddy and the coffee was intended to bring them back down. Water and juice were also served, which Anna consumed in large quantities.

Several of the dancers, however, missed out on these beverages and were found passed out under one of the awnings. More than one local had joined them.

Anna was just pouring herself another glass of water when the heavens opened. Immediately, the sober and not-so-sober attendees made a dash to the awnings or any available hut. This forced a large volume of people into a small area.

The main awning where the sisters and Father Neel took cover, withstood the downpour with no problem. Everyone sat around a large table as the rain came down.

A giggling Sister O'Keefe set her glass of wine down and stammered loudly, "What a hooley we just had! Just like the charlady's ball. There was one step and two step and the devil knows what new step."

Not realizing Sister O'Keefe had overdone it, one of the locals said to Anna, "I no sabi."

Laughing, Anna explained. "A 'hooley' is an Irish party, something like what we had today. A 'charlady' is a British cleaning woman, and the last part is a line from an Irish song called the Charladies' Ball. Actually, what we had here resembles a charladies' ball."

The local shook his head still not understanding while Sister O'Keefe giggled louder. There would be more than one headache in the morning.

Anna was about to get up from the table when Kim appeared and whispered in her ear. "Father Neel would like to see you. He's in the infirmary."

Anna jumped up, carefully picking her way through the slippery mud and falling rain while trying to avoid a nasty spill. Making it safely to the infirmary, she pushed open the door and saw they were alone.

"Kim said you needed to speak to with me."

"Yes. Please have a seat." His face wore a pale shade of misery.

Knowing the answer, Anna asked anyway. "Did we get the money?"

"I'm afraid not. There was a letter from Mother Mary Martin saying they are working on getting it together, but I'm afraid it will be too late. We are unable to pay you or provide the sisters their stipend. I am also unable to pay the staff. It's them and the construction workers I worry about the most."

"What about the babies?"

"Oh my," he said slapping his cheeks, "I was so consumed in my own world that I completely forgot about them. I suppose I could have Patrick drive the babies to the Scottish mission and tell them our dilemma. Perhaps they could take them. Of course, while he's doing that we'll have to head towards Lagos to catch a steamer for home."

Anna felt her eyes sting with tears. "The thought of losing them hurts me deeply. Maybe one of the sisters and I could stay behind and care for them."

Father Neal shook his head. "I couldn't allow it. I'm responsible for everyone's safety. You must come with me when this settlement is closed down. It would be too difficult for you, especially with no paid staff around. You would starve, not to mention the babies. No, I'll tell everyone tomorrow before we dedicate the new building. No sense in moving in when we are moving out."

Suddenly large headlights flashed through the fields scattering the partygoers.

"What is all this?!" Father Neel said. "Those don't look like kit cars."

The two moved closer to a window and peered at the headlights coming towards them. When one vehicle illuminated the other, they could see they were the same military vehicles that had been there before. They both stood transfixed as a soldier came running towards the infirmary.

"Man injured! Need doctor!" he shouted.

Father Neal turned to Anna. "Go and find Dr. Chapley. I'll see what this is all about."

Anna ran to the main tent, which was the last place she'd seen him. Finding only Sister Browne, she yelled out, "Have you seen Dr. Chapley?"

"I believe he was going to the latrine or his hut. Try those."

She found the doctor coming out of the latrine. "Thomas, come quick. A man is injured and needs assistance."

He said nothing as he fell in behind and jogged to the vehicles. Father Neel was there talking to the military commander.

"Doctor, I had him taken inside. See what you can do for him."

"Will do!" he said, hurrying through the door.

Father Neel pulled Anna aside. "I'm afraid they caught up with that fellow they were looking for. He's been shot several times."

Anna registered shock. "Did you see his face?"

"No, I didn't. Why?"

"I'm worried he could be Grant Eaton," she whispered.

"The fellow that came over on the ship with us?"

"Yes, he visited in January and asked me to marry him."

Father Neel blinked several times. "I've had some whiskey, but did I hear you correctly?"

"Yes, and he was here at my hut last night."

Father Neel grabbed her arm and led her away from the scene. "I suppose it's none of my business who you see, but let's not mention any of this right now. These military men are aggressive and I don't know what they might do. The two English chaps that were with them Saturday morning are in another vehicle and not here yet. No telling what these men might do. In the meantime, I think I'll go to the infirmary and inspect the man myself, see if I recognize him."

A few minutes later, he returned with a long face. "My dear, I'm afraid I have bad news. It's Grant, and he's dead. The doctor couldn't save him."

Anna stepped away and lowered her face into her hands, sobbing. Father Neel hugged her.

"I'm so sorry dear. All I can think about were his last words to me on the ship, 'Beware the Bight of Benin, for few come out though many go in!' For him, it has come true."

He continued holding her. "I suppose we can take his body back with us if we can preserve it properly. That's the least we can do. Perhaps you can see to it that he's properly buried."

Anna jerked her head up. "Oh my gosh, I have to go to my hut right now!"

She left a bewildered Father Neel standing there with empty arms.

Night had fallen and it was dark. Anna lit her lamp before looking under the bed. Sure enough, the satchel was still there, the same satchel with more than enough money to keep the leprosy settlement up and running for decades to come *and* her precious little ones alive. Thinking of them, she sat there in her hut, fingering the money and wondering what she should do. Finally, she strapped it up and left her hut.

Father Neel was talking to two English officers when she walked up to them. Through watery eyes, she handed them the satchel. "Here is the money he stole, or at least some of it."

The closest man took it and undid the straps. Seeing the contents, he glared at her. "How did you come into this?"

"He was our shipmate coming over and he visited me Saturday night. He gave me this for safekeeping. Now I realize he wasn't who I thought he was."

The second officer spoke up. "Ma'am, I think we need to speak to you. Is there some place we can go?"

"Yes, please come to my hut. That will be private enough." To Father Neel she said, "Could you please send Kim with some hot water, coffee and refreshments?"

"Certainly. I'll take care of it right now."

"Thank you. Now gentleman, please follow me. I have a lot to tell you."

It was early the next morning when Father Neel, head down, trudged along the dirt path. He had just performed a mass in the Ogojan mission church—his last one—and was headed back to tell everyone to start packing. Someone was waiting for him halfway.

"Anna, what brings you here this early? I hope you got a little sleep."

"Before you tell the others we're leaving, I have something for you." She held out a small box.

"What's this?" he said, squinting his eyes and studying it closely.

"It's what Grant—or Gene—gave me in January. He told me to keep it and open it when he came back, but I never got a chance. I showed it to the officers last night and they said with the money they recovered, they didn't want to look at what was inside. They said they were going to assume it was nothing more than a cheap carving. Since there was a reward for his capture and no one was going to collect it, they thought I should just keep the box and whatever is in it, especially since I could've kept the money and no one would've known. Of course, I couldn't keep this, so I'm giving it to you. Whatever's inside, I don't want to know. Maybe you can sell it and use the money to pay everyone, at least until the money comes from home."

"Are you sure you want to do this?"

Anna nodded. "Yes, I'm sure. My little ones are all I can think of."

He tore away the paper and string as Anna turned her back, refusing to watch. Briefly looking inside, he closed the box and shoved it in his pocket.

"It's a miracle, just what I asked God for. I'll have Patrick take me into Enugu today and load up on imported milk. I think we will be staying a while."

"Then I guess I'd better get back to my babies and teaching."

Father Neel's face was aglow. "I suppose you should. And don't be surprised if at breakfast you hear me say a prayer thanking God for some unnamed miracle! It's the least I can do!"

12

June 1, 1947

Dearest Molly,

It's amazing what a new building can do for the bush. Do you remember when I wrote about the first rains bringing the grass up from nothing? Well, the lepers have immediately come out of the bush to help make this small camp a thriving village. It's truly amazing!

We dedicated the building on May 1st when Father Neel presided over the high mass. The leper children's choir sang Full in the Panting Heart of Rome. It was a beautiful rendition. After mass Father Neel blessed the building and then said it was the happiest day of his life. He was so humbled to be able to bring the lepers closer to help and community. Then there was a second blessing, followed by a benediction and another big feast. I'm sure I've gained a pound or two!

We moved into our new quarters the next day even though it was not by any means completed. In fact, we had to become virtual trapeze artists, ducking and dodging around all the scaffolding. By May 5, there remained only the interior decoration of the oratory, office and chop room on the ground floor. (Chop room is our dining room). The workers were still painting and putting on the final touches. To call it hectic would be an understatement!

I must say though, this sort of life isn't for the inflexible. I've come to the conclusion that to be a Medical Missionary of Mary, one must be versatile and full of many different skills. We've had to direct the builders, teach the art of brick making (as Sister Flores has done in the village), lay out gardens, carry out repairs on a disabled car, and so many other tasks far outside what one would expect that it's too long to list. If you are a person who likes the easy life, this is the wrong place!

By now, everyone has moved into the new quarters except me. A nurse from the Scottish Church Leprosy Hospital in Uburu (about 120 miles southwest of us) has taken my room in the new building for the moment. She arrived for the dedication and will be staying for several months in order to pass on the medical techniques they've learned treating lepers in their area. She also hopes to learn something from us as well, although Thomas told me she seems to know more than he does, which is saying a lot. He feels more like a pupil when he's around her. Her name is Isla McGinty. She's about fifty years old and very rigid like Sister Flores. As such, they get along famously. If everything is not shipshape and in its place, you can hear their voices in unison setting it right. I stay clear of them, if I can.

I could've stayed in the new house if I wanted to. Father Neel left me that option. There are four rooms for each of the sisters and Thomas and Father Neel each have their own room. That left my room or a meeting room for Sister McGinty. He was prepared to convert the meeting room to a bedroom for me or even ask the sisters to double up, but I begged him off. The truth is, I'm quite used to my tropical hut by now and it provides far more privacy than the upper floor of the new building (we call it the house), especially since my room would've been next to Sister Flores. With my current arrangement, I can still have visits from Clarence and play cards with Thomas and no one is the wiser (or listening in). The only negative to all of this are the animals. More days than not I see long lines in the mud telling me a large snake has been by my hut looking for a rodent or something more. The other day several lepers were causing a commotion. I went to investigate and discovered that they were examining leopard tracks. Because we have so many villagers now, they were very surprised to find it wandering through our camp. They couldn't believe it had visited me in my hut all those months ago. To be honest, neither can I.

Once the house was fully occupied, the babies were moved from my school to the old infirmary (now the nursery) and are now very happy. Even though our imported milk shortage was solved by the new funds, we can't be sure milk will always be available. To make it last longer, we're giving the babies and young children palm oil soup, yam fou fou, and orange juice. Some take it better than others. My two babies—Jonah and Lily—will take just about anything put in front of them. Of course, they're still the objects of my affection several times a day. I love watching them get bigger and bigger. Sometimes I even feel like they are my own children. (No surprise, right?) I guess they are mine since their mother and father have abandoned them. We'll discuss that later.

With the house built and the babies in the nursery, we can now see all the patients in the hospital—the ground floor of the house. It's very organized. All the records are there and they patiently stand in the shade while waiting their turn for examination and injections.

On a new subject, things did not work out between me and Grant. I decided not to accept his proposal and gave up the box he had given to me. Apparently, he is headed back to England, where the government has great interest in him.

As for money, Father Neel says we have enough to last through to the fall. Medical Missionaries of Mary is holding a raffle in Ireland and publicizing it, hoping to bring more funds in. I helped Father Neel write a long letter describing our work here and God willing, it will bring us everything we need to stay past the fall.

When everyone vacated the huts for the house, the lepers moved in. Father Neel and Sister Flores had everything set up with a proper list as to who would receive which hut. There were six huts available so two lepers were assigned to each one—three huts with males and three with females. That singular event seemed to be the push the lepers needed to come in from the bush and help us make the field a real village. In no time, and with a little money from our purse, the lepers began building more huts everywhere. Now they are tilling the earth and planting the seed we purchased for them. One man—a burned out case—is responsible for laying out the paths and roads and does a creditable job. He is very happy to have that responsibility. All this activity and commotion makes it a living, breathing community, one the lepers can finally call their own. They are so happy that whenever I pass one, he or she always smiles and says "Morny O." Hope is an amazing remedy for the hopeless.

We also employ many workers—all of whom are lepers. They spend their days felling trees, weeding, planting, and caring for our crops. Four sawyers are engaged in cutting up felled trees for timber suitable for building material. They take the wood to a small carpenter's shop, which was erected in just a matter of days. It keeps two men fully employed constructing things and making house repairs—a continual task. On general workdays, the lawns are cut, not by a mower but with the all-purpose machete, without which no Nigerian is complete. The burned-out cases (those lepers missing toes, feet and/or hands) are given tasks too, which they seem to greatly appreciate. Some of them clean the grass for the thatch (this is also permanent work, for each new hut requires roofing). One woman with missing hands pounds fou fou all day, which is a big help to the cooks. Watching her wrap the stumps of her arms around the tall staff, then raise and lower it directly onto the fou fou is a true testament to her determination. We would have all the money we needed if a film was made showing her at work. It's quite heartwarming.

With the village now organized, there is work and pay for everyone except the hospital patients. Even the children may earn money by gathering grass in the bush. A small plot of land is given to those who can hold a hoe. One boy, Thames, is too small to hold a hoe. He's so small he cannot even be seen as he walks through the eight-feet high elephant grass and frightens the other lepers when he suddenly pops out. (Most of us can be seen coming through the tall grass because we are pushing a lot of it to the sides and that gives us away.) Once, he even scared me. It was just after I had seen the leopard tracks. I was sure I was done for!

Thames (a name he chose after hearing Father Neel talking about our great English river) wanted his own plot, but was denied by the village chief. (Yes, the lepers have a village chief and sub-chiefs). The next day he found a broken hoe and was seen crouching over a small patch of dirt. Father Neel went to investigate and after hearing his pleas, felt his heart touched so much that he bent over and began helping the boy hoe. Then he gave him a small piece of land to work (much to the dismay of the chief) and Thames hasn't stopped smiling since. I noticed Father Neel finding various reasons to check on Thames throughout the day. Perhaps he has found his own Clarence.

Recently, we tried dipping our toes in to the chaulmoogra oil business. This is the oil we use to treat the lepers. It comes from the hydnocarpus tree, which is grown in South America. The Nigerian government provides the oil for free, however we worry about the supply lines, much like with the imported milk. To deal with this, Father Neel sent off for seeds to grow our own hydnocarpus trees. Fifty seeds arrived in early May and the lepers planted them straight away. They tend to them like they are gold, or perhaps holy ground. It will be some time before we see if they produce oil.

Leprosy, as I have written before, is a slow, deforming, wasting disease. What I haven't told you is something I recently learned. The natives have a term for leprosy. It's called 'Opo'. The term originated in southern Nigeria and is rarely used for fear that repetition could cause the speaker to contract this disease. They wholeheartedly believe this superstition. It's that important to them. That's why none of us had heard the term until Isla came over from the Scottish mission.

Another thing that's very important to each leper is their mat. Everyone uses a mat for his bed to keep the ground from "getting inside them." The mats are the same kind of bed to which our Lord referred when he said to the man sick with the palsy, "Take up thy bed and walk." The first use of the mat is to give the person a resting place at night and the last use is to enclose his worn-out body when it's lowered to its final resting place. This is done while the soul sings out its glory to God, begging Him once more "to reward with eternal life all those who did it good for His name's sake."

With the wet season came a large swarm of white ants. They have been climbing up the bamboo of our mud huts and other structures and eating everything in sight. Several of the lepers are assigned the task of locating any white ants and killing them. Believe it or not, it's a full-time job. I'm constantly on the lookout in my little hut. The rest of the staff are in the new house and well protected from the white ants since they can't eat through metal and concrete. Yet!

*As for me, my six little ants have grown into a full colony. I now have twenty-four ants—or stud-**ants** in my school. I even have a gong with which to call them. Last week an old car wheel appeared out of nowhere and a sub-chief suspended it from two posts and a horizontal branch. I select the students* with the best behavior to ring the gong each morning. It's proved itself very effective at controlling them during class since they fully behave now, hoping they might be the chosen one to ring the mighty gong. With so many students, I've had to divide class into three sections: senior boys, junior boys, and girls. Hopefully, it won't take long to bring up the oldest to earn their Primary Certificate Standard Six.

Each morning, my school begins with assembly and prayers. We follow the usual curriculum of English, history, geography, hygiene, handwork, and religion. Then we go to our various classes for physical training. We all love this part of school and there is sometimes an audience of adults wishing (I'm sure), that they could join us. Then comes rural science, which is usually taught outside where each section of students have their own farm and are growing yam, cassava, ochre, red pepper and so forth. We have one rice field, the crop from which we use for a school feast. Anything left over is distributed among the children. Perhaps you won't believe me, but it truly tastes better than any rice bought in a market—even a market like Clarence G. Pyle and Son Grocers.

We have recess from 11-11:30 a.m. during which time we prepare our chop. I have a cook who prepares mine. Afterwards school continues until 1:30 p.m. By this time, we're usually glad to get to the cool shelter of our mud block huts. Before long its chop time again and then time to relax.

It's a nice little life I have. To fully illustrate it I'll leave you with this story, which pretty much sums up everything. As a preamble, you should know that a patient is supposed to pay a small fee to be in our settlement, but many have nothing beyond the smile and loincloth they come in with. If they aren't really poor and have some means, someone will inform on them. I had one boy tug on my sleeve and this is the gist of our conversation:

Boy: "Sista, that man give charity-money dere plenty, him brudder get big farm." (We are giving money to someone who has a rich brother.)

Me: "So what do you want me to do about it?"

Boy: "That man he fool sista. Make sista no agree for house until he agree for money." (Don't give him a hut until he pays for it.)

So I went to the accused, whose name is Oluwa, and asked, "Which man bring you?"

"No man, Oluwa come me one." (I am alone.)

"You get father?"

"No father." Shaking his head.

"You get mother?"

Still shaking his head. "No mudder. Father and mudder done die long since."

"Which man look you for your place?"

"Brudder he dere. Brudder take other wife, wife no agree for Oluwa to stay. She say, 'You be leper-man, make Oluwa go.' She done drive Oluwa out!"

I did a little more investigation. Sure enough, the village chief said Oluwa had been cast out from his family when a new wife came. They sent him away with no food, not even a yam! So I started talking to him and saw that Oluwa had a weakness for tobacco. When I gave him a pipeful, he sat on one of the walls and entertained the crowd with a song and a dance, occasionally adding a loud cry of "Bip!" and "God He dere. God savvyies prayers small."

Now, whenever we need entertainment, I try to find a little tobacco for him. One time he started singing, "Oluwa get no father, no mudder. Sista be father and mudder now. Oluwa get no tobacco, sista bring tobacco now." He's very funny and the fact that he amuses me so much tells you how integrated I am with the bush. When I come home one day, you may not recognize me.

That's it from Ogoja. Please write and let me know the latest Maghull activities.

Still your best friend,
Anna.

A brief rain passed through the settlement. It was a hot June day, the rain adding more humidity to the already thick air. Anna had finished school and was back in her hut where she cast off her shoes and stretched out on her bed for a much-anticipated nap. She was ten minutes into a nice dream when a loud rap on the door caused her to bolt upright.

"What is it?" she said, somewhat shaken.

Clarence flung open the door. "Sista! People plenty for road. Some don die."

Anna tried to clear her head. "What are you saying? Slow down."

He came inside and grabbed her arm, pulling her towards the door. "No be small wahala o. This one crazy o. Make we comot o! (*There is a big problem. Please come with me.*)"

Anna put her shoes back on and stepped outside. By this time, Clarence was running to find Patrick so he could explain to him what was happening. When Anna finally caught up to both of them, Patrick was able to tell her the problem.

"Many don hurt o. We need a doctor wey go help dem shap shap. (*Many people are hurt on the road. We need to take a doctor and go help them.*)"

"Okay," Anna said. "Let me get Thomas—I mean Dr. Chapley. You get the kit car ready!"

Anna hurried to the new hospital and found him sitting at a desk, filling out some records.

"Thomas, Clarence just told me some men are injured somewhere on the road. He will take us there. Can you come to the kit car?"

Thomas jumped up immediately. "Yes! Let me find my bag and get some things. It will only take a moment." He stuffed his medical bag with various supplies and said, "Lead the way!"

The ride to the site was ten hard miles through twisting roads, two steep gullies and one rickety bridge. Anna couldn't understand how Clarence had found them, much less traveled back to the village for help. This boy continued to amaze her.

They arrived to find fourteen lepers—ten men and four women— scattered on the side of the road, all in terrible shape. After a few minutes of hurried examination, Dr. Chapley pulled Anna aside.

"Six of them are gone. The other eight are in bad shape. They haven't had food or water in days. We don't have room for all of them in the kit car, so we need to make some quick decisions. Patrick is the driver so he has to go back. Clarence can stay behind since he knows his way around. That leaves you and me."

Anna touched his arm. "Stop. You have to go back so you can treat them. I'll stay behind with Clarence and tend to the sick."

Thomas sighed. "Fine. That's what I was hoping for. As soon as we unload them, I'll send Patrick right back. It took us forty minutes to get here so we won't be back for at least an hour and a half. Is that all right?"

"Enough! Stop worrying and tell me which ones we need to load."

Dr. Chapley pointed out the six worst. They were helped into the kit car and secured with rope to keep them from falling out. Meanwhile, Patrick worked with Clarence to tie three dead bodies to the top. As soon as Dr. Chapley gave the word, they were off.

Anna pulled the two still alive closer together and gave them some of the water Dr. Chapley left behind. After several sips, one of them began to revive. He was an older man with a small, firm mouth and dull red lips. Anna studied his long, thin nose and hazel eyes, and guessed he was from the Fulani tribe. His white head sprouted tight little curls, which further distinguished him from all the other dark faces and black, kinky hair. Anna gave him the last of the water causing him to sit up and begin talking to Clarence in a tribal dialect. This went on for twenty minutes as the man had to take breaks and gather his breath along with his thoughts. When he was done, Clarence explained in pidgin what happened.

In the large town of Onitsha, over 150 miles away, a rumor of a wonderful cure for any person who was sick with leprosy had spread from town to town, village to village, and compound to compound. All one had to do was to bathe in and drink the waters where the white men were treating the sick. It was said that on certain nights the waters moved and a white man would rise from them. At this place the sick men would become healthy and the weak men, strong. It was a powerful story, one easily believed by desperate people. But there were many such stories floating around. The difference with this one was the fact that several witnesses were present, two of which were lorry drivers. For a fee, they could drive the afflicted person all the way there.

These fourteen had heard the story and saved their money—most of it either begged or given to them from desperate family members who wanted them back home in their villages. They hired one of the eyewitness lorry drivers to take them there, wait for them to become healed, and return to Onitsha.

On the appointed day, with no belongings other than the clothes they had on their backs or wrapped around their loins, this little company piled into the large lorry and set off for their miracle healing. It was a joyous event. As they travelled the winding and sometimes washed-out roads, they dreamed of the moment when they would drink the magical water, bathe in it and do everything the rumor required. It couldn't be long before this ju-ju started working. What happiness! What joy they would feel to be free of the opo and be readmitted to the loving embrace of their spouses and families. To be able to shout to all the world: "We're clean! We're clean!" These thoughts made the miles of rough, pot-holed road easy to take.

This man, who was seated in the front, began to see worry in the driver's face. The driver continued looking around and asking if anyone had died. He was worried that they would give him the opo.

At some point, the driver stopped the lorry and said he had mechanical problems. He needed everyone to get on the side of the road while he made repairs. While they were waiting together, they watched him start up the lorry, and to their horror, turn around and head away from them. It was terrifying.

After waiting for a while to see if he was coming back, they realized they'd been cheated. Still, the little company decided to press ahead. They knew the place was east, so they gathered whatever information they could along the way and kept walking. Unfortunately, two of the lepers were burned-out cases. They had trouble keeping up. It was either leave them behind or slow down. They decided to slow down.

When they reached the point where lack of food and water dropped the two sickest, they carried them. Many nights passed before they reached a small stagnant creek and drank their fill. Directly afterwards, a young girl came by and pointed out the direction to the white man's village. They were almost there. If they could just keep going they would all be healed.

That night they found a nice, cool spot on the side of the road and settled in for a good rest, feeling confident that tomorrow could be the end of their journey. Unfortunately, during the night they all got sick, a likely result of contaminated water. The two weakest ones never woke up. When no one could get up and move, they simply stayed where they were and hoped for the best. Several more days passed before a young boy spotted them. It was Clarence.

After hearing this story, Anna shook her head in disgust. A dishonest lorry driver was a well-known danger. So were the ridiculous rumors of magical water. Yet Anna didn't have the heart to tell him that there was no magical healing awaiting him at the end of his journey. Instead, she tended to both him and the young woman and waited for Patrick to return, hopefully before it got too dark and the beasts of the bush appeared, looking for their next meal.

13

T he small group looked at the trees and found the shadows beginning to stretch across the road, creeping their way towards them. Anna glanced at her watch. Patrick had left a full two hours before, and there was no telling when he would be able to make it back. After four months of rainy weather—the kit car could rarely reach twenty miles per hour as it picked its way among the large ruts, slippery mud, and damaging potholes. And that didn't cover the hard part: getting across the rickety bridge. To accomplish that feat they had had to line up the wheels perfectly with the rail boards. It had taken Dr. Chapley standing on the other side waving hand signals to Patrick to make sure a tire didn't go off the bridge. Coming back a second time, Patrick would be by himself, navigating that same bridge in the fading light. If something tragic happened to him—such as driving off the bridge—no one would know for a long time. They would be stuck all night without food or water and at the mercy of any wild animals. With three dead bodies next to them, that was like ringing the dinner bell.

Anna considered her options. If Patrick didn't arrive soon, she could send Clarence back to the settlement on foot. He not only knew where it was and how to get there, he also had excellent night vision. But that would leave her alone with two sick people. She would be the only one available to fight off predators.

The other option was to stay together and wait for help, however long it took. Surely, Father Neel would launch another party at sunrise, and they would be picked up by noon. Neither option was particularly appealing, especially for the two sick people next to her. She was about to ask Clarence a question when he jumped up and pointed down the road.

"Dem dey come! Dem dey come!"

Anna tilted her head, but heard nothing. "Are you sure?"

"Yes!" he said, continuing to point.

It was a minute more before Anna heard the grinding of gears and squeaky axles. She didn't dare let a smile appear on her face until she saw Patrick waving through the windshield. It was a huge relief.

Patrick pulled up and jumped out. He had food and water with him, along with several lanterns. They had to hurry to get everyone loaded in the fading light. The three dead bodies were tied onto the back, leaving plenty of room for Clarence, Anna and the two survivors inside the kit car. It was only after Patrick said his prayer, crossed himself, and started up the kit car that Anna felt free enough to let out a deep sigh.

Back at the village, everyone was stirred up with their arrival. The two survivors were unloaded and the sisters worked quickly to bathe, dress and bandage them. Afterwards they were soothed with cool drinks, while soup and yam simmered nearby. After seeing that there was nothing more she could do, Anna pulled Father Neel aside and asked for an update.

He turned his back to everything and whispered, "Two more from the first group died. With your two survivors, that leaves six alive and eight dead. I've arranged for graves to be dug at first light and we'll have a burial service for them. Do you know where they come from and how they came to be there?"

"I do and it's not a pleasant story. Let's go to the kitchen so I can have some tea. I gave all the water to the victims and I'm very thirsty."

"Of course. I had Kim hold the dinner until you were back. The others will join us shortly."

Once Anna had a steaming cup of tea sitting in front of her, she told him everything she'd heard from the old man. When she was done, Father Neel leaned back in his chair and shook his head.

"What a dastardly deed for someone to commit, especially on people as sick as these. It challenges one's soul to pray for criminals like that!"

"It sure does. Seeing all the dead bodies at once is hard to digest. It's like a tornado came through and killed them all."

"An evil tornado. An evil, *human* tornado."

Anna held the cup in front of her lips and paused. "But is it any worse than taking a three-year-old child and casting her into the bush?"

Father Neel frowned. "I suppose not. But still…"

He didn't have a chance to finish his thought. Instead, the sisters arrived for a delayed dinner, along with Dr. Chapley. Everyone was starved.

"Where's Sister Flores?" Father Neel asked.

"She's staying behind to feed two of the survivors," Sister Browne said. "She'll come in later."

They said a prayer and Father Neel asked Anna to repeat the victims' story while they ate. It didn't get better with a second telling and the reactions were the same. They were still discussing the situation in detail when Anna excused herself and went off to the hospital to check on the old man.

The village chief was there and had already selected a name for him: Gran'pa. From what she could make out, Gran'pa wanted to stay in the settlement and was asking the chief to find a hut for him. Gran'pa thanked her several times for her kindness, before Anna took her leave to check on the other five survivors. They appeared to be doing better. She stayed a bit longer before heading to her hut and collapsing in her bed. It wasn't that she had physically worked so hard; it was just the break from her routine and the uncertainty of being away from the settlement. Within seconds of her head hitting the pillow, she was out.

The next day, Anna discovered that Gran'pa was feeling much better and even walking around. He told the fellow lepers his story, which angered them. They, too, were sorry for their brother's trouble.

Dr. Chapley gave the surviving victims various pills and powders and added them to his already full quota of regular patients. A week later, with his hard work and the sisters' good care, all the survivors had fully recovered and were undergoing leprosy injections.

Surprisingly enough, everyone but Gran'pa wanted to return from where they came. Anna wondered why, especially since they would be outcast to the city's fringes where the other lepers lived. Perhaps they wanted to point out the lorry driver to their fellow lepers. Either way, it was only Gran'pa who made it clear he wanted to stay. He said there was nothing for him to go back to. This place was probably the best he'd be able to find, especially with free leprosy treatment.

Their departure was arranged and a small party planned. Gifts were handed to the survivors and good wishes imparted. Once the party was over, Patrick loaded everyone into the kit car and left on the long drive to Onitsha.

❧

It was a Sunday in late June when Dr. Chapley began making preparations for a trip to Otukpo, eighty miles to the northwest. With the Leprosy Settlement in Ogoja on solid footing, it was time to start expanding their leprosy treatments. Father Neel had been overseeing all the preparations, including the packing of home cooked food from Mama Mimi. He'd been on these journeys before and knew that the quality of the food was a hit or miss proposition. A little whiskey wouldn't hurt either.

Anna picked out her clothes from a sparse selection and packed them, along with a week's worth of tea. She also tucked some money in a small luggage compartment, but knew the chances of buying anything worthwhile were very slim.

Dr. Chapley spent his last day organizing the medical supplies, since invariably a patient or two would need to be treated for some ailment or injury. He needed to be prepared for anything.

That afternoon, Sister Browne suggested to Anna that they take one last bath in the river so they could catch up on things before she left. Anna agreed. She went to her hut, grabbed a towel along with her kit and headed to the river.

When she saw Sister Browne already in the water, she said, "I thought I'd beat you here, but the muddy tracks gave you away."

"I was going to surprise you by walking in the grass, but then I thought of all those snakes and didn't feel like stepping on one."

Anna giggled. "That was wise, especially with the only doctor around these parts leaving tomorrow morning."

Anna disrobed and slid into the swollen river. "Any news for me?" she asked.

Sister Browne raised her hands out of the water and rubbed them together in excitement. "Yes, several scraps. I overheard Sister McGinty talking to Sister Flores. She was saying that when you three return, she was going to have Patrick drive her back to the Scottish mission."

"That's rather sudden," Anna said. "I thought she was staying two full months?"

"Well, by the time you return, it will be close to two months since she's been here. Maybe a few days short."

Anna thought for a moment. "I suppose that's right. I've lost track of time."

"Once she's gone her room will be open. Are you going to move in to the house or stay in your hut? I have to say the breeze is nice up there, but the noise is quite distracting. There always seems to be a commotion going on and Sister Flores is usually a part of it."

Anna surrendered her head to the cloudy water, giving herself time to think. When she popped up, she said, "I don't know. I would like to stay clear of Sister Flores. Despite all my best efforts, we're not destined to be friends."

Sister Browne laughed. "I've noticed, although 'best efforts' are not the words I would have chosen."

Anna splashed her with water. "Aren't you being smart today!"

Sister Browne dodged the water. "Oh, I almost forgot, I heard Father Neel talking to someone from the village. They heard one of the Nigerian soldiers saying that they planned to ship Grant's body back to England, but instead it was buried in Calabar somewhere. No one wanted to pay to ship it back. I didn't know if I should tell you this or not, considering how close you were to him."

This was sobering news to Anna. She still had feelings for him, having come so close to being his wife. To know his body was buried so far from home bothered her deeply. She couldn't imagine being left in a distant, foreign country such as this, even if it now felt like home. Every now and then her mind flashed back to the missionary cemetery she'd seen with Grant in Lagos and it always darkened her mood.

She sighed. "Yes, I'm glad you told me. But that's all in the past. Now, do you have any other news to brighten my day?"

"Not really, unless you want to know what we're having for dinner?"

"No. Let that be a surprise, although I daresay fou fou will be involved."

This time Sister Browne splashed her. "That's right! If you would just find a sauce you liked to dip it in, you might acquire a taste for it."

"I doubt it. But there's always hope."

♌

The next morning, the three travelers finished breakfast and went to get their luggage. Anna detoured briefly to make one last trip to see her precious Lily and Jonah. Sister Flores was there keeping a stern watch on everything, but Anna didn't care.

"Now you both be good and eat all your food," she said, touching their noses. You need to grow up big and strong. When I come back I'll expect many kisses from each of you."

Both babies cooed and giggled and even appeared to wave good-bye as she turned to leave. Anna stopped and waved back. She would only be gone a week, but at the moment it felt like a distant journey to a far-off land. She choked up a little before finally turning away and heading toward the kit car.

When they were all loaded up, Father Neel touched Patrick on the shoulder. "All right. Say your prayer and start the engine. I want to get there before it's dark."

"Yes sir," he said, turning the engine on. "Let us go!" He was sounding more and more British every day.

He put the kit car in gear and took off. As he did, the three passengers turned in their seats and waved goodbye to everyone who had come to see them off. Little Thames was standing close to the car, making sure Father Neel saw him. By now they had grown very close. Anna located both Gran'pa and Oluwa and waved to them too. Oluwa was already smoking some of the tobacco she had left for him. Sitting next to Anna in the rear seat, Dr. Chapley touched her arm.

"I guess I don't need to reiterate my advice about not allowing the lepers to smoke. It's truly bad for their lungs."

"I know, Thomas," Anna whispered. "But he has leprosy. He needs a little pleasure in his life, don't you think?

Dr. Chapley grinned. "It's your money and his lungs, I suppose."

Anna tossed her head back and laughed. She had heard him say this before, usually over several glasses of wine and hands of gin rummy. Still, she had a soft spot for these lepers and despite his professional demeanor, he did too. Anna was sure he would soon find his own Clarence, or Oluwa, or Thames. It was just a matter of time.

The journey got off to a solid start with the kit car carefully making its way over the muddy, washed-out roads. Occasionally, they saw a few Nigerians waving to them as they rolled by. The women were usually topless with colorful fabric wrapped around their waist and carrying heavy loads on their heads. The men had nothing on besides loincloths. Even in both Ogoja and the leprosy settlement, they were dressed like this. It was only the rare male like Patrick who had a shirt of some kind.

As they passed by, these people called out for rides. With passengers in his car, Patrick didn't stop, though everyone understood that when he had the vehicle to himself, it was normal to pick up riders, charging them a few pence or *naira*—the Nigerian currency. It's just the way things were. Nothing was wasted, not even an empty seat.

After an hour of steady climbing, they came to a cliff and faced a bridge to cross. This one was more than simple logs set over a swollen stream. This bridge spanned at least 300 feet, and like all the wooden bridges in the bush, it could only hold one vehicle at a time. Luckily, there were very few vehicles so this was no inconvenience.

Patrick stopped the car at the edge of the cliff and got out to inspect the boards.

"The bridge done spoil small," he said.

Let's check it out," Father Neel said.

As Father Neel and Patrick walked slowly across the bridge, Anna and Dr. Chapley took this opportunity to get out and stretch their legs.

Anna said, "What do you think, Thomas? Does it look safe?"

"None of the bridges look safe. There's no transportation department out here to maintain them. With the rainy season sending river debris slamming into the supports below or better yet, washing out the soil underneath the caissons, they could go at any moment. Truthfully, my hair stands on end every time I have to go over one."

"Didn't you ride your bike over this bridge?"

"No, I walked it over, which is actually quite difficult because this is the highest bridge around. Look down there. If we fell off, we'd take a full ten seconds to hit the water."

Anna looked down and swallowed hard. "My goodness! Is ten seconds really that long?"

"Maybe not in other contexts, but if you're falling it would seem like a lifetime. Just crossing it on foot seemed like a lifetime to me. I tried hard not to look down. It was very tense."

Anna watched Father Neel carefully picking his way back.

"There seem to be some boards that are broken," she said to Dr. Chapley.

"Of course there are. See those sleepers lying across the bridge? They're like railroad crossties and many of them are broken. Also, notice the three long pieces of wood on top of the sleepers? They are barely fifteen inches wide. That means Patrick has a flat surface of only fifteen inches to guide the tires over. If he goes off those long pieces, he'll land the tire in between the sleepers and they'll break. If enough of them break, the long pieces have no support. So you see, our kit car can easily end up in the river."

Anna shuddered. "Don't talk like that. You're scaring me."

"If you're ever driving over a bridge, you need to be scared. That fear will help you to remember to first inspect it for broken sleepers and then make sure to keep your tires within those fifteen inches of track."

Anna tried to put the grim thoughts out of her mind. They said nothing more until Father Neel and Patrick returned. The pale look on Father Neel's face was plain to see. "There are quite a few broken sleepers and a few spots where the rails are split, but I'm going to try to guide Patrick over it. He suggests you two stay on this side until we've made it across. Then, I'm afraid you'll have to walk over."

Anna understood the message. *If disaster comes, no sense in everyone dying.*

They stood near the edge of the cliff while Patrick shifted into first gear, touched the pedal, and started inching forward. Father Neel positioned himself thirty feet in front and made furious hand signals. Watching from behind they could see Patrick trying hard to keep each wheel in the middle of the fifteen-inch rail. Foot by precious foot they progressed over the bridge, stopping twice to make sure Patrick steered past a split rail. Eventually, they pulled off the other side of the bridge and up the cliff. When Patrick stopped the car and got out, Father Neel waved for Anna and Dr. Chapley to start walking.

"Now listen, Anna. I want you to walk on the same rail I do and stand back about fifteen feet in case the one I'm standing on breaks. Okay?"

"Okay. I'll step exactly where you step."

"Good. And even though you'll be looking at the rails, try not to look past them. That's what almost tossed me over when I walked my bike across the last time."

Anna nodded as Dr. Chapley started out. When he got far enough ahead, she began walking behind him.

The boards near the edge of the bridge were muddy and slick. She had to be very careful not to take too big of a step.

As they progressed to the middle of the bridge, the rail was drier and free of mud. Even with solely focusing on the boards, Anna couldn't help but see the muddy water below. Each time, she caught herself and refocused on the rail. She couldn't imagine how anyone could navigate this in the dark.

Dr. Chapley slipped a few times, but he kept his feet underneath him. Anna could see that each rail was too far apart to walk together. There was no way to put her left foot on the left rail and her right foot on the right rail without falling and doing the splits. If she did that, she might even fall between the sleepers, which had a gap wide enough to fit a slender person through. It was truly nerve-wracking!

After several tense minutes, she finally stepped onto solid ground and congratulated Dr. Chapley. Anna now had an even clearer understanding as to why drivers like Patrick always congratulated each other when they got together. Just surviving made one want to celebrate. They were about to climb back into the kit car when Anna's smile turned into a frown.

"What the matter?" Father Neel asked.

Anna stared at the bridge. "I just realized we have to cross it again when we go back."

Dr. Chapley laughed. "Don't worry, after you see the next big crossing, this one will seem like a party!"

৶

Three hours later they'd worked their way back down to a low-lying area and were approaching yet another swollen river. Below threatening skies, a small pontoon rested against a crude dock. Anna saw a cable stretched tightly across the river and a device connecting it to the pontoon. Patrick asked everyone to get out while he worked with the operator of the pontoon to steer the vehicle onto the raft. Anna waited with the other two and watched as the right front wheel slipped off a plank, forcing the operator to use a lever to guide the tire back into place. Meanwhile the pontoon dipped left and right under the shifting weight of the car. The car was clearly too big and heavy. Each time the pontoon dipped down, a wall of water rushed over the wooden deck—a deck barely wider than the car—and disappeared down numerous holes and cracks. After a few minutes of watching, Anna pulled Dr. Chapley aside.

"Is this what you were telling me about?"

"I'm afraid so," he said, grinning. "What do you think?"

"I think the pontoon can't hold our car. It's too small. We'll need to find another route!"

"This is it. This is our only crossing."

Anna leaned away. "That can't be! Besides, it's about to storm. How many trips can it make before the weather turns nasty?"

Dr. Chapley grabbed her arm and walked her onto the raft. "One will be enough."

Anna was about to protest when the pontoon shoved away from the bank. With the first good push, the entire raft dipped to the left causing Anna to fall into Dr. Chapley arms so he could keep her upright.

"Hang on!" he said. "It's going to get bumpy!"

Anna gazed into Thomas' face and found her arms had instinctively wrapped around him. Once she was standing solidly, she released them and looked away.

Then a wave of water soaked her feet, bring her back to the moment. "Thomas, this is crazy! Please, let's go back. Please!"

The operator came up to Thomas and handed him a large piece of wood. He pointed to some metal posts and went back to the front.

"Anna, hold this and help me ship the oar rudder in these posts. We have to pull it back and forth to gain some steerage."

Too dazed to speak, she grabbed the thick, long oar and helped him guide it in place. Then, standing opposite of each other, they alternated between pushing and pulling it back and forth. Each time they did, it caused an exaggerated dipping of the pontoon, but propelled it forward.

"This is mad!" Anna said again. She couldn't see how they would survive this.

Patrick and Father Neel stood at the front, on the left and right sides of the pontoon. Each held a large oar and pushed water backwards. If one of them pushed before the other, the pontoon made yet another big dip. As for the operator, he had a device clamped tightly on a suspended cable, allowing him to stand on the deck and walk towards the rear, pushing the raft forward. When it was at the very rear, he unhooked it and walked it forward, clamping it on again and repeating the whole process over and over. It was extremely primitive, but nevertheless effective—until the clouds opened up.

They weren't even half way across the river when lightning cracked over the water, barely a few hundred yards away. The earsplitting noise confused all of them. The pontoon dipped hard to the right. At the same time sheets of rain pounded the wooden deck, throwing everything into further confusion. The operator said something to Patrick, who yelled across to Father Neel, who then turned around and yelled back to Anna and Dr. Chapley.

"Stop rowing! It's too rough. Keep the oar straight! And stand apart! We need to balance the…"

Father Neel didn't finish. Anna watched in horror as a wave spilled over causing him to slip and fall hard to the deck. His shoulder met the deck followed by his head. This caused his arms to relax allowing his body to slide easily off the deck and into the water, disappearing from sight. In less than a second, the violent rain removed all trace of him. Father Neel was gone.

14

"Oh my God!" Anna screamed through the pounding rain. "Somebody get him!"

Dr. Chapley handed her the end of a rope. "Pull me up when I jerk three times, and pull hard!"

She blinked and saw his body form a perfect arc, hanging above the water for the briefest of moments before disappearing into the turbulent waves. The rope slithered after him like a snake on the deck, boring rapidly into the water. Seeing that the rope was almost gone, she wrapped the end two times around her wrist when the operator unwrapped and snatched the loose end from her, expertly tying it to a cleat. Then he got down on his knees and held the rope for any sign. With his free hand, he continually wiped away the rain cascading off his forehead, doing anything he could to keep his attention focused on the line.

A crack of lightning caused Anna to snap out of her trance and tap the man on the shoulder. "He said to pull him in when he jerks three times on the rope."

The man nodded and crawled with the rope to the rear of the pontoon.

By now, Patrick was there, ready to help. Just as the operator's body stiffened, the rope twitched, then jerked.

Instinctively Anna yelled, "Pull! Pull him in!" But they were already ahead of her.

The two men pulled hard, taking turns gripping the wet rope and walking backwards. The deck was slick with unrelenting rain that pummeled everyone and everything. As the raging river forced water up over the sides and around their feet, the men found it nearly impossible to get solid footing. With the only rescuer underwater and out of sight, falling into the thrashing river would be a sure death sentence.

Without being told, Anna took up the slack and kept it out of their way. It was hard work, especially when one of the men backed up and released his grip to walk forward to grab a section of rope closer to the water. The weight on the unseen end was tremendous, certainly more than these two thin men should have been able to handle. But they didn't cease pulling.

What felt like hours were mere seconds as a large shape floated to the surface. A face lifted out of the water, frantically choking, in search of air. River water washed over the face, revealing it was Dr. Chapley. He coughed several times before he managed to pull a large mass to the edge. Staying in the river, he helped the two men lift Father Neel out of the water and onto the deck, his lifeless body falling backwards and his face pointing to the heavens. Anna dropped to her knees and grabbed Father Neel's armpits. Surprising herself, she dragged him to the middle of the pontoon, just behind the kit car, where water dripping off the bumper formed two small pools in each of his eye sockets. The pale face of her mother sitting in that chair flashed through her mind and she fell back, cupping a hand to her mouth. Like her mother, she knew he was gone.

In a blur, Dr. Chapley was out of the river and rolling the lifeless figure onto his stomach. Pressing hard on Father Neel's back, he yelled, "Lift his legs up!"

Patrick took up the task and raised his legs straight up, causing even more river water to spill out onto the deck.

"That's enough! Set him down," Dr. Chapley commanded. Patrick obeyed.

The Irish priest lay face down on the deck while Dr. Chapley continued back compressions. Anna stared helplessly, struggling to make sense of it all. She focused on his left hand when it twitched. Moving closer, she wondered if she was imagining it. A gurgling sound. Spitting. Coughing. More spitting.

Dr. Chapley rolled him on his side. "Can you hear me?!"

Father Neel coughed several times, sending out more water.

Anna watched as his sides heaved in and out. Patrick continued rubbing on the lungs, both front and back. Another crack of lightning accompanied by a large wave sent Patrick and the pilot back to the cable to move the ferry across the river. Whatever life Father Neel now had would be wasted if the pontoon capsized, which was a very real possibility.

Through the sheets of rain, they squinted upstream and saw walls of mud sliding into the river, carrying tree stumps and other debris with it. If any of that hit their pontoon, they'd be done for.

"Stay with him!" Dr. Chapley yelled to Anna. "I need to help get us across before it's too late." He shipped the long oar and began its back and forth motion to push the large raft forward. The operator was walking the cable device, which provided the most power. Not to be left out, Patrick worked the oar like never before. Knowing their lives were seriously at risk, all three men gave every ounce of energy they had. Even the operator seemed frightened, which kept the other two highly motivated.

Through the angry torrents of rain and the ripping waves, the ferry pulled to within a stone's throw of the far bank. The men could see they were almost home. Anna continued tending to Father Neel, who still hadn't uttered a word. When a bump sent her falling forward, she knew they'd made it. Yet another miracle.

Dr. Chapley and Patrick slid to the rear and lifted Father Neel up, carrying him off the pontoon. Anna promptly followed behind, not wanting to stay one more second on this raft of death. While the men

set Father Neel in a tiny shack on the dock, the operator was busy tying every rope down, hoping to keep the ferry from being damaged
or carried away.

"Stay with him," Dr. Chapley said again, as he wiped rainwater
from his eyes. "We have to get the kit car off before it falls into the
river."

He grabbed Patrick and ran back to the ferry to untie the straps.

Anna used her bare hand to wipe water off the priest's face. He
was breathing steadily but still didn't appear to be conscious.

She yelled, "Father Neel, can you hear me?"

He blinked his eyes, apparently understanding her words.

"Can you say something?"

He blinked again and winced, his eyes tracking only up and
down. Even though his face was now dry, Anna continued wiping and
caressing it.

Through cracks in the walls, she saw the kit car roll off the pontoon and up the muddy bank. When it started sliding, Dr. Chapley
ran to the rear and pushed while Patrick steered. The operator ran
to help, pushing with Dr. Chapley. With all three struggling to stay on
their feet, they were finally able to guide the kit car to a flat portion
of road about a hundred yards away from the shack. By now, the rain
had slackened, making the two-wheel path that served as a road, easier to see. Leaving the kit car be, the three men carefully picked their
way through the mud, back down the river bank, the operator stepping on his pontoon and the other two heading toward the shack.

Dr. Chapley stuck his head in. "How's he doing? Did he say
anything?"

"No, he blinked a few times, but he's still out of it. He seems to be
in some pain."

"Let's carry him to the car and we'll spread him out in the backseat. We need to keep moving and get to the village before dark. He
may need help, and I can't do it out here in the bush. Patrick, grab his
legs while I grab his arms."

Instantly, the shack filled with a primal scream.

"Set him down!" Dr. Chapley yelled. "Something's wrong."

When they did, his screaming stopped. The doctor ran his hands over the patient's shoulders, arms, chest and neck. Looking at Anna, he shook his head. "The shoulder's broken. You have to help us."

Anna jumped up. "Sure, tell me what I can do."

"Switch places with Patrick and grab his legs. Patrick, you put your hands under his left side and I'll carry his right. And don't pull from his armpits. Understand?"

Patrick nodded. "Good. Everyone lift on my command. Reeaddyy... Now!"

The three lifted the body up which brought forth more screams. "Keep walking! We have to get him to the kit car no matter what!"

Father Neel tossed his head violently from side to side, screaming, crying, doing whatever he could to make them stop. They didn't. It was a painfully disturbing journey.

They gently lowered him into the backseat, letting his bare feet hang out the left side of the kit car. This gave them a chance to catch their breath.

Dr. Chapley was the least physically affected. "I guess all the bike riding got me in shape for this," he joked.

Anna took in lungfuls of air. "I can't believe what I just saw. You dove into the water, found Father Neel and brought him back to the surface. Then you helped row the ferry in and carry him to the kit car. I don't know many athletes who could do what you've just done!"

Patrick, breathing hard, nodded in agreement. In the silence, the three stood next to the kit car, letting the light rain cool their skin. Dr. Chapley was the first to snap out of it. "There's no sense in getting dry now. Let's put a blanket over him and all squeeze into the front seat. It's the only way to allow him to take up the entire backseat."

Anna dug through the luggage and found a thin blanket. She carefully draped it over Father Neel, tucking one end under him and the other in the fold between the backrest and the seat. Hopefully, this would keep him from rolling forward and falling onto the floorboard. Satisfied this was the best they could do, Patrick said a prayer, started the engine, and took off.

Anna opened her eyes and stared at the strange ceiling. Nothing made sense until it did. She was in Otukpo, sleeping in a hut they had cleared out for her. She remembered how completely exhausted she'd been when they finally arrived. Even a cup of strong tea had not been enough to bring her out of her utterly beaten state. After she had changed out of her wet clothes, she collapsed on the bed. That was all she remembered.

Anna glanced out the window at the bright sunlight. It was much later than her usual waking time. Forcing her legs out of bed, she scooted her feet around searching for her shoes. When she found them, she didn't even bother reaching down to lift them up and empty any night crawlers that may have established residence. Instead, she slid her feet in and stood up wearing the same outfit she'd worn to bed.

Checking her pockets, she found a bit of leftover bandage. The memories flooded back. Dr. Chapley had needed her help in wrapping up Father Neal's shoulder to prevent it from moving. When that was done, she had remained behind and fed their patient soup, as his right arm was immobilized and he was still not fully there, the shock of what he'd been through obviously still lingering.

During all this, Father Neel hardly said two words to her. After he consumed all the soup he wanted, she bunched up his straw-filled pillow and lowered his head gently onto it. That's when she had joined Dr. Chapley and Patrick for a hearty supper of Mama Mimi's cooking.

The villagers provided ample fou fou and water—both cold and hot. Anna remembered gulping down a cup of Ceylon and chatted a few minutes before giving up and heading to her hut. Even the power of her strong tea wasn't enough to keep her awake.

She smoothed down her dress as best she could and brushed her hair back. From her bag, she fished out some tea, and left her hut in search of hot water.

It didn't take long to find some. Dr. Chapley was seated at a small table outside, two huts away, with a steaming pot in front of him.

"There you are," he said. "I thought I was going to have two patients."

"What time is it?" she mumbled.

"Half past eight. I heard you stirring so I ordered another pot of hot water."

"Thank you, Thomas, you're a dear. I hope my English breakfast will cut through the fog." She sat down and spooned tea leaves into her infuser.

"I've already eaten but I'm sure you're famished. Let me signal the girl for some food."

He raised his hand catching the girl's attention and pointed to Anna. She nodded and took off in the opposite direction.

"How's Father Neel doing?"

"Better. He's talking now, and I don't think he has any other injuries. He seems normal other than the pain he's feeling, and doesn't remember much, which is a blessing."

Anna set her tea infuser in a cup of hot water and waited for it to steep. "That *is* a blessing. Can we take him back the way we came?"

Dr. Chapley sipped on his tea and placed the cup back down on a piece of wood. "That's an interesting question because it has two contradictory answers. The first one is no. He's too injured to travel and couldn't endure that route. The second answer is yes because it's the only way back. Of course, we could head north for a hundred miles then work our way east and perhaps find a route back after traveling across Africa. But realistically, it would take too long. If our kit car broke down, where would we be then? No, Father Neel must go back the same way we came."

"So I'm going to ask you the question you're waiting for me to ask, even though I'm not in my normally upbeat mood. I assume you already know what it is?"

Dr. Chapley mischievously grinned. "Are you saying you're occasionally less than chipper?"

Anna said nothing and frowned just as she took a sip of her tea.

"Okay. Here's the butcher's bill. We're going to be here for at least six weeks; maybe longer."

"Six weeks! I have students to teach. Injections to give Clarence. Children relying on me. This won't do!"

"Don't you think I'm needed there? I'm the doctor."

The impact of the situation was slowly sinking in. Dr. Chapley could see this, so he let her digest it.

The girl brought a plate of plantains and dried meat, placing it before Anna. She waited for the girl to leave before speaking.

"What will we do? Can I go back without you and Father Neel?"

"That's what you and I need to discuss. I must stay with him until he's healed. Out here, this far in the bush, if he took a turn, we'd lose him. I can stay with him and have Patrick take you back but you saw how that road is. Do you want to make the journey like that without another man to help Patrick over the bridge? Or over the river? Or to push the kit car out of the mud? It's very risky. You might make it but why would you want to take a chance?"

Anna shook her head in frustration and remained silent.

"And what about me? If you two get into any trouble, I wouldn't be able to help you. How long would I be stuck here before they sent out another kit car looking for us?"

Her dark mood lightened. "No, you're right, Thomas. Without you, Father Neel would be dead, and we would've capsized. I wouldn't feel safe without you." She sighed. "So you're saying we'll be here for six weeks?"

"Yes, that's what I'm saying. We were going to be here for seven days, anyway. You can spend the extra time looking for all suitable staff to train while I check out the locations for a medical facility and school. We may be able to stretch those tasks to two weeks, if we're really thorough. But I propose we work together and stretch it to four weeks. I can give you my opinion of the staff you want to train, and you can help me look at the various locations for a leper settlement. You might enjoy the exercise, strengthen you up a bit. Maybe you could be the one who rescues me next time. What do you say?"

"Spending time with you is always enjoyable," she said, cracking a smile. "This is a lot to take in. Let me have my tea and eat something before I comment. Okay?"

"Certainly. I'll check on my patient again and be back to listen to any alternative proposal you care to offer."

Anna laughed because she knew there was none. This wasn't like Maghull, where she could take a taxi or bus if the train broke down. No, this was Africa: sometimes primitive and unpredictable. Life adjusted to Africa, not the other way around. She would just have to 'get used to it', just like her first week in the bush when she forgot to bring toilet paper to the hole in the ground she and the nuns were using as their bathroom.

Alone, Anna sat there eating. From her table, she took in the circular village of Otukpo and noticed how it differed from the rectangular Ogoja. She rather liked this layout because from her chair she could see just about every hut in the village. This wasn't the case in Ogoja, where one had to stare down a long row of huts—some hiding in recesses behind others—and huts laid out in a haphazard fashion.

The center of Otukpo held several large chairs, presumably for the village chiefs. A few tables stood over the chairs, providing cover for the naked children who played some kind of game. A few others ran around chasing chickens and goats. At least that much was like home.

"Home," Anna said aloud to no one. "I guess that's telling me something."

"Telling you what?"

Anna saw Dr. Chapley coming out of Father Neel's hut. "Oh nothing. I'm just talking to myself."

"Talking to yourself is a symptom of loneliness. I may have to examine you."

Anna chuckled and smiled. "I thought of Ogoja as home without even thinking. It came right out."

Thomas took a seat next to her. "It sounds like you're now a permanent part of Nigeria. Welcome."

She laughed again, her dark mood completely gone. "I guess so. Look, I don't want to make the trip back without you, and your plan is the most reasonable. Let's stay as long as we need to get Father Neel well. I'll simply have to make my tea last."

Now Dr. Chapley laughed. "Oh! So that's the real issue troubling you. Well, I've been asking around, and we might be able to get a bit more. I brought some money but not enough for six weeks. Maybe we can pool our money and buy what we need."

'Don't worry. I brought more than enough, even though I had no thought of spending it."

Thomas reached over and touched her hand, something he hadn't done since they met. "Then it's agreed. We'll be a team. I'm so looking forward to it. Now, finish your tea and let's get to work."

Anna glanced at his hand over hers and said nothing, the corners of her mouth lifting ever so slightly.

❧

Two weeks later, Anna and Dr. Chapley selected a site for both the school and the infirmary. Father Neel, though unwilling to speak about his ordeal, was well enough to start negotiating with the chiefs for the land. While he did that, the two spent two more weeks interviewing close to a hundred prospective nurses, leprosy control officers, clerks, and teachers. They drafted a comprehensive list of the top candidates. Instead of informing the ones they wanted to come to Ogoja for training, they waited until they were ready to leave as circumstances could always change. As Dr. Chapley had said, "They may lose interest, get married, leave the village, or God forbid, get eaten by that leopard that roams this area freely."

"You know, it came into my hut once, and I surely don't want to see it again. I'm glad the man you sent to Ogoja made it back safely, without running into it."

"I am too. I wouldn't want to make that trip on foot alone."

The first week Dr. Chapley had paid a villager to make the three to four day walk to Ogoja and inform them what had happened. When he returned, he reported that everything was fine there and that they were praying for speedy healing. He brought back a signed note from Sister Flores to prove he'd been there. And the best news was he hadn't seen the leopard.

"How much longer do you think we'll be here?" Anna asked.

"He's healing nicely. I should say six weeks should be plenty of time. Why? Are you looking to get rid of me?"

"Of course not, I would just like a change of clothing, although I must admit I am missing my babies and Clarence."

"How about going on a picnic? It's a nice day, and we can go to the site of your school and spread out a blanket."

Anna's face brightened. "Of course. Let me grab my straw hat and I'll be ready in a jiff."

They made a long walk to a beautiful clearing and unfurled an elaborately patterned quilt stitched by one of the elderly women. The woman had playfully grinned at Anna when she handed it to her causing Anna to shake her head several times. This prompted the rest of the women to laugh and gibber in their tribal language as Anna left their company. She got the message.

Once they had the food set in front of them, Anna said, "Tell me Thomas, what are your plans? Are you staying with us much longer?"

Dr. Chapley sliced a tomato. "You know, I was a temporary solution. And my previous employer at Obubra—the Nigerian government— filled in nicely for me with another doctor, who is said to be leaving soon. I thought they might call me back but recently, or at least before we left Ogoja, I learned they received a letter from a doctor who may be coming over and willing to work at Obubra. I expect to find out if the government wants me to come back when we return."

"Gosh Thomas, I'd hate for you to leave."

He handed her some sliced tomato. "What about you? What are your plans?"

"I think I'm likely to stay longer than you. With every passing day, my former life in Maghull disappears. I'm not sure I could handle the pace of life back there, or leave my babies and all. I just don't know."

Dr. Chapley uncorked some wine and poured her a glass. "This is my last bottle so I saved it for something nice."

"Thank you," Anna said taking the glass. "It's been a while. Did you bring other bottles I didn't get to enjoy?"

They clinked glasses. "Actually no. This was my only bottle. I just wanted you to think I traveled with a cellar of wine. It's sounds so rich."

Anna giggled and sipped her wine.

"Would you like to get married and have children?" he said casually as he tilted his glass.

Anna froze. Was he asking her to get married? Or was he asking if she would consider it one day? This was just like Thomas to do this. She picked the safer of the two options.

"Yes, I still have hope. You know how much I love Lily and Jonah. I would love to have two of my own one day."

Dr. Chapley let the moment hang there, before lifting his plate of food and eating. Anna did likewise, fairly confident this little test was the first of more to come.

⅋

The dust was everywhere, settling all around them as the car came to a stop. They were three miles outside of Ogoja and Patrick was pulling the kit car over to inspect something that had come loose. The three passengers took advantage of the stop and stretched their legs.

The journey had been relatively uneventful. The river crossing was smooth, with a new operator telling them the last one quit after a rough experience. The rickety bridge hadn't worsened, which was also a relief. With a bright, clear sky, they'd covered the eighty miles fairly quickly.

Dr. Chapley stretched his legs and went to help Patrick, which gave Father Neel a chance to speak to Anna privately.

"I want to thank you for all you've done. I'm very grateful."

"Oh Father, please," she said honestly. "It was my pleasure. You were an easy patient. Besides, I'm just grateful you're here. After all, we almost lost you."

"Yes, I realize I almost entered heaven. Thankfully, it wasn't my time. But I'm not just referring to me. I'm talking about the money you provided. If you hadn't brought more than enough along, we would've been quite thin." He patted her shoulder. "You've bailed me out once again."

"I'd like to think God had a hand in it. Or maybe it was my strong desire for tea."

"Either way, I'm not complaining. Still, I want to thank you. I'll reimburse you when we get back."

"You do whatever you think is best. I won't miss the money if you don't."

Father Neel nodded. They both knew how tight funds always were. He couldn't guarantee anything to anyone. Without support from the Medical Missionaries of Mary, or donations from caring British and Irish citizens, they'd have to abandon their work and head back England. This thought was always nagging their minds.

"Well, I think we have it," Dr. Chapley announced. "Shall we?"

He eased Father Neel into the front seat, which was more comfortable. Then he helped Anna into the back allowing his hand to caress hers as he stepped in and slid next to her.

Anna blushed. The memory of him leaning over and kissing her on their picnic was as vivid as if it had happened a few moments earlier. She smoothed out her dress, for no good reason, and sat back for the final few miles to home.

The kit car moved down the dirt road kicking up dust, which signaled their arrival to the settlement. Surprisingly, no one came running. It was late afternoon, when there should be plenty of activity, yet it was as if the place was abandoned. Even Patrick was confused.

"Wetin dey do like dis? Dem dey play with us?"

"I don't know," Dr. Chapley said. "Maybe they're going to surprise us."

The car rolled to a stop and all four of them got out. Father Neel stared intently across the large field at an area near the forest.

"I think I've solved our mystery," he said, pointing with his left hand.

"Oh no," Anna cried. "A funeral. I hope it wasn't one of my babies."

"I'm afraid it's going to be someone important," Dr. Chapley added somberly, "because the entire settlement is there." That tensed up everyone.

"Oh dear God!" Father Neel pleaded. "Please don't let it be one of the staff." He quickened his pace sending his arm swinging back and forth in its sling. The rest picked up their pace behind him.

As they neared the settlement's cemetery, they could see a large group of people standing around an inner group which wasn't fully visible. A few in the rear noticed their approach and touched the ones in front, slicing a path through the mourners. When they had made their way to the inner circle, Anna looked around in panic for the people she cared for the most. She didn't see Clarence, but that wasn't a surprise. He rarely left the woods and certainly couldn't be expected to mingle with a group this large. She didn't see her two babies who were likely in the nursery. Then she found the nuns. They were standing next to the grave, as two strong men readied themselves to lower the deceased to the bottom.

In an instant, Anna studied their faces. There was Sister Flores, conducting the service. She wore a serious expression. Next to her was Sister Whelan, crying softly. On the other side of Sister Flores, stood Sister O'Keefe, with a tear-streaked face.

Could it be the visiting nurse Isla McGinty who died? Surely she had left by now. If it wasn't her, didn't that account for everyone? Or did it?

Suddenly, Anna panicked and spun around the inner circle searching for one more face. "Wait a minute?" she cried. "Where's..." She pushed closer to the deceased. "No! It can't be!" she screamed, the panic and fear rising up from deep inside her. "Please God, no!"

Dr. Chapley grabbed her arm to pull her close but she was able to break free, and stumbled towards the burial cloth that held the deceased. Without asking for permission and with no one having the courage to stop her, she lifted the veil and saw the face. Her knees gave out and she collapsed next the body. Crying hysterically, she stared at the sky and screamed, "No!"

15

The two Irish sisters held Anna up while Dr. Chapley propped the door open.

"Let's put her on the bed," he said. "Help her in there."

Sister O'Keefe eased her through the small opening while he continued giving instructions.

"Easy now. Watch her feet."

Sister Whelan, the last one in line, released her hold on Anna to wipe the tears streaming from her own face. She stayed outside since the tiny hut was already crowded with three people.

"There you go, Anna," he said soothingly. "Lie down and let me give you something to help you sleep."

He opened his medical bag and pulled out a vial while Sister Whelan removed Anna's shoes and placed a sheet up to her neck. Squeezing a dropper into a cup of water, he handed it to Anna.

"Here, drink this. It's the tincture of laudanum. It'll help you sleep. I'll check on you before I turn in tonight and see how you're doing. Okay?"

Anna mindlessly nodded. She drank the water and let her head fall to the pillow, praying for sleep.

"Let's go," Dr. Chapley whispered. "She needs to rest."

When the door to her hut closed, he pulled the two sisters over to the side. "I know you have a lot to do but if you can, please keep an eye on her. Can you do that for me?"

They both nodded.

"Thank you. Now, I need to see Sister Flores and find out what happened to Sister Browne."

The next morning, Dr. Chapley ducked under the low thatching and peered through a small crack in the door. Sister Whelan had told him his patient was up and dressed. He could see she was at her writing desk, taking some food along with her beloved tea. This was a good time.

"Knock. Knock," he said, lightly tapping on the door. "Care for a visitor?"

"Come in," she said flatly.

Dr. Chapley creaked open the door and closed it behind him. Finding the only other chair available, he sat down and studied Anna's appearance. She looked wide awake, yet appeared very tired. He knew from the opium drops he gave her, it was expected.

"How are you feeling?"

Anna continued staring at her food. "Miserable. We were very close. I'm going to miss her terribly."

Dr. Chapley knew enough about these matters to go easy. "Yes, I'm very sad too. I worked with her many times. She was always a joy to be around."

Anna twisted her head towards him and glared. "May be, but you seemed to have already moved on. I can't just do that. I have feelings."

He let that pass. "We are all hurting. But everyone has a different way of mourning."

She poured herself another cup of tea. "I didn't even see you cry. Do you have any feelings at all?"

He was unable to let this pass. "Yes Anna, I have deep feelings. But I'm a doctor. I have a mask on. It keeps me safe and enables me to perform my job. I see death all the time, certainly more than you'll ever see. But I am sure you know this already."

She said nothing as she swirled her mother's cup on the saucer, lost in her thoughts.

"Clarence, the boy you're so fond of? Sat outside your hut all night listening for anything you might need. Only when the sun rose above the trees, and Sister Whelan came to check on you, did he leave. You know his condition is not improving. During the time we were gone, he did *not* go to the infirmary to continue his injections so the patches are bigger and spreading. He may have five years, or five months. Who knows?"

"And that girl you love to watch pound fou fou, the one with stumps for hands, her name escapes me just now."

"Maria," Anna muttered.

"Yes, Maria! Thank you. She will die in two weeks, maybe this week. In fact, we will probably bury two or three lepers this month. So you see, to me death is a constant."

He kneeled next to her. "Look, I'm not asking you to stop grieving. And I know that it was a shock to find out about her death the way we did, but these people here need us. Today! Right now! Clarence needs you. Your school children need you. Oluwa is looking for more tobacco from you so he can entertain us with God knows what." He paused a moment. "Your two babies need you."

At the mention of her babies, she looked at him through tear-filled eyes. He continued talking. "And I need you, Anna. I do!"

She turned from her chair and fell into his waiting arms, sobbing hard. He said nothing for several minutes as he waited for her to cry it out.

When she finally tapered off, he said, "Your students asked me if you were coming in to teach them today. Don't tell them I told you, but I think they have a surprise for you."

Anna wiped her eyes with a handkerchief. "Tell them I'll be in, just a little late. Will you?"

"Of course," he said, as he stood up to leave.

"Thomas wait! Can you tell me how Victoria died?" She held the handkerchief close to her mouth in case it was bad.

"Yes. She first complained of chills and a fever. When she started sweating and became delirious, they knew she had malaria. She passed away almost a week after she fell ill. It was not pleasant for the nuns to witness this but at least they had time to prepare themselves. Even though we take quinine, I'm surprised that none of the other missionaries including you, haven't come down with it before.

"I wish we had been here!"

"If you or I had been here, there wouldn't have been much we could do. The patient either fights off the disease on their own or dies. It was God's will to take her so she can be with Him."

"God's will? Sure… I guess. But that doesn't make me feel any better. It's hard to feel so out of control, like we could die at any moment. Right?"

"Perhaps. But it's a matter of perspective. I never told you this but back at the river when I was underwater, I was almost out of breath. Out of nowhere came this black mass. It was Father Neel's robe. I stretched out and gripped a piece of his collar but when I pulled him to me, the fabric slipped out of my hand. He was just too heavy. I knew I was about to drown so I tried to swim up to the surface when somehow, that slight tug had pulled his body an inch or two closer. As I made a swimming stroke, my hand ran into his rosary and it got tangled in my fingers. Now I was even more sure of my death. Rather than trying to free my hand, I pulled hard, assuming the cheap string would snap. But it didn't. It held. We were both going to die together with the violent river consuming our bodies. It was a terrible feeling knowing all was lost. I have never felt so helpless, no—*hopeless*—in all my life."

Anna stared at him with both confusion and astonishment.

"The moment I surrendered to my fate, a wave, I suppose, or some unseen force pushed him closer to me and then both of us towards the surface. At one point, I felt him lagging so I jerked on the rosary and it held. How we made it to the top, I have no idea."

"The men pulled you up when you jerked on the rope. Remember?"

He shook his head.

"Thomas, I saw the rope jerk three times!"

He placed his hands on her shoulders. "No Anna. I never jerked on the rope. I was out of breath and not thinking clearly. How that rosary held Father Neel's waterlogged body, I have no idea. Or actually I do."

Anna's jaw hung open. "So do I. Now run and tell those children I'll be right there. She would want me to move on."

"Good. They'll be waiting so hurry up."

He closed the hut door, happy knowing at least one of his patients was feeling better. Now, he had to spend the next eight hours treating forty more.

The children peeked below the edges of the roof until they saw that unmistakable gait.

"Shhh! She come now," Esi said.

They all scattered to reach their desks and tried to keep quiet, all except Esi. She stood at the entrance, hands on her hips, waiting.

Anna ducked under the roof and then straightened up. Blocking her path was a little bundle of determination.

"Well, hello Esi. Did you miss me?"

Esi pointed to the ground. "Madame, see the shine?"

Anna focused her attention on the bright reflection coming from the red and black mud floor. She knew it was a result of the students polishing it with coconut shells. It was their way of saying how much they missed her.

"My my, this is very nice! Thank you, dear students, for all your hard work. I'm sorry I'm late."

"Madame, here. We work on dem tings you give us." Esi handed her a stack of papers.

"I have to thank you again. It looks like you have used your time wisely."

The papers Anna had left behind were a week's worth of assignments. She didn't think they would be disciplined enough to get them completed, but she also didn't know she'd be gone for more than a week. When one week turned into six, they obviously found the time.

Glancing around the classroom, she spotted something different. "It seems we have some new students. Could the new students raise your hands?"

Five children raised their hands. Suddenly, she had twenty-nine students. With the carpenters having constructed only thirty desks, she made a mental note to ask them to build more.

"Esi, I want to thank you for keeping everyone organized. You've done a very good job."

"Madame, I want to be dey teacher one day. You dey teach me."

Anna chuckled. "I assumed as much. And you're off to a great start. Now, please take your seat and we will begin today's lesson."

Esi beamed all the way back to her desk. Once she took her seat, Anna began the lesson.

Six hours later, class was over and the children scattered everywhere, heading to their work or huts, or perhaps just to play which each other. Anna collected her things and decided to take a trip through the village to see what had changed while she was gone.

The sun, still high in the sky, brought out all the vibrant colors she'd come to know. The air was cool, at least according to Nigeria's standards, making it a pleasant walk.

The first change she noticed was the land. Where there used to be empty fields, now there were crops growing. Large cabbages burst through the soil. So did tomatoes and cucumbers. Closer to the ground were yams, potatoes and ground nuts.

Most lepers had some plot of land they were responsible for, including little Thames. She spotted him, holding a proper hoe, having traded in his broken one. He was struggling to use it as Father Neel stood over him, inspecting some seedlings he'd planted. Anna stopped and watched the exchange as Father Neel offered some farming advice, pointing with his left hand and trying not to become too animated. As sad as she was about the recent events, a tiny smile formed on her cheeks for there was Thames, with stumps for arms and Father Neel, with one arm completely immobilized. Between them, the two had only one functioning arm, making them quite a pair. When Father Neel patted Thames on the shoulder telling him how well he was doing, she had no doubt he had found himself a 'local son'.

Anna turned to continue her journey when she heard her name called out. "Anna, could I speak to you for a moment?" It was Father Neel.

"Yes Father, what is it?"

They stepped away from Thames for some privacy.

"How are you feeling today? I heard you taught your class."

"Yes, I'm... I'm dealing with it. That's the best I can say."

"I know. We all are. I, for one, have had some very dark moments since our return. But getting back to the routine has certainly helped me. If it's not too troubling, would you have the time to come to my office? I need your help in drafting some letters. With the sisters working extra hard, I just can't spare them."

"Of course. Let me do a few things first and I'll be there in, say, thirty minutes?"

"That would be fine. That will give me plenty of time to show Thames how to thin the weeds."

He turned back to the little boy. "Now, don't hoe too close to those seedlings..."

Anna smiled as she walked away. There was so much to do here, so many people to help that it was almost overwhelming.

Her next stop was the carpenter's shack. Like everything, it too had grown. Where there once were supplies stored under a lean-to up against a small hut, now there was a spacious building with another smaller shack for various wood sizes. Anna searched among the six men working there for the master carpenter and told him she needed more desks. He summoned an assistant who was three feet away and told him to get the desks built. The assistant summoned another carpenter two feet away and assigned him the task. The importance they gave to titles, status and authority was almost comical. Anna shook her head, unsure if any of her desks would get built. However, she thanked the master carpenter and left them to their work, moving on towards her intended destination: the cemetery.

At the edge of the forest, just before the earth sloped down to the river, was a flat piece of land, shaded by tall trees. It was the perfect spot to bury their dead. Anna found the freshly turned earth with a large white cross protruding out of it. This was Victoria's final resting spot. Bright flowers ringed the plot, the earth below it dark from a recent watering. As she stood facing the cross, tears welled up in her eyes. Memories of all the river baths and gossip sessions they had enjoyed replayed in her mind. With Victoria gone, there was no one else she could confide in. That would make it a lonely existence.

She stood there taking in the sounds of the forest. Wings flapped above her as a bird moved from one tree to another. Insects buzzed and hummed all around. Noise of leaves being stirred told her unseen ground animals were moving around in search of food. This place of death was truly alive.

She lingered awhile before saying a prayer and leaving. She was already missing her good friend terribly.

Anna stopped off at her hut to store her school papers and books. On her bed was a single flower someone had left her. It had to be Thomas. He must have come to check on her and left it as his calling card. She'd have to thank him later.

As she headed to see Father Neel, Oluwa appeared, touching his hands to his pipe.

"Oluwa get no tobacco, Sista. You bring tobacco come?"

Anna reached into her pocket and produced two shillings. "Here, that should tide you over."

"Sista, I go make you laugh now!"

He started dancing a ridiculous routine that looked more like he was drunk than actually dancing. Gesturing wildly with his arms, he plastered a large smile on his face doing everything he could to cheer Anna up. Finally, she laughed a little.

He kept dancing until she cut him off. "Oluwa, you have your money. Now run and get your tobacco. You can make me laugh later."

"Oluwa go come and make Sista laugh later." With that, he took off to find his tobacco supplier, whoever that was.

She finally reached Father Neel's office and saw papers scattered everywhere.

"Just look at this mess," he said. "I will never get it straightened up!"

Anna started gathering up the papers and stacking them in a pile. "Yes you will. I'll come and help you until your arm works again."

Father Neel sighed. "That might be quite a while. Dr. Chapley thinks I should keep it immobilized for at least four more weeks, to make sure it's healed."

"Four weeks? That is a long time. Still, I'll do what I can for you. Besides, where else do I have to go?"

"Anna, you're a Godsend! Truly you are."

She pulled out a chair. "Alright Father, enough about me. What's first?"

He tapped his finger pointing down on the desk. "We have to deal with Sister Browne's affairs. I know it's painful for all of us but it won't take long."

Now it was Anna's turn to sigh. She found a fresh piece of paper and loaded a pen with ink. "I assume we need to write to her parents first. Do you have their address?"

Father Neel shook his head. "She had no parents, not even siblings, for that matter. Didn't she tell you?"

"Tell me what?"

"Why, she was an orphan. Someone left her on the doorstep of a convent. The sisters took her in and raised her up from a little baby. That's why she volunteered to come out here. She wanted to help all the poor orphans like her."

An open-mouthed Anna pushed back from the table.

"I'm sorry," he said. "I knew you two were close. I thought you knew."

Anna had been close to Victoria but she never learned anything important about her. They had always talked about Anna's issues instead of Victoria's. The fact that she didn't know this about her close friend wounded her even more deeply, made her feel self-centered. She put the pen down.

Father Neel, seeing her reaction, was unsure of what to do. "I can see you are surprised by this information. Perhaps we should deal with this paperwork at a later time."

Anna rubbed her eyes and collected herself. "No, I owe it to Victoria. We have worked too hard to let everything go now. But I can tell you this is very hard on me."

"I understand. I do. I just wish Nurse McGinty didn't have to leave. She stayed three extra weeks but we were gone six. She went back to the Scottish mission two weeks ago, and with Victoria's death, things are quite difficult to manage now. The three sisters are barely keeping up, with the babies to care for and all. As hard as things are for you, I believe you can help me with all this and possibly relieve them in the nursery. I've already talked to Sister Flores and she's amenable to you working in there—under her supervision, of course."

She smirked. "Of course."

"Have you been to see your two babies?"

Anna breathed deeply. "No. I awoke and went to the school, then came here. I'm planning on seeing them as soon as we are done."

"Well then, let's not delay your visit any longer than necessary. It will likely do you some good."

Anna nodded. "What's the first order of business?"

"I need you to take a letter to Mother Mary Martin about Sister Browne. I must tell her what's happened and I want her to send more sisters, including a nurse! Oh, and more money! It's always money and people, isn't it?"

"Yes it is. More money and more *good* people."

16

Anna poured herself a cup of Black Ceylon and lifted it to her lips, engrossed in deep thoughts. So much had happened in the two weeks since they returned, it was hard to process it all. Her first visit to the nursery to see Lily and Jonah was supposed to be a thirty-minute love fest but turned into a three-hour shift. While she was there, it was obvious the three sisters were pushed to the limit. They had delegated more tasks to local women but there were a few things they just had to do themselves; feeding the babies was one of them. That's where Anna came in. But first, she and Sister Flores established an uneasy truce. There was no choice. Sister Flores needed Anna and Anna wanted to work. So they said very little to each other and did their jobs.

When Anna first saw the babies, she couldn't believe how much they'd grown. They were crawling more and wanting to play, so placing them in a makeshift wooden playpen with cloth for walls was part of her chores now. Of course, Anna couldn't just set the babies down in the playpen and leave them on their own. She had to tickle and play with them for a few minutes before going back to feeding and changing diapers.

There was one piece of good news related to the milk supply. While they were in Otukpo, a new supplier delivered at least several months' worth. They wouldn't have to start worrying about milk for some time, and hopefully they would be eating mashed up food by then.

At first, Lily and Jonah desperately clung to Anna, not wanting to go into the playpen. This tight bonding was very apparent and Anna did nothing to dampen their enthusiasm. She didn't share her feelings with anyone but she couldn't get enough of the babies. At times, she thought about their mother. How could a woman simply give them up? It broke her heart thinking about the misery their mother must now be suffering.

One of the good things about being away so long was the mail. She had received three letters from Molly, two of them having been stuck on a freighter which detoured to Ghana due to engine problems.

Molly's letters contained the usual interesting gossip and the comings and goings of Maghull. She was still dating her deliveryman, Francis, and saying he might be the one. That must have been the reason why she finally gave Anna the man's name; before, she had simply called him her deliveryman.

Since she had been back, Anna wrote several short letters to Molly and sent them with Patrick on one of his trips to Calabar. But when he returned, she got a surprise. It was a fourth letter from Molly, a very recent one. And the news it contained was shocking.

So now, with hot tea to keep her awake, Anna sat at her desk ready to write a letter back to her best friend.

Dearest Molly,

It's mid-August here, and I have just received your letter informing me about the loss of Clarence's wife during childbirth. I can still see her face at the bank, which was the last time I saw her. They were going out for lunch. And now she's gone. It's tragic! I'm sure Clarence must be devastated! You said the little girl she had was healthy; I thank God for that. If you see Clarence, please tell him how sorry I am for his loss.

I know by the time you receive this letter, you will have received my other letters about our journey to Otukpo and Victoria's (Sister Browne) sudden death, so I don't want to dwell on that anymore. But I am quickly learning how much death is a part of life out here. The lepers are suffering and they are dying all the time. Father Neel is even looking at clearing more land to expand our cemetery. God only knows how many more missionaries will be taken. Just pray, I'm not one of them.

To give you an example of what death out here is like, let me tell you about my routine today. I awoke at six a.m. and proceeded directly to the nursery. There I fed and played with the babies for an hour and a half. This relieves the sisters who are completely exhausted. Then I took some breakfast, spending barely twenty minutes, before going to my school to teach class. However, at ten a.m., the sisters were overwhelmed with lepers at the infirmary, so I had to cancel the class and help them out. I've become an expert at giving the intradermal injections of Chaulmoogra oil and tending to their white patches. Thomas tells me how much to administer, and I do it. Cleverly, he has set up all the patients with a special disc they wear around their necks. This disc tells us the dosage of oil they should receive. It makes us very efficient.

When I wasn't treating patients, I worked with two local women, whom we are teaching to help the doctor. We are paying them so they are willing to learn these valuable skills. Their job is to inject pilocarpine into the skin of the new patients. If the skin is normal, it will start to sweat. If they have leprosy, they won't. That's when we move to the next stage—we paint the injection sites with iodine and sprinkle dry starch over them. The starch will stay white and dry on infected patches but turns dark blue on normal skin. This prevents us from accidentally treating healthy skin. The patients have no idea what we are doing. But when we see the dark blue, it's like a boost of joy to the entire staff since the patient is healthy and free to go back to their village with a certificate to prove they are safe. Sometimes, though, we are so overloaded that Thomas asks several intelligent lepers to give themselves the injections. Really, it's all hands on deck.

As I treat some of the lepers, I'll ask them how they are doing. Sometimes they say, "I am getting better small." This means I'm getting a little better, but is said with disappointment. Usually, I will raise my eyebrows, which causes them to add, "I thank God!"

If the leper is not doing well, they might hold up their feet and hands and say, "Too pain." Or they will point to the body and say, "Is one big ache!"

Despite all this, I need to make it clear that there are no rebellious spirits but instead a feeling of gratitude and a "God bless you!" when I am done treating them. It is the best payment in the world!

After working at the infirmary all day, I went straight to Father Neel's office to help him with paperwork. He's now started to use his right hand but I'm still writing his letters. I'm hoping this extra work will stop in another week or so.

Before dinner, we had a funeral for an older woman, Maria. She was a burnout case and finally died. I had treated her many times and she was well aware she was going to die soon. She even begged me to do her a favor. She had a pair of lovely shoes she wanted to be buried in. We put the shoes on her and conducted the burial service. When we finished the prayers, we left to get some tea. When we came back to make sure the gravediggers lowered her down properly, the shoes were gone. Her poor feet were sticking out of the mat bare. Father Neel was outraged and organized a search everywhere but they were never found. Since she had specifically asked me this favor, I was crushed. But on the other hand, the shoes really could help another woman. So, I guess that's how it is out here.

With all this talk of death, let me tell you some positive aspects as well. Our settlement here is very alive. We have a leather shop now, along with twenty more huts. There are little fires everywhere as the lepers use the food from their land to cook the food for their chop. Everybody works and is grateful for it. There are occasional disputes of boundaries and responsibilities but the village chief or one of his sub-chiefs handles it. Two days ago, a chicken disappeared and one man suspected another of stealing it. There was pushing and shoving until several of the men found leopard tracks. There's a female leopard in the area that has been causing problems. Anyway, a few hours later they found the feathers in the woods where the leopard had devoured it so the man apologized to the other man for accusing him. The chief made sure it was completely settled. That's our justice system.

My little Clarence has been letting me treat him. I've been stealing supplies from the infirmary because now I have access to it. We have regular dates when he comes to my hut and allows me to tend to him. I love helping him, but I fear seeing new patches, which means his days are slowly being whittled away.

Because of the time we are spending together, we are even closer. He doesn't say much, although I did find out something from him. Each afternoon, when I returned to my hut after school, there was a single flower on my bed. I had thought it was from Thomas and was going to say something to him, but I found it was Clarence. He knew how sad I was at losing Victoria and it was his way of trying to cheer me up. These lepers have so little but give so much. I assume he's roaming the woods each day and can find the flowers since he doesn't appear to work. With all the theft that goes on here, I also assume he's part of that business. But at least, nothing has been taken from me since the previous incident. Perhaps he has placed my hut out of bounds to his fellow thieves. Who knows?

Do you remember Gran'pa? He was the leper with white hair from Onitsha, who stayed with us when their taxi driver abandoned his group. Honestly, I thought he would be deceased when we came back from Otukpo because he was so frail, but he's doing just fine. In fact, for some reason Thomas can't explain, he actually seems to be getting better. He's even taken up with a woman leper in the settlement. She's a very sweet person with a plot of land on which she works every day. He helps too but really, he can only do so much. Later, she pounds fou fou for both of them and they sit by the fire like a happy couple, though marriage here is not always a formal affair like in our part of the world. Who can complain when it saves on the cost of a wedding?

Speaking of marriage, as you know from my previous letters, Thomas and I have gotten very close. He has been waiting to receive word to return to the Nigerian Government since they're the ones who paid his passage over here. However, Father Neel, through me, writes to the government and begs them to let him stay. We are even sending them some money for the loan, although we shouldn't have to do it. I know all of this because I write the letters for Father Neel. I make sure those particular letters are dripping with desperation and the best-spelled words with the neatest handwriting ever. So far, it's worked. Father Neel also trusts me not to say a word to Thomas that we are writing these letters, which is very awkward. But, I've kept my word.

Father Neel is trying hard to convince a doctor from London to come here permanently. When a new doctor does finally come and Thomas has to leave, I will know where I stand with him. So, we will see.

On a final note, we seem to be making progress on the image of leprosy. Before we came, the Nigerians felt that anyone with leprosy was dangerous. They still mostly believe that however, with the white man in close proximity to the lepers and treating them each day, several locals have decided they could work for us in the settlement, for pay of course. And taxi drivers and delivery-men, where they used to stop in Ogoja and drop off their loads, they now find it acceptable to drive into our settlement. Although it seems like little progress, it makes us feel that we are accomplishing something.

I am fairly exhausted and have to get up early tomorrow morning, so I will end this letter. As always, thank you so much for your letters. They cheer me up to no end, and I read them at least ten times. Please keep them coming.

Your Best Friend in the Bush,
Anna.

October 7, 1947

It was a rainy, overcast evening when a strange kit car pulled into the leprosy settlement and parked in front of the two-story building. Father Neel pushed back his chair and shuffled to the window. Staring down at the kit car, he noticed a driver he wasn't familiar with.

"Now who do you think that is?" he said to his assistant.

Anna got up and joined him. "Are we expecting anyone?"

"Always. And never."

They both watched as the driver exited the kit car holding a piece of fabric to protect himself from the rain. He went to the door behind him and opened it. Out stepped an older woman, in her later forties, followed by one in her twenties. They were both dressed as nuns and took a moment to shake out their clothes, before running to the shelter of the building and out of sight of the watchers.

"Well, my dear Anna, we may have some relief. And two of them! I'd hoped for more but we'll take whatever we can get, right?"

"Yes, we all could use some rest."

"Let's go and greet them," he said.

They made their way to the ground level where the two nuns were rubbing their legs, obviously fatigued from the long drive. Looking around the settlement, they chatted quietly with each other. When they spotted Father Neel and Anna, they straightened into a formal stance.

Father Neel stuck out his hand. "Hello and welcome to the Leprosy Settlement in Ogoja. And who might you be?"

Shaking his hand, the older one spoke first. "I am Sister Evelyn Bissett. This is Sister Janey Landon. Mother Mary Martin sent us. Are you Father MacKenna?"

"I am, although out here, I request everyone call me Father Neel. It's two less syllables and saves energy." They politely laughed.

"We have some news that will change that, I'm sure." Sister Bissett said it confidently, as someone with her age and experience might. "Mother Mary has given us documents to give to you. Shall we do it now or would you rather wait?"

"Well, that's sounds interesting; there is no reason to wait. Let me show you to my office."

They approached the stairs when Father Neel stopped them. "Oh, I almost forgot. This is Anna Goodwill. She is our only teacher out here. She helps me with administrative matters and will join us."

Anna shook hands with the two nuns and followed the group up to Father Neel's office. When they were all seated, Sister Bissett said, "Will our luggage be safe down there?"

"Oh yes. The driver won't leave until I pay him. Only then will he begin to unload it. Since he will be staying in Ogoja tonight, he has plenty of time, don't worry."

He leaned forward placing his palms flat on the desk. "So, what is the news you have for me?"

Sister Bissett pulled out two sealed packets. "I am allowed to tell you before you open the seals and read them."

She handed him the first one. "This packet contains news of the Irish raffle. It was a great success and raised over £7,000. One woman gave £1,100. Mother Martin was extremely happy and excited. She has enclosed the draft information in this packet. We delivered a confirmation of funds to the bank in Calabar before we made the trip up here. You may begin drawing the funds immediately."

Father Neel clapped his hands. "Oh my, what a gift from God! We are blessed indeed, and believe me, I have a hundred uses for that money. You two are turning into angels right before my eyes."

They both laughed along with Anna, who sat just behind them.

"Wonderful," she said continuing. "Mother Martin knew you would be extremely pleased. This brings me to the next order of business."

She slid the second packet to him. "It is with great pleasure that I have the task of informing you that his Holiness the Pope has signed your appointment to bishop. It is inside this envelope. Bishop Reynolds from Calabar received a letter from us instructing him to proceed to Ogoja for your ordination. Congratulations *Bishop* MacKenna."

Bishop MacKenna's eyes swelled with tears. He was speechless. With trembling hands, he opened the packet and read the order. It held a wax seal embossed from the Pope's ring. He lifted it up in the fading sunlight to see if it was real. It was.

"I-I think I would like to be alone please. Anna, would you show them a room to share for now until we sort everything out?"

"Certainly... *Bishop* MacKenna."

He seemed too stunned to reply as Anna led the two sisters to a vacant room—the one Isla McGinty had been in—the one Anna should have taken.

Once they were inside the room, Anna said, "I will have the workers prepare another bed and pay the driver so he can bring up your luggage. Why don't you wait here for your luggage to arrive? Then you can unpack and freshen up. When you're ready, I will escort you on a tour of your new home. Supper should be served soon, so I need to tell them to cook for two more. If you will excuse me, I will get everything set in motion."

"Thank you," Sister Bissett said. "We'll be waiting right here."

By the time the tour began, the rain had stopped and the sun was barely over the tree tops. As the women walked through the village, most of the lepers came out from their huts and lean-tos to get a glimpse at the new arrivals. Some were excited to see new white people coming to help, while others no doubt were sizing them up for a handout or worse, a little theft.

Anna introduced Sisters Bissett and Landon to the chief and sub-chiefs. She also managed to get Oluwa, Gran'pa and Thames in too. She was surprised at how well the women held their shock at seeing Thames' stumps protruding from his little body. They were seeing everything the place had to offer, both good and bad. Even

Esi came running out to shake their hands. "Mesdames, I make you black soap."

She pulled out two small bars of dark gray soap and handed them to the nuns. It was obvious she hadn't made the soap for them since no one had known they were coming. Yet, it didn't diminish the sincerity of her gesture.

"Thank you Esi," Anna said. "That is the soap we use here. It's made from palm oil. It doesn't look nice but it works fairly well."

Sister Landon, the younger one, stared at the misshapen lump, and tried to hide a frown. She might have no problem with a burnout like Thames but having regular soap was a basic necessity. For both of them, this was just the beginning of experiencing the differences between the bush and back home.

"Don't worry," Anna said, patting her shoulder. "You'll get used to it soon enough. That reminds me, let me show you the toilets."

Esi jumped up and down. "May I go, Madame?"

"No, I can handle it. But thank you for asking."

She was clearly disappointed and ran somewhere else, quickly forgetting all about the rejection.

"Here it is," Anna said, leading them to an area where two outhouses stood. "The W is ours and the M is Father Neel's—I mean Bishop MacKenna's and Dr. Chapley's. Inside, there's a collection of dried banana leaves, bits of paper and so forth to use. If we're lucky, we might have toilet paper." She opened the door letting dozens of flies out.

Holding up a metal tin, she continued. "We keep it stored in this. But first look for bugs and other creatures as they like to nest in it. Sometimes, a small brown snake curls up here but only during the rainy season. He's harmless and eats insects so don't hurt him. Just take your time and be careful. And depending on what you do here, this tin has lime powder. Drop a handful down the hole to keep the odor down please. The occupant after you will greatly appreciate it. Oh, and do this *after* you have used the leaves because you do *not* want to get lime on your private parts. And please wash your hands free of the lime powder when you are done. Don't wait on that."

"Does it ever get full?" Sister Bissett asked.

"Yes, it does. During rainy season, it can also flood which makes a mess. However, we will instruct the workers to dig a new one when it gets close to the top. They will come and move the structure over the new hole and cover up this one. Simple and effective."

The sisters nodded. It wasn't pretty but it was necessary.

They started the walk back to the building when Anna had something else to add. "Oh, and we have pans for your room so if you have to go during the middle of the night, use those pans. We don't want you walking around in the dark."

Sister Landon shook her head and chuckled. "No more flush toilets, I suppose."

"No, I'm sorry. There are many modern conveniences that we don't have here. However, there is so much that is better than back home. Give yourself a month and tell me how things are then."

"We will," they both replied.

They arrived at the supper table just as it was being laid out. The three sisters were already seated. Anna introduced everyone and watched as each one sized up the other. Sister Flores wore a polite smile, one Anna had seen many times. It always seemed as though she was pained to have to smile.

They waited for Bishop MacKenna but finally started without him. He showed up fifteen minutes later both excited and in shock. Dr. Chapley and the sisters congratulated him, and then asked him about the ordination.

"I will have to begin organizing it tonight. I'm sending the driver back with a letter for Bishop Reynolds to come this Sunday, which is only five days away. There is so much to do. Even though this is my honor, we will have another celebration like we had for Easter. Except there will be one mass held in Ogoja at the mission's church. Then, we will come back here to celebrate. The lepers will enjoy it, I'm sure."

Sister Flores spoke up. "Please make a list for us, and I will see that it all gets done."

"Of course I will, thank you. Anna, I'm going to depend on your writing and organizational skills to help me get everyone started in the proper direction."

"Certainly. Whenever you need me, let me know... *Bishop*."

He laughed. "Yes, Bishop MacKenna. It rather rolls off the tongue, don't you think?"

"Definitely," Dr. Chapley said, chuckling. "It does indeed."

"Oh, that reminds me Thomas. We have received the funds from the Irish raffle and I want to talk to you about plans for more infirmaries. Can you see me right after the meal?"

"More Funds? Now I'm eating even faster!"

The group of diners had a good laugh as they watched him pretend to shovel in food.

Soon, everyone at the table had welcomed the new sisters, asking them about their past, their experiences, and news of home. The first two to excuse themselves were the men. They went up to the bishop's office to discuss the expansion of the leper settlements.

When Anna finished, she left the new arrivals in the care of the other three nuns and excused herself. She first went to check on her two babies before going to her hut to work on lessons for the next day.

Around eight, an excited knock jolted her.

"Anna, are you in there?" This was a common greeting, although with a lamp on inside, every visitor knew she was there.

"Thomas, come in."

He burst through the door with a bottle of wine. "I've brought my best red. Not only are we celebrating the bishop's step up, but we're also celebrating that northeast settlement I wanted to start. Do you remember me talking about it?"

"Yes, I think so. Refresh my memory."

He removed the cork and poured two glasses. "Cheers!"

They touched glasses. "It's that piece of land that sits about twelve miles to the northeast. There's a trail to get there, a good one. It runs along a ravine for a good portion of the way and rarely dips down to the river. Because it's mostly elevated, it can't be washed out or flooded. It takes a good two-hour bike ride to get there. I know. I've made the trip twice. The influx of lepers we're experiencing come primarily from the northeast. If we expand there first, we can stem the tide and then focus on the bigger prize: Otukpo."

He swallowed some wine as he stared past Anna, deep in thought about all this. Anna could see how thrilled he was about the plans.

"Then, once Otukpo is in place, we are in business because we can establish an outer ring. It will allow me to ride counterclockwise—east to west—and stay a few days in each village before coming back from Otukpo. That's why I'm excited. We can finally make some progress. Some real progress!"

Anna held her glass up. "Well, here's to your progress. I mean *our* progress."

Thomas gulped some more wine and set his glass down. "Anna, I have an idea. Would you like to ride out to the northeast settlement site with me? Get some exercise? I need to make some topographical notes, which will take an hour or so. We could take a small basket of food and make a day of it."

"Gosh Thomas, I've ridden a bike around here but not out in the bush. I-I don't know."

He was determined. "Oh please! I'll be with you. Nothing will happen. Besides, I'm a doctor. If you fall, I can fix you. What do you say?"

Anna felt the wine and his excitement go to her head all at once. Four hours was a long time to be on a bike. But then again, how often did she ever have any real privacy with him? Even in her hut, there were always people around, listening, peeking in the windows. With a few more sips of wine, she made a decision.

"Sure, let's go. It'll be fun."

"Wonderful! We'll have a grand time, you'll see. And you'll get to see some new territory. I can't wait!"

Anna beamed. "Thomas, I'm excited that you're excited."

He slapped the table. "Great! Let's see how you feel after I beat you at cards."

"Yes, we will indeed. Just remember that prediction when the final tally is in. Now, pour me some more wine and shuffle up the cards."

The forest crunched softly under her feet, the air cool and dry. This was the 'tweening' time—the part of the day that wasn't yet evening and past the afternoon. The lepers loved the tweening and usually relaxed or talked with friends before they had to begin preparing the chop for supper.

It was during this slow time that Anna made her way to the secluded spot. There, standing where it was supposed to be, was her barrel. And it was full of fresh rainwater.

Anna's kit was tucked under her arm tightly, so as not to drop any of it. It was stuffed with two new items: a half coconut shell for rinsing and a small bottle of coconut milk for her hair.

She watched her steps, careful to avoid anything that might make a noise. That's when she noticed tracks in the earth—leopard tracks. It was impossible for her to know how old they were; she wasn't that skilled. Since it was coming on the dry season, the ground was loose and dusty. Deep prints like these appeared to have been made after a rain, the last one occurring two days ago. They were probably not recent. Still, she had to be cautious.

Anna undid her long tresses and leaned back into the barrel, letting her hair sink to the bottom for her ten-minute soak. Five minutes in, she heard a sound. Something in the forest was moving towards her.

Panicked, Anna pulled her dripping hair out of the barrel and looked around for a stick. She cursed for not having something to defend herself. She thought about dropping everything and running, but before she could decide what to do, a figure appeared from behind a large tree.

"This place dey okay, sista. No wahala. I dey for you."

Anna's heart raced. "Oh, Clarence! You scared me. I thought the leopard was coming to get me for sure."

"No wahala sista. Go wash una hair. I go watch."

She slowed her out-of-control breathing and collected herself. Scanning the entire forest, she resumed her soak.

When ten minutes were up, she pulled her hair out and mixed in the last of Grant's special shampoo. Once she was satisfied with the coverage, she combed it for another ten minutes while staring at Clarence. He said nothing. Although he was barely thirteen, she thought of him as a young man. Growing up in the bush made people age fast. He was a prime example of this.

When her hair was thoroughly combed, she dipped the coconut shell in the fresh water and rinsed the shampoo out. Then she applied the new ingredient: coconut milk. She brushed in the white liquid for another ten minutes, making sure it reached every strand of hair. With that accomplished, she rinsed it out and looked over to thank Clarence but he was gone. He always did that. He was more ghost than boy.

Because she had already bathed, she waded across the shallow river and walked back to the settlement. Now, she thought, I'm ready for Thomas, the bishop's celebration, and the next two days.

୨

The first of 'the next two days' was Sunday. It was Bishop MacKenna's ordination. After many meetings and discussions, it was decided that Anna would supervise the nursery and thus miss the actual ceremony. The nuns explained how they were required to witness the event and couldn't be at the nursery to watch the babies. They discussed the possibility of trusting the local women, which they did at night, but Sister Flores insisted someone from their staff be there. When Dr. Chapley offered to do it, Anna wouldn't let him.

"I get to play with my babies uninterrupted. To me, that's priceless!"

Anna spent her Sunday morning rolling around the nursery floor lifting Jonah and then Lily. She played with the other babies but those two always got the most attention from her. They were too big to cradle in her arms so their ritual was mostly playing with toys Anna put in front of them. A few toys in Nigeria went a long way.

The ordination would last an hour and a half and included a mass. With an extra thirty minutes before and after the ceremony for the nuns to get ready, Anna had a total of two and half hours of nursery duty. Two local women were there to help. The babies had been fed before she arrived with most of them eating a tiny bit of mashed food. So, all she had to do was let them crawl around until they stopped from exhaustion.

The final hour found the babies breathing steadily, deep asleep in their beds. Anna took the time to relax and think about her upcoming trip with Thomas. They were leaving tomorrow morning. She sat in a chair, brushing her hair and marveling at the effect of pure coconut milk. It didn't seem possible, but her hair was even softer and more luxurious. The suggestion from one of the women in Otukpo had been correct. It was a wonderful new twist to her hair care regimen.

She was sitting there, daydreaming about Thomas when Patrick appeared. "Sista, mail don come for you from Calabar."

He handed her a letter. She recognized the handwriting instantly. It was unmistakable. The return address confirmed it. Her hands trembled as she turned it over.

"I dey take the mail and go Calabar tomorrow with bishop, yeah?"

Anna dumbly stared at him. "Oh, yes. I understand. If I have some mail to send, I'll give it to him. Thank you, Patrick."

When he was gone, she nervously slid her nail along the flap and opened the envelope. Pulling out the pages, she found there were only two.

"*Dearest Anna,*

I hope this letter finds you well. Molly has told me she wrote to you about the tragedy that struck me. I lost Florence in childbirth and buried her with her family. Our girl was saved though. I named her Angelina as she is my little angel. I dote on her probably too much, but is that bad? I hope you are shaking your head no right now."

Anna was.

"What I am telling you, I know you will keep in the strictest of confidence. Without going into details, due to various wartime expenditures and debt, my father was desperate to receive financing from the Hatterton Bank of Liverpool. We thought we had everything set when suddenly, the loan was denied. When I enquired of the officer in charge of lending, I was met with the answer that our business was too risky. He assured me it had nothing to do with my recent breakup with Florence. However, my father had a source who discreetly informed him that because Florence was so upset, the bank decided not to move forward with the loan. This same source said that should I proceed with the marriage, my new father-in-law would approve the loan since he was not willing to see his daughter marry the son of a bankrupt grocer. When we announced our engagement, my father received a call from the bank to come in and discuss that loan. After we were married, the money came through and barely in time. You will never know how close it was. Now, I will spend the next ten years paying off my debt to my former father-in-law. Please understand that I did care for Florence and mourned for her, but now I must move on with my life.

When I heard you were leaving to help the lepers in Nigeria, I couldn't believe it. I had become extremely fond of you, as you know. However, since I was marrying, I could not place a hold on you. Now that I am a widower, the circumstances look different to me. I know life is fleeting. The war taught us that, which brings me to my point. You couldn't have known this, but I fully intended to ask you to marry me when the situation with Florence came up. I wish to remedy that now. Though I would have loved to say this to you properly, circumstances with my daughter won't allow me to come down there to see you. So, here it is: Would you give me the pleasure of becoming my wife? I hope you are shaking your head up and down now."

Anna's head wasn't moving. She was too stunned to do anything.

"Please write back to me as soon as you can due to the time lost in transit. However, if you must take your time, that's fine with me. You are worth the wait.

Lovingly waiting for your answer,
Clarence."

Anna's shaking hand set the letter down. Eyes wide-open, she was taking in everything around her: the babies, the local women, the room. Out of the window, she could see the lepers getting ready for the big party. They would perform special dances for the bishop. There would be food and plenty of drink. The celebration was soon to begin.

Could she leave all this and go back home where she would be Mrs. Clarence Pyle? Where she would have his children—her own children? Where she would live a genteel life? It was all too much, too sudden. She fully understood offers like this come around once in a lifetime. She needed to decide quickly but what her answer would be, she didn't know.

๙

"Are you ready?" Thomas said, sticking his head into her hut.

"Yes, I'm just finishing up something." She sealed the envelope, grabbed her hat and joined him outside. Oluwa was standing nearby with his hand out.

"Well, you're just the man I need," she said reaching into her pocket.

"Oluwa dey here for you," he said.

She placed a coin and the envelope in his hands. "Here's six pence for you. Take this letter straight to Bishop Reynolds and make sure he takes it back to Calabar. Understand?"

"Yes sista. Many thanks!" He took off running towards a kit car that was being loaded.

"Boy, he seemed excited," Thomas said plainly.

"Yes, anytime he has money for tobacco, he's excited. And please don't tell me again, I know it's bad for him."

"I'm not going to tell you that. But I am going to tell that I received a letter from a colleague about a promising new treatment for lepers. He told me that it actually retards the spread and in most cases, cures infected skin. They are still checking out the results but he's going to send me a sample to try as soon as he has an extra dose. I thought I would try it on your Clarence if you are okay with it?"

"Clarence?!" Anna jumped at hearing him say that name.

"Yes, Clarence. Are you okay?"

Anna caught herself. "Oh yes, Clarence. Of course. That would be wonderful," she said, still preoccupied with other thoughts.

"Alright," Thomas said, tabling the matter. "We can talk about it on the road. Saddle up and follow me."

Anna fastened her hair behind her head, tightened the hat's leather strap under her neck, and climbed on the bike. In the bush, riding a bike twenty-four miles was nothing, unlike back home where most people travelled no more than three or four miles. There were too many other options to ride that long.

As they headed out, the weather was perfect—cool and dry, yet sunny and bright. With a slight breeze, they were confident of not being knocked off the bike from a strong gust of wind.

In ten minutes, they had cleared the settlement and found the special path Thomas loved. It was surprisingly in good shape, its base made of shale covered with a few inches of soil. For the bush, this was as good as it got.

The ride out there was fast but at times scary. For a two-mile stretch, they paralleled a deep ravine. When the trail narrowed, pushing them close to the edge, Anna grew nervous. Her nervousness eased when the ravine disappeared and the path came level to the dry creek bed.

Along the way, they discussed the big party Bishop MacKenna had thrown to celebrate his ordination. There was the usual overindulgence in both food and drink, neither of which Thomas or Anna experienced. They knew they had this trip planned and didn't want to spoil it.

The time raced by as did the miles. Finally, they arrived safely at the spot.

Thomas put the bikes away checking them first for any mechanical issues, and then took off with notepad in hand to survey his proposed new settlement. While he was busy doing all of this, Anna took the provisions from the kits attached to their bikes and arranged a nice lunch. She watched him standing in the field pointing this way and that. Clearly, he was excited about this project.

It took him half an hour to complete his task and walk back to the lunch Anna had set up.

Spreading his arms wide like a conquering general, he announced, "I'm done with the work! Let our feast begin."

They had been eating for a few minutes in silence when Thomas spoke up. "You seem distracted by something. Is everything okay?"

Anna blinked several times. "Why yes, I'm sorry. With all the planning and work that went into the ordination, my head is all a jumble. But, I'm back now. I'm all yours."

"Okay," he said warily. "It's just that we have a long trip back and I want you paying attention. Fatigue can cause you to go over the edge and down into that ravine which would be serious trouble."

"Yes, I know. Now, let's talk about pleasant things, shall we?"

They passed the time going over his plans for where all the buildings would go and how it would all get built. He told her a school would go over there by a tall tree and the infirmary in that large clearing. He wanted it to be smaller than their current settlement.

"However, this site has plenty of room to grow. And, we wouldn't have to pay any chiefs for the land. It's here for the taking!"

Anna grinned at his unbridled enthusiasm. She wished she could share it with him.

When they had eaten, Anna packed everything up while Thomas checked the bikes one more time.

"You can never be too careful. Take care of your equipment and it will take care of you. That's my motto!"

"I'm glad one of us knows something about bikes," she said. "I feel safer knowing you have checked it out for me. Let's get going, shall we?"

"Absolutely," he said mounting his bike. "I'll lead."

They were halfway home when his bike stopped with a gnashing sound. Thomas checked it and saw the chain had caught something. He worked on it for a few minutes, believing the problem was fixed and mounted back up. By now, Anna had moved her bike ahead of him.

"Mind if I lead for a change?"

Thomas was surprised. "Why of course. By all means, lead on."

He fell in behind and maintained the standard hundred-foot gap to avoid visibility problems from any dust being kicked up. Soon, they approached the dangerous ravine section of the path, requiring their intense concentration on exactly where to steer their bikes. Anna picked a spot on the path ten feet in front of her and focused on that. That's why she didn't see the leopard crouching on an outcrop above the path, watching her prey draw nearer. And waiting.

As the first one neared, she tensed up shifting her stance to pounce. Anna came closer and closer to the danger, completely unaware of what was about to happen. The leopard waited and waited for the right moment. When Thomas was almost in its range, he looked to his left and saw the big cat.

"What the...?" He jerked the handlebars to the right—too hard—sending the bike off the edge.

"*Aaaiiieeeee!!*" he screamed, half riding and half falling down the rocky slope. Fortunately, this was a shallow section, barely twenty feet to the bottom, and his fall ended quickly. Yet there were hundreds of the jagged rocks, most having recently fallen down from the adjacent slope. The rocks had not been worn smooth by the river which ran fast in the rainy season.

Thomas lay on his back among the sharp rocks and next to the twisted heap that used to be his bike. Something was wrong. He could barely breathe.

In front of him, Anna had already stopped, turned around, and was coming back along the path to see what had happened. Panicked, she couldn't find Thomas anywhere. With the ravine being the only other place he could be, she feared the worst.

When she reached the spot he had gone over, she saw his tracks veer off the edge and knew the worst had happened. Immediately, she got off her bike and looked over. There he was, face up with blood everywhere.

"Oh my God, Thomas! What happened?"

He barely moved, not answering her. She looked farther back down the trail and saw a flatter portion that would allow her to safely make it down the slope and then back to where he lay. The trip was not totally without risk. Anna had to pick her steps carefully, slipping several times before scrambling along the rocky bed to his side. She fell to her knees and placed her hand on his ripped shirt. It was soaked with blood.

"Thomas!" she said hysterically. "Oh my God, how can I help you?"

He could barely lift his eyelids. "J-just stay with me p-please. It won't be long." His voice was weak and raspy.

"Let me go for help. I'll get someone and be back."

"No!" he said with an unexpected burst of energy. "Don't leave me here. She'll come and finish the job."

Anna looked around to see whom he was talking about. She saw no one.

"Who did this to you?"

She followed his gaze to the edge of the ravine where the cat had her head over the edge, watching them.

Anna whipped her head back to Thomas. "Did that knock you down here? Were you attacked?"

He nodded.

Anna glanced back up and saw nothing. "The leopard's gone now. Let me go for help."

"No!" he said again, forcefully. "I'm the only one w-who can f-fix me and I'm... bleeding internally."

Anna began crying. "Please don't leave me Thomas! Not you too. I can't take one more death."

He struggled to nod his head, the injuries and lack of blood taking their toll. Then he whispered something.

Anna placed her ear close to his mouth. "What did you say? I can't hear you."

He coughed up blood as he spoke. "Bury me next to Victoria."

Tears raced down her cheeks and splashed on his face, washing some of the blood away.

"Please don't go!" she cried placing her hands underneath his head.

"P-promise me, you'll stay here. H-help the lepers. Jonah."

"Jonah! What about Jonah?" She watched his lips for any movement.

"You are like Jonah. Read about him." He paused to take in more air. "Stay here… c-complete the mission. Have faith…" His voice gave out.

Anna looked over his tattered clothes. "No Thomas, you're going to be fine. Tell me what to do to help you. Please!"

It seemed as if calmness enveloped him suddenly. "Look, she's c-coming for me. It's my time to go." He was staring back up the ravine to the edge he had gone over.

Anna twisted her head around, fearing the cat was coming down the ravine to kill them both. She grabbed a rock ready to defend herself and searched frantically for the big cat. But it was not there.

"She must be gone now," Anna said. "I can't see her anywhere."

She turned back to Thomas as a light breath slipped out between his bloody lips.

"I l-love…" he coughed out.

Instinctively, she leaned down to kiss his cheek. As her lips touched his warm skin, she felt his chest slump, and he was gone.

Anna lifted her head to the heavens and screamed. Then, she buried her face in his bloody chest and sobbed.

17

October 13, 1950 – Three Years Later

"Students, please make sure you're ready for a test tomorrow on fractions. I expect your best effort. If you need help, my assistant will stay behind to work with you. Now have a good day!"

In unison, fifty-one children rose to their feet and clapped. Anna gathered up some papers, stacked them neatly, and then glanced at the girl beside her.

"Esi, please grade these tonight and have them ready for me in the morning."

"Yes Madame."

Anna closed her satchel and walked outside, leaving Esi to handle the necessary tutoring. Drawing in some of the fresh air, she stopped and looked around. It was a beautiful afternoon, and for that matter, a beautiful time of year. The rainy season had ended three months earlier, and the dry season still had two more months before it started. With moderate temperatures daily and the occasional rain shower to shake things up, life in the Leprosy Settlement in Ogoja was just right.

Anna stood a few feet away from the new school building when she heard her name called.

"Sista, I get wine for you!"

Anna saw a man leaning against the building, holding a dark glass bottle.

"Oluwa, you got it! Wonderful."

She walked over to him and took the bottle in one hand.

"Mama Mimi says she dey bring food for una chop tonight. You fit look for her when da sun is no more."

"Thank you for checking. I'll make sure my girl brings some plates and silverware to my hut. I'm hungry just thinking about her cooking."

Anna was lost in her thoughts and about to resume her stroll when she noticed Oluwa touching three fingers to his mouth.

"Oh, I almost forgot. Thanks for reminding me."

She handed him the bottle back while she reached into her pocket and pulled out a change purse. It took a few seconds before she found what she was looking for.

"Here you are," she said, handing him the money.

Oluwa's eyes widened. A full shilling! Usually she gave him a few pence, enough for two pipefuls of tobacco. But today, she gave him more. This would buy a small pouch loaded up with Nigeria's finest.

"Bless ya Sista! Bless ya."

He gave her back the bottle then performed a crude cartwheel, sending his shilling flying through the air. Anna stood there laughing as he panicked over the lost coin.

"It's over there," she said, pointing to a patch of grass.

When he found it, he put the coin up to his lips and kissed it. "Oluwa money miss road! (*I'm throwing money around.*)"

"You sure are, now don't lose it. Have a nice day."

He immediately ran off in search of the settlement's exclusive tobacco vendor, an arrangement that no doubt put free tobacco in the pipes of a chief or sub-chief.

Each time she gave Oluwa money for tobacco, she heard Thomas whispering in her ear. "That smoke is no good for these people. Or any people for that matter."

"I guess if the leprosy doesn't kill him first then the tobacco will," she said out loud.

"Are you talking to me?" Janey Landon said, coming up from behind Anna.

"Oh, sorry. I was talking to myself. Thomas is punishing me again for giving Oluwa tobacco money."

"If that's the case, he's going to be mad at me because last week I gave him a few pence for some unimportant errands here and there."

"Don't we all. Are you already finished at the infirmary?"

"Yes. I wanted to catch you before you disappeared somewhere. Would you like to join me for a river bath in an hour or so? Since we're all out of patients, Sister Whelan wants to take advantage of the free time and dip her toes in the water, and more likely the rest of her too."

Anna shook her head. "No, I can't. I have my favorite bottle of wine and Mama Mimi is bringing supper to my hut. Plus, I'm going to spend time with Thomas."

"I understand. We'll just have to get clean without you."

Anna patted Janey on the shoulder and continued her stroll through the sprawling settlement. After four years of steady growth, it had fairly stabilized. With three outlying leprosy settlements now in operation, their infirmaries absorbed a large amount of the new lepers. Thus, migration to Ogoja had almost stopped, allowing for a consistent daily life.

She moved along the well-worn dirt path, the main one that had been compacted from years of use. It was as hard as any concrete block. Wisps of smoke drifted over the huts as the inhabitants prepared their daily chop. Some of it smelled good.

Anna looked around and noticed how every hut bore some unique touch. Any bit of waste and scrap was fastened to the walls, covering up openings or simply making a personal statement about the occupants. Even though the huts had started out the same, that was no longer the case.

Completely surrounding each hut were rows of plants. Not only did the land provide food for the entire settlement, but it kept curious busybodies from getting too close to the window openings. Anyone willing to pick their way through tomato vines and okra plants to peek into someone's hut would be easily seen. Then they'd be summarily dealt with. Anna had witnessed the tribal court and the whippings handed out afterwards. Thank God it was rare!

As she approached the leatherworker's shop, she spotted Gran'pa inspecting some of the leather goods made in the settlement. She laughed to herself knowing he had no money to buy anything. At least looking was free.

After a pleasant stroll, she reached her destination: a small plot of land bordered by a low wooden fence. Anna gently and quietly lifted the latch and entered. To her left was a rectangle of freshly turned earth. The white cross at the head bore the name Thames. Bishop Neel had performed the service, struggling impossibly to get through it without completely breaking down. Thames was the son he'd never have. Even this morning at breakfast she'd noticed his red eyes. He would certainly be grieving for a long time.

She said a prayer for Thames before walking over to Sister Browne's grave. There, she spoke out loud.

"Victoria, every time I take a bath in the stream I miss you. I really miss talking to you about all the comings and goings in the settlement. You always knew more about it than I did, although that sounds rather selfish of me to say. I truly regret not getting to know your background more. I wish we would've had more time together."

Anna drew in a deep breath and exhaled. The noise of the settlement suddenly went unnoticed as she shifted over to another grave. At this one, she went to her knees and set down the wine bottle. Pausing for a good while, she again spoke out loud.

"Thomas, it's been three years to the day since I lost you. Today, I purchased your favorite wine and will have a nice meal this evening. If you care to join me, I'll have a plate for you."

Her eyes filled with tears.

"Three years and you still do this to me," she said, taking out a handkerchief to wipe her cheeks.

The grass completely covered his grave and it had been recently cut. She could still smell it.

Anna silently said a prayer before finally dusting herself off and leaving the cemetery with a heavy heart. It was a ritual she did every year.

Two hours later, Anna was comfortably seated at the table inside her hut with two glasses of wine. She had already refilled hers once and was feeling the effects of the second.

"Thomas, I have a glass of wine ready for you. The cards are shuffled and ready for our usual game. If you'd care to join me, I'd be grateful."

Suddenly, there was a knock at her door. Anna stared at it, confused. It had to be the wine.

When the next knock repeated itself, the door visibly moved. Someone was actually there.

"Come in?" she said weakly and confused.

The door swung out and the opening was filled with a large black figure.

"Sista, I don bring for una to chop."

It was Mama Mimi. Anna had completely forgotten. She jumped up and helped the woman with the stacked plates.

"Oh, I'm sorry. Let me take these from you."

Anna set the plates down gently and paid Mama Mimi. When she was alone again, she returned to her chair and stared blankly at the food. It was all her favorites, names she still found hard to pronounce.

Most of the food was spicy and all of it well cooked. It took her a moment to clear her head from the wine before saying a blessing over it. When she was done, she began eating her meal in silence, drinking only a little more wine.

She had almost overdone it. And with no food in her stomach! It was stupid. After she had eaten as much as she wanted, she lifted her glass and made a toast.

"To the best, most caring doctor who ever came to the bush. I miss you every day, Thomas Chapley, M.D."

She finished off her glass then poured the remainder of the bottle into her glass leaving his full and untouched. Then she continued talking to him as if he were there.

"You know, I never understood your final words, but I think I do now. You mentioned Jonah, my little boy. I thought you were talking about him but you were actually talking about the prophet Jonah, who God told to go to Nineveh. He wanted Jonah to tell the citizens there that they would all be destroyed if they didn't repent and accept Him as the one true God. Yet Jonah was scared and didn't want to go because he knew as soon as he told them, they would kill him. Instead, he went on a boat in the opposite direction. However, a storm came up and the crew members threw him overboard assuming he was the cause of their misfortune. A giant sea creature swallowed him and it was inside the belly that he prayed and repented. Three days later the creature spit him out on land and Jonah carried on with his mission. When he reached Nineveh, he preached God's message and instead of killing him, the citizens repented and were spared destruction. After that, Jonah became an incredibly effective prophet.

"Now I get it. You saw clearly my mission: I must stay here and help these lepers, no matter what might come my way."

She raised her glass again. "Thomas, your good works continue and your dying words shall not go to waste. Please watch over me if you can, and keep me away from danger."

She took a long sip of wine. "I still miss you, but I plan on moving on just as soon as I beat you at cards. Are you ready?!"

A few rays of sun had filtered through the trees as Kim set the hot water pot in front of her. Instead of making her precious tea, Anna sat there rubbing her temples. Last night was one of the few times she had finished off an entire bottle of wine by herself, even trading glasses with Thomas to drink the last of his. Now, she was paying the price.

"Morny-O," Esi said, plopping down next to her. "Here are da papers, Madame."

Anna gazed at the stack in front of her, touching the hot water pot. That's when she remembered to fix some tea, ignoring her assistant while she set the leaves to steep. Only then did she pick up the papers and begin to review them.

"Madame, I'm afraid it catch me."

"Speak *English* please," Anna said, irritably.

"Sorry, Madame. I'm afraid of the test. I want to get certificate very bad."

"Esi, you want to get *a* certificate very *badly*."

"Yes, Madame. I'm sorry."

Anna poured a cup of tea and drank a good portion of it. She also took in some fresh water. As she did, she felt the coolness of the morning and the shade they were enjoying. The breakfast table was under an enclosed section of the new building which housed the kitchen, dining room (both indoor and out on the patio) and food storage. This structure had been built at the same time the school was built thanks to the money from the Irish lottery.

Anna addressed the only other occupant at the table. "I know this test is important to you, but I also know you can pass it. You are ready to obtain your teaching certificate."

She placed her hand over Esi's. "Why don't you take today off and study. That way, you'll be good and ready for your test tomorrow. Okay?"

"Okay, Madame. Thank you!"

Like a jackrabbit, she hopped up from the table and ran back to her hut. Even though she usually acted like an adult, she was only fifteen—a mere child in England.

Just missing her was Dr. Hampton. He watched as she ran right by him.

"My, she's quite excitable today."

Anna looked up at the tall, bearded man. "Yes, she has to take her certificate test tomorrow and she's very nervous."

"She seems fairly bright. I'll bet she passes."

"I sure hope so because frankly, I need the help. The bishop has been after me to travel to the other settlements and supervise their teaching methods." She took a sip of her tea, holding the cup with both hands. "By the way, how is your wife adjusting?"

"Slowly. Between the bottomless pit of the latrine, the ugly looking soap and the dangerously large bugs, there have been a few heady moments for her. But I believe she's turned a corner now. The sisters took her for a bath in the stream yesterday afternoon and once she got over her lack of modesty, she very much enjoyed it."

Anna chuckled. "Good. We're all looking forward to the physiotherapy and rehabilitation techniques she can teach our sisters and locals. Hopefully I can pick up on some of it. I also understand she's a musician."

"Yes, she excelled in just about every stringed instrument. She's a rare talent—one who had many options, the least of which was following me around the world."

"That's wonderful! I've wanted to start up a band for the lepers. They love being involved in activities like that. Perhaps she can help?"

"She'll be along shortly. You can ask her yourself."

Dr. Hampton had been at the settlement for four months. His wife had arrived several days earlier. While he was committed for another eight months, his wife would leave in 60 days.

"I have to tell you Doctor that we plan to use her up before she heads back home."

He laughed. "Well, leave some for me!"

Kim arrived with breakfast and they made small talk before Dr. Hampton brought up another subject.

"Say, I examined that Clarence of yours yesterday. The last doctor put him on a new drug, mostly as an experiment and I've continued it. I can't believe I'm saying this but his patches are no longer growing. Some of them actually appear to be shrinking. I've ordered more of the drug because I want to spread the experiment to a select group of patients."

Anna put her fork down before she dropped it. "Are you sure?"

"I am. Whether or not it's the drug remains to be seen. However, several medical journals have touted it as the latest miracle in treating leprosy. I believe it may have come just in time for your Clarence because he was showing signs of burnout, especially in his fingers. Now, it's entirely stopped."

Dr. Hampton went on to explain that the drug he was using was a tablet of DDS (diaminodiphenylsulfone) and taken by mouth twice a week. The generic term was Dapsone, and the doctor was very excited about it.

"If the reaction by Clarence is typical, we could possibly see a repatriation of lepers to their villages. Wouldn't that be something to write home about?"

"Indeed!" Anna said, feeling better. "But even if it only stops the disease's progress, I'd be happy with that."

Dr. Hampton was about to say something else when an ashen Bishop Neel appeared.

"Excuse me for interrupting your breakfast, but Anna, could I speak to you in my office?"

"Certainly. Besides, I'm finished."

She rose from the table and excused herself. When she came close to the bishop, she put her hand on his shoulder. "I know how much you miss Thames. How are you getting along?"

"Huh?" he said, distracted. "Oh, Thames. Why yes, his departure still wounds me deeply. Thank you for asking."

Anna was confused. Whatever was on his mind had nothing to do with Thames' death. She said nothing more and followed him up to the second floor.

Bishop Neel let her into his office and looked both ways down the hall before closing the door. As he sat down, she noticed his deep-set, sunken eyes and poor color. Something was definitely wrong.

"Anna, I need your help once again. As you know, Patrick came back yesterday from Calabar carrying the funds from the bank. I hid the money here in my office in what I thought was a safe place. It has always been so before. However, between last night and this morning, some monster found my hiding place and took the money. *All of it!* Oh, it's such a despicable act! All we want to do is help these people and somebody did a thing like this. Sometimes, I just want to give up!"

Bishop Neel shook his head several times. It seemed as if he was near an emotional breakdown.

"Look," Anna interjected, "this money was ours, not just yours. The thief stole from all of us. You don't need to bear all the weight of this crime."

He took out a handkerchief and dabbed at his eyes. "Oh yes I do. I'm a bishop and the leader here. Everything is my responsibility. *Everything!*"

She let him work through his feelings before speaking. He had done the same with her before.

"How can I help?" she asked.

That brought him back to the present. "Ah yes, your help. I called you up here for a reason. I need you to do two things. First, I need you to locate your little Clarence and see if he can discover who took the money and possibly recover it. Of course, I would reward him. Then I need you to go with Patrick back down to Calabar. You must carry another withdrawal slip and obtain more funds. I know you haven't been away from the settlement for quite some time and hoped that perhaps you'd like to do some shopping there or whatever. It would be a great help to me."

"Do you really need me to go? I have to teach class today and my assistant is studying for her teaching certificate test, which I was going administer tomorrow after church. With today being Saturday, you know I can't even access the funds until Monday."

"There's a lot going on here that you don't know about. Patrick has been taking more and more time to make the trip down there and back. He says he has to repair the vehicle, yet every trip takes more time than the previous one. I'm assuming he has a girlfriend along the route and is spending some time with her. The reason I need you to go is because the last few times I've sent Patrick with a withdrawal, especially right after I have withdrawn funds, they have refused, suspecting some type of fraud. Whenever this situation has come up, I have gone down there myself. With the church service on Sunday and the upcoming baptisms, I simply can't be spared. I know you have an account there, and they are familiar with you. I can't send one of the sisters because they have no money, or at least not in any bank accounts. This trip is urgent because I need the money to pay the workers. I was supposed to pay them today."

He leaned towards her. "Anna, I promise I wouldn't ask you to drop what you are doing and leave unless it was urgent. If you leave within the hour, you'll be there by evening before it gets dark and unsafe on the roads. Then you can shop on Sunday since the markets never close and by Monday morning, you can make the withdrawal and be on your way back."

Anna exhaled, absorbing all his words. "Okay. I'll go pack and make the arrangements. Is there anything else you need while I'm down there?"

"Oh yes! Please check on the mail. Patrick said there wasn't any for us, but I feel he was less than truthful. Something is up with that boy and perhaps you can find out for me."

"I'll do my best. Please have the withdrawal slip completed and I'll meet you at the kit car after I've finished packing. I'll talk to Clarence right away."

Anna left the bishop and hurried to find Esi. She was studying on a bench near the sisters' garden, her usual spot to read and relax.

"Esi, I need you to find Clarence right away. Then I need you both to come to my hut. If you can't find him, come anyway. Do you understand?"

"Yes Madame."

Fifteen minutes later, Anna was almost packed when Esi arrived with Clarence in tow.

"Esi, I have to run an urgent errand for the bishop to Calabar. I'm leaving in a few minutes and won't be back until late Monday. I need you to stop studying for your test and teach class today. Here's the lesson."

She handed Esi a sheaf of papers.

A large frown spread across the young girl's face. "But, when do I take the certificate test?"

"I'm sorry but that will have to wait. I'll give you plenty of time to study when I get back. Now, please run along to the class as I need to talk to Clarence privately."

Esi made eyes at the boy before leaving which Anna noticed. "I guess you two are growing closer. Esi seems to be able to find you whenever I need you."

"She be the right woman for me. We get married but ground no level (*We would get married except I don't have enough money*)."

Anna grinned. He was a year older than Esi, who was too young to get married. But here, that didn't matter. With life expectancies very low in the bush, and with lepers even lower, things happened fast. Marriage. Babies. And not necessarily in that order.

"Short of money, you say? We may be able to fix that. The bishop had some money stolen and obviously, someone around here took it. It had to be someone who saw Patrick return from Calabar. The thief must have crept up to the bishop's office on the second floor, either last night or early this morning. The bishop told me he will give you a reward if you can find it. The money was in a black leather pouch almost this big."

She formed her hands into the size of the pouch.

"Listen, the bishop is really worried. See what you can do and bring it directly to me. Do you understand?"

"I dey hear una word."

"Good. Now get to it!" Before she could finish her sentence, he was gone from her hut.

Ten minutes later, Anna set her bag down on the hard mud floor of a large hut. "Where are my hugs today?"

A little boy turned around to check out the familiar voice, and started running towards it.

"Moda! Moda! (*Mother! Mother!*)"

She scooped him up in her arms and kissed his cheeks while he giggled loudly. "There's my Jonah. How are you doing today?"

Before he could answer, another child came running, shouting the same thing. "Moda! Moda!"

Since she was long past being able to hold two four-year-olds at one time, Anna went to her knees. "Lily, my love. It's been less than a day since I've seen you. Did you miss me?"

She buried her head in Anna's chest. "Ya Moda, ya!"

"Play now?" Jonah begged.

"No, I'm sorry. I'll be gone for a few days and needed to give you some hugs before I left. I want you to know I love you both and will see you when I get back. Please be good for the piccan watcher (babysitter). She tells me when you've misbehaved."

They all stared at the woman at the rear of the hut, who nodded.

Now that Anna had their attention, she picked each one up, inspected their bodies and kissed them on the cheek. Then, she got up, dusted herself off while pushing the children back until finally, she managed to close the door.

Patrick was sitting in the kit car with the bishop standing next to him, leaning against the frame. He helped her load her suitcase in the rear before handing her some documents.

"Here's the paperwork for the bank. Everything should be in order. If not, I'm sure you can make them understand."

She tucked it safely away and was surprised when he hugged her.

"Patrick," he said, "please drive carefully. And Godspeed to you both."

"We'll be fine Bishop," she said. "Don't worry. Besides, Patrick will take good care of me. Right Patrick?"

"Patrick get you safe to Calabar. Just hold on."

Bishop Neel patted him on the shoulder and stood there as Patrick said a prayer. When he was ready, he started up the kit car and took off down the long settlement road leaving a trail of red dust behind.

⚘

An hour south of Ogoja, Anna shifted uncomfortably in her seat. She was having a hard time forgetting the small white patches she had just seen on both Jonah and Lily. She knew from experience that the earlier patches hit a child, the shorter their life expectancy. This new drug Dr. Hampton was using on Clarence wouldn't be fit for the children since Thomas had said he was worried about using it on Clarence, especially with his kidneys and liver not fully developed. While the drug was powerful and might save a child from leprosy, it would likely cause organ failure and kill them even faster than leprosy. It was a cruel choice. For the next hour, she could think of nothing else.

When Patrick pulled off the road at their usual stop, she fixed her mind to change the subject. But first, she needed to refill her canteen and go to the bathroom. She left Patrick to fill the kit car with petrol while she went off to take care of business.

She was in the outhouse when she heard yelling. A man with a deep voice boomed out something in a tribal dialect. He sounded extremely passionate. When she was done, she stepped from the outhouse and searched for the voice. It was fifty yards away, obscured by some dense trees. Whatever was going on there sounded important.

With her canteen full, she went to the kit car and sat down, yet Patrick was nowhere around. This was unusual since someone always stayed with the kit car. Luggage and other valuables had been known to sprout legs and walk off. She assumed he was off paying for the fuel. With some free time, she opened a sack and decided to have some of the food Kim had packed.

It wasn't long before she finished her food and looked around for Patrick. He had vanished. This could be the first clue as to why he had been taking so long to make the trip to and from Calabar.

When it was long past the time they should be on their way, Anna reluctantly left the kit car and made her way towards the deep voice in the woods. As she came nearer, there were at least fifty men standing before a man perched atop a tree stump. He was passionately waving his arms and pointing here and there. There was much clapping and hoots in agreement with whatever the man was saying. Anna finally spotted Patrick on the fringe of the group and quietly went to him touching him on the shoulder. As soon as he recognized her, he looked panicked and quickly walked back to the kit car with her. After a brief inspection to make sure nothing was missing, he started it up and took off.

Anna waited until they had covered several miles before bringing up what she'd just seen.

"Patrick, what was that man talking about?"

"Dat no be for you sista. Everting dey fine, no worry."

She decided to remain silent and let him drive. There was nothing worse than a preoccupied driver in Nigeria. It usually resulted in someone crashing.

When they arrived at the Catholic mission in Calabar, Anna was tired and went straight to bed. Patrick, though, had plans to head into the city. He said he'd sleep at a friend's house and would meet her at the bank Monday morning at nine. Anna agreed.

Since her bag was light, she bid him goodnight and carried it inside the mission residence where an extra cot always awaited, along with several kind sisters in need of fresh conversation. It was the usual price of admission.

The next morning, Anna slept late and awoke refreshed. She dressed in a light cotton dress and comfortable shoes, perfect for walking around Calabar and shopping.

After traveling a few blocks, she found the town wasn't much different than her last trip eight months ago. From past experience, she knew the safe parts to explore and seedier areas to avoid. She looked over her list of items to buy, which included shampoo, tea and possibly some nice fabric.

By two o'clock, she had a sack filled with all three items, plus two bottles of wine and was wandering back to the mission when she spotted a cemetery. It was a smaller one, which told her it may be a 'white man's' cemetery. When she saw some of the names on the first headstones, she realized it was. Against her will, she strolled through the cemetery looking at each one.

At a crude concrete block set in the ground, she felt her heart stop. The inscription read: "Gene Eppers or Grant Eaton—shot in Ogoja." There was no date of birth or death. With no money to ship his body back to England, someone—likely the Nigerian government—buried him as cheaply as possible. There was no other choice.

Anna stood there staring at his grave. She wasn't sure what she felt. She remembered him on the ship and the times they had spent together in Lagos and Ogoja. She also thought about all the nights she'd contemplated marrying him. That's when feelings for Thomas came up. Now her heart truly began to ache. Death was such a cruel separation. Before she grew too emotional, she turned away from his grave and left.

It was Monday and Anna counted the money again just to make sure it was all there. Satisfied, she carefully folded the bills up and put them in a pouch that happened to fit in a large pocket on her dress. When she was confident it wasn't going anywhere, she thanked the bank teller and went outside.

The hot sun was just hitting the bank's entrance and felt warm on her forehead. She looked around for Patrick but didn't see him. It was twenty minutes after nine.

Where is he?

By ten o'clock she was very concerned. Occasionally, she thought she spied a local hidden in the shade of some doorway, staring at her as if they knew she was carrying a large sum of cash. One of the reasons they went everywhere with a driver was protection. Not that

Patrick would lay down his life for them, but he would certainly put up a fight. Now, she was standing here waiting for Patrick to drive up in the kit car with her luggage safely in back, so they could get back to Ogoja in one piece and avoid the dangerous road at night.

Reluctantly, she went back inside the bank to get out of the scorching sun. Staring out the front window, she saw the locals walking by or riding bicycles. The occasional truck sputtered past, belching smoke everywhere. Still, there was no sign of Patrick.

The tall wooden clock behind her chimed twelve times. When a bank clerk politely shooed her outside so they could close at noon for lunch, she knew something was seriously wrong. As she stood in the alcove, her hand over her pouch, she was certain Patrick wasn't coming. She would have to find someone else to drive her back to Ogoja, someone she could trust.

Anna thrust her hand back into her pocket.

A person could get killed for the amount of money I'm carrying.

She shook her head in disgust and thought about crying. Instead, she backed up against the bank's door and prayed for help.

18

Bishop Neel lowered his feet to the cool concrete floor and searched for his glasses. After finding them, he took several deep breaths to clear his mind. Then he struck a match to light an oil lamp. This gave him the ability to read his pocket watch, which told him it was past three a.m., way too late for a kit car to arrive. He removed a thick robe from a wall hook and wrapped it tight around his knee-high nightshirt, before sliding his feet into a pair of well-worn slippers. When he heard the car doors slam, he shuffled to the hallway and awaited his visitor.

The footsteps tapped out a rhythm as they climbed upward. Whoever it was, they knew the way to his quarters. When they reached the top landing, Bishop Neel was able to see the person.

"Ah, Anna it's you," he whispered. "Please come to my office."

They walked in silence—Anna carrying her travel bag—until he had closed the door and fit himself into the chair behind his desk. When Anna was seated and facing him, he noticed her haggard face.

"Please tell me that you are alright," he said.

She reached into her pocket and produced an envelope. "Here's the money. I can't tell you how relieved I am to be rid of it. It was more than an adventure. I also believe I can tell you what has been going on with Patrick."

Bishop Neel counted out the money and placed it in his robe pocket. "When you didn't appear for supper, I knew something was up."

Anna gave him the details of the first stop on the road to Calabar and the man speaking in the woods. Then she told him how Patrick had been hours late to meet her at the bank. Apparently, he had been to another rally and lost track of time. She wasn't sure what it all meant, but it was clear that Patrick's mind was on something other than his job.

"What do you make of all this, Bishop? I was extremely afraid holding the money and waiting for him. He doesn't even seem to be the same person we've known all these years."

Bishop Neel removed his glasses and rubbed his eyes. That's when he noticed Anna's normally lustrous dark hair was ratted and dirty. There was dust all over her face too, common from such a long drive.

"I'm afraid the independence bug has bitten Patrick. And it may have bitten a few others around the settlement as well. I have been corresponding with my brethren throughout Nigeria and the movement is just starting. After a time, the people dislike being lorded over by foreigners. It happens in every British colony… *eventually*."

"But what does it mean for us?"

"It's hard to say. If it grows large enough, the Crown will have to make a decision. Either we hand the keys over and wish them the best or we bring in the troops to put them back in their place. Either option can mean trouble for us, especially where war is involved. Even if we hand them back their country without firing a shot, within a short time there is usually a civil war as various factions fight for control. I'm fairly certain that would happen here."

Anna stared at a spot on the wall. "Patrick simply lost his desire to drive me or show up on time. It was like he has already quit his position but didn't tell anyone."

Bishop Neel scribbled some notes to himself. "Yes, I'm going to have to talk with Patrick and perhaps sack him. I don't know. He's been such a superb driver for so long. And he knows how to repair that kit car. He's saved us a great deal of money. I hate to lose him, but I may have no choice. These rabble-rousers serve up a mighty powerful tonic, especially to empty vessels like Patrick. It can be intoxicating for a young man with little to look forward to."

"Gosh, I would hate it if this movement forces us to leave this place, especially when we're getting so close to finally helping these people. I mean we are now providing real care!"

Bishop Neel put his glasses back on. "Don't you worry too much. There are three main tribes in Nigeria and each one wants to rule the entire country. Patrick is from the Igbos. They are the only tribe that would be happy returning the country back to its individual parts, just like they were before we pasted them all together. The other tribes are all so fractured, it will be very hard for them to put together a united front and accomplish anything of real importance. However, I shall keep an eye on the whole mess. Now, did you find any mail?"

Anna stood up and opened her travel bag. "Yes, there was quite a bit. One letter was for me so I removed it but here are the rest."

She handed him the stack.

"I talked with the postman and he said it's been sitting there for a month. Obviously, Patrick forgot to pick it up last time."

He looked through the envelopes and shook his head. "It's just as I thought. Well, I'm wide awake now, so I'm going to stay up and go through all this. I'll let you turn in for the night."

He rose to show her out.

When he opened his office door, he whispered, "Please let me know if your Clarence has found anything. I am most anxious about that matter."

"I will," Anna whispered back. Then she left Bishop Neel to his work and staggered through the darkness to her hut where she collapsed on her bed and passed out.

A hurried knock on her door made her sit upright in her bed. Anna reached over, lit her lamp, and looked at her watch. It was almost two in the morning. It had been two days since she had returned from Calabar and still, she hadn't caught up on her sleep. "Who is it?" she called out.

Without answering or asking for permission, a dark figure jerked her door open and lurched in. Anna swung the lamp around and saw Clarence's bloody face. A shot of adrenaline raced through her body.

"Oh my goodness!" she said, as she grabbed a small towel and dipped it in her water basin. "Clarence, sit down and let me tend to you. What happened?"

"I find the stealer and e dey bad. I go dig 'em out."

"Let me take care of you. My goodness, you have cuts and scrapes all over. Did you get the money?"

"I don recover una money." He produced the leather pouch and opened it up. It was filled with bills.

"Who was it? Who took the money?"

Clarence's face grew dark. In a low, angry voice, he said, "The man don die."

The shock of those words stopped Anna. "Okay…" she said, before continuing her nursing work. "I suppose we will find out soon enough"

She worked on him for a few more minutes until she was out of bandages.

"I have to go the infirmary and get more supplies because I can't send you out with these deep cuts." She cupped his chin with her hand, lifting his head so she could stare directly into his eyes. "I'll be right back and you'd better be here. Understand?"

Clarence reluctantly nodded.

In the darkness, Anna picked her way along the beaten path carefully, having left her lamp behind. In her pocket was the leather pouch full of money along with a key. The key had been Sister Victoria Browne's and was among her personal effects when Bishop Neel asked her to go through them. Surreptitiously, Anna had kept the key in case of an emergency—like now.

There was barely enough moonlight to help her avoid stepping off the path, although she probably could've closed her eyes and made it there just fine. As she walked through the settlement, the bugs made their presence known, chirping and buzzing loudly. Occasionally, she heard bats fluttering overhead in search of the same insects making all the noise. She breathed in clean air, devoid of the smoke so common during the day. Instead, the fresh smell of garden vegetables and fruits which flowered in October filled her head.

Moving slowly and deliberately, the trip took several minutes before she finally arrived at the infirmary door. The overhang from the upper floor created a dark shadow and prevented any moonlight from reaching the lock hanging from the hasp. Anna fumbled with the key, dropping it on the concrete floor. The sound of metal striking the floor echoed off the walls like an alarm. She lowered herself to her knees and spread out her hands searching for the missing key. When she had it again, she looked around to see if anyone had been alerted. Nobody was stirring.

This time Anna carefully inserted the key into the slot and quietly unlocked it. She set the lock down on the ground and gently pulled the door open avoiding a loud squeaking sound. Then she gingerly picked her way to the nearby unlocked supply cabinet. In total darkness, she felt for the bandages and gauze, wrapping up a small bundle with a large bandage. With this done, she closed the cabinet and slowly retraced her steps back to the entrance.

Again, falling to her knees, she thrust her free hand out searching for the lock. She felt something but it wasn't a lock; it was more like a piece of hard leather. A hand clamped hard around her wrist and jerked her into the dull moonlight.

"Now I have you, you *thief!*" a voice shouted.

Anna lay flat on her chest with two shoes near her face. Another hand gripped the same wrist ensuring she would stay in this position.

Again the voice yelled. "Our supplies are always missing, and I bet you thought I'd never catch you, huh?!"

Anna recognized the voice. Twisting her face up, she managed a weak response. "It's me, Anna! I can explain. Please, let go of me."

Sister Flores bent down and inspected her catch. "So you're the thief. Well, now we will all know!" She released her grip sending Anna's hand smashing into the dirt. "Get up! We're going to see the bishop right now!"

Anna dusted herself off and rubbed her wrist. Sister Flores had squeezed it tightly, surely leaving a bruise. "All right, let's go," Anna said.

Sister Flores locked up the infirmary taking Anna's key with her. Then the two walked up the steps to the residence floor. Sister Flores knocked hard on Bishop Neel's door.

"Bishop! Bishop Neel, I need you now!"

"Okay," an exasperated voice said. "One minute please."

A light filtered under his door while they stood there, listening to him put a robe on and locate his slippers. The door opened revealing the bishop.

"Ladies, it's very late. What is it that can't wait till morning?"

Sister Flores stood close to him. "I've caught the thief stealing the medical supplies from the infirmary."

She forced a bundle of bandages on him, which he looked down at.

"Good work ladies. Where is the thief?"

"Right here!" she said, pointing at Anna.

Bishop Neel glanced at Anna and looked behind her. "Where? I don't see him."

"Right here!" she said putting her index finger on Anna's chest, who was smiling nervously.

The bishop laughed. "I still don't see him. Please ladies, I'm too tired for this."

By now, Sister Flores was even madder. "Bishop, Anna is the thief!" Her shouting was waking everyone else on the floor.

Sister Landon opened her door. "Is everything okay?"

"Go back to sleep, Janey," Anna said.

Sister Flores could see this was getting out of hand. "Bishop, may we go to your office to discuss this?"

He dropped his head and shook it several times. "Oh for goodness sake, let's go. And please make it quick."

The three shuffled into his office where Sister Flores explained in dramatic fashion how she'd made the collar. The bishop sat there, nodding several times and trying to look interested. As Sister Flores wrapped up the tale, her face was a bright red. She was really wound up.

"All right Sister, excellent work. Now, please leave us so I can discuss this serious matter with Anna and determine her punishment."

"I most certainly will, and if I may give my opinion, she should be sent directly home! We can't have thieves in our mission. We are an example to these people here. How can a thief be an example? After all..."

Bishop Neel cut her off. "All right, all right, I understand your position. Now let me deal with this matter."

Sister Flores had more to say but knew when it was time to shut up. Giving Anna one more nasty look, she closed the door and went to her room. When the bishop heard her door close, he spoke in a low voice to Anna.

"Now, what's this all about?"

"Before I plead for mercy from your Honor, I hope this little token of my esteem will cause you to be lenient."

As she removed a black leather pouch from her pocket, the bishop's eyes widened.

"Oh my, your boy recovered it! What a blessing!"

He pulled the bills out and counted them. "Thirty pounds are missing but a small price to pay. I assume your boy helped himself?"

"I don't think so. He said this was how he found it and I believe him. In fact, he's very injured and in my hut right now. I was stealing—I mean *borrowing* these supplies when Sister Flores caught me. I must go back and tend to him and I'd like to bring him a reward."

"Certainly." He handed her the bundle of medical supplies. "Keep this in your pocket and don't let Sister Flores see it. How much do you think is appropriate?"

"He said he needs ten pounds to have a hut built for him and his wife-to-be. Judging from the injuries he suffered, I would say at least fifteen pounds if not twenty."

"Here you are, thirty pounds. You never know when I might need his services again. But if he's in that bad of shape, how's the one he got it from?"

Anna looked away. "I'm not sure, but I think someone in the settlement will be permanently missing tomorrow."

"Oh, dear! That's fairly drastic—bush justice if you will. I guess that sometimes sacrifices are necessary for the greater good. Perhaps the thieving around here will stop, although I doubt it. I suppose your boy won't be showing his face in the settlement, at least not until he heals."

Anna hesitated. "Probably not, though he didn't say. He usually hides out in the forest and I assume this time will not be any different."

"I have an idea, one that will help your boy out and us too. Let me tell you what it is."

Dear Mrs. Francis Lucchese,

    Molly, I'm writing you this letter because I'll be away for several weeks. There has been another incident with Sister Flores. Bishop Neel believes now is a good time for me to check the outlying leprosy settlements. We call them Segregation Villages with ours being the Central Settlement. It's like a bicycle wheel with a hub and spokes. I guess we are the hub and the Segregation Villages are at the end of the spokes. Anyway, I need to get out there and check on the teaching. This will be my first trip as all the teachers had come to Ogoja where I taught and approved them. Now, I need to see how they are doing in the field. I'm somewhat nervous as to what I will find. I hope they are all working hard.

    The normal route is by car to the northwest, but I told the bishop that there was no way I was going over that rickety bridge and ferry again. It's been three years since our disaster (where he almost died) and it feels like yesterday. Instead, the only other way we can go is northeast, the same route Thomas and I traveled the last time. That makes me nervous too. The problem with that route is that a car won't fit on the first leg. To solve this problem, Bishop Neel is arranging for a horse from someone in the village. He is also getting a cargo donkey to carry our supplies. 'Our supplies' mean the supplies for my little Clarence (although he's not little anymore) and me. He's sixteen and knows the bush like a cartographer. I will ride the horse and he will lead the donkey with our luggage, I guess. We will start for the Katsina Village. It's named Katsina Village but it's not even close to Katsina. (At least we are close to Ogoja.) After staying there for a few days, we will travel west to Adinya, and finally west again to Otukpo. When we're done, we will retrace our steps and come home. Each leg is about a full day by horseback and foot (I think!). I will let you know how it goes in a later letter.

    I received your last letter regarding the baby's bib and you're welcome. A leper in the colony fashioned it out of leather and twine and when I saw one she had done for someone else, I knew you'd love it; I mean little Owen would love it. Hopefully it keeps him clean.

It's hard to believe you have a child and he is already one, but I am glad my gift arrived in time. I tried to plan it out when I received your letter telling me you had given birth to a boy. I was so thankful you were healthy (considering what happened to Florence). I set the woman to work on it immediately. It took her a month and cost me less than a shilling so don't think I'm a big spender. Everything out here is cheap!

In the same vein, I'm happy to hear that Clarence has married again. She sounds like a wonderful girl. He deserves to be happy and his daughter deserves a mother too. Give him my best when you see him next.

Dr. Hampton's wife recently arrived, and he told me she is a musician. I met with her today and she agreed to help get a band together. I'm hoping by the time I get back, we will have beautiful music out here in the bush. Dr. Hampton also gave me good news about a leprosy drug called Dapsone. My little Clarence has taken it and the results seem promising. Please pray that the progress continues!

I know you always ask me about Gran'pa so here's an update. Each day I'm amazed he is still here with us. You cannot possibly miss his white head with its tight little curls. He has been with us now for three years, during which no relative or friend has ever visited or enquired about him. The years and suffering have told their tale in his bent body and drooping shoulders, but for all his years, there is no laziness in him. Each morning, you might see him stoop beside a big dome-shaped stone we have to fight against erosion. This particular stone lies half-buried in the soft, sandy shoulder of the road, and it's there he will sharpen his machete. Then, after some difficulty, he will straighten himself up and with quick, short steps trot off to do his quota of work, or to make farm, or to cut his firewood. Few of his Igbo tribe are in the settlement. (Our driver, Patrick, is one of them.) Gran'pa's house companion is also from Igbo. She is a big, strong woman who seems quite attached to her man. She is a leper too but I'm not entirely sure who is taking care of whom. It's a mystery I may never solve.

Here's another story for you. Six months ago, a Mohammedan came to our settlement. The leprosy was very infectious and deeply rooted in him, as was his faith in Islam. He struck up a conversation with another leper and watched each time as he went off to attend mass. One day, he decided to attend mass and receive the sacraments even though this has never been a condition of receiving treatment or pushed on anyone. He continued coming to mass and observing Catholics at prayer. During this time his Islamic friends came to see him often and would stay for hours talking and laughing in their tribal language. Three weeks ago he became very ill and asked to be baptised. Once he was baptised, his friends refused to visit him. He died this week and we buried him wrapped in his mats in an unmarked grave like hundreds of others consigned to mother earth. It never ends.

My school population has stabilized at fifty, give or take a few. With the outlying settlements, any growth we have now is from births within the settlement, though they are all still too young to attend. My precious Lily and Jonah will not start for at least another year so I spend time reading to them. They are fast learners and Lily is quite clever.

I will close my letter with this humorous story. You will recall we planted fifty hydnocarpus seeds and in over three years, with the fertile soil and excellent growing climate, they are nice looking trees. However, none of them produced any oil. Recently, Bishop Neel heard about a plant expert visiting the bush and had Patrick pick him up in Abakaliki. We made sure he was filled with good food and wine, so he would take a look at our trees. It turns out each of our trees is male, although I have no idea how one can tell that. He told us how to order female seeds and we have done so. I hope to write you in several years and tell you what a success it's been since the oil is vital in helping the lepers.

I must go now and get some sleep, but I want to tell you as I always do how happy I am for you and Francis. At times, I still can't believe you are married or that I missed the wedding! I can't wait to see your precious little Owen. Wishing you all the best,

Your Friend in the Bush,
Anna Goodwill

19

The small group headed out before there was barely enough light to see. It had been a day and a half since Clarence returned with the stolen funds. The bishop was adamant that they move away quickly to avoid more fallout with Sister Flores. He had told Anna how important the nun was to the entire settlement and didn't want to lose her. He was right, and she really did need to check on her teachers. It was a win-win situation.

The prior evening, during her last visit with Bishop Neel, he had whispered to her that he heard one of the important sub-chiefs was missing. "Since I assume those close to him know full well what he did and how much money he had on him, they will suspect foul play. They'll be looking for revenge. It's the way with these tribes."

Anna considered this as they slowly picked their way along the well-defined trail. She glanced up at the dark gray sky and was grateful when, an hour later, it lightened to a nice shade of blue. Clarence walked with the donkey ahead while she rode a big horse from a local villager. He told her the horse was gentle and as long as she didn't mistreat him, wouldn't easily spook or try to buck her off. All she had to do was keep her legs wrapped around the horse's belly and hold on to a crude rope saddle he had fashioned for her. As for guiding it, she simply held on and let the horse follow the donkey in front. Riding in this manner was fairly easy.

Anna loosened her jacket as the cool morning air warmed up. It was now enjoyable. Clarence, on the other hand, was wrapped in a blanket as he walked in front of the donkey. During her time in Nigeria, she discovered that the black skin of all Nigerians was excellent at repelling heat and keeping them cool. Yet the slightest bit of cold weather caused complete shivering and misery. It seemed to her that the cold was magnified in their bodies and thus, they built raging fires and wrapped themselves in multiple layers of anything they could find unless they had the means for thick clothing and blankets. In a few months, the hot, dry season would be firmly in place and all Nigerians would be happy once again.

Anna shifted on her horse. It didn't seem to mind her awkward movements. When the sky was light enough to see far down the trail, she pressed down on the horse and lifted herself up a bit to see if anyone was coming towards them. They were all alone. That would change soon when the travelers from the Katsina Segregation Village were up and moving. They would either be traders in search of Ogojan customers or lepers in search of Dr. Hampton. A few might simply be coming for a change of scenery, not happy with where they were staying. Regardless, their loneliness on the trail would surely change in few hours.

After two hours of easy lonely riding, Anna called out to Clarence to stop. She needed to take in a little water and relieve herself. Clarence pulled the donkey off the path and into a small clearing, and then helped her dismount. A few minutes later, they were drinking from their canteens when Anna inspected his face.

"You still have some deep wounds but at least you're a fast healer. I'm thankful you allowed Dr. Hampton to tend to you. He gave me a large bundle of bandages so I can change them when needed. And he wants to make sure you continue taking your Dapsone. I can tell it's definitely working!"

Clarence felt her fingers around his wounds and tried to change the subject. "Sista, where una fada and moda dey?"

"Oh, they have both passed away. But now that you've brought it up, they kind of remind me of Esi and you, especially with the reward money the bishop gave you. When I saw you give some to the hut builder to make you a hut while you are gone, it made me smile because my father also went through something like that. You see, my parents were Irish even though my surname—Goodwill—is English.

"It started with my grandfather, who was raised near London but for reasons I'm not quite sure, he moved to Ireland when he was twenty and took up life as a fisherman. There he met my grandmother, married and had my father. That's why my father grew up as an Irishman.

"Later when he was eighteen, he joined the Royal Irish Constabulary—Ireland's armed police force—and was stationed in Cavan. That's where he met my mother. Her father didn't approve of her marrying an RIC member so they eloped to Dublin and were married in a Pro-Cathedral. My father quit the RIC and had a job waiting for him from a cousin in Maghull as plumber and pipefitter.

"My mother's father came to Dublin and checked the marriage register. When he saw that they were properly married, he followed them to Maghull and bought them a house. That's where I'm from."

"Shey una sabi make pipes for water?"

"He didn't make the pipes; he installed them. When he was done with a project, the water was flowing through the pipes as it was supposed to. In fact, when I was a little girl, he brought some pipes home. One time, I was playing with them, and I stuck my fingers inside the opening. There was a lot of nasty oil and grease. When I showed it to him, he said all the pipes are made like that so when they installed them, they had to run water to flush it all out. Until they did that, the water wouldn't be safe to wash with or drink. From that day forward, I didn't let water from a pipe touch my hair if I could help it. And it's been thick and dare I say beautiful ever since."

Clarence stared at her hair. "You get nice hair sista. Real nice!"

"Thank you. And thank you again for that rain barrel. We left so fast I didn't have a chance to wash my hair in it. I'll have to take care of that in Katsina if I can find some rainwater."

Anna took a swig of water and put the cap back on her canteen. "Say, the bishop told me before we left that one of the sub-chiefs was missing. He assumes the man was our thief. How is his absence going to affect you?"

Clarence looked down at the ground and pushed a stone with his sandal. "He be powerful wit plenty, plenty friends. Dey go come find person whey kill ham, if dem hear."

"Yes, *if* they know. That sounds dangerous. Very dangerous…" she said, her voice trailing off, wondering what it would mean for them.

They stood there for another minute, silently, before loading up and resuming their trek.

Halfway into the journey, the fierce sun forced Anna to reposition her large straw hat. She wanted to shield her face as much as possible so as not to burn her sensitive English skin. Clarence, feeling warmer, abandoned his blanket. Now he walked with only a loose white shirt hanging lazily over heavy cotton trousers which were tied by a rope. His trousers stopped just below the calf, in the typical style of the locals.

They began seeing other travelers headed in the opposite direction. Some of them were alone wielding large walking sticks, while others walked in groups of two or three. Each time they passed one of these, Anna waved and said hello. Usually, it was returned with the standard, "Morny-O!"

Near noon, they rounded a rocky outcrop which Anna recognized. She called out to Clarence, "Please stop! I need a moment here."

Anna thought about getting off the horse but decided against it. This was the first time she had returned to this spot and it brought back many painful memories.

After Thomas died, she had placed a blanket over him. Then she put some large rocks on the sides of the blanket. As an added protection, she placed his bicycle on top of his body hoping to keep away any animals that might be around. The men from the settlement had gone back out and recovered his body. She had never asked them what condition it was in or where the blanket and bicycle ended up. It was all too excruciating.

She looked down the trail's edge at the exact spot. The sunshine hit the riverbed and made several of the shinier rocks shimmer. A few pieces of wood lay rotting right where the receding water had left them. Anna studied the vegetation around the area and it appeared to be larger, fuller than before. Otherwise, the place was the same.

She said a quick prayer and was done—with all of it. "Let's go!"

Clarence started up the donkey and the horse followed. An hour later, they stopped for lunch and allowed the animals to graze on some elephant grass. Clarence watered them at a nearby small pond hidden by the tall grass. This amazed Anna. How he knew where everything was, she had no idea.

They reached the leprosy village by 4 p.m., which was a good time. Starting out very early made the difference as the last thing Anna wanted was to get stuck on a trail at night. Clarence might be comfortable with it, but she sure wasn't.

Their arrival surprised the staff, who immediately called for more food to be cooked. While all this was happening, a hut was cleared out for Anna. As she was tired after the long ride, she took her time washing up. When she came to the table, the seat of honor was reserved for her. She looked for Clarence but he was nowhere in sight. He was probably taking care of the animals since it was unlikely that the staff would want him at the same table or that Clarence would even want to be there. Before she could think about him again, people were placing a variety of dishes in front of her. After Anna gave a blessing, everybody started eating.

For the next two days, Anna observed her teacher—a young girl from Otukpo—at work in the classroom. She had been in the first group to come to Ogoja and was one of the brightest. Her school held thirty-two students and from everything Anna could see, she was doing well. This was a huge relief because the girl was the youngest of all her teachers. Anna had been worried about sending her off on her own but she had no choice. Now it looked like her trust was well placed.

During the last full day, Anna spent a few hours with the medical staff going over records and scribbling notes to take back to Dr. Hampton. It was important that they knew how many medical supplies were being used so they could replenish them in time.

With that done, she made a sketch showing the layout of the huts. Bishop Neel would then send the sketches and progress reports to the MMM to show not only where the money was going, but also how much more was needed. They had been told that in six months, Mother Mary Martin herself was coming over with a film crew. The plan was to shoot the Leprosy Settlement in Ogoja to help with fundraising back home. Bishop Neel was already making plans for it. That's why Anna was glad to get this trip over with. It would give her plenty of time to prepare the choir and boy scouts to welcome Mother Mary properly.

It was almost time for dinner when Anna noticed several of the village men trotting off somewhere. After a few minutes, she located her teacher and asked what was going on.

"Dem dey go see a man talk."

"Please speak proper English. Does this man talk about independence?"

The teacher looked scared. She pulled Anna inside a small room and whispered to her. "Yes, many men are talking. Please don't ask about this openly."

"It's okay. I'm not going to tell anyone. Let's forget about it and go eat supper."

Despite Anna's assurance, the teacher acted uncomfortably during the meal.

Early the next morning, they mounted up and started for the next village, Adinya. When they reached it, a welcoming committee rushed out to greet them, having received advance notice from the Katsina residents.

This village was larger than Katsina which surprised Anna. When he saw her sketch, Bishop Neel would be very pleased. However, her good feelings quickly faded when she discovered her teacher was down with malaria. Thoughts of Victoria came flooding back, giving her nightmares.

Anna stopped what she was doing and taught the class for three straight days, until Sunday. Then, she checked on her teacher and found she'd passed through the disease's critical point and was still alive. She would likely survive now.

To celebrate, Clarence found a large barrel near a stream that had collected rain from a recent thunderstorm. This gave her the chance to trot off with her 'tools' and soak her dry and dirty hair. By combing in her shampoo for longer than normal, she was able to stretch the event out to an hour. Then she stripped down and took a bath in the cool river. It was wonderful being clean again. And her hair had instantly sprung back to life. If she ever returned home, she'd never appreciate a bath and hair rinse as much as she did out in the bush, where simple pleasures were transformed into lavish experiences.

With her teacher on the mend, they spent an extra two days in Adinya before heading out to Otukpo, a place where she had spent six weeks a long time back. On the trail, they were rarely alone as people traveled in both directions in greater numbers. There was obviously a good deal of trade going on between these two villages.

When they crested a small hill just outside of Otukpo, these villagers had an even larger welcome ready. Anna was shown around like the Queen of England, with everyone coming out of their huts to greet her. This was by far the largest of the three outposts, with sprawling huts and nice staff facilities.

Near the edge of the village was a steam plant. It was situated in the center of a large workshop and received various fruits and vegetables to process.

The staff showed Anna where oil was pressed for use in the food and how soap was made. In addition, alcohol was being drawn from sugarcane for medical use. It was a very efficient operation.

The next three days were a repeat of her visit with the first village. The woman at this school was the oldest of three teachers and it was a good thing because she had over seventy students! Wisely, she had been training two assistants and it appeared that everything was running very smoothly.

One evening, Anna again saw the men leaving the village and discreetly asked her teacher about it. Sure enough, she discovered another man was rallying up the local men for independence. She made notes on all this for Bishop Neel since he would want to know about this activity. There was no doubt in her mind that this issue wasn't going away.

At the end of her two weeks, Anna concluded that her time had been very productive, even with the three extra days due to the malaria-stricken teacher. Anna had a lot of information to give to both Dr. Hampton and Bishop Neel, and she couldn't wait to get back and sleep in her own bed.

Clarence told her he wanted to rest the animals in Katsina, which would add a day to their return trip. He felt the animals were currently rested enough to make the two-day trip from Otukpo to Katsina, but making them work a third straight day would be pushing their luck. So Anna agreed to spend a full day in Katsina before heading home.

As they pulled out of the Otukpo Segregation Village early one morning, Anna gazed ahead at the sun just coming up over the horizon. It was a beautiful sight, one that only Africans saw. British citizens certainly never enjoyed a sunrise like this in England. Again, it was one of the simple pleasures that made life in the bush worth it.

On the trail to Adinya, Clarence was in charge. From her high mount, she couldn't believe how Clarence had changed from a boy to a young man. His body was more developed, with lean muscles. And his life experiences gave him confidence that many adult men didn't possess. The boy leading the donkey was not the little boy she had seen playing hide and seek so many years earlier, but a solid young man. He would surely make a good mate for Esi.

At Adinya, Anna was pleased to find her teacher now fully recovered from malaria and back to teaching her class. After dinner, Clarence showed her to the rain barrel again where she washed her hair before bathing in the river. Refreshed, they had a good night's sleep before taking off early the next morning, and arriving safely in Katsina before supper.

This time, the staff was not caught off-guard. They had prepared a huge feast for Anna with plenty of wine. By the time she made it to bed, she was completely full and totally exhausted. As her head hit the pillow, she was grateful they had a full day to rest. She wasn't sure about Clarence, but she certainly needed it.

Deep in the night, a rustling at her door brought Anna out of a heavy slumber. She blinked, trying to decide if she was dreaming when a strong hand suddenly clamped onto her arm.

"What's going on?!"

"Shhh sista. Do quick!" the grip tightened. "We dey go now!"

"What? Why?"

"Dem dey come!"

"Is it the independence men?" she whispered.

"No know. Do quick!"

Anna fumbled for her lamp, but by the time light filled the hut, Clarence was gone. She threw some clothes on and stuffed her bag with everything she had. Then she glanced at her watch—3:30 a.m.

Her heart raced. She'd never seen Clarence act like this. If he was worried, something was really wrong.

With bag packed, she took the lamp and slipped out of her hut. In the moonlight, her horse grazed at the edge of a leper's garden. Anna jumped when Clarence tapped her on the shoulder, gesturing for her bag. He stowed it on his donkey and held the lamp so she could mount her horse. When she was firmly mounted, he doused the lamp, grabbed up the rope, and led them out of the village.

They traveled south quickly, Anna listening for any sound behind them. Occasionally, Clarence would freeze, hugging the donkey's neck and tilting his head. It was too dark to see more than a few feet so she could only assume he was listening for pursuers. Anna clenched the reins and forced air into her lungs. She couldn't remember ever being this scared.

Worries filled her mind as they made their way slowly along the trail.

What if these men didn't want her telling anyone about their speeches? What if the animals tired out? What if her horse broke his leg? What if they encountered robbers along the trail? Her dangerous thoughts churned out of control.

By daybreak, Clarence led them off the trail, deep into elephant grass. After listening for a few minutes, he took two large stones and secured them to the ropes of the horse and donkey. With his machete, he carved out a small clearing.

Anna watched him work while she rummaged for some food, discovering they had very little; just a few bananas and some bread. She ate some of the bread and saved the rest for Clarence since he was doing most of the work.

Picking up her canteen, she sighed. Her water was almost gone. Their hasty exit left them totally unprepared. This was often fatal in the bush.

Clarence went back to the trail to listen. When he returned, he told her he couldn't hear anyone coming. He believed they were several hours ahead, if they were coming at all. He offered her his water, but Anna declined, saying she was fine. Soon, she wouldn't be.

This break lasted no more than ten minutes before they got back on the trail. Whatever lead they had, Clarence was determined to keep it.

An hour of hard traveling brought another stop to water the animals in an open stream. With his machete in hand, he stood guard while Anna searched for water. Unfortunately, the stream was too dirty.

She took a few small sips from her canteen and paused as the water slid down her parched throat. This might be the last comfort she would feel for hours.

Overhead, the light gray clouds kept the air cool. This was the first morning Anna had seen Clarence without a blanket wrapped around him. Even though it was probably cold for him, he was dressed as if it was blazing hot. A thin sheen of sweat covered his exposed skin which explained the lack of a blanket. She wondered if it was nerves or if his disease had him feverish. Either one was bad.

After the animals had their fill, they headed south again. In the clearing light, Anna could see far enough to spot any trouble coming. When the sun finally appeared, the straw hat went back on, its leather string tied snuggly against her chin. By 9 a.m., she was so thirsty that she tilted the canteen and impulsively drank the rest of her water. It was barely two mouthfuls but felt good going down. All she could now was hope they would either find safe, clean drinking water or arrive home before her thirst was out of control.

An hour and a half later, they came to the flat, rocky part of the trail. Clarence stopped them unexpectedly and handed her the animals' reins. He scrambled up a boulder and looked back towards Katsina. He was there no more than thirty seconds before he raced down.

"Dem dey come. Four of dem."

"Oh God!" she cried. "What do we do?"

Anna's horse whinnied at her voice.

"I get one idea."

He led the animals back behind the boulder and pointed for her to duck.

"Stay put!" he commanded, before heading back to the trail.

Anna heard him brushing their tracks a good distance back towards Katsina. Suddenly, he appeared from the other side of the boulder surprising her. She let out a small scream and clapped a hand over her mouth.

"Shh sista! Shhh!"

He held his machete at the ready. Anna climbed down from her horse and picked up two good sized rocks, gripping them tightly. Twenty agonizing minutes passed until they heard the gang coming nearer and nearer. The men were no more than twenty feet away from them. Anna felt like passing out, her hands clenched around the rocks, aching. Clarence's desperate wide-eyed gaze scared her even more.

They listened intently as the men passed by, the sounds of their footsteps fading. Clarence put a finger to his lips and crept back to the trail. When he returned, he sheathed the machete and led the animals out.

"We go go to Katsina," he whispered.

"No!" Anna protested. "We must go home."

"Shh!" he said angrily, starting the donkey to the northeast.

Left with no choice, she mounted her horse and followed.

They traveled for two long, hot hours before pulling off the trail. Clarence led them for twenty more minutes through tall elephant grass, thick brush, and finally, dense trees. He gulped down some water from his canteen and told her to stay put. Then, removing the machete, he was gone.

Anna sat against a tree, tears and sweat running down her cheeks. She was hungry and thirsty but too scared to do anything about it. She just sat there as the horse and donkey grazed on what little vegetation they could find. An occasional noise in the forest made her twist her head in fear, yet there was never anything to see. It was maddening.

She tried to breathe deeply and think of Molly or her little ones—Jonah and Lily—but the sounds in the forest were hard to ignore She felt helpless as time, unnoticeable but unerring in its course, slid by like thick molasses.

When the sun was dipping through the trees, she assumed Clarence wasn't coming back. Anna got to her feet, shaking. She wasn't even sure how to get out of the forest.

If she started now, she might read the tracks they had made coming in and at least get back to the trail. Perhaps she would have a chance to make it to Katsina, even if she set the donkey free. Before she could reach a decision, she heard someone coming.

Anna looked around frantically for a weapon and picked up a small stone. Just as she pulled her arm back to throw, she spotted Clarence making his way towards her.

"Where have you been?" she said, dropping the stone. Her heart sank when she saw his dejected face.

"Dem dey come now o," he said grimly. "Dey don sabi where we dey."

Anna pressed a hand to her mouth. "Oh God, who is it?"

"Dem be men of the sub-chief. Dem fit kill me o."

"What do we do?!"

"Follow me," he said.

Clarence took the donkey's rope and led them deeper into the darkening forest. After a bit, he took a wide left turn and made a semicircle with their tracks. Then he took the ropes and tied them to a tree. Anna watched him study the ground with a furrowed brow. The pursuers would be able to see them much easier here than if they had kept to a straight line, moving away from the men. Stopping was completely insane. It was then that she realized she would die in this place. Anna prayed for someone from the village to find her body and bury it next to Thomas, though that seemed highly unlikely.

Clarence walked ten feet back towards the approaching killers and tossed some stones ahead. She followed the arc of each one before it disappeared in the ground. He was throwing them into a hole the size of a rain barrel. Where the stones went or why he was doing it, she had no idea.

The men drew closer and closer. There was no chance to run now.

Clarence strained over a large stone and moved it to a spot he was happy with. Then he found another large one. Just as he lowered it to the ground, the first man appeared and spotted them standing there. Clarence was unarmed, his machete lying on the ground a few feet away. Instead of following the animals' tracks and making the large semicircle as Clarence and Anna had done, the man came straight towards them, bisecting the circle, just as Anna feared. The man strode with anger and purpose, his machete flashing in the filtered light. There was nothing she could do now but pray.

20

The man was thirty feet away when he raised his machete to begin the attack. For a brief second, he was there—a ruthless killer on a mission—and then he was gone, into Clarence's hole. A second man appeared with two others closely following behind. The leading man took the same path as the first one, stopping when he came to the spot where the first man had disappeared. But he too lost his footing and fell. The men behind him rushed to his aid.

Clarence did nothing and merely watched. When the two men dropped to their knees to pull their comrade to safety, Clarence picked up one of the large stones at his feet and hurled it high in the air. Anna thought it would hit one of the men but the stone landed wide left and to their rear. With a deep thud, it too disappeared.

The rescued man was on his stomach between his two comrades, partially out of the hole. All three men looked towards the thump behind them. Then they turned their gaze back to Clarence, but he had already sent the second stone flying through the air. Anna was disheartened when she saw he'd miscalculated again. This stone landed to their rear but wide right and disappeared.

The men, realizing their attacker had missed a second time, sneered at Clarence and got to their feet unwilling to wait for a third stone. Suddenly, the earth behind them collapsed in a straight line connecting the two holes where the large stones disappeared. The three men didn't move, unsure of what was happening. With a groaning creak the ground around them gave way and they fell, bringing a crushing wave of soil and brush with them. The hole stopped mere feet from where Anna and Clarence stood. She closed her jaw with a click and swallowed. Her throat was raw as though she'd screamed, but she never managed a sound.

Clarence sheathed his machete and untied the animals. As he worked, a long, painful wail rose from deep in the hole. Anna edged close and stared into the dark maw of the sinkhole. It was four stories deep and wide enough to fit six kit cars. Large puddles of water surrounded massive mounds of dark soil. Sticking out of one of the mounds was a man, buried up to his chest. He wailed in a language she didn't understand, waving for help and straining toward her.

"Oh my God! What do we do?"

"We dey go now."

Clarence led the animals back to the path.

The man continued wailing and waving, sinking deeper into the wet, soft soil.

"But we can't leave him to die!"

"He fit kill us if he get free o. We dey go now."

Anna swallowed hard. The man was up to his neck, his cries fainter and tears streaming down his cheeks. Ahead of her Clarence was making his way back out. Anna stared up at the sky but it was hidden by the thick canopy of trees. She knew it would be dark soon and they might be stuck in the forest, or possibly find another sinkhole. Pulling away, she followed Clarence with heavy feet. A minute later, the man was silent.

∽

Anna sat atop the horse staring at the landscape illuminated by a full moon. Shadows danced in and out of the elephant grass like animals prowling their tracks. Yet nothing attacked them.

Clarence was ahead, guiding the donkey over the undulating path, leading them home. Three hours of straight riding had put some distance between them and the four dead men. Three of them had been instantly digested whole by Mother Earth. The image in her mind of the man being swallowed by the soft pile of muck burned, as did her thirst.

She swayed with the horse's gentle gait, fighting to keep her eyes open. Even though her body was well acclimated to Nigeria, she was not used to being out in the open air all day long. Without water, she could very well join their pursuers.

The two-animal train continued on a south by southwest track, silent save for hoof-beats and the occasional snuffling whinny. After they crested a small hill, Clarence veered the donkey off the dirt path into the high elephant grass, his machete whistling through the air. Anna twisted in her saddle and scanned the horizon.

Was someone else coming after them? Did he see something that we need to hide from?

Her horse picked up his gait for some reason. As they waded through the grass, her horse grew excited. A lantern flickered to life, throwing light over Clarence's dark face. He took the horses reins.

"Make you fill your canteen before I free the animal go drink o."

Anna slid off the horse with the canteen around her neck and took the offered lantern, moving quickly to where Clarence had pointed. She set the lantern down on a flat rock and leaned down to taste the rainwater. Taking a mouthful in, she swished it around, to see if it was safe. It tasted like fresh rainwater and Anna gulped down the water, coughing and spitting and forcing the clear, sweet liquid down her throat. She made herself stop and breathe, chills chasing the water as it dripped down her face and neck. She scooped up handfuls until she was satisfied and then filled her canteen up before going back to Clarence. He released the reins of the two animals and stood by watching them move rapidly to the pond.

Anna glanced at Clarence out of the corner of her eye and cleared her throat. "Listen, we need to discuss what happened back there."

Clarence chewed on a piece of sugarcane and said nothing.

"Are there more men coming after us?"

He spit and kept chewing. "No."

"How can you be sure?"

He spit again, sending a piece of cane flying into the grass. "Dem select four men and all of dem don gone."

"They could have sent some more."

He stared at her flatly, chewing.

Anna sighed. "Okay, well, what do we tell the bishop, then?"

Clarence reached into his mouth with two fingers and pulled out the rest of the sugarcane, shaking it off his hand. "No'tin."

"Nothing? You can't be serious!"

"Yeah, I dey serious!"

For the first time Anna could remember, his face was drawn in anger.

"If anyone finds out these four are dead, will they send more?"

"Yeah!"

Her mouth dropped open. "So, what, it never ends? They'll seek revenge forever?"

Clarence looked down and then away, his face smooth once again. "Na our way. (*It is our way.*)"

"And as it is now, they'll think these four are still out looking for you. Or that they found another man responsible and killed him."

Clarence nodded.

Anna felt the slap of cold, hard truth. "They won't think you killed all four, especially without a trace of the bodies."

She folded her arms and took a deep breath. "They'll think they might be roaming through the bush still looking for you. It might be years before they wonder where the revenge-seekers are."

"Yeah, we dey go now."

Without another word, Clarence retrieved the animals from the pond and helped Anna back on her horse. He grabbed the reins of the donkey and led it out of the grass. When he was on the main path, he doused the lantern and continued to the leprosy settlement without looking back.

☙

Anna pulled her sheet closer to her neck. The steady noise outside her darkened hut lulled her back to sleep. After another long interval of deep dreams, she woke and stretched, checking her wristwatch: 1:30 p.m. Anna rolled on to her side and struggled to open her eyes. Her whole body ached. The events of the past hours were slowly coming back.

They had entered their village at three in the morning. After pulling all her belongings off the horse and helping Clarence get the two animals to their stalls, she had trudged head down to her hut, lit a lantern, and set to washing her face. Unfortunately, there was no water in the pitcher so she had to go pump some. Then she brought it back and washed her face and hands. When she was done, she could barely turn the lantern off before falling into a deep sleep.

Now, she lay there in that state between I-know-I-need-to-get-up and I-don't-feel-like-getting-up. As Anna stared up at the underside of her thatched roof, she remembered more clearly the gruesome events of the past twenty-four hours. That got her adrenaline pumping.

She sat up and looked at her watch again. 2:10 p.m. Impossibly, another forty minutes had disappeared. She splashed her face with water and quickly dressed.

Stepping outside, the bright sun made her squint. Striding briskly down the nearby path was Sister Landon.

"Janey, what's with all this activity?"

The nun stopped, eyebrows flying up. "Anna!" she exclaimed. "When did you get back?"

"Early this morning," she said through a yawn. "I was exhausted so I slept in. What did I miss?"

"Yesterday, a telegram came in that Mother Mary Martin had arrived with a film crew," the nun said excitedly. "She's being brought up here by some drivers from the Catholic Mission in Calabar. Bishop Neel thought we had over five months before they would arrive so somehow, the wires were crossed."

"Goodness, I would say so. How can I help?"

"Well, Bishop Neel and Sister Flores are in a panic. Everybody's doing something. My job is to get the lepers to clean the outsides of their huts and tend to their gardens."

Sister Landon made a frustrated gesture at one of the messier huts. "We think they're arriving late this afternoon, but who really knows. If you want to help, I suppose you should see the bishop since you and Sister Flores aren't exactly chums."

"I will. Thanks!"

Sister Landon took off faster than Anna had ever seen her move before, and that quickened her step.

Before she knew it, she stood before a stressed bishop. "I'm back," she said, as cheerfully as she could. "I just heard about our visitor. How can I help?"

"Anna!" he said. "I'm grateful to see you, but I fear we've been caught with the draw bridge down and the castle door open. I'm sorry, but your report on the segregation villages will simply have to wait."

"I assumed as much. Do you have something for me to do?"

"Oh, bless you a thousand times," he said. "I need you to organize a presentation of the Boy Scouts. And if you could, help organize the musical band of lepers Mrs. Hampton put together. She's busy with the doctor getting the infirmary and nursery in shipshape condition, so she doesn't have time. We may have only a few hours left but if you could somehow make it appear as though we have a certain level of competence, I'd be eternally grateful! After all, it's not every day that your main benefactor shows up to inspect the goods."

"Of course! I'll get to it right now."

Five months earlier, Anna had come across a man with crippled legs propelling himself along the ground with his hands, mangled legs protruding in front. At first, Anna thought he was building concrete steps for a Celtic cross over a tomb. But as she talked to him, she discovered he was actually building a flagstaff to fly his flag, for he was a soldier, injured in some regional fighting.

He said his name was Sergeant Stanley Ringer, a native Nigerian raised by British parents who worked for the British government. He had been injured near Ogoja and was being treated by a local hospital when he contracted leprosy. They promptly removed him to the bush and left the wounded soldier to fend for himself.

With no money or possessions, he begged his way to Ogoja leprosy settlement and began receiving treatments and food. He was determined to make the most of his new life.

Because he spoke excellent English, he and Anna had had wonderful conversations. It didn't take her long to find crutches for him and soon, he was strutting around like he owned the place.

One day, he asked if they had a Boy Scout troop. Anna said they did not. Within days, he set about making plans and writing a list of everything he would need. Anna was willingly drafted into his plan, and before she knew it, they had a dozen leper children in the Ogojan Boy Scout Troop.

Each boy wore a basic uniform, made from fabric purchased in Calabar. With Sgt. Ringer's direction, the boys felt like a special military organization. They had their own leaders and were assigned tasks and challenges to earn badges and ribbons. Anna's job was to procure the necessary supplies and keep track of it all. Being in the troop gave the boys confidence and comradery. It was a huge success!

Anna located Sgt. Ringer and told him what was happening. Together, they found the two Boy Scout leaders and gave them instructions to find the scouts and get them into their uniforms. Anna told the leaders they had one hour to meet her on the soccer field for a drill. Stanley agreed to make sure they were all there. Then she took off to find Mrs. Hampton and arrange the band members, whoever they might be.

For the next few hours, brooms and paintbrushes and needles and suds flew. Busy were the woodsmen, the washermen, and the carpenters. The head tailor was in a fit preparing the Bishop's cloth, having already completed the canvas for a dozen chairs. The settlement buzzed like a hive of bees, swarming here and there and occasionally running into each other.

At just after 6 p.m., two young girls came running towards the settlement waving their arms frantically to announce the film crew's arrival. Seconds behind them, two kit cars made the long drive up the main avenue, dust trailing behind them. Movie cameras stuck out from the open windows, capturing everything, including the few lepers who hadn't completed their tasks.

The lepers standing in formation whispered with wonder as the cameras trundled past them. Each one stiffened their backs to appear even more respectful to the visitors who seemed like royalty.

When the kit cars finally stopped, Bishop Neel appeared from under the large tree and hustled over the short grass. He waved a hand and Anna hurried out from behind a tree, a Boy Scout troop on her left and a small band of musicians on her right. They proceeded towards the new arrivals, who had already opened the doors to stretch their legs.

When the bishop raised his hand again, Anna stopped and the band began playing. The wailing horns and pounding drums made a less than proper sound and it was certainly nothing that would be acceptable in a local school back in England. But it was the effort that counted.

The Boy Scouts, with their khaki short sleeved shirts, bandanas, and dark brown shorts made a nice picture. The ones who wore badges and pins thrust out their chests as far as possible, the two leaders standing tall behind them donning distinctive brown berets. The scouts with white splotchy leper's skin stood behind the clean-looking ones without anyone telling them do so. To the side stood Sgt. Ringer, the brightest smile that ever sat atop a pair of crutches and mangled legs.

Hidden from view was Sister Flores with two sets of workers running around throwing whitewash on any wall they could find. They had already used up most of their paint supply and were on the last two cans. Bishop Neel had instructed her to paint the world white, and she was determined to do just that.

The bishop approached the visitors and introduced himself, addressing the man designated as the producer.

"Sir, I am Bishop Neel MacKenna. Welcome to the Leprosy Settlement in Ogoja."

He swept a hand behind him. "I trust your journey was a safe one?"

Andrew Wiggins shook his hand. "Yes, safe, though it was quite bumpy. I'm not sure I'd want to do that more than once in a lifetime."

The bishop chuckled. "Of course, of course. You can stay with us forever and thus, won't have to go through it again."

The men laughed.

"Thanks for reminding me about the return trip to Calabar," the producer said with a grin. "But let me introduce the crew."

He brought forward two men and two women as the bishop grew concerned.

"But where is Mother Mary Martin? Your telegram said she was coming. Is she behind you?"

"I'm afraid not. I told the clerk at the mission to send you a telegram stating the film crew from MMM was coming and wondered too late if he fully understood it stood for Medical Missionaries of Mary and not our founder's name Mother Mary Martin. Apparently, he got it wrong."

He offered a sheepish smile. "Anyway, she decided that with her past malaria, it was best to stay in Ireland for now. Upon her decision, we were presented with an opportunity to immediately hop a comfortable ship to Port Harcourt at a steeply discounted price. Mother Mary couldn't turn down a chance to save money, so we packed in two days, caught the ship, and here we are."

Bishop Neel tried to hide his disappointment. "I understand. Welcome, then. Let us show you to your quarters so you can freshen up. Supper is being prepared as we speak. You must be hungry."

"That sounds wonderful. However, with the Boy Scouts here and the band playing, we would like to shoot some film before the light fades. We aren't here many days and need to take advantage of all the daylight we can get. Our drivers will carry the luggage to our rooms if you show them where they are."

"Of course, sir. Is there anything we can do to help you?"

"Yes, just act normal and provide us a guide."

By now, Sister Flores had arrived and heard the last words of the man. She was about to step forward when the bishop spoke.

"Anna, will you please show the film crew around? We will be busy getting their rooms ready and supper served."

"Certainly. It would be my pleasure, Bishop."

While Anna gathered the five visitors, she caught Sister Flores' narrow-eyed gaze. They had had no contact since the theft incident weeks earlier and it was doubtful Sister Flores even knew she had returned. Now, out of the blue, Anna had been selected for this key role.

"May I take you on a tour of our settlement?" she said to Andrew Wiggins.

"Please. And give us some explanation along the way of what we are seeing and why it's important. We will edit everything when we return home."

As they walked off, Bishop Neel turned and barked out orders. Soon, sisters and lepers ran in all directions to finish the few items that had not been done. Everyone except Sister Flores, who simply stood there, her intense glare burning into the back of Anna's skull.

∾

Over the next several days, everyone in the settlement made contact with the film crew. It was hard to say they were 'acting normal'. Even though the lepers had never seen a moving picture camera, they somehow discovered how to be actors. Often, a leper or two would wander near the film crew hoping to gain their attention. Oluwa, a natural performer, made a frequent appearance in their vicinity doing cartwheels that mostly ended when his legs crashed to the ground. Sadly for him, the film crew was unaware of the need to tip their performers and his tobacco habit was not fully satisfied.

And there were other issues.

One of the new canvas seats had not been tested and ripped with the first guest. That brought howls of laughter from everyone but the unfortunate guest. Bishop Neel even said a prayer of thanks that the crew hadn't caught it on film.

The supper each night was followed by generous amounts of wine and Irish whiskey. Anna noticed several bottles of Bishop Neel's favorite whiskey discreetly smuggled into his room, a present, no doubt, from back home.

Each night, there was another round of celebration and each morning, the crew got up and shot more film. They barely rested, as their time was limited to four days in Ogoja.

Anna visited one of the women who had come and learned more about Mother Mary Martin, their missing benefactor. Apparently, she had lost her brother, Charlie, in the Great War. In 1915, he was waving men back into the trench to retreat when he was struck in the arm and leg. He kept directing them until he took a bullet in the spine. He died three days later. Ever since then, she had worked hard to help people around the world in Charlie's memory. This film, Mother Mary Martin hoped, would not only show potential donors what MMM did, but also highlight the crucial need for more leprosy mission donations and more missionary volunteers.

Mother Mary Martin had obtained the best film equipment at the time and was set on making the best film she could. This crew was very experienced and professional. Everyone had high hopes for the project.

Anna had Esi teaching class while she spent all day with the film crew, showing them everything the settlement had to offer: the doctors and nurses at work, the babies being cared for, the children at play, and the workshops which produced towels, shoes and many utensils needed by the settlement. They also captured the lepers working the land, and explaining how they grew yams, cassava, groundnuts, peppers, sugar cane, plantains, tomatoes, bananas, soya beans, rice, and palm trees. It was a complete tour with nothing left out, including the latrines, the bathing spots and the cemetery.

On the last full day, Anna took them into Ogoja and filmed the markets where settlement products from weaving to shoe-making to pottery were sold. Mama Mimi provided a wonderful lunch and, of course, ended up on film.

All in all, the crew said they had had a successful shoot, especially with the weather being perfect each day. Andrew Wiggins felt confident the film would be very good.

That final night the crew had one last party and for the first time, found it difficult to get up for an early breakfast. Bishop Neel had the band out to play them some departure music and the entire settlement clapped and waved as the two kit cars drove away, leaving a trail of dust behind along with a year's worth of stories for everyone to tell over and over again.

21

Bishop Neel leaned back in his chair. Over the rims of his reading glasses, he studied the sketch.

"I'm very impressed with the expansion at the segregation villages," he said, clearing his throat and waving a hand at a fly. "According to your sketch, they're ahead of schedule."

"Yes, Bishop," Anna replied. "Each village is progressing nicely. I got the real impression that there is some competition among the three, perhaps even with us."

Bishop Neel chuckled. "That's wonderful. A little competition is good for business. Even the various religions compete against each other. It adds urgency to one's steps."

Anna smiled. "My teachers are even aware of how many students the others have and how many pass their tests. Since all the students must either take the certificate test here or wait until I travel out there, I can be assured that the teachers are doing their jobs—not simply passing them on without the proper education."

"Good. A little quality control won't hurt anyone either." He slipped Anna's report into a folder. "I noticed your boy's wounds were completely healed when he returned. And since you left so early, I can't imagine anyone saw his battered face. That should throw suspicion off him. But tell me, did you run into anyone looking for him while you were in the hinterlands?"

Anna stiffened and fought the urge to play with her hair. "Uh…
no. We didn't see anyone that gave us any cause for trouble. We did
see men leaving the village," she added quickly. "They were going to
hear someone speak about independence. The locals tried to hide it
from me but my teachers told me what was happening, although they
promised me to secrecy. Which reminds me, have you decided what
to do with Patrick?"

The Bishop sighed and shook his head. "I'm afraid I must sack
him," he mourned. "That independence fever has got him in its
grasp. He's not the same anymore."

Anna frowned. "What will he do?"

Bishop Neel removed his glasses. "I don't know, probably help organize the movement. They don't have much money, although I heard
they take up donations when they give those," he waved his hand,
"*speeches*. Still, I don't know how he'll eat. I talked with one of the drivers that brought the film crew and he'd be willing to live up here. From
what I understand, he has relatives in Calabar that he'd rather be free
of. The prospect of a new job up here interests him a great deal."

"I hate to hear that about Patrick. He's like part of the family."

"He *was*, my dear, but now it's time to set him free. I cannot have
you or me standing at the bank with a pouch full of money and no
driver. We might get conked over the head or worse." He grimaced.
"And don't forget, he could stop along the way, hear someone speaking and leave you behind. Your safety is my responsibility. But on a
good note, Mother Mary Martin sent a lengthy letter to me through
the film crew. Among the many things she had to tell me, she said
MMM is set well in funds and she's confident this film will loosen
more purse strings. She wants me to be ready to expand to three
more segregation villages. I have some locations in mind which I'll
discuss with you and Sister Flores separately. I assume you haven't
made up after that incident at the infirmary, although it seems you
two were rather cross from day one."

Anna hesitated. The Bishop had always been a friend to her, but
so much had changed in the last few weeks. The man from the trail

still screamed and sank to his death each night in her dreams. She took a deep breath and pushed the thought from her mind—nothing could be done for him, but perhaps the Bishop could help ease this other pain.

"I remember when I was teenager back in Maghull. This was before the war. I injured my arm on the playground and had it bandaged up with a strap around my shoulder to keep it from moving too much. None of the boys had ever paid me the slightest glance, but when I showed up with that bandage, well, you can guess. They stumbled over each other to open doors and pull out chairs and carry my books—anything to prove themselves. That's when I noticed a girl in my class come alive.

"Her name was Lenora Camphurst and she had never talked to me before. Of course, I had never talked to her either. She was pleasant girl, fairly attractive, if one considered how the boys spent their attentions. When I showed up with my arm in that bandage, everything changed. Before I knew it, she was saying horrible things about me to anyone who would listen, and playing nasty little tricks. She liked to act as though she was holding the door open for me before letting it slam. And silly me, I'd fall for it.

"Two weeks later, the bandage came off and the boys went back to plying their attentions elsewhere. But Lenora Camphurst continued hating me. Not for the rest of school year or even for the rest of high school, but even now she hates me. And it's so terrible, you know, because I have no cause to dislike her at all. That's what it's like with Sister Flores. You can't make a person like you who's already made up their mind not to. You can pray for them but it's truly out of your hands. That's where I am with Sister Flores."

Bishop Neel fiddled with his glasses on the desk. "I assume you have no idea why she dislikes you?"

"Well…" Anna shifted uncomfortably. "Back at the convent in Ireland, Mother Walmsley told me that Sister Flores worked closely with another sister during the war, a sister whose name escapes me."

"Sister Fent?"

"Yes! Did Mother Walmsley tell you?"

Bishop Neel sighed. "No. But Sister Flores has spent years trying to convince me to put in for her transfer to this settlement. I wrote many letters to Mother Mary yet never had a response."

"Well, that certainly fits. They're both so valuable; they didn't want to waste them on the same mission. Still, I heard if I hadn't come along to teach, Sister Fent was coming here instead."

"Yes, it all makes sense. You being here blocks that scheme."

Anna shrugged. "And she's held it against me ever since."

"Well, I am sorry for that, my dear." Bishop Neel tapped the desk. "I wish I could change things, but it's those above me who make all the decisions. I can only carry them out. And speaking of my duties, I understand I have a wedding ceremony to perform?"

Anna brightened. "Yes!" she said, clapping her hands. "My Clarence is marrying my Esi."

Bishop Neel reached for a blank piece of paper. "They are like kin to you, aren't they? Let's set our plans straight, so we can make it a special event."

Anna left Bishop Neel's office with a long list of tasks to complete. She first went to see Mrs. Hampton in the infirmary, where she was working on a patient's flexibility.

"Mrs. Hampton, I would like the band to play at an upcoming wedding. Would you have time to discuss this?"

"Certainly. And please, call me Sam."

She patted the patient's leg and the young man eased his leg down with a groan. "Do you have some songs in mind?"

The women pulled up chairs to a small table and took tea while they talked. There were six players in the band and although they were still learning, they could occasionally produce a full song that sounded almost professional. Anna proposed a standard wedding song which they had never played. With the wedding in five days, it was doubtful they could get up to an acceptable standard. But Sam agreed to give it a try, so Anna marched off to see Oluwa, who always had a knack for knowing the right people for a job.

"Oluwa, I need some flowers gathered. Would you know who I should contact for that?"

"Oluwa sabi the right people. I beg tell me wetin you want."

Anna went over the details and slipped him a few coins. He took off while she headed to her hut. That's when Gran'pa's woman approached her.

"Sista, I beg come," she said motioning for Anna to follow.

"What's the matter?"

"I beg," she urged, "waka here quick!"

Gran'pa lay face up on a mat, his body sweaty and strained. Anna sighed, for it was clear his days were nearing an end. Between her trip to the segregation villages and the frantic time with the film crew, she hadn't noticed his poor health—she barely had time for her own precious children.

Anna knelt carefully next to him and moved her face close to his. "How are you feeling today, Gran'pa?"

He closed his eyes and coughed. "I made this for una." His voice was weak as he handed her a wooden stick with a thread through it.

Anna took the stick from his frail hands and studied the carvings. "Oh, it's beautiful."

"When you don lost, it go save you."

"Thank you Gran'pa. I'll treasure it always."

He grabbed her hand and squeezed. "I never chew how una stay with me on the road."

She cupped his face. "I haven't forgotten that either. Not until the day I die."

He coughed again and moved his dry, cracked lips, but no sound escaped.

Anna offered a shaky smile. "I'm so glad you stayed with us instead of going back to Onitsha. I hope we made a difference in your life."

He nodded, tears filling his eyes. Again, he mouthed soundless words, gazing into some unknowable distance. Anna's eyes swelled too. She patted his shoulder and thanked the woman for coming to get her. With another touch on the shoulder, she left Gran'pa's hut for the last time.

✆

Bishop Neel slipped on his white vestment and picked up his bible.

"Is everyone ready?" he said.

"Yes," Anna replied. "The band members are just retrieving their instruments. By the time we're there, everything should be in place."

"I have to say this is the first time I've performed a funeral immediately before a wedding. I'm glad we were able to get the order straight."

Anna helped him brush off some plant spores and smooth out his vestment. "I hated to see Gran'pa leave us, but he certainly outlived everyone's predictions. His is quite a story to tell one day."

The bishop nodded. "Yes, one day we all will have hundreds of stories to tell. Now let's get out there and see if we can add one more."

Sam Hampton raised her hand and the band assembled around the ceremonial area of the village. Bishop Neel walked to the center and called out for the bride.

Carrying a bouquet of flowers, a young girl stepped out of one of the huts wearing a white blouse, waist and thighs wrapped with blue fabric and cinched in front as so many women in the village wore. An older woman took the girl by the hand and led her back through the crowd to Bishop Neel.

With this ceremony having no duties for them, the nuns sat along one row watching with the rest of the crowd. Anna was next to them, smiling at Esi. The young girl had come a long way from being just another abandoned child in the bush.

Bishop Neel cleared his throat. "Ladies and gentlemen, we are gathered here today to join a woman to a man."

No sooner had he said the word 'man' did a leper holding a large jug rise to his feet. He seemed unsure of what he should do next.

"Excuse me," Bishop Neel said, waving his hand in a downward motion. "But we're not quite ready for that. I have a few words to say first."

The man sheepishly sat back down as the bishop launched into a short homily about marriage and the duties of a man and wife. He had learned from dozens of leper weddings that the crowd could basically care less what he had to say. They were mainly interested in the food and drink afterward.

He talked for less than five minutes before signaling Anna to come to the center. She slowly walked to stand beside Esi, bringing with her a decorative wooden cup. Wearing a big smile, she took the flowers from Esi and handed her the cup. Then she nodded to the bishop who pointed to the man. "Now you may bring the wine."

The man jumped up with enthusiasm; his task was one that gave him some status in the village. He came to Esi and held the jug out, doing nothing more.

Slightly frustrated, Bishop Neel huffed. "You may pour the wine now."

Esi whispered a few words in her language and he popped the cork, pouring her cup half full.

"Thank you," Bishop Neel said. "You may return to your seat."

Once again Esi whispered something to him and he took his place back on the log.

Bishop Neel nodded to Anna. "Now, Miss Goodwill, do you have something to say?"

Anna cleared her throat. "I am here to announce to all of you that Esi has obtained her teaching certificate and will now be teaching the students on her own!"

There was chattering among the crowd as they spread the word. The volume continued to rise so Bishop Neel raised his hands and called out, "It is now time to find the groom. Esi, you may begin your search."

A band member picked up his drum and lightly slapped it while another member hit two sticks in rhythm with the drummer to build tension.

Esi held the cup with palm wine and started at the far right, walking up to each male and looking him over carefully. Most of the men did nothing. A few smiled and pursed their lips as if they wanted a kiss. Esi smiled and wagged a finger at them as she continued working the circle looking for her man. Finally, when she was almost done with the entire circle, she found Clarence hiding three deep in the crowd. She stretched her hand out and he took it, allowing her to pull him through the crowd to the center. Once they were there, the bishop commanded them to share the wine, taking turns until it was all gone.

"Bring the cloth please," he said.

A different man and woman approached, carrying a long, thin cloth.

Bishop Neel raised his arms. "Now, we will bind this couple in holy matrimony."

The man and woman each held on to an opposite end of the cloth. Smiling, they pushed the new couple so that they faced each other and made seven passes around while muttering strange words.

Clarence and Esi wrapped their arms around each other, pulling each other close until the cloth was spent. The man tied seven knots and clapped his hands.

"Now we take an offering for the new couple," Bishop Neel announced.

Another villager stepped forward. He lifted a large barrel with a small pot attached to the lip inside. Anna was first and placed a pound note in the small pot. The nuns were next, tossing coins in. They were followed by the doctor and his wife.

Once the 'rich people' finished, the crowd formed a single file and offered their gifts. The lepers, having no money, placed food items in the barrel—yams or cassava root—which thudded at the bottom. A few gave cucumbers or lettuce, with the poorest dropping in a stick of wood for the cooking fires the newlyweds would soon build.

Bishop Neel offered a prayer for blessing and then gestured to one of the many huts. "It is time to consummate the marriage."

With that, the band took up their new song. Several of the lepers grabbed the now heavy barrel and lifted it before the couple, while others guided the newlyweds along. Once the barrel and the couple were inside the hut, the door was closed with another piece of decorative cloth tying it to the jamb from the outside.

The band reached a crescendo as the crowd gathered around the hut chanting and yelling tribal words of encouragement. The party had truly begun!

Calabashes of palm wine quickly made their appearance and towards evening, the beating of the drums made both the good feet and weak feet dance. There were feet with toes and feet without, "For this is a day to be remembered," the bishop cried out. "Praise be to God!"

After the party had reached its crescendo, Anna found herself at a small table with Bishop Neel, Doctor Hampton and his wife, Sam. Dr. Hampton drained a glass of wine then placed his hand over it when Bishop Neel tried to pour him some more.

"No thanks. One glass is it for me. I still have more patients to see today."

The bishop poured himself another cup instead. "I guess we don't want you sauced now, do we?"

"Definitely not. I have to distribute some DDS tablets to a few new patients. I've increased my sample group because I believe that this drug is going to make a huge difference. I placed an order for a large quantity. Did you get it?"

"Yes, I did," the bishop said, taking another sip. "As soon as my new driver gets here, I'll have him take me in to Calabar and send the order off. We'll have all the DDS you need soon and then you can tell me if we need to keep it up."

"As I have said before, it's working miracles on Clarence. I'm sure it's going to eventually put us out of business."

Bishop Neel swigged some wine. "Nothing would please me more!"

Dr. Hampton and his wife returned to the infirmary leaving Anna alone with Bishop Neel.

He leaned forward and whispered, "Did you see those rough-looking characters on the fringe, staring hard at Clarence?"

"No." Anna frowned. "Who were they?"

"I recognized one of the men as kin to the missing sub-chief. He did not look happy."

Anna bit her lip. Just that morning Clarence had told her the builder he hired to construct his hut was worried that he might not be pleased. It seemed that people feared him. Rumors were flying that he not only killed the sub-chief, but had done away with the four men sent to kill him. When Anna discussed these rumors with Clarence, he admitted he was scared but it had nothing to do with the men. He was terrified of being a husband. He had no idea what to do or what his new bride would expect. Since Anna had no advice on the subject, she reassured him that he would be a wonderful husband and off he went.

Anna cleared her throat and glanced cautiously at the bishop. "Now that I have Esi teaching," she began, "I plan to use our new driver to check on my teachers in the segregation villages more often, along with possibly, scouting out new expansion locations."

Bishop Neel slammed down his cup causing Anna to flinch. "Anna, are you telling me you will now risk the bridge and the ferry?!"

She shook her head. "After the long, hard ride on that horse, I have no choice."

The bishop grinned. "I suppose you don't. A horse is a hard way to go! I prefer the kit car myself. Say, would you consider going down to Calabar and dropping off this DDS order?"

Bishop Neel brightened at his own idea, taking another sip from his remaining wine.

"I was going to have to do it because I want to make sure it's done properly. We need to file a form with the government as well as send off requests to supply houses in England. I want all the DDS we can get in case one source dries up. This stuff is saving lives. What do you say?"

"Of course!" Anna replied quickly. "I have a few things I want to buy, anyway."

"Excellent!" he said, topping off both their cups. "I always feel better staying here to keep an eye on problems while they're still mole-hills and not mountains."

Anna drained her glass, and excused herself. She wanted to visit her babies.

She found them just outside of the nursery with two babysitters watching them kicking a ball made from trash.

"There you are my sweet." Anna swung Lily up and kissed her. "My, you are getting bigger. I won't be able to do this much longer."

Lily giggled. No sooner had she set her down did Jonah come running.

"And how are you, my little man?" Anna squatted down and pressed her lips to his smooth face. His neck and shoulders sported the white splotches, creeping ever closer to his poor, lovely nose, his small mouth, and his bright eyes. She closed her eyes and prayed the DDS could soon be taken by the children and help them too.

"I still haven't forgotten what happened that night at the infirmary!" a voice from behind said.

The child squirmed in her arms as anger surged inside, a yellow-orange flash like brushfire. Anna gritted her teeth and glared at Sister Flores.

"Listen, I've had it with your bloody attitude," she said, releasing the boy. Standing up, she squared her shoulders to her tormentor. "You've had it out for me from day one, and I ha—"

A hand grabbed her arm. Anna reacted, spinning around.

"Just me, Anna," Sister Landon said, her eyes were wide with shock. "They told me to come get you. It's time to untie the door and let them out."

Anna sighed heavily. "I'm sorry Janey, it's just that I…" She turned back to face her opponent but Sister Flores was gone. Taking a few more deep breaths, she frowned and said, "Alright, alright. It's meant to be festive today, isn't it? I'm not going to let her get to me."

Janey put her arm through Anna's and tried to comfort her. "It's alright, dear. You'll feel better by the time we get there."

Anna lowered her head and went with her friend, trying to picture Esi's bright and shining face while leaving the angry image of Sister Flores behind in the dust.

※

Two days after the wedding, Anna had calmed down and gotten back to her duties—which seemed to grow every day. She was head of the Boy Scouts. She worked with the band more and more so she'd be able to take over when Samantha left. She gave Oluwa money for tobacco in exchange for petty chores he did for her. She ran a crafts center and inspected the quality of the stitching, painting and pottery goods the lepers made to sell in the Ogojan market. Occasionally, Anna even helped out in the infirmary or the nursery. She did all these things on top of all her teaching duties, which were soon to expand. She hardly had time to worry about herself and her children, much less Sister Flores.

"There you are!" Sister Landon called. "I checked at the children's hut, but they said you had already left."

"Yes." Anna smiled. "I played with Lily and Jonah for an hour and then went back to get my kit. You said to meet you here at four, yes?"

Blushing, Sister Landon glanced at her watch. "Oh, yes. It's just that I was early for the first time in my life and went to the children's hut thinking you'd be waiting there for me. By the time I got back here, I was five minutes late."

"Ah, so you have an excuse, then," Anna teased. "Trying to be clever, and all that."

Sister Landon giggled. "I believe you have the gist of the matter."

"You sound like Victoria now. That's the kind of thing she tried to pull on me. Shall we?" Anna offered her arm.

"We shall."

The two began their short walk to the river, arm in arm.

After a few minutes, Sister Landon spoke. "Listen Anna, I have some news for you, but I want to wait until we are relaxed in the river."

Anna glanced at her friend. "It sounds serious. I hope it's not bad news."

"I'll let you be the judge of that," she replied, her face blank.

Anna went through the list of her worries, wondering if it was Esi or Clarence. She'd seen Janey helping them decorate their hut's interior as she was somewhat of an expert on the subject. Her ability to use what was available to make a hut cheery and colorful was highly valued by lepers. Thus, fashion in the bush would never be the same.

When they finally sat in their favorite hollowed out sand chairs, river flowing up to their chests, Anna nudged Janey's shoulder and gave her a pointed look. The nun sighed.

"Alright, alright, here it is," she said. "You know that new driver who came in last night? He brought the mail with him. One of the letters was from Mother Mary Martin. She's..." Janey took a moment. "She's, well... sending me to Poland and replacing me with another sister."

Anna's heart sank. "Janey—I—you're my best friend out here. After I lost Victoria, you were a godsend."

She put a desperate hand on Janey's shoulder. "Do you have to go?"

Sister Landon looked down at the water. "I'm a nun. I have to go where I'm told." She sniffed and wiped her eyes. "I leave in two weeks. At—at least we'll have that time together."

She offered a watery smile. "And at least you'll inherit all of my bush property. That should be something."

"Have you told Sister Flores yet?"

"She's the one who told me."

Anna straightened up. "Did you see the letter? She would send you away just to spite me."

Sister Landon grimaced. "Actually, I didn't. But I might see if I can sneak a look at it. I know where she keeps things."

Anna sighed and stared down at the flowing water. Janey lowered herself deeper into the water so that it was touching her chin.

"Look, I felt bad just thinking about telling you."

They said nothing for several minutes while Anna tried to imagine life in the bush without her dear friend. She bit her lip and shook her head.

"Let's talk of cheery things now," Anna offered. "I have to go into Calabar tomorrow. I don't want to think about this the whole trip."

"Of course," Sister Landon said.

The two continued bathing and sharing gossip about the activities in the village until they were out of topics. As they neared the end of their bath, Janey felt her forehead.

"I told you I felt bad about telling you, but now I really feel ill. Is my forehead warm?"

Anna scooted over and placed the back of her hand on Janey's forehead. "Oh, Janey, you need to see Doctor Hampton right now!"

Sister Landon moved to the bank and dried off. "I hope I'm not coming down with malaria. Not with my leaving in two weeks."

"Go see the doctor right away!" Anna ordered. "I'm going to stay here a bit longer, but I'll come check on you, alright?"

Janey slipped her dress on. "I'll be in the infirmary unless I die along the way."

Anna splashed some water in her direction. "Don't joke, Janey! Not out here in the bush."

Anna finished her bath as she watched her friend walk up the well-worn path and disappear in the woods. Even though she was worried about Janey and wanted to spend more time with her, she was all alone—a rare event. She took this opportunity to slip farther down the river and wash her hair in the hidden barrel. It had rained the day before and she knew it would be full of fresh rainwater. With her trip to Calabar in the morning, she could replenish her shampoo there, which was almost gone. And she wanted to look good for who-ever might be there to see her. Besides, dipping her long hair in that rain barrel was Anna's special treat to herself, in a place where treats were few and far between.

The next morning, Anna brought her bag to the kit car and was sur-prised when a young man ran towards her and snatched it from her hand.

"You don't need to carry bag sista. I will do it for you!"

"Thank you," she said, surprised. "That's very kind. My name is Anna Goodwill. What's yours?"

"My name is Patrick."

Anna stopped in her tracks. "Did you say Patrick?"

"Yes sista."

"That was our last driver's name. Is it a coincidence?"

"What is that word?"

"Is it mere chance that you have the same name?"

He shrugged. "Dunno, sista. Many boys named Patrick. Many drivers named Patrick. It's St. Patrick's Society."

Anna mused. At one of the hundreds of parties she had attended, she talked with a priest from Calabar. He said that during his time in Nigeria, he had run into at least a thousand boys named Patrick. His theory was that it was the fault of the Irish. They had a long history in Nigeria.

He explained how the Irish priests from the Order of the Holy Ghost established a mission in southern Nigeria in the 1920s and the St. Patrick's Society set up two missions: one along the Ogoja River and the other in Calabar. In 1932, when the Catholics set up the St. Patrick's Society for Foreign Missions (aka the Kiltegan Fathers), the die was cast. Waves of Nigerians named their boys Patrick believing that he was extremely important to the white man. She had seen three or four Patricks in the segregation villages, but Anna had never thought about it until now.

"Patrick, can you wait here for a few moments?" she asked. "I need to see Sister Landon."

"Yes sista, I stay here."

Anna hurried to Sister Landon's room and tapped on the door. "Janey? Janey, are you in there?"

"Come in," a feeble voice replied.

Anna pushed open the door and saw her friend in bed with a wet towel resting on her forehead. On her nightstand were two glasses with different liquids. Anna started to come to her side when Janey stopped her.

"Don't come any closer! The doctor doesn't know what it is. I might be contagious."

Anna stayed where she was. "Goodness, I hope not. Is Dr. Hampton taking good care of you?"

"Yes," she managed, voice cracking. Janey licked her lips and tried again. "Yes, very good. He thinks I might be fine after tonight if the fever breaks."

"That would be wonderful."

Janey's face was pale and sweaty, and her chest barely moved with her breath.

"Is—is there anything I can do for you, dear?"

Sister Landon shook her head. "Just," she coughed wetly, "just tell me about the new driver when you come back."

Anna smiled. "I sure will. And if I don't come back, please don't get in the car with him."

Sister Landon tried to laugh but was too weak to manage anything more than a cough.

"Get well Janey."

Anna spun around and collided hard with someone. Startled, she stepped back and saw it was a glaring Sister Flores, who was holding a fresh wet towel.

"Excuse me," Anna spat out.

A few moments later Anna sat in the kit car headed south to Calabar, hands clenched in her lap.

The trip was fairly uneventful and quick. It made a huge difference when the driver wasn't stopping to listen to independence speeches. Anna wondered how many of those stops were actually necessary from an automotive standpoint. She did learn that the new Patrick had been taught how to drive and speak decent English by a nun. That made it nice not having to struggle through Pidgin, although she mostly understood it now.

They arrived in Calabar and Anna checked into her usual church quarters just as the sisters were about to serve a meal. She enjoyed eating with them—they served different dishes than in Ogoja.

The next morning, Anna waited at the government building before it opened and filed a form for free DDS. Incredibly, this task took three hours. Such was life in Nigeria.

With that done, she walked to the post office and mailed several DDS requests to England. This left her with plenty of time to shop.

Walking through the streets of Calabar with her freshly washed hair was nice. The air was cool and massive mangroves threw long shadows over the dirt. She even found all the items she needed, including a new brand of shampoo from France. That excited her the most.

With everything done, Anna went back to her quarters where another array of new dishes and interesting conversation awaited her.

The following morning, there was the new Patrick—waiting just outside her quarters with the kit car running. He was certainly showing himself to be a worthy driver. They hadn't had one mechanical issue. She was going to give an excellent report to the bishop. Their driving problem was solved!

The trip back to Ogoja was fairly pleasant, if a long dusty drive could be called that. As they pulled into the settlement, children came running alongside, waving and cheering as if the King himself had arrived. Anna waved back until they fell behind.

When they came to a stop in the parking area, Patrick said, "I take luggage to your hut."

"Thank you Patrick! And let me say you are an excellent driver. I intend to tell the bishop just that."

"Many blessings sista!" he said with a big smile.

After such a long drive, Anna walked up the stairs as fast as her heavy feet could carry her, but Janey's room sat empty. She knocked on the bishop's door and received no reply. In fact, no one was in their quarters. Anna thought it was good news—perhaps Janey felt better and was back to work.

At the bottom of the stairs, Oluwa waited.

"Oluwa, do you know where Janey—I mean Sister Landon is?"

His face went tight. "She dey here." He pointed to the infirmary. "She no dey well."

Anna's heart stopped. The last time she had returned from a trip like this, they were burying Victoria. Dr. Hampton caught her at the door of the infirmary. His brow was furrowed and his face bore long, grim lines.

Anna gripped his arm. "Doctor, I just got back! How is she?"

His eyes dropped and he shook his head. "It won't be long, dear. The CSM got inside her and there was nothing I could do. I'm so very sorry."

Anna covered her mouth and turned away. CSM was cerebrospinal meningitis, a disease that brought on a stiff neck, rashes, violent headaches, and finally delirium. They had no cure for it and few people survived it.

She stared at the sun hanging high above the village, curling the green treetops and cracking the hard earth. Lepers moved about the village in their rhythmic circles, shouting and smiling and carrying on their business. Anna wanted to scream.

Dr. Hampton put his hand on her arm. "I'm sorry, Anna. We don't have a way to treat it. I feel so helpless."

Anna couldn't answer. The door to the infirmary opened and Samantha Hampton stepped out.

"She heard your voice and would like to see you."

Holding the door open, she said, "Right now!" when Anna failed to move.

Anna steadied herself and forced her feet to move. Sam led her to a bed veiled by mosquito netting. Anna drifted closer to the feeble voice calling out to her.

"Janey, I'm here. I made it back safely." She didn't bother to wipe the tears from her cheeks.

Sam touched her arm. "That's not Janey. She's sleeping in the other room. She's almost fully recovered."

Anna stiffened. "She's going to be alright?"

"Yes. Janey is fine. This is Sister Flores. She is the one who called for you."

Anna's stomach dropped like a stone. She opened her mouth but her voice caught. She coughed and tried once more: "Sister Flores, did you call for me?"

"Yes," she croaked. "I... need to... tell you something."

Anna wiped her cheeks with her sleeve and lifted the veil. Sister Flores was pale and sweating with death, her dark hair plastered to her face. Anna swallowed.

"I'm—I'm here."

Sister Flores muttered something but Anna couldn't make it out. Dr. Hampton came back into the room and pulled Anna away.

"Not too close," he warned her. "You know CSM is contagious."

"But I can't hear her. She's trying to speak."

"I know, but you must stand back. Doctor's orders," he said firmly.

Sister Flores' voice floated weakly out again, unintelligible.

Anna pulled Dr. Hampton down and whispered in his ear. "How much longer does she have?"

"Minutes," he whispered.

She bit her lip. Then, before either Dr. Hampton or Sam could stop her, she went to the edge of the bed, lifted the mosquito netting, and peered directly into the dying woman's eyes.

"I'm here, Sister," she soothed, peering into the nun's eyes. "It's me, Anna."

"Isabel," Sister Flores croaked.

"Isabel? No, I'm Anna."

The patient was now breathing heavily, flirting with unconsciousness.

"My... first... name."

"It's beautiful," Anna said, full of emotion. "All these years and I never knew."

Sister Flores barely nodded, trying desperately to form a smile with the corners of her weak lips. Suddenly, her eyes rolled back.

Panicked, Anna reached over and shook her. "Isabel! I'm here! Please don't go."

She rolled her face over towards Anna and opened her eyes. Her lips parted and something came out but again, Anna couldn't hear it.

"Please, I can't hear you!"

Staring straight up, Sister Flores licked her dry lips with tears filling her eyes. She drew in as much air as her empty body would allow. Then she turned her head towards Anna causing several tears to drip on the pillow.

Anna, sensing more words, moved to within inches of her face. Finally, Sister Flores was able to release her desperate message.

"Anna... I'm... s-sorry."

Stunned, Anna leaned back. Her eyes threatened to spill once more. All these years, and for what? All the lepers they had buried, all the friends, and neither one of them could ever find the courage to apologize. Perhaps that would have ended everything and they might have been close friends. Now, at the very end, the words had finally been said. But it wasn't from Anna's lips.

Anna's chest went tight and her heart jumped. "Isabel..."

But it was too late. The eyes of Sister Isabel Flores lay open, empty—she was gone—another missionary lost in Africa.

22

May 27, 1968
18 years later

The conditioner soaked into Anna's long hair as she brushed it, pulling the same small strokes she had done thousands of times before. But no longer was her hair a solid display of dark caramel. Streaks of gray wove in and out of light browns crowding out the few dark strands of her original color. Soon, it would all be gray, and then white, like her mother's. Still, she felt like the young, vibrant, thirty-year-old girl who had come to the bush, but her appearance told a different story.

Sun spots dotted her hands and arms and cheeks. It certainly wasn't the life she envisioned when she was eighteen, nor when she was twenty-nine. But she had learned to be comfortable with herself, and now she couldn't imagine anything different.

Anna washed out the comb and used the barrel's edge to tap the water off the spines. This was the fourth barrel Clarence had set up for her, the other three having rotted out the bottom.

Or was it the fifth?

She couldn't be sure. She only knew this would be the last time she washed her hair from a rain barrel in Ogoja and Anna wanted to savor the moment—make it last.

She drank in the forest as if to keep it inside her somehow, so she could play it back years later sitting next to some hearth fire, listening to the wood crackle and pop. The trees here grew so thick, with their large canopies blocking out much of the light, the shadows filled with the cries and rustles of unseen creatures. Anna wanted to remember it all.

She poured the rainwater over her long tresses, more than she usually did. And why not? No one else was going to use it except for a few birds.

She wrapped up her things and waded across the shallowest part of the stream. Then she walked up the dirt path to the edge of the village trying hard to remember the first time she made this trip, no doubt dirty and dusty, and completely unprepared for all she would face.

In the village, many of the humble huts now had concrete blocks around the bottom. As the settlement gained the ability to make its own blocks, the lepers either purchased or commandeered them.

In a small field, there were the fifty original male chaulmoogra trees with their female companions, delivering the oil the doctors no longer needed. The lepers still collected the oil and sold it in the market to the locals, who used it as a remedy for a variety of conditions. All around, the normal hustle and bustle was quite diminished.

She had no formal count but guessed the settlement was less than a fourth full, with most villagers having fled south to better security and more food. At least, that was what the rumors promised.

Anna wandered past the two hospital wards—twenty-five beds each. Then the midwifery school and the maternity clinic, both of which were modern and spacious. These last two allowed the missionaries to catch leprosy at an early stage and prevent the babies from being dumped in the bush. They considered it one of their greatest accomplishments.

Just before she reached her residential building, Anna passed the library, a small building attached to their residence. There they kept donated books from America, India, Ireland, and England. The lepers who had learned to read, borrowed the books and returned them within a specified period of time. As Bishop Neel had said many times, "How many of these people would've never been educated but for contracting the disease? It makes one marvel at God's plan."

Right outside the library was a small amphitheater where they made announcements to the villagers and held the all-important graduation ceremonies. When someone was deemed free of leprosy, they were given special papers in this ceremony and encouraged to return to their village (if they knew where they were from). Hopefully, they could reunite with their family. If not, they could travel to other villages and live, although most stayed in the village where they were loved, cared for, and cured. It had taken a great deal of time and effort to get to the first graduation, but the new drugs had worked, and family reunions were common now.

Anna walked up the stairs of the first building they had built so long ago. She lived in Janey's old room. It had been Victoria's before that. Across the hall, Anna used Sister Flores' old room as an office. With just her and Bishop Neel on the floor, they had spread out.

Anna draped her wet towel over the exterior window sill to dry and packed her bathing kit in one of two bags, before sighing. She wondered what would happen to the room when she left. She was certain anything she left behind would disappear moments after her departure. Yet the space itself held so many memories, so many conversations that they couldn't take away. Only she could.

There was knock on her door. It was Bishop Neel holding a bottle.

"As this is our last day here, I thought I could persuade you to enjoy a glass of single-malt."

Anna placed a folded blouse in her luggage and glanced at her watch. "I guess we've done enough work for the day. I was about to make some tea but I suppose a taste of Scotland will do rather nicely."

Bishop Neel laughed. "It's high time to let someone else treat you, although I must say, I think this will be a treat for both of us."

He tried to hide a grin. "Actually, it will be more of treat for me than you."

She chuckled and followed behind him, watching him slowly shuffle to his desk and arrange his chair just so. When he was situated, he opened the bottle on his desk, struggling a bit with the wax seal. After pouring each of them some scotch, he handed a glass to Anna and raised his own to make a toast.

"Here's to both the Queen and Mother Mary Martin, not necessarily in that order."

Anna laughed and lifted her glass up, smacking her lips on the brown alcohol. "Goodness, that's stout! What is it?"

The bishop lowered his glasses and turned the bottle around so she could see the label. "It's Glenlivet," he said. "Distilled in 1946 and bottled in 1961. I picked it up at that meeting a few years back in Umuahia. The Scots were there and I persuaded one of them to turn loose of it since they could easily replenish their stock."

"1946? That's the year we came here."

The bishop smiled. "I thought I would save it for my seventieth birthday, you know. But we'll be on a ship back to Dublin soon, and I might have to share it with too many people. This is my next choice."

Anna sipped the potent spirit. "It's hard to believe we made it twenty-two years."

"Yes," he said, smoothing back his thick white hair. "I must admit I told Sister Flores you wouldn't make it a month, which, looking back, may not have helped her... *disposition*."

Bishop Neel smiled wryly. "Sister Flores! Now there's a name for you. Seems so long ago."

"Eighteen years," Anna said. "We're leaving her behind, along with Thomas and Victoria. Our work here has taken quite a toll."

Bishop Neel swilled his glass while he stared up at the ceiling. "Don't forget that other doctor. What was his name?"

"Oh that's right! Cedric Longbottom," Anna said, nodding. "He died along with Patrick Number Two, as we called him. Poor Patrick. Remember when he got too close to the edge of the ravine and rolled our kit car down that embankment just before Abakaliki? We lost them both right there. And Sister Crozier, too, bitten by that large snake."

"Yes," he said leaning forward and setting his glass on the desk. "And there was one more. That tiny girl who died of malaria."

Anna closed her eyes trying to remember. "It was… Sister Cornell! Yes, she was only staying six months but died after three."

Bishop Neel poured himself more scotch. "I'm sad to say I'd forgotten about all that."

Anna pursed her lips. "Memories of death tend to stick with me."

She took another sip and sighed. "I can't believe the very people we helped are forcing us to leave."

The bishop leaned back cradling his glass. "Well, it's not the very people we helped. I doubt many of these soldiers are recovered lepers. We are in the new country of Biafra, my dear, home of the Christian-Igbo. Of course, the rest of Nigeria say we are in rebel territory and everyone here must die. Not a pleasing thought!"

Anna frowned. "Too bad we were restricted from setting up missions outside the Igbo controlled areas when we first came here. I can only imagine how much good we could've done in the rest of Nigeria—the Muslim Nigeria. And I suppose independence only made it worse. I can still see our original driver, Patrick, so many years ago. His young face as he went off."

Bishop Neel lifted his glass high again. "Good for them! He and all his brethren throughout Nigeria finally gained their independence from the Crown without firing a shot. Unfortunately for Patrick Number One, he was Igbo. The Igbos ended up on the outside of the new government looking in. It's always the case. Being united for independence is the easy part. But they don't think about what happens afterwards, when only one party can rule. And Patrick's party wasn't it. That's when the coups and civil wars come. They always do. Now it's the Igbos who have declared Biafra a new country, and we have to leave before one side or the other shuts down Port Harcourt and traps us here!"

"It seems ridiculous," Anna scoffed. "We are British citizens, after all."

"My dear, war turns man into a savage beast, making his blood run hot. They will beat this old man to death and do unspeakable things to a woman no matter what papers you present them. Without order and discipline and skilled officers, these Africans—be they rebels or federal troops—will pillage and plunder without a second thought."

"If we would've built these settlements in federal territory, would we now be safe?"

Bishop Neel hummed, staring into his glass. "It depends. If we were in federal territory and the rebels took that section over, they would be the dangerous horde we now fear. The only way we would've been safe was to be surrounded by disciplined British regulars—the backbone of a civilized society."

Anna nodded. "How many lepers would you say we healed?"

"Thousands! I have the records in my valise. It has to be a very large number. After all, we achieved eighteen segregation villages in addition to what we accomplished in this settlement. I'm going to carefully study the records on the ship back to England. It will give me something to do."

Anna clapped her hands. "I can't wait to know the number. You really made the Nigerian Leprosy Control Programme something the world could be proud of, especially the way you helped them become self-sufficient."

Bishop Neel leaned forward and grew serious. "No, Anna. It was you and the sisters from MMM teaching them to be self-sufficient—that was the difference! The Leprosy Control Officers. The midwives. The nurses. The teachers. I can't imagine how many souls would long be buried if you hadn't been here. You helped them multiply among themselves. You were the key! I want you to know I've put your name in to the Queen." He leaned back in his chair. "We'll see if I still have some pull left."

Anna's mouth hung open, her humbleness coming out. "I-I can't thank you enough. But I—don't forget the film *Visitation* brought in all that money and all the work the sisters did. That's what really pushed all the expansion."

"Yes, it sure did. Mother Mary Martin was brilliant when it came to marketing our cause. And of course, the sisters of MMM were invaluable in our efforts to sustain and grow the villages. Certainly better than I ever was."

Anna reached across the desk and covered his hand with hers. "Well, if I was so important here, it was your speech in Maghull that sold me. So I guess you're not as insignificant as you think."

"I'll drink to that," he said, as they clinked glasses.

Suddenly, a loud explosion rattled the building.

"What was that?!" Bishop Neel said, setting his glass down, struggling to his feet.

Without answering, she raced downstairs in time to see a boy emerging from the woods and running across the field. Anna moved to intercept him.

"What was that explosion?" she called out to the boy.

"Federal troops coming!" he yelled, waving his arms. "They through Abuochicie!"

"That's only four miles away! Are you sure?"

The boy continued running and yelling. "Federal troops coming! Federal troops coming!"

She ran back up the stairs to find Bishop Neel on the landing.

"What is it?" he said with a worried voice.

"The federal troops have run through the rebel defenses at Abuochicie! They're coming to Ogoja!"

"Oh God no!" he said covering his mouth. "I'm afraid we have overstayed our welcome. Grab your bags! We must hurry!"

Anna dashed past him and into her room. She tossed a few more items into one of the bags and snapped them both shut. She was almost out the door when she stopped. There, hanging on a nail was the decorative stick Gran'pa had given her so long ago. She carefully lifted it off and put it around her neck. Then she ran downstairs, tossing her bags into the rear of the kit car before flying back upstairs to help the bishop. She found him struggling with his bags, his round face reddened.

"Here, let me help you with these," she said, panting. Anna lifted them as he turned around for something else. "Hurry Bishop! Please, we must leave now!"

"I almost forgot this!" he muttered.

Anna didn't wait to hear the rest, instead hurrying back out to the kit car. She knew the bishop was moving too slowly. Sometimes, he needed a cane to get around. It seemed to be getting worse.

She was just about to go back for him when he appeared, clutching an old Bible in one hand and the bottle of Glenlivet in the other. He shuffled as quickly as he could to the car.

"I couldn't leave these behind," he said.

Anna closed her door. "Okay, let's go!"

Bishop Neel scrunched his forehead. "Yes indeed, let's go! The key is in the ignition."

Anna jerked back. "You're not expecting me to drive, are you?"

"Certainly. I'm too old to drive. I'm sure I can't even see the road at night, which is soon coming. Besides, I never learned to drive."

"Oh no!" Anna said, slapping the seat in front her and startling the bishop. "I never learned either!"

He moaned. "Oh dear. Apparently, having your own driver all your life *does* have a drawback. I'm afraid I sent him off to say good-bye to his family. He won't be here until morning. By then, I'm afraid there will be nothing to drive."

Her shoulders slumped. "We can't wait that long. What are we going to do?"

More explosions cracked through the bush.

Anna stared at the direction from which the boy had come and gasped. "Oh my God! There!" she cried, hitting the bishop's arm. "See those men? They're coming! Let's hide!"

He grabbed her arm. "Wait a minute. My eyes may not be so bad after all. Those are the rebels fleeing. That one chap appears injured."

She squinted her eyes and stared harder. Sure enough, he was right.

"What do we do? We can't sit here."

"We can. Perhaps one of the fleeing soldiers can drive us. This is as good a place as any."

Anna ignored his comment and opened the car door. "I'm going to see how far behind the federal troops are."

Before the bishop could say a word, Anna was halfway to the fleeing soldiers.

One of them called to her. "We have wounded. Do you have doctors?"

"No, they're all gone. But we do have medical supplies in the hospital. It's over in this building. I'll show you."

Two men helped another rebel between them, who was dragging his feet in the dirt. Blood dotted his uniform. When they got him inside and into a bed, the lead soldier stared at her and froze.

"What is it?" she said, afraid her life was in danger.

"Miss Anna?"

Anna backed away from him in fear "Do I know you?"

He slapped his chest. "I'm Patrick! Your driver. Remember?"

Anna blinked. "Patrick! We were just talking about you. The bishop is in the kit car and we need to leave right now, but we can't drive." She gripped his arm and pulled him close. "Can you drive us south to Calabar?"

He pulled his arm free and shook his head. "I cannot do this. The federals have seized the coast and blockaded all of Biafra. We were just attacked at Abuochicie. They have gone ahead of us and taken over the road to Calabar. You cannot go that way. You must head west."

"West? We have to catch a ship in two days' time. We have to leave!"

"I'm sorry Miss Anna. I must stay and fight. You must leave or the federals will kill you." His face was harder than she remembered, a thin scar running past his left eye. "Go west to Abakaliki," he insisted. "You will be safer there. Take the small-small road through Ekuaro. Do not go on the Calabar Road."

Anna was desperate. "We can't drive the kit car. We don't know how. Can you spare a driver?"

"I cannot."

A loud explosion vibrated the floor getting their attention. The troops were close, less than a mile away.

"Miss Anna, they are coming! I must lead my men."

He was gone before she could say goodbye.

Anna went back to the kit car and told Bishop Neel what had happened.

"Just our luck," he cried, slapping his thigh. "We need a driver and Patrick comes along to save us. Yet, like before, his interests lie elsewhere."

Anna was frantic. "What are we going to do?! I guess now is as good a time as any to learn how to drive."

The sound of another car racing up the road distracted her.

"Look!" she yelled. "Maybe we can ride with them."

A kit car skidded to a stop behind them and a man slid behind the wheel; it was Clarence—no longer the boy Anna remembered.

"Clarence!" Anna cried. "You came to rescue us!"

He nodded, wiping sweat from his forehead. "As I don hear the explosion, I try my best to run outside. Jonah go dey follow behind us."

Clarence jumped in, started up the engine, and took off down the settlement road. In the late afternoon light, Anna stared out the rear window at the village she had lived in for the last twenty-two years. A fireball crashed near the path to the river Anna had taken earlier in the day. Trees splintered and fell. The crackling of gunfire was heavy now. She watched as dozens of remaining lepers ran in different directions unsure of where to go.

Anna squinted and saw Patrick leading a charge of men towards the federal troops. A man next to him fell. The last thing she saw was the little village sign planted firmly in its flower bed. "Welcome to the Leprosy Settlement in Ogoja,"—her home.

Bishop Neel tugged on her sleeve. "I have no regrets about this place, you know. Even with all those we've lost, it was worth every year."

Images of Thomas, Victoria, and Sister Isabel Flores floated through her mind.

"I certainly have regrets," she said, wiping her eyes. We're leaving some wonderful missionaries behind. No one will ever know what all they did to save lives."

Bishop Neel sighed. "Well, I do wish we would've left a week ago, and I think you're wrong about them being forgotten."

They drove southwest for twenty minutes and pulled into Ekuaro just as dusk settled. The panic from Ogoja had not yet spread there, but the sound of the explosions had been drifting in their direction for quite some time. This quickened the leisurely pace of life in Ekuaro. Hurried movements were now the norm and Anna feared that would soon change to panic.

The two kit cars came to a stop outside a small market. Clarence yelled something to Jonah causing him to sprint off. Anna leaned forward and touched Clarence on the shoulder.

"Where did you get that kit car? Did you buy it somehow?"

"No, someone leave ham behind."

Anna went no further. She knew Clarence all too well.

"Listen, I saw Patrick, our first driver. He's a soldier now. He told me to stay off the Calabar Road and head west to Abakaliki."

Clarence nodded. "Na the truth he dey speak. We dey go west."

"We?"

"Yeah, Esi, me, Jonah, Lily and Isabel. The soldiers go kill me and take the women for dem use. We go also!"

Anna leaned back, biting her lip. This was getting serious. She sat there with Bishop Neel watching Jonah help his mother and sisters carry their bags to the kit cars. Three years ago, Clarence and Esi had moved to Ekuaro where a distant relative of Esi's owned a market. With the relative getting too old to manage his affairs, Clarence and Esi took it over. Because they had basically raised Jonah and Lily (with Anna's financial support), and considered them their own children, they went to Ekuaro too along with Isabel, the child of Clarence and Esi.

In less than five minutes, the other kit car was loaded up and ready to go. Clarence directed Isabel to sit next to Anna while he started up the engine. With dirt and dust flying, the two kit cars took off, heading west.

In the light that was left, Anna studied the girl sitting next to her. "Isabel, I can't believe how you've changed. How long has it been since I've seen you?"

"Two Christmases ago," Isabel replied, smiling.

"Oh, my! How old are you now?"

"Seventeen."

She looked every bit of that and more.

Anna clasped the girl's hand in hers. "You are simply gorgeous! The boys will go wild."

Clarence heard this. "We dey leave the wahala boys here," he yelled over the engine's roar.

Isabel blushed and changed the subject. "Father says he wanted to name me Anna—after you—but you refused."

"Yes, I wanted him to name you after another person who deserved the honor more than I did. I'll tell you about her someday."

Isabel grinned.

When it was completely dark, the kit cars turned on their lights. A cool breeze whipped through the open windows as Clarence pushed the speed. They were on a back road and had almost reached Abakaliki when the kit car Jonah was driving, slowed and drifted to the side of the road. Clarence turned his kit car around and came alongside him.

"What dey the matter?" Clarence asked.

"Out of petrol," Jonah replied.

Clarence parked the kit car and told everyone to stretch their legs while he and Jonah worked on transferring some petrol from his tank to Jonah's. When they had finished and were putting things away, a military jeep approached, catching them off guard. With nowhere to run, they froze.

A wide spotlight flashed on, blinding them.

"Who are you?" a deep voice boomed.

Leaning against the kit car, Bishop Neel waved his hand at the light. "We are missionaries—British citizens—on our way to catch a ship back to Dublin."

One of the men exited the jeep while the other pointed a rifle at them. "Papers!" he said.

Anna and Bishop Neel handed him their passports. He looked them over and handed them back.

"Who are they?" he said pointing to the others.

"They are my family!" Anna said desperately. "The boy driving is Jonah and the girl with him is Lily. I raised them from babies before Esi and Clarence took them in as their children. Then they had Isabel, this one next to me. Both Esi and Clarence worked for me in the Leprosy Settlement in Ogoja until a few years ago."

"Is that where you come from?" he said moving closer.

"Yes," Bishop Neel chimed in. "The federal troops were fighting with the Biafrans. It was too dangerous."

He turned and gave a signal to the man in the jeep. The spotlight lowered to the ground, no longer blinding them.

"We are Biafran officers. The roads are not safe. You should have left Ogoja weeks ago. Where are you going?"

"To Abakaliki," Bishop Neel said.

The officer shook his head. "There is starvation and death there. You may be attacked for your food and water. You should not go there."

"Where then?"

"Go through Abakaliki without stopping and on to Onitsha. You may be able to pay a man to take you across the Niger. The British are stationed on the other side in Asaba. If you can reach them, you can surrender, but it will be very dangerous. If the federal troops find you first, they will kill all except you two." He pointed to Anna and Bishop Neel. "Maybe they will keep you," he said staring at Isabel. "How old are you?"

"Seventeen," Anna replied, pulling the girl close.

"If you stay on this side, food can be smuggled across the river for money. You might buy some to stay alive. But be careful. A starving person doesn't care what they do to get food."

Bishop Neel nodded vigorously. "Thank you for the advice sir. We are grateful."

The man said nothing. He climbed in the jeep and turned towards the east, dust clouding in his wake. When the jeep was out of sight, the bishop spoke.

"I suppose we should follow his advice."

Clarence pulled Jonah aside and privately spoke to him in their language with Esi chiming in periodically. When they were done, Clarence nervously rubbed his hands together.

"We dey take the kit cars go a hill before Abakaliki. We go wait until night don come. Then we ride fast go the city. We go keep silent and suppose stay dark-dark when we don reach near the city."

Everyone nodded in agreement. The two vehicles loaded up and took off.

They waited silently on the hill overlooking Abakaliki until all the light had faded and clouds covered the moon. Then, with headlights off, Clarence led the two vehicles through the heart of Abakaliki. When they were safely through the city, he turned on his headlights and continued west until he reached the outskirts of Enugu.

Once again, he stopped the cars to tell everyone that they were going to repeat the same routine though this city. Anna kept her head down and prayed, not stopping until Enugu was miles behind them.

Before them was a long stretch of heavily, forested land with only the road as clear space. They had gone a mile into this land when Jonah's kit car quit again. He let it coast as far as it could before pulling over.

Clarence drove back to him and shut his engine off. With Jonah's help, Clarence examined the gas tank. After more discussion, the verdict was in.

"Our petrol don low. Both cars no fit make it to Onitsha. We dey make one."

"Will we all fit?" Anna said. "What about our luggage?"

"We be seven. That don dey too plenty to carry. We go leave luggage behind. You na go carry wetin dey important only. If the weight don too much, we no fit make it to Onitsha."

He didn't have to say anything more. If they didn't make Onitsha, they would be stuck on the side of the road, a place more dangerous than in a starving city. Roving bands of criminals could appear at any minute and strip them bare. Anything could happen! And there was Bishop Neel. He would be left behind since he couldn't walk more than a quarter mile, if that. They would have two choices: Stay together and die, or walk into Onitsha without the bishop and perhaps live.

Clarence lit two lanterns and hung them from the kit cars. In the dim light, Anna set her two pieces of luggage on the side of the road and opened them up. She placed everything she wanted to keep in one bag and items to be left behind in the second bag. It was agonizing. When she was done, Clarence came over and inspected her work.

"No! Too plenty."

He held up his hands and formed a small box to show her how much stuff she could take. This devastated her.

By the time she was done, she had one set of undergarments and a single spare blouse. The clothes were wrapped around her precious whale bone comb, and even more precious teapot and saucer—her mother's. There was also a package of Ceylon tea, Sister Flores' pocket watch—which ran the entire settlement while she was alive—and a photo of Victoria. Thomas' favorite deck of cards was carefully hidden inside a leftover tea package next to Molly's letters. She had everything shoved into a light fiber hand tote. This, Clarence approved.

Anna wandered over to where Bishop Neel was undergoing the same painstaking process.

"It's funny how you value things differently when you have to really choose."

"Yes," said the Bishop, clearly distraught. "I have these special vestments but when forced to choose, I must keep the records from the settlement and my Bible."

Anna noticed he also had rolled a pair of underwear around his special bottle, but said nothing. It too passed Clarence's detailed eye.

After everyone was finished, Clarence inspected the weight of all the belongings and with many frowns, finally approved it. Esi had another bag that contained food and water, which they decided to eat right then. There was no sense in having it taken from them in Onitsha. The only things they kept were two canteens full of water. The empty skins they tossed in the back in case they had a chance to fill them up later.

Once they had eaten all the food, they said a prayer for their safe passage and crammed into the kit car. With four adults in the back-seat and three up front, it was hard for Clarence to steer properly.

Finally, dawn arrived. The weather was good and the air fairly cool, which was a blessing. They wound their way steadily along the dirt road finally leaving the forest and entering a long stretch of flat, desolate land. Still they saw no one.

An hour later, they were climbing a small hill when the kit car sputtered to a stop. Clarence tried to start the car again several times, but to no avail.

The sun was rising and growing hot. Any breeze had sputtered out long ago with the petrol. They stared ahead and could see no shade for miles and it was many miles they still had to go.

Anna glanced at Clarence who was studying the old man and her heart sank.

"Bishop Neel," she blurted, unable to finish her sentence. She knew he would be left behind to fend for himself. And to die.

23

Clarence and Jonah stood in front of the kit car, looking back at the rest of the group. No one dared say a word. It was almost noon, but the relentless sun had already warmed the land all around them. Soon, it would be blazing hot.

Hands on hips, Clarence spoke to Jonah away from the kit car. The other five sat in their places, waiting for the order they knew would eventually come: They would have to start walking.

Meanwhile, Bishop Neel would remain behind, hiding under the only shade around—the kit car—and hoping for the best. Maybe someone would come along and rescue him, some soldiers perhaps. Even though no one was on the roads, they needed something to justify what they were about to do. Finally, the bishop himself broke the tension.

"Well, what are you all waiting for? Start walking! I'll stay here and guard the kit car." He smiled, despite the sad faces staring back at him.

"Oh don't worry," he said. "I have my special weapons to keep me company."

Anna sprung from the car. "There has to be something we can do, Clarence! Let's push the car with Bishop Neel in it. If we all work hard, surely we can make it!"

Clarence shook his head before shrugging his shoulders and giving in. "We dey try."

Anna clapped her hands with excitement, attempting to build enthusiasm about something that was sure to be a lot of hard work. The others got out of the kit car and went where Clarence positioned them. He moved the bishop to the driver's seat, since he seemed capable of steering. Once everyone was in place, Clarence slipped the engine out of gear and released the brake.

Running around the car to the rear bumper, Clarence cried, "Push!"

They all leaned in and pushed hard. The car moved up the hill, but at an excruciatingly slow pace.

Anna was positioned on the passenger's side rear bumper and looked ahead. The top of a hill was coming into view. She assumed that when they crested the hill, they could hop in the car and ride down the other side, which hopefully would be a long way. But they had to reach the top first.

They agonizingly watched each inch below them crawl by. After five minutes, the group could feel their initial energy running low.

Sensing this, Clarence yelled out, "Push! Push!"

They dug down and fought against the road, often slipping on the smooth, polished clay. Just as they were about to reach the top, some of the pushers relaxed. That brought the kit car to a stop, which threatened to send it back down the hill. Jonah and Clarence dug their feet into the road and groaned loudly. Their effort spurred the others on.

With a final burst, the kit car started rolling easier. The road had flattened out. They still had to push hard, but it seemed like things were going to get better. Then Anna stepped out from behind the vehicle.

"Oh no!" she cried out. "You've got to be kidding!"

There was no downhill slope on the other side. Instead, there were several more miles of flat road, leading to another small hill.

Who knew what lie behind that?

They all stopped pushing, allowing the kit car to roll to a quick stop. No one had the strength to push that far—and certainly not up another hill. This was the end of the road.

They breathed heavily. Esi and Anna bent over in exhaustion as Clarence and Jonah walked away and began talking again. Jonah was getting upset. For a few minutes, he frantically pointed at items on the kit car. Then Clarence retrieved some tools, and they talked more calmly as they worked. Eventually, a plan evolved, and Jonah relayed it to the rest of the group since his English was more like Anna's.

"It's way too hot to walk during the day. We'll take off parts and use them for shade. At night, we'll walk and push the kit car again. You'll see!"

Anna didn't fully understand their idea, but she could tell Jonah was excited about it. They climbed back in the vehicle or sat on the road, where the kit car provided the most shade. The two men pounded and ratcheted away. Throughout all this, Bishop Neel remained silent, while the others chatted among themselves.

Ten minutes later, Clarence and Jonah removed the large hood and fastened it to the roof, so that it hung over the side and created even more shade. Now Clarence had easier access to the engine. They banged on it for an hour, occasionally cursing, until the engine dropped to the road. Both men stood back like proud fathers of a newborn, the kit car having just lightened its load.

By now, it was 2 p.m. and very hot. Sweat glistened on their bodies, wicking away precious water they would need to survive. Soon they would be dehydrated. They had only one shot: They'd have to find Onitsha by morning, or they wouldn't last another day.

As the sun began its descent, the kit car was no longer recognizable. Clarence and Jonah had removed all the doors and hung them over the roof for more shade. A welcome breeze rewarded their hard work.

Their last task was removing pieces of the engine from under the car, so it could roll without getting stuck on the parts. When they finished that, the car was completely stripped.

Anna couldn't believe what she saw. This might actually work!

Everyone sat on the ground on the passenger's side, which was bathed in shade. Clarence and Jonah were sprawled out sideways on the car seats, their legs hanging over, and snoring. They were exhausted.

The shadows grew longer and longer and swallowed up the piles of car parts scattered everywhere. A cool breeze returned with occasional puffs of dust, which made them cough.

Anna looked at everything they'd removed. She was sure the kit car would now be easier to push. The engine alone had to weigh 150 pounds.

The big issue was the hill. If that was still too difficult, they would have to leave the bishop behind and wish him the best. Anna didn't want to think about what that scene would be like.

At 9 p.m., the road was illuminated by only a bright, full moon. Clarence stirred. He nudged Jonah awake. In just a few minutes, they removed the doors and hood from the roof and cast them aside. If they didn't make it to Onitsha by morning, the extra shade wouldn't matter.

Anna tried to lick her dry lips and desperately wished for a drink of cool water. The last time she'd faced a deep thirst like this was when those men were coming to kill Clarence—and probably her too. Even though that happened a very long time ago, her thirst made it feel like yesterday.

Anna knew they had a lot of work ahead. Even if they couldn't push the bishop up the hill, they still had to walk. That alone was going to be tough.

She convinced herself that for the next ten hours she would do whatever she had to do to survive. She wasn't ready to join Thomas and Victoria.

Once again, death was in the vicinity, looking for another missionary to claim. She balled up her fists, determined that it would not get her.

"Not today," she whispered to no one.

Clarence put the bishop back in the driver's seat and arranged everyone around the car. With no gears to worry about, he simply called out, "Push!"

Incredibly, the kit car moved easily. It was almost like rolling a toy. If there was a slight dip in the road, only two pushers were needed. The rest hopped in the car and relaxed. It was unbelievable!

When they reached the second hill, they found it wasn't that hard to push it all the way up. At the crest, not one of them was exhausted. And now they had a bigger treat waiting for them: A long, downward slope which allowed everyone to ride for a good bit. This idea was working out even better than walking!

After coasting for a while, two of them got out and pushed. They continued like this for hours—pushing and riding. And since the land gently sloped toward the Niger River—which they knew was waiting for them in the distance—they never had to climb a hill the size of the first two again.

While they pushed, Bishop Neel regaled them with Irish songs. Though they'd heard them all before, they still enjoyed the melodies. In other circumstances, this might've been a fun adventure. But too much hung in the balance; it was a matter of life and death. Bishop Neel was barely hanging on, and they all knew it.

It was still dark when they saw dozens of small fires ahead. They had almost reached Onitsha. The city was now entirely lit by these small fires since the electricity had stopped working long ago.

Clarence warned them to keep pushing no matter what. They shouldn't talk to anyone. The last thing they needed was people rushing them for possible food. If that happened, they would have to fight.

When they reached the city's edge, Anna saw people sleeping everywhere. It wasn't dawn yet, which turned out to be very convenient. None of the sleepers noticed them roll by, which wouldn't have been the case two hours later. It occurred to her that many of these people were probably waiting for someone like them to roll by. More newcomers to rob.

A gray light filled the sky when they reached the center of the city. Clarence pointed to a large mangrove tree where they rolled to a stop and found they had the entire tree to themselves. They all got out and rested against the massive tree.

With each passing minute, the sky provided more light, allowing Anna to see their surroundings. What she saw horrified her.

Emaciated figures of starving people were everywhere. Many of them were gathered around a nearby government building—hoping for some type of handout. At that moment, she understood the warnings of the rebel soldier. But the one thing he hadn't mentioned was that people might lack the strength or energy to attack anyone. That fact might keep them safe... for a while.

Clarence fetched the skins from the back of the kit car and handed them to Esi. "Take Jonah. Go dey find fresh water." He pointed to a distant building. "Maybe dey pump there."

Esi nodded, and she and Jonah left.

The bishop found a hollowed-out spot between two large roots. Weak but comfortable, he said, "I suppose we wait until we've replenished our bodies with water before we decide what's next."

Since Clarence remained silent, Anna answered the bishop. "Let's make sure we have enough water before looking for a way to cross the river. Perhaps later, we'll send someone out to look for food. We could combine our money."

"That's an excellent idea," the bishop said. "Maybe the rebels have some food they wouldn't mind parting with for the right price. I'm sure it won't be Mama Mimi's, but I promise I won't complain."

"It's Kim's Place now," Anna said. "Remember? Kim took it over."

"All I remember is the rebels fighting the federals. God help all of our people there, including Kim," Bishop Neel said, his voice trailing off.

That thought lingered in silence. Finally, Esi and Jonah came back with full skins.

"The pump is there," she said, pointing to a cluster of people a half-mile away. "We drank already. This is for you."

Anna and the bishop shared one of the skins trying not to act desperate. They consumed as much water as their mouths could hold. Lily, Clarence, and Isabel shared the other. When the skins were completely dry, Clarence popped up and took them back to the pump to be filled again. With a fresh supply, they all took one long swig before they collapsed against the tree.

Then their bellies rumbled with hunger.

Anna spoke up. "Clarence, should we send someone to go look for food?"

"Food cost big-big money," Clarence replied. "We dey pay man to cross river."

"How much do we have?" Anna asked.

They pulled out every pound they had hidden away and placed it on the car seat. Clarence divided the notes and coins into two stacks: one large and one small. He handed the small stack to Esi and said something in their indigenous language. She motioned for Lily and Jonah to join her, and off they went.

"They will look for food," was all he said before resuming his spot under the tree.

When night fell and they hadn't returned, Anna feared the worst. "Should we go out looking for them?"

"No!" Clarence said abruptly. "Dey go come."

The small fires around the city began popping up. With no food to heat up, the people used them to illuminate the nearby area, to protect them from desperate souls sneaking up and robbing them. Or worse.

Around midnight, they spotted three figures hobbling toward them. It appeared that Esi, Jonah, and Lily had been attacked. Clarence and Isabel ran to meet them.

Sure enough, Esi and Jonah had both been beaten. Only Lily was uninjured.

Anna gave them water to drink, and wet a rag to wipe the blood from Esi's face.

"What happened?" Anna whispered.

Esi cried, "They took the money!"

Jonah dabbed at some of his wounds. "Lily grabbed a piece of wood and beat them off. I think one of them is dead."

Anna put her arm around Lily. "I knew you were tough. Are you okay?"

Lily nodded.

"I want you next to me tonight, understand?"

Lily hugged her. "Okay."

Anna realized that this situation could rapidly turn into tragedy. "We can't stay here. We need to cross that river."

"I agree," said the bishop. "But how are we going to accomplish that?"

Clarence volunteered. "I fit go find someone in morning. Make we sleep tonight."

He took Esi over to his spot and wrapped her up in his arms. Anna did the same with Lily, and Isabel joined them. Bishop Neel stayed in the backseat of the kit car, where he was most comfortable.

No one in the city was stirring. For those who had the energy to move, it wasn't safe after dark. People were getting injured or killed. It was a lawless mess.

A slight breeze wafted smoke throughout the downtown area. Anna had gotten used to it long ago, especially after being in the Leprosy Settlement—where fires were burning all the time. At least it kept the bugs down.

Soon, Anna drifted off, into a deep sleep.

♉

Anna lifted her head to another day of misery. They had been stuck under this mangrove tree for five full days—without a thing to eat. There was nothing to buy anywhere.

Occasionally, rebel soldiers raced through the city in jeeps. They were too fast for anyone to try and stop them, even if one dared to ignore the rifles.

Each day, Clarence and Jonah roamed the city, looking for food or someone to help them across the river. So far, they'd found no one with the means to help.

The only good news was that plentiful freshwater was available. They made constant treks to the pump, only to find fewer and fewer people there.

All around them, the stench of death filled the air. Every other day, a large truck rolled through the city. It loaded up the bodies and carried them to the city dump. It was disgusting and shocking. So many of their new neighbors were now dead. Describing the scene as a nightmare didn't do it justice. It was a humanitarian crisis, which was drawing comparisons to the Holocaust in newspapers across the globe: the Christian Igbos had replaced the Jews as the latest victims.

Anna bent over to check on an even weaker Bishop Neel. "How are you feeling?"

He reached up to touch her face. "I didn't think I'd be celebrating my 70th birthday like this, but here we are."

Anna blinked. "It's your birthday? That's right!"

She jerked her head away to tell everyone. But his hand caught a string around her neck. The string snapped, sending the small stick off the cushion and onto the floorboard.

"Oh my," Bishop Neel said. "I'm afraid I broke your necklace."

"Don't worry. It was just a string. Nothing fancy."

She reached down and picked up the stick, showing it to the bishop.

"Gran'pa made it for me. I'll just keep it in my pocket now."

"Gran'pa," he said, his voice hoarse and dry. "I barely remember what he looked like."

"Let me get you some water and we can remember together."

She helped him sit up to drink. Then she reached into her pocket, pulled out the stick, and inspected it for damage. A piece of wood had dislodged from one end, so Anna looked around on the floorboard. But she couldn't find it.

"What're you looking for?" he said.

"This stick is missing a piece. See?"

He took the stick from her and studied the markings. "You know, I believe it's some kind of flute. The two holes for the string are something you cover up to make different sounds. But there's no place to blow into."

Anna took it back and looked closer. Sure enough, he was right. On the undamaged end, she could see that a piece of clay had intentionally been put there. It was clogging up the stick. She used her fingernail to loosen it, and then banged the stick on the kit car until it fell out. Suddenly, she was holding a tiny flute.

"I think you were right. I'll see if I can play something."

She started blowing on it, making a high-pitched sound. Using two fingers, she could cover up the sides and make different sounds. With a little practice, she was able to play three separate notes and by varying the intensity and alternating the notes, she got quite good. At least it distracted them from their misery.

By noon, Clarence returned from looking for a way to cross the river. He was tired and out of energy. With all the walking and no food, he was nearing the point of simply dropping to the ground. If that happened, Anna was sure they were doomed.

For the first time in a long time, Bishop Neel got out of the kit car so Clarence could rest. Clarence immediately slumped back over the seat, too tired to say anything. Seeing this, Esi grabbed a skin and made him drink some water.

From her spot under the tree, Isabel turned and cried on Lily's shoulder. She was so hungry she was becoming distraught.

With nothing left to do, Anna played her tiny flute. A woman walked by with two buckets slung over her shoulder. She turned her head at the sound and came over to Anna. Speaking in an indigenous dialect, the woman said something, and Esi stood to answer her. They exchanged a few more words, and the woman left.

"What was that all about?" Anna asked.

"The woman, she dey want to know where you got that. I told her."

"Oh," Anna exhaled, leaning back and staring at the roof. She too was reaching the point of collapse. She wondered why she didn't just walk over to the river and try to cross it. If she was shot to death, it beat dying of starvation. With so many people around them dying, there was no sense in waiting for help that wasn't coming. As she considered the possibility of this plan, she closed her eyes and fell into an uneasy sleep.

"Wake, Miss Anna! Wake!"

Before her stood two large Nigerian men. Behind them were two women. One of them was the woman who'd earlier passed by carrying the buckets.

Anna reached for her money but remembered Clarence had all of it. She was sure that was what they had come for. Now, it was survival of the fittest.

The first man spoke as Clarence eased out of the kit car, ready for action. Jonah crept from the other side of the car, which would at least provide a decent line of defense. Anna spun around and saw everyone on their feet, except Bishop Neel. He was leaning against the tree and had no strength to rise. Anna searched for a weapon but saw nothing suitable, so she balled up her fists. This might be the end, but she was going down swinging.

Clarence said something to the woman. She stepped from behind them and spoke up. Soon, Clarence, Esi, and the woman were talking in their native language.

When they stopped talking, Esi said, "Miss Anna, these people, dey go help us."

Lily stepped in and spoke in clear English. "They are family with Gran'pa and have heard about your work in Ogoja. The ones who returned to Onitsha told them what happened. When Gran'pa died, a man from our village sent word back to these people about how well he was cared for. The flute you've been playing belongs to their clan. They say they can help us. We should go with them."

Anna studied these people. "Do you trust them, Esi?"

Before Esi could answer, one of the men spoke in mostly clear English. "We must return what you give our family. We have small-small food but know dem who can help you cross. Please, you trust us. Come now. Come!"

Anna looked back at Bishop Neel. He might not make it another day. They were out of options.

"Alright," she said. "Let's go. But you will need to help the bishop."

One of the Nigerians went over and easily lifted the bishop in his arms, and another helped with his legs. The rest of the group collected their meager belongings and straggled behind, unsure of where they were going. Regardless, it had to better than staying under the tree waiting to die.

They walked less than half a mile before coming to a poorly constructed two-story building. The outside shell had clearly been repaired many times. It looked as if a strong storm could knock the whole thing down.

The men showed them inside, where two other large men waited. They were obviously protecting the place while the others were gone.

Anna noticed that all of them appeared well-fed, at least by current standards. She also saw machetes and clubs leaning against the wall. Maybe they did have food.

The man lowered Bishop Neel to the ground and barked out orders. Shortly, a woman brought out some moldy bread and several bananas. She divided it up among the group and stood back as the hungry Ogojans devoured it in seconds.

After everyone had a little food inside of them, the Nigerians waited an hour before bringing out some cold stew. They dished out a cupful per person. Isabel was so grateful, she began crying as she sipped on her stew.

These people kept divvying out food to them for several hours. At various times, one of the Ogojans jumped up and ran to the bathroom. Their digestive systems weren't used to food.

By nightfall, Bishop Neel was actually sitting up and talking. "I feel much better," he said. "It's a miracle we found you."

The lead man spoke. "Yes, it is. We know men inside the army. They smuggle goods across the river. We talk to them tonight, see if they come and take you."

"God bless you, sir. We have money and can pay you," he blurted out accidentally, contrary to their plan to say nothing about their funds for fear of being robbed again.

The lead man held up his hand. "We no take your money. But the man crossing the river, he will tell us how much it costs to take you over."

Nothing more was said until 2 a.m. Someone entered the building and talked to the Nigerians in a back room. A door swung open, and the lead man appeared with a very slender, light-skinned male. He wore all black, including flaps for his face, which were unbuttoned now. He walked close to Anna and the bishop, studying them.

After a few moments, he said, "150£ for you two. We can cross now."

"Wait!" Anna cried. "All seven of us must go, not just two of us."

The man shook his head. "I can't fit all of you in one boat. That will cost too much money. Besides, these five are Igbo, they will not be treated well."

Esi touched Anna's arm. "It's okay, Miss Anna. You go."

"No, I'm not leaving you here to starve or be killed. You are my family, and you will come with me. If we can get to the British, we'll be treated well. You'll see."

The smuggler shook his head. "For all seven, it will cost 700£."

Bishop Neel coughed before speaking. "Could we have a moment in private to discuss your offer?"

The Nigerians and the smuggler left the room. Clarence came over to a small table and set a wad of notes down.

"How much do we have?' Bishop Neel asked.

He counted it out. "484£."

The Bishop clasped his hands together. "Oh dear, we're short. Perhaps we can haggle with this man."

"Hold the money, Clarence, and call him back in," Anna said.

When they stood before the smuggler, Anna said, "We can pay you 400£ for the seven of us."

The man again shook his head. "No. For 400£, I take four people."

"Please, you must take less than 700£! We don't have that much. Please!"

The smuggler folded his arms. "You don't know the danger. I don't have to do anything." He paused and said, "I'll take 600£, but no less."

Anna jumped on this. "Okay, we can pay you 500£."

He leaned his head back and laughed. "600£. That's it! Too many of you. I have to make two trips and get a longer boat."

Anna grabbed Clarence. "Give me the money."

He pulled the wad out of his pocket and handed it to her. She went over to the table and began slowly counting it out in the candlelight. She watched the smuggler's eyes sparkle at the sight of fresh money.

"460... 470... 475... 480... and one, two, three, four... That makes 484£. That's all we have."

The smuggler stared at the money and glanced at the seven desperate passengers. "I need more. What else do you have?" He pointed to their bags. "What's in those?"

"That's our luggage," Anna said. "There's nothing there you'd want."

"Let me see."

They opened all five of the Igbos' bags. They were poor people in a poor country, so it was no surprise that they had nothing of value. Then the bishop opened his bag. The smuggler held his Bible up, turned it over, and set it back down. He found a half-empty bottle of Glenlivet. Being interested in scotch, he removed the bottle and set it on the table.

"Open," he ordered Anna.

She opened her bag and unrolled a blouse she'd packed, which was protecting a cup and saucer. When he quickly snatched it up, she gasped.

"No please, that was my mother's. It's very dear to me."

He took the tea set and put it on the table next to the bottle of scotch. Next, he unrolled the undergarments she'd packed and found a pocket watch.

Anna reached over and touched his arm. "Please, not that. Please!"

He jerked his arm away. Suddenly, his eyes widened. He found her father's silver-handled whalebone comb. Now tears streamed down her cheeks.

"I beg you no. Please!" But she could tell her protests were actually creating interest in all her precious items.

He unscrewed the shampoo, smelled it, and kept that too. "Your watch. I want it."

Anna looked down at her wristwatch. "This? You can have it, but please don't take my comb. It's all I have of my father's. I beg you, sir." Her voice cracked.

He didn't care. Instead, he piled everything on the table next to the cash, including her wristwatch. "I'll take all seven of you across for all of this," he spat out, pointing to the table.

Esi put her arm around Anna. "You go, and we'll stay. Take your belongings. Please!"

Anna jerked away from her. "No! I could never live with myself—knowing I left you behind because of material possessions. I'll get over it. You are my family, and there is no choice here. You will cross with us, and the British will protect you!"

She wiped her tears and turned towards the smuggler. "Okay, sir, you have a deal."

He quickly gathered everything up and placed it in a dark bag. "I come for you tomorrow night. Wear dark clothing. And you two," he said, pointing at Bishop Neel and Anna, "cover up your white skin. All of it!"

Anna blocked the exit. "Wait! You can't take our money until we've crossed. Leave it here!"

The lead man stepped close to Anna and pushed her out of the way. "He will take it now, as he must find a long boat. He may hire another man to row back. The current's strong."

Anna wasn't giving up. "We have no way of knowing if he'll come back for us tomorrow night. Do we?"

The lead man grabbed her shoulder. "His family lives near. If he doesn't come back, we take payment from his family—one way or another."

The smuggler's expression didn't change after hearing this. Apparently, it was just business.

Anna watched the smuggler leave with all their money and her most prized possessions. Gritting her teeth, she muttered under her breath, "You'd better come back for us!"

24

They spent the next day preparing for the return of the smuggler—and eventually crossing the river. The Nigerians gave them more food, which improved their strength and energy.

Bishop Neel's recovery was most remarkable. Not only was he up and moving around, he was also telling jokes as the women fashioned black cloth around him. He found it unfortunate that he'd left his black robe behind, as it would've covered his skin perfectly.

Laughing out loud, he said, "A bishop dressed in black crossing the Niger to freedom! Sounds like a great movie, doesn't it?"

"Are you planning on standing up in the boat?" Anna asked.

"I shouldn't think so, as only Christ walked on water. And after that nasty spill at the ferry crossing, I know which direction I'll go in once I hit the water."

The group laughed at his jokes and comments. It was a welcome relief from the anxiety they were all feeling. Each one knew they'd be placing their lives at risk very soon. Either side could shoot them. All they could do was hope and pray.

By evening, Anna and the bishop were covered in black—between the women stitching black cloth, and Clarence applying black dye that the lead Nigerian had found for them.

The bishop picked up his Bible and held it above him. "I guess this will be all I need to carry over. Everything else can remain behind. We shall either make it, or we won't. A fresh change of clothes won't matter."

Anna lowered her head in sadness. Most of her belongings were gone. She still had Victoria's photo, which she slipped into Thomas' deck of cards. She slid the deck into one of her pockets with her passport and other papers. She would leave everything else behind.

At 11 p.m., the Nigerian women served up a large loaf of bread with some thick soup. The smell was intoxicating, which caused everyone in the room to salivate. One thing was certain: This smuggler was bringing over plenty of food.

"Eat all you can," the lead man said. "It will be a long night. You may not eat again for some time."

Right before the group dove in, Bishop Neel said a brief prayer over the food. In five minutes, the food was all gone. Then they each found a place to lie down and relax. It was time to wait.

Just after 1:30 a.m., the smuggler reappeared. "Stand up!" he ordered.

They got to their feet, bleary-eyed, while he inspected his passengers. When he lingered a little too long on Isabel, Anna put an arm around her to make sure he moved on. He smirked at her.

"You must walk in single file behind me," he commanded the group. "We'll walk at least a mile along the tall riverbank. Step where I step, and don't stop for anything—because I won't. Let's go."

"One moment," Bishop Neel said. "Let us pray."

The smuggler rolled his eyes. "Your god will not help you tonight. The only things that will protect you are me and my boat."

"That's what you say, sir. However, we shall still put on the breastplate of righteousness."

He bowed his head. "Dear Holy Father, please bless our crossing, and see us safely to the other side. Let us find the British, and let no harm befall us. We ask all this in your Holy name. Amen."

The others who were praying repeated, "Amen."

The bishop dusted off his clothes and picked up his Bible. "Now we're ready, sir."

The smuggler shook his head and gave a signal to the Nigerians. All the lamps and candles were immediately doused. Then, the seven of them filed out behind a man who would either lead them to freedom or death.

The walk was long, slow, and tiring. During much of it, they trudged through mud. However, the smuggler mostly kept to solid ground. Once two of them had stepped in his footprints, the ground was firm for the rest of them.

The smuggler hadn't lied about the distance. By the time they reached a large pile of driftwood and garbage, they were exhausted. Anna turned her wrist to see what time it was, but she remembered the smuggler had taken her watch too. Instead, she watched as Clarence and Jonah helped the man remove debris from his overturned boat, and pull it towards the water.

The moon was obscured by clouds, casting just enough light to see a hundred feet or so in front of them. They turned the boat upright.

The smuggler pointed to Clarence, Jonah, Bishop Neel, Isabel, and Esi. He wanted them to cross first. Keeping the bishop with two women on the federal side was the best way to protect them.

He came back and whispered to Anna and Lily, "You hide in the trash right there and cover up good. I will come back for you. Do not make a sound or leave this spot."

Within seconds, he was gone, leaving Anna and Lily alone under the dark shadow cast by the high bank.

Anna pulled Lily down to the ground. On their knees, they crawled under the wet paper, cardboard, driftwood, and other debris. It didn't stink, since it didn't include food.

With a little creativity, Anna was able to lie on her back with her head tilted up. She and Lily were covered with debris, making it almost impossible for anyone to know they were there.

Through an opening, she had a good view of anyone approaching. She wrapped her right arm around Lily and pulled her close. They were both terrified.

They remained like that for some time, until Anna dared to whisper. "Lily, you are like my daughter. I hope you'll always know that."

"I know, mother," she said hugging her tight. "I know, and I love you."

"I love you too."

A noise from the riverbank above them caught their attention. Neither of them could see what it was, but the sound of a rifle being readied was distinct. It had to be a rebel soldier.

Anna felt Lily's body tense. They held each other tighter.

Anna glimpsed wisps of cigarette smoke floating high above, illuminated by the moonlight. She counted the seconds, hoping the soldier would finish and leave. Eventually, a burning cigarette butt flipped through the air and landed just beyond them, near the water's edge. Anna relaxed, and Lily followed suit.

After about an hour passed, Anna began to panic. She thought no one was coming back for them when suddenly, she heard a noise.

The noise turned into a figure, which pulled paper and debris away from them. It was the smuggler.

"Hurry!" he said quietly. "We must cross now!"

Anna grabbed his hand and stood up. He helped Lily up next, and they followed him to the water's edge.

Clarence and Jonah had the boat ready and pointed across the river. Without saying a word, Anna and Lily slipped into the long boat and crouched down, as far as they could. Clarence started paddling as Jonah and the smuggler pushed them into the dark water. They were off.

The three men used short, smooth strokes, angling the boat slightly upstream. Occasionally, a cloud shifted and cast more moonlight on them. The increased light made things more dangerous. They needed almost complete darkness to safely cross. Anna stayed low and tried not to think about anything but getting across the river safely.

When the boat scraped on sand and gravel, Clarence hopped out and pulled it up on the riverbank. The smuggler pushed Anna, and she and Lily jumped out of the boat into the shallow water.

Anna whispered, "Thank God we made it!"

The three men lifted the boat and carried it as short distance. Anna and Lily followed them. After they traveled 200 feet, Anna saw another river.

"What's this?" she asked the smuggler.

"Shhh. The river forks here. One more to cross."

They repeated the boarding process. In seconds, they were heading to the next shore, which was now visible in the bright moonlight. Paddles dipped in and out of the water less silently than before, the men realizing they were visible. They could not afford to be spotted, especially on this side of the river.

The smuggler was intent on landing at a certain point. With hard paddling, it took several minutes before they hit the west side of the Niger. From a dark spot against the high bank, Esi, Isabel, and Bishop Neel approached the new arrivals. They motioned for them to follow.

Anna, the last in line, turned to say something to the smuggler about her whalebone comb, but he was already in his boat, headed downstream. They were truly on their own.

The Ogojans scrambled up the bank and saw some thick vegetation just ahead. Clarence led them toward it. In seconds, they were safely hidden among the bushes.

Clarence whispered to the group, "We wait here. See if dem dey spot us."

Anna took this time to quietly remove her shoes and clean out some of the sand.

Next to her, praying and gripping his thick Bible, the bishop whispered, "Where do you get your fortitude? Besides the Almighty, of course."

"The same place that you do – Irish blood," Anna said with a smile.

Suddenly, the sounds of vehicles grew louder. Brakes squealed as jeeps stopped very near them. Spotlights blinded them. And this was followed by distant gunshots, bullets whizzing all around. The spotlights snapped off.

A man barked orders, and flames exploded from rifles. In blinking moments of flashing light, they could see eight soldiers firing back at the other side. Anna and Clarence motioned for everyone to hit the ground. A few minutes later, the shooting stopped.

Two flashlights flicked on just a few feet away. The soldiers were studying the ground for tracks. Anna could barely breathe. There was no possible way they could escape detection now. Sure enough, the silhouettes of two soldiers with rifles appeared in the bushes.

Esi yelled at them, which likely saved their lives. They weren't expecting to hear a female voice.

The soldiers ordered them out. Anna was the first to leave the bushes. As the soldiers cleared the rest of the group, a rough man dragged her to a jeep and tied her hands. When everyone was loaded up, they took off.

⚲

Anna had no idea how much time had passed since she'd been thrown in the small, dark cell. It was at least two days. There were no windows or natural light to gauge the time—only a meal service, which was not on a regular schedule. She received some water in a tin cup, a bowl of thick porridge, and a slice of bread. The only light sneaking into her cell came from a flickering oil lamp on an opposite wall, somewhere out of view.

When they initially brought her to this building, it was still dark. They thoroughly and roughly searched her; no modesty was preserved. Her few remaining belongings were thrown into a small basket. Now there was nothing to do but wait and see what happened. At least she was alive.

A guard appeared and unlocked her door. He motioned for her to come out and led her to a room with several oil lamps, causing her to shield her eyes from the extra light.

A table and two chairs occupied the middle of the room. The guard pushed her in and closed the door. Anna walked around the room, trying to calm herself.

Ten minutes later, the door opened to reveal a young British officer. He came in, closed the door behind him, and set a file on the table.

Seeing him, Anna threw her head back and cried out, "Oh thank God! The British are here!"

The officer sat down opposite her and opened the folder. "Yes ma'am, the British are here. But the question is, what are *you* doing here?"

Anna placed her palms on the table and took a deep breath. "We were living in Ogoja. We fled the fighting that was taking place at our settlement. On the road, a Biafran soldier told us that our best chance of reaching the British was crossing at Onitsha. And thank God, it worked!"

"You said we. Who is *we?*"

"The people I was captured with. There are seven of us."

He pulled out a pen and clicked it. "Could I have their names please?

Anna gave him the information. "Can we please go home now?"

The officer appeared confused. "Home to where? Ogoja?"

"No, of course not! We have a ship—or had one—waiting to take us to Dublin."

He stared at the names he had just written. "You and the bishop are British. But these five—are they British as well?"

"No, they're Nigerian. I raised Lily and Jonah as leper babies. Esi and Clarence were lepers too, but they were all healed when we got DDS. Then they got married and had Isabel. They are now parents to Lily and Jonah."

"Isabel. She's the beautiful one?"

"Yes, she is quite fetching. They are all with me. You can ask the bishop. He will confirm all this."

The officer smiled. "He already has. His story matches yours, and your papers check out. I'm going to make arrangements to take you and the bishop into our custody, and transport you to the coast. Our foreign attaché will help arrange transportation for you to get home. Though I don't know how long that will take. As you know, we are at war."

Anna slapped the table. "But I have to take the other five with me! They need to go too!"

He shook his head and avoided eye contact. "I'm sorry, but they're Biafran. Once I take custody of you and the bishop, the federal soldiers will immediately execute them. If we had caught your group, we may have been able to save them. But we didn't. We have an uneasy relationship with the federals, and I'm sure my colonel won't risk jeopardizing it for five Biafran—especially Igbos."

Anna covered her face with her hands and started crying. "PLEASE GOD NO! Don't do this!"

"Ma'am, it's not me that's doing it. It's the federals. They were caught sneaking into federal territory, so they're considered spies. Surely you can see that. And yes, I know they aren't actually spies, but most of these soldiers have no training. They're also Muhammaden. It's war. People die. Although they may keep the young one—Isabel—for, uh… personal reasons."

Anna was now wailing, close to breaking down. She pounded the table hard, alarming the officer.

"Ma'am, please! Restrain yourself. I was going to leave you in this room until I could get the paperwork signed off, but now I'll have to put you back in the cell. It may take me a few hours."

He looked at his wristwatch. "It's 9 p.m. right now. I think I can have you out of here by 11 p.m."

Anna was still bawling when he opened the door and called for the guard. She could barely stand, so the guard grabbed her arm and forced her down the hall.

The officer called out, "If you have any problems, just ask for Lt. Lucchese."

Anna clutched her chest and fell to her knees, catching the guard by surprise. Seeing this, the lieutenant took a few steps back down the hall to help.

At first, it seemed that Anna was just hysterical, but then she cried out for him. "Lieutenant! Lieutenant!"

The guard regained control over her and said, "Ma'am, you need to stop this. Please! You're not helping things."

Anna caught her breath and tried to calm down. Making direct eye contact with the lieutenant, she said, "Are you Owen?'

He jerked back in surprise. "What did you say?"

"Are you Owen Lucchese?"

His eyes narrowed. "I didn't tell you my first name. How did you know it?"

"Your mother and I are close friends. But between the Biafran war and problems with the mail, we haven't been in touch for the last several years."

"My mother? I don't believe you. What's her maiden name?"

"Tomlinson. She's missing her left leg, unless she's found a way to grow it back—and I wouldn't doubt it."

His mouth hung open. "What?"

Sensing her advantage, Anna continued. "And I sent you presents from Africa, which you played with as a child. Surely you remember some of them."

He looked back at his folder with the names listed. "Please come back into the room."

When the door was closed, he said in a low voice, "Anna Goodwill! Of course! I had completely forgotten. Mother told me about you. I thought it was just some crazy story, since no one would come here of their own accord."

"Yes, it's me," she said, patting him on the shoulder. "And just like Molly is to you, these Biafran are to me. They are my family. I'd rather die than lose them."

His smile turned to a frown. "I'm very sorry, but they are likely to die. I'm just a lieutenant—and a new one at that."

Anna clutched his hand in hers. "Please help me, Owen. I'm begging you with all my heart and soul!"

He took her hand. "Miss Goodwill, I could get court-martialed and shot myself."

Undeterred, she set her jaw. "Then can you please arrange for me to die with them? Tell your mother I will miss her dearly."

He pinched his lower lip together. "I'll think about it. Now go back to your cell, and I'll come for you later."

"Owen, please! I, and many others have spent the last 22 years helping these people survive leprosy, and we have lost a lot of Britons in the process. These five are the best examples of our work. Please don't let their lives and mine be for nothing. Please!"

He nodded. "I understand. Now go back to your cell please, and let me see what I can do."

When the guard slammed her cell door shut, she stayed near it to see if she could hear anything that might help her save five lives.

A loud noise rattled around the cell walls, waking Anna from a troubled slumber. Once again, the guard removed her from the cell. But this time, he led her to a different building. Inside, a single lamp was lit, which cast eerie shadows across a large room. Tables and chairs were arranged in a pattern, which she assumed was a makeshift mess hall for the soldiers. Because it was early in the morning, the building was empty.

The guard ordered her to sit, and she complied. When he left, she thought about getting up to see what was behind the double doors. But she thought better of it.

A few minutes later, the guard reappeared, pushing Esi in front of him. She ran and hugged Anna, as the guard turned around and left.

"Are you okay?" Anna said, her voice shaking.

"Yes, Miss Anna, but I fear what they will do to us."

"So do I. Say nothing, and let me do the talking."

They stayed close to each other and held hands, waiting for what was to come.

The door creaked open again, and there was Isabel. Next was Lily. All the women hugged each other and cried, but Anna did her best to calm them down.

A noise behind the double doors silenced them. Anna crept closer but didn't dare cross into the dark space, which she assumed was a kitchen. Instead, she peered through a heavily scratched window in the kitchen door. Over the large sink, there was something metal scraping on the window frame. Then a figure looked in, but she couldn't make it out. With a final pop, the window flung upward. Anna pushed the kitchen door open but didn't go in.

"Esi, Miss Anna, come!" a voice said.

Anna recognized the voice and ran to the window. Clarence was on the other side, holding a pry bar.

"Pull it up and come. But be quiet!"

Esi was at the kitchen entrance, holding the door open. Anna waved to her. "Esi, get the girls."

In seconds, they stood in front of the large kitchen sink. Anna pulled over a chair and barked out orders. "Isabel, crawl through first!"

Isabel stepped on the chair. Using the bottom of the sink for support, she made her way through the window. Clarence was on the other side, pulling his daughter through. In one continuous stream, the rest of them followed. When Anna landed on her feet, Bishop Neel and Jonah were there to welcome her.

Clarence signaled to stop the greetings. It was dark, but the sky was clear—which allowed the moon and stars to help them see where they were going. They made their way a short distance, until the outline of a jeep appeared.

"Get in," Lt. Lucchese whispered, "and stay down."

It was extremely cramped for eight people to fit into a four-seat jeep, but in their desperation, they found a way. The lieutenant started up the jeep and eased it into gear. Without using headlights, he slowly rolled away with his group of 'spies'.

They traveled slowly and quietly for several miles, until the jeep veered left towards the river, easing to a stop. Lt. Lucchese killed the engine and gestured to them. "Get out and be quiet."

All seven scrambled out of the jeep and stood, waiting for the next order.

Lt. Lucchese pulled Anna and Bishop Neel to one side, and turned back to the rest. "You five follow this path along the river. It's easy to see in the moonlight, and you should be safe for several miles. If you see any federal soldiers, slip down the bank until they pass. You can walk along the river's edge. It's muddy but beware: You might get shot from the other side since they can see you. I can't promise that you'll make it, and you'll need lots of luck. But it's better than what they had planned for you."

Clarence spoke softly. "Where we dey go? Back to Biafra?"

"Yes. If you stay on the federal side, you'll be killed. You must go back to Biafra."

"But dem dey starve there," he said despondently.

The lieutenant went back to the jeep and grabbed two backpacks. "Here," he said, handing one to Esi and the other to Clarence. "I stole these. Inside, there's a compass, a knife, and plenty of food and water. The food should last you more than a week if you ration it carefully." Reaching into his pocket, he handed 50£ to Clarence. "This is all I have. Really, it's the best I can do."

Lily approached and hugged him unexpectedly. "We will never forget you!"

Surprised, the lieutenant hugged her back. Then he added this advice: "Listen, if you get caught, you *cannot* tell them I helped you. Remember, you broke out of your cells and escaped with these backpacks. If you don't get caught, bury the backpacks when you're done with them. Do you understand?"

"We do," Clarence said, shaking Lt. Lucchese's hand.

Anna noticed Clarence's eyes were glassy, and his voice was cracking—something she'd never seen before. She flung herself at Esi and Clarence and gathered them close to her.

"So this is goodbye." Anna hugged them harder. "I want you to always know that I love you and will be praying for you."

Clarence had tears streaming down his cheeks. "Miss Anna," he said, trying to use his best English. "I don died many—many years ago in the bush, but you saved me. No person on this earth could ever done more than you. I'll never know why you dey did it."

Now Anna was crying. "Love, Clarence. And God. That's why!"

Jonah, Lily, and Isabel joined in. They were all hugging and crying.

Standing alone, a voice near the jeep cried out. "Can a bishop get a hug too?"

They moved as a group and hugged him. Then they kissed Anna on her cheek one more time.

Lt. Lucchese stepped forward. "Please, you need to go now! Please!"

They looked back, as if to permanently capture Anna's face. Before she could say another word, they were gone.

"What about us?" Anna asked,

Lt. Lucchese pointed away from the river. "You two will start walking towards that star just over those trees. It leads to my base camp about three miles away, though you probably won't make it before a British soldier spots you. Raise your hands immediately, and identify yourself as British citizens. I have all your documents with me, so tell them I was interrogating you. When I didn't come back, you didn't trust the federals, and felt you had to escape. Do you understand?"

"Yes, we do." The bishop said, choking up. "I can't believe you did this for us—for *them!*"

"I did it for her." The lieutenant gestured at Anna. "Otherwise, my mother would have disowned me. She loves her a great deal. Now I just have to avoid getting caught myself."

Anna hugged him hard. "May God bless you. You have done a very good deed."

He nodded, saying nothing

"Do they have a chance of making it?" she asked fearfully.

He frowned and looked downcast. "Because the ground is damp, their tracks will easily be seen when the sun comes up, which is in a few hours. But at least they have a better chance than they did in front of a firing squad."

Anna slumped, but the bishop did his best to hold her up. "Dear, I need you for support, not the other way around. That's the way it's always been."

Anna straightened herself up.

"Perhaps we should start walking, and pray for a miracle," Bishop Neel said.

"Yes," Anna said. "That's what we'll do. Pray!"

"Once you're captured and mention my name, I'll be summoned. Then I'll come take custody of you." Lieutenant Lucchese held his arms out to herd Anna and the bishop along their path. "Please, you must start walking now, before we're all caught!"

Anna and Bishop Neel gathered themselves up, shook his hand, and looked for the star to guide them. Lt. Lucchese hopped back in the jeep, and with his headlights off, disappeared from sight.

After walking for a few minutes, Anna heard the bishop muttering under his breath. "Are you praying, Bishop?"

"Of course. We've had a lot of miracles, so one more shouldn't be a problem."

Anna glanced up at the sky. "Can you see the star we're supposed to follow? I've lost it."

"No, I can't. The clouds appear to be covering it up. I think we should keep walking in the same direction until we see it again."

Anna felt something on her arm. "What was that?"

"Were you bit by something?"

"No, it wasn't a bug. Oh, there it is again! Do you feel it?"

The bishop dabbed at his hand. "A raindrop. Oh my, I'm afraid we're about to get wet."

Anna began laughing. "Yes, it's raining. It's the miracle we needed!"

The bishop pulled his clothes tighter, hoping to avoid the rain as much as possible. "We're going to get soaked to the bone."

The rain intensified.

"Yes, we will be soaked!" she yelled through the now-deafening rain. "But their tracks will be washed away too. They'll have a better chance. In fact, I bet they're going to make it! And all because of *your* prayers and *my* secret weapon!"

Anna closed her eyes and tilted her head back, lifting her hair to let the fresh rain soak in, and take her back home.

EPILOGUE

Over 3 million people died in the Biafran war—and untold millions more from leprosy.

I visited Anna in 2016 when she was 100 years old. I found her in a nursing home in England, and she was as full of life as ever. Even though she was slipping a bit, she was able to show me the Member of the British Empire Award that Queen Elizabeth bestowed on her. She also showed me the Pro Ecclesia et Pontifice medal she received from the Pope. There were other awards and newspaper articles about everything she had accomplished in Nigeria. And of course, there were the letters to Molly. I looked through all of them, and listened to her as she told her stories of Africa—amazed by her ability to still recall details.

During tea breaks (yes, she still had her special blend of Ceylon, Kenya and Assam next to the English Breakfast and Molly's favorite—Darjeeling Orange Pekoe), she introduced me to her friends at the home, even though they were mostly decades younger than her. When the excitement of my visit waned, she finally got down to business and told me the important details.

Molly's husband died in 1989, and Molly followed him in 1999, right before "the coming of the new century," as she put it. She and Molly remained friends until Molly's death. She was looking forward to seeing her best friend in heaven soon.

Clarence Pyle, Jr., successfully expanded his father's grocery stores to dozens of small towns in western England. One day in 1982, one of Clarence's stores was robbed, and he saw his clerk being threatened. Despite being in his sixties, he jumped on the assailant and wrestled with him. In the process, he suffered stab wounds. The other clerks beat the robber with glass bottles of ale and held him until the police arrived. Clarence was laid out on his back and tried to calm the worried employees and customers who stared down at him. He died a few minutes later. His estate sold the store chain, and his family was well taken care of for the rest of their lives.

When I asked Anna what happened to Esi, Lily, Jonah, Isabel, and the other Clarence, a brightness filled her eyes, and she started to say something. But she got confused and told me about some friends in her retirement home. Since she had clearly had enough for one day, I stopped and told her I'd be back the next day to resume my interview.

As I was leaving, she smiled and said, "You take good care of my story. It's the most precious thing I have left in this earthly world."

I kissed her goodbye and left.

The next morning, I arrived to find an ambulance at the main entrance. One of the head nurses had tears in her eyes and pulled me aside.

"I've been here for twelve years, and she was like an aunt to me— dispensing advice whenever I needed it, and what a great sense of humor she had. I can't believe she's gone."

When I realized she was talking about Anna, I started crying. That's when she caught herself, not realizing we were related.

"Oh dear, I'm sorry. I didn't know."

We consoled each other, and I left to go back to the hotel and make arrangements for the funeral. Eventually, I returned to Dallas, where I live with my family.

Several months later, I received a package from a barrister in England. He had closed out her estate and was sending me her personal items. I tore into the box and found Thomas' favorite deck of cards, along with Victoria's photo tucked between the queen of hearts and the queen of diamonds! The box also contained a well-worn Bible. Hidden inside its pages was her birth certificate, the letter from the Queen, the medal and (most importantly) a letter from Esi that was dated 2003.

It read:

Dear Miss Anna,

I hope this letter finds you in good health. We have sent many other letters and have never received a reply. I visited the church in Calabar, and they explained that the church in Ogoja had the wrong information for you all these years. They felt sure this would reach you, and I pray that it does.

The night we left you, God was with us. It rained hard, keeping the watchers on the river inside their warm huts, allowing us to slip by. We 'borrowed' a boat (you know Clarence) and traveled many miles down the Niger until daybreak. We hid the boat and ourselves until darkness returned. Clarence paddled us to a small village, Kaiama, where we left the river and traveled east through the great forest. One day later, we found several families hiding in the forest, and we decided to stay with them. Jonah proved an excellent hunter and provided us meat for many weeks. We stayed there for close to a year until the federal troops crossed the Niger and pushed us east.

Over the next two years, we lived near the coast, where the smuggling of food and relief from other countries was widespread. With Jonah hunting and Clarence 'borrowing', we all survived, though at times we were quite thin.

In 1971, with the war over and Biafra no more, we made the long journey back to Ogoja, and we found the federals had taken the leprosy buildings for their own. I found a teaching position in Ogoja, and Clarence took odd jobs. Somehow we made it, although so many others didn't.

As Igbos, we were discriminated against and found life hard for many, many years.

Clarence was using a machine at work, and it broke. His leg was cut deep, bleeding, and the doctor was called. When he said there was nothing he could do, I was able to be with him. We held hands to the bitter end, and he made me promise to find you. Then he took his last breath and died in my arms. That was 1980, and I never remarried. No man ever seemed good enough.

Jonah is a preacher and has a church just south of Ogoja. He married a nice girl, and they have three children. Lily married a businessman, who sells vegetables in the market. They also have three children and live well. Isabel married a handsome man, who is a regional representative and hopes to be President of Nigeria one day—perhaps when the Igbo people are forgiven for the Biafran War. They have one child, a daughter they named Anna.

I get to see my grandchildren quite often. However, my days are numbered now. My fingers are gnarled and twisted, and I can't write letters. I had an educated friend write this for me, so I could tell you this: Because you and the sisters of MMM and the doctors cared for us long enough to get the new drug, we have been able to lead full, rich lives and have wonderful grandchildren. The people you all saved will bear fruit for centuries to come.

But I fear the old disease has shortened my life, and the doctor tells me it won't be long now until I see the Kingdom. If you ever come back to Ogoja, I will be buried with Clarence in the same cemetery with your dear Sister Browne, Sister Flores, and Dr. Chapley. Patrick, the driver, is also there, as he was killed in fighting near Ogoja. He must have been brave, because they have a special marker on his grave. I hope you have the chance to come and see me, though I know it is not likely, given both our ages.

I have been blessed to have lived so long. I thank God that I was able to live through all of this. If this letter finds you alive and well, it will be the greatest joy of my life—that I (a humble leper from Nigeria) was able to thank you for the life you gave me. When Clarence died in my arms, his last words were, "God bless Anna Goodwill."

So I will close out my letter to you with the same words: God Bless Anna Goodwill.

PS: Clarence told me about your rainwater secret, and it's still safe with me.

NOTE FROM THE AUTHOR

I'd like to thank my family – Tony, Katie, Sam & Sarah for encouraging me to continue with the book and for not rolling their eyes every time I brought it back into the conversation. I love you with all my heart. Many thanks to Jeanie Galvin for being my guinea pig and being the first and only person to read the book – but most of all for being my friend for more years than we can count. To Sister Catherine Dwyer at the MMM's in Drogheda – thank you for all the hard work you have put into the MMM archives and for allowing me to research your files and answering the hundreds of questions I've had through the years. Tricia Chinn, thank you for making that first trip to Drogheda, Ireland with me that began this adventure. Thank you to Emily Galvin for my Author photos www.emily-galvin.squarespace.com. Thank you to Carol Barnes for our many years of friendship and for helping me with decisions regarding the artistic features of the book. A huge thank you and kudos to Josiah Jones www.theartjones.com for my beautiful cover and for putting up with me until we got it just perfect! Thank you to Michael Gray for editing and Liane Larocque for proofreading. Finally, thank you to my parents, grandparents, Lily and Eileen Paterson, all in heaven, for pushing me and encouraging me in subtle ways to tell this beautiful story to whomever is willing to listen.

http://www.therainwatersecret.com/

49456189R00217

Made in the USA
Columbia, SC
21 January 2019